HE WHO PLAYS THE KING

The future King Richard the Third was a boy of only seven when he watched an even younger child coping determinedly with a large boarhound. Never again was Richard to have so clear a view of Henry Tudor, who, twenty-six years later, was to cost him his crown and his life at the Battle of Bosworth Field.

Mary Hocking tells an absorbing story of kingship and kingmaking, of the deep-rooted rivalry between the houses of York and Lancaster, and of the lives of these two young claimants to the throne. Richard, a man of sharp wit and formidable energy, became a vigilant, unrelenting king. Henry, for years a powerless exile, remained patient, forbearing yet shrewdly calculating, until the opportunity for action came.

HE WHO PLAYS
THE KING

By

MARY HOCKING

1980

CHATTO & WINDUS

LONDON

Published by
Chatto & Windus Ltd
40 William IV Street
London WC2N 4DF

*

Clarke, Irwin & Co. Ltd
Toronto

British Library Cataloguing in Publication Data
Hocking, Mary
   He who plays the king.
   I. Title
   823'.9'1F   PR6058.026H/
   ISBN 0–7011–2521–7

© Mary Hocking 1980

Printed in Great Britain
by Ebenezer Baylis & Son Ltd
The Trinity Press, Worcester, and London

To Glyn

ACKNOWLEDGEMENT

I am most grateful to Dr. Pamela Tudor-Craig for permission to use her translation of Richard's prayer, part of which is printed on page 219. This prayer is written in Richard's Book of Hours, which probably originated in the Warwick family somewhere between 1430 and 1450, and is now in the Library of Lambeth Palace.

M. H.

CONTENTS

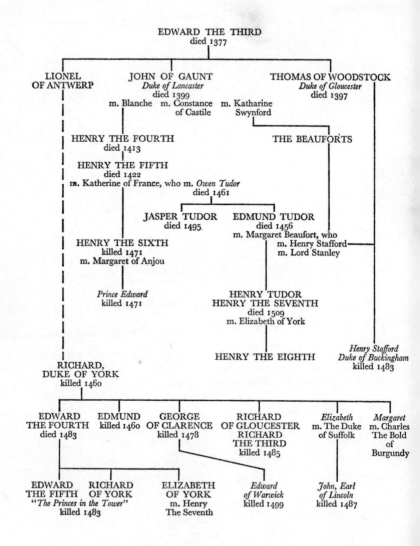

EDWARD THE THIRD
died 1377

LIONEL
OF ANTWERP

JOHN OF GAUNT
Duke of Lancaster
died 1399
m. Blanche   m. Constance   m. Katharine
of Castile   Swynford

THOMAS OF WOODSTOCK
Duke of Gloucester
died 1397

HENRY THE FOURTH
died 1413

THE BEAUFORTS

HENRY THE FIFTH
died 1422
m. Katherine of France, who m. *Owen Tudor*
died 1461

JASPER TUDOR
died 1495.

EDMUND TUDOR
died 1456
m. Margaret Beaufort, who
m. Henry Stafford
m. Lord Stanley

HENRY THE SIXTH
killed 1471
m. Margaret of Anjou

Prince Edward
killed 1471

HENRY TUDOR
HENRY THE SEVENTH
died 1509
m. Elizabeth of York

HENRY THE EIGHTH

Henry Stafford
Duke of Buckingham
killed 1483

RICHARD,
DUKE OF YORK
killed 1460

EDWARD
THE FOURTH
died 1483

EDMUND
killed 1460

GEORGE
OF CLARENCE
killed 1478

RICHARD
OF GLOUCESTER
RICHARD
THE THIRD
killed 1485

Elizabeth
m. The Duke
of Suffolk

Margaret
m. Charles
The Bold
of
Burgundy

EDWARD
THE FIFTH
"The Princes in the Tower"
killed 1483

RICHARD
OF YORK

ELIZABETH
OF YORK
m. Henry
The Seventh

Edward
of Warwick
killed 1499

John, Earl
of Lincoln
killed 1487

Part I

A CROWNED CALF

'A crowned calf, a shadow on a wall. . . .' Commynes

Chapter 1

A formation of starlings; the first squadron of the evening.
Bats flicker under huge elms. The long line of hills, veined with
gullies where dark rivers foam, is now reduced to uniform
blackness, and the valley is a desolate sea of grass in which there
are strange flickerings of light where water lies in patches of bog.
A landscape difficult to set in time; this scene can have changed
little in hundreds of years: England on a peaceful autumn night.

But come closer, through the picture frame, into a village
which the moon has conjured out of the darkness. A silver shaft
of light penetrates the window of a cottage where a priest kneels
at prayer. He seems utterly absorbed, gazing down, his nose
pinched at the nostrils as though offended by his own breath.
But then there is the sound of running feet on cobblestones. The
priest looks up and smells burning tar; one wall of the grim
little room is softened by the rosy glow of torchlight. His
devotions are not proof against this distraction; he rises and goes
into the street. Women are running from open doorways,
carrying mugs of ale. Men are shouting and bragging, rehearsing
punishment meted out and mimicking the abject surrender of
the Lollards whom they have smoked out.

The priest walks along the street, taking no part in the
jubilation. At one point, he stops to glance up, perhaps to stare
into the face of God despairing at the behaviour of His creation.
It is, however, the face of a girl at a window which arrests his
gaze. His ugly face becomes distorted by lust.

The moon tires of this scene and now discovers a road which
stumbles across the very spine of England. A rough road, and
lonely; scrubland on either side with here and there a tree bent
by the prevailing wind. On one such tree something that was
once part of a man sways when the breeze catches the rope from
which it hangs. The limbs are being hacked apart so that they
can be distributed to various dwellings as a warning to those who
favour the white rose of York that this is Lancastrian country.

While the men are thus engaged, the victim's son, a sprightly lad, has taken advantage of their preoccupation to steal his father's horse, and once out of ear-shot he mounts and rides away.

For a time, the moon lights a path for this enterprising lad. But there is little amusement in mile after mile of rolling heath-land repetitively patterned with manor or monastery and its attendant cluster of cottages; so the moon leaves the lad on his lonely path and rides leisurely over a dark forest with trees standing so close that not even a needle of light can penetrate their ranks. It idles on towards a tall, horned bank of cloud, and now it has fun on its journey, peppering a winding river with darts of silver and, being no respecter of power, however sub-stantial, making a shadow play across castle walls. In the meadows beyond the castle, the tall grass sways in a breeze so light that it barely lifts the standard struck where one of the camps has been set. The moon, losing interest in the game, hides behind the cloud. And out of the darkness, there comes a great cry, 'Treason!'

That cry, which echoed around the outer fortifications of Ludlow Castle, was repeated within the keep; it rang across the inner courtyard and resounded in the great hall, it reverberated on the stairs and climbed to the room where two children slept. The older boy, who slept heavily, coughed and snuffled, fumbling to wakefulness; but his seven-year-old brother woke instantly. The great cry belonged to the world of nightmare, that unexplored territory which lies beyond understanding in which evil is never explicit and terror cannot be identified. The fire had burnt low, but one flame stirred still, casting shadows on the wall. The younger boy watched and waited, rigid in the narrow bed. But this nightmare did not gradually peel away as the room took shape around him; an examination of the bench with the familiar tumble of clothes across it brought no re-assurance.

George, the older boy, feeling sick because he had been wrenched too violently from sleep, said irritably, 'What is it? Why are they making so much noise?'

His younger brother, Richard, replied, 'Something terrible has happened.'

'What?'

But if it had been possible to say, it would not have been terrible.

George said impatiently, 'Get up and find out.' He was reluctant to rise from bed at the best of times; and now there was another reason, which he could not have explained although he felt it in his stomach, why he did not want to get up. He looked at his brother. In the firelight the red hair fell like a dark stain across the blanched face and the eyes seemed black as pitch. George acknowledged grudgingly that age made certain demands on him, 'All right,' he said, '*I'll* go.'

He got up, breathing heavily, and made a great labour of drawing on his hose. After a few moments Richard, not wishing to be left alone, came padding across the floor and announced that he was coming, too. When they had dressed, for there was always the chance they might not come back and it was important to be warm, they went quietly out of the room. Richard, who had wet himself, moved awkwardly and was wretchedly uncomfortable in his tight-fitting hose. Earlier, there had been some activity outside their room, but now there was no one about. The two children hesitated. Then George took his brother's hand and they went down the twisting stairs towards the sound of voices in the great hall. As they passed a window, they stopped to look out. There were men in full armour hurrying across the courtyard, torchlight burnishing breastplate and helmet. Orders were shouted, then the voices died away as the men entered the castle by the door just below the window. 'It's all over and we've won,' George said; but he was careful to keep his voice low and he proceeded down the stairs with caution. When the children rounded the last turn of the stair and the hall came into view, they sat down huddled close together in the shadows, partly for concealment but mostly for physical comfort. Above them, the stair climbed up like a half-opened fan.

The scene in the great hall was one they had witnessed many times, servants bringing food and drink, the fire being rekindled. The smell of wood and oil, roast meat, spiced wine, had until now denoted conviviality and was normally accompanied by a great deal of noise. But tonight all was silent, like the entertainments performed by the mummers at the country fairs. The little knot of armed men by the long table stood mute, looking all ways but at one another. No sooner had a servant laid down his tray than he was hustled away by the children's mother. When all the servants had gone, she seated herself on the bench by the fire, half-turned from the men, although she watched them out of the corner of her eyes. She sat upright, her hands folded in her lap. The bodice of her green dress was drawn tight across her breasts, but she sat so still that the only shimmer of movement in the bright cloth was caused by the flicker of firelight. It was the restless hands which betrayed her unease.

The children's cousin, the Earl of Warwick, dominated the

group of men by the table, but the children had eyes only for their father. The Duke of York stood beside Warwick, nodding his head vehemently yet not seeming to attend to what was being said. Once, he thumped his fist on the table and then unclenched the fingers slowly, staring at them so intently that the children supposed he must have something concealed in the palm of his hand. Warwick went on talking; their father curled his fingers into a fist again and shouted, 'Trollope, my God! Who could have thought that he would betray us!'

Warwick stopped talking. Heads turned, eyes probed the corners of the room and then had difficulty in meeting those of their companions. In the torchlight, the face of the children's father seemed dark with blood.

The children understood little of what was going on. But though they did not understand, they sensed the harm that had been done. In this small gathering of armed men were a father, two brothers, an uncle and a cousin, with none of whom they were well-acquainted but of whose exploits they had heard much. They knew that their father was the greatest lord in the realm, that he had ruled it as Protector, that all the people loved him and wanted him to be king (though quite why this had not happened was not clear to them). They never tired of hearing of their uncle Salisbury's defence of the West Marches. Most splendid of all were the tales told of their cousin Warwick, who had the power to fire men's imagination so that they spoke of him as though he was twice the size of other men and he bore himself accordingly. To the children, these men now gathered round the table were figures of great glory whose invincibility had never been questioned. Yet now, they were disturbed by the doubt that transformed a confident face, the darkening of a bright eye, the confusion of resolute features. One person alone provided reassurance. Their eldest brother, Edward, interrupted Warwick to ask whether it was indeed impossible to meet the enemy.

'Now that Trollope and his men have deserted we are lost,' Warwick said brusquely. 'They are the best trained of our army.'

'Certainly no one can know their merit better than you,' Edward acknowledged, 'since they are your men.'

Warwick looked at him angrily but Edward seemed unaware of causing displeasure. He was seventeen, confident and un-afraid. Richard, watching from the dark stairs, thought him dazzlingly beautiful. The children returned to their room. They heard the metalled impact of horses' hooves, the shivering jolt of armour; they listened while the martial noise diminished to a jaunty jingle and then died quite away. Leaning from their window, they could see nothing but the upthrust walls of the keep bruising the night sky. George sneezed. In the distance, the cock crew; but his message was not needed, already those left behind were preparing for the grim business of the day.

But when the time came, and the children stood before Ludlow market cross, one on either side of their mother, each holding a hand of hers, it was not so very hard. She was magnificent, erect and proud; so they could be erect and proud, too; and since no one harmed them, it was not difficult to maintain their poise. Around them, there was much screaming and cursing, smoke and flame and the smell of burning thatch. Their mother, who would not plead for herself, pleaded for the townsfolk, but no one heeded her except the pale, elongated king.

'I will not have these outrages committed in my name!' he protested, almost in tears, to an attendant, who bowed to conceal his contempt at yet another instance of the King's madness.

The King was kind to the children, but they had no respect for him; they had heard their father call Henry the Sixth a holy fool and they had been told that he was in the power of his French queen, Margaret. They were taken to his camp where he made a fuss and said, 'The children must have food immediately.' None of this impressed them: a king should have better things to do than bother about children's food while his army rampages through a town. George remarked to his brother that the meat was heavily spiced to disguise the fact that it was bad: he was attentive to matters concerning food and drink. It was a pleasant afternoon, the sun warm for the time of year, and after they had eaten the two boys were allowed to sit outside the tent while their immediate future was debated. George was a big, florid child already tending to overweight, but lively and attractive nonetheless. Attention was important to him and he was not discriminating as to whence it came. Now, he took an eager interest in the comings and goings of those around him and could scarcely refrain from attempting to make their acquaintance. The dullness of sitting quiet was almost insupportable; he had much to talk about, he was prodigiously well-informed on all manner of subjects so that an audience was of considerable importance to him. As he watched a man hammering out a dent in a breastplate, another polishing a pair of boots, a third mending a leather strap, it was a great hardship to George not to be able to give advice; but as he realized this to be beneath his dignity, he had to satisfy himself by pointing out to his brother the mistakes which each man was making. Richard was used to receiving instruction from George, and as it was given with the wholly good-natured intention of improving his mind, he was usually grateful. His, however, was a very different disposition from that of his brother, and at this moment he was unable to respond. He sat huddled forward, his thin face peaked with fatigue, his lips pressed closely together, his eyes not resting on any of the men around him but concentrating with surprising intensity for one so young on a patch of ground a few feet away, as though by staring long enough he might bore a hole in the earth and make his escape; in his rather sombre attire he looked not unlike a little mole who has come up for air and found it has little liking for what it sees. Richard was well aware that he was among his family's enemies and firmly resolved to hate all who supported the red rose of Lancaster.

The sun was bright and the children had had a heavy meal; after a while George could not concentrate on the mending of straps nor Richard on his hatred, and soon they both dozed. They had been through an hour of danger, but they were not marked by it. The danger that is faced squarely in the full light of day is one that can be accommodated; but the sight of mighty men, magnificent in armour, devastated by disillusion and bitterness, is very frightening. Richard dreamt of his father, standing in a room with his head turned away, the face hidden. Try as he might, he could not see the face. He was so frightened by this dream that he could not speak of it; but when, some weeks later, his mother had time for him, he asked to be told of his father's exploits.

'What do you want to know?'

He wanted comfort but did not know how to ask for it. He was fortunate, however, in that his mother was disposed to give him her attention. She and the children had been committed to the charge of the Duchess of Buckingham, and the Duchess of York found the lack of occupation more testing than the petty indignities to which she was subjected. Over the years, she had seen little of her children; now they were all she had and, since she was a woman who must be usefully employed, she bent her energies to the task of instructing them.

During these weeks when they were confined together, she told the children not only of armies bravely led, but of responsibility on a less heroic scale. She had as much reason as any of her menfolk to know that loyalty must be earned. Indeed, she was perhaps better aware, having spent more time on her husband's estates than had he, that demands for good service are more readily answered by men who are content; and she had had the opportunity to observe that while the great lord has noble aims such as the defence of the realm and the pursuit of foreign wars, the common man is more concerned with pasture rights and the price of perch.

Richard listened because it was his habit to listen. But George soon became restive; matters of law and administration, as well as being hard to grasp, were in his opinion very boring and inappropriate to himself. He sought, by eager questioning, to divert his mother's discourse to more martial matters worthy of a man's attention.

Once, Richard, who was usually silent, asked, 'What is treason?' But the questioning was taken over by the more volatile George and Richard received no answer. By the time he understood, fear had put down roots.

Their life continued uneventfully for a time. They had limited apartments in one of the Duke of Buckingham's manors on the Welsh Marches. The Duchess of Buckingham was in residence briefly and during this time she received a number of visitors. One of these was Margaret Beaufort, Countess of Richmond, a girl of sixteen, a mother and already widowed. She was to marry the Duchess' second son who would leave her a widow again before many years had passed.

One morning, Richard was drawn to the window by a mêlée in the courtyard. A child of some two years had been knocked down by one of the boarhounds, and now victim and aggressor, the one held by the hand and the other the collar, were being encouraged to make truce. The dog was the more eager to please; the child responded to its wet embrace by poking it in the eye. Remonstrances followed and the dog was brought forward, tail wagging forgivingly, but the child held out against this unwanted friendship with remarkable determination. Richard watched with no idea that he and this tenacious child were to be the protagonists in a story of two men who were strong, of one who lost and one who survived. After a few minutes, he turned away in search of more interesting distractions and never subsequently had so clear a view of Henry Tydder.

Chapter 2

I

In July of the following year a battle was fought on the outskirts of Northampton. This time it was the turn of King Henry's

men to cry 'Treason!' as a wing of their army deserted to the
Yorkist lords. News of the outcome of the battle was soon
spread by men fleeing to their villages: rumour was rife, facts
were harder to come by.

The man who came to the priest's house in the village of
Foxlow, near Tewkesbury, was in search of facts. Dr John
Morton, acting on behalf of his patron the Archbishop of
Canterbury, was on his way to see Lord Stanley in Cheshire
when news of the battle reached him. He made enquiries at the
inn but soon realized he must look elsewhere for facts. What Dr
Morton sought he was accustomed to find; but he listened with
good grace to the innkeeper's unlikely tales. Something about
Morton's face, the hint of a desire to please, suggested that he
was a man who had worked for his advancement. But the bright
eyes were not ill-disposed towards life and there was no resentment in the line of the mouth. Advancement had so far kept
pace with expectation.

'And Lord Stanley?' he interjected eventually.

Invention failed the innkeeper at this point and he admitted
that it was uncertain whether Lord Stanley had taken part in
the battle. This, Morton thought, was not surprising since
Stanley was subject to chronic uncertainty on such occasions.
But whether he had fought or no, he was not one to seek glory
on the field of battle and Morton had few qualms for his safety:
it was with the fate of King Henry that he was concerned. The
innkeeper now discovered that he had much business to attend
to and suggested that Morton should pay a visit to the priest.
'He knows everything there is to know.' The recommendation
was made with such evident dislike that Morton approached
the priest's dwelling anticipating a storyteller as loquacious as
the innkeeper but less likable.

The door opened so quickly that Morton guessed the priest
had observed his approach. Morton saw a man some ten years
younger than himself, perhaps still in his twenties. Before he
could introduce himself, the priest said, 'I recognized you.'
Morton looked at him closely. He was very thin and his face
was remarkably ugly, the eyes not aligned, the nose bent to one
side and the full mouth purple with sores. In spite of its repulsive
appearance, there was, however, an arrogance about the face,
and an unmistakable intelligence in the eyes, which made it
possible to accept the next statement. 'I heard you discussing
Wyclif's *De Domino Divino* when I was studying at Oxford.'

As soon as they were seated, the priest began to talk about
Wyclif with more enthusiasm than discretion. He ranted about
the corruption of the monks and said that if, a hundred years

ago, Wyclif could speak of the monastic life as 'the religion of fat cows', what would he say now? Such talk was well enough at Oxford where it was understood that half of what was said was not meant, but elsewhere one ran the risk of being taken seriously. 'Perhaps Wyclif would be taken aback at the way some of his ideas have been misrepresented by ignorant people?' Morton said gently. 'Were there not three Lollards burnt at the stake in this very district last year?' The priest had the wit to look uneasy.

This would have been the moment for Morton to plead the urgency of his mission and ask for news of the battle. But his curiosity was aroused and, obeying his intuition, he encouraged the man to talk about himself. So it was that after an hour he was still sitting in the dingy room that smelt of damp and the priest's bad breath. The wind was up; he could see it thrashing the branches of a pear tree and blowing straw across the yard of the inn where his horse was tethered. He said, 'And so you came to Foxlow?' He was by now aware that this man, like himself, was not of noble birth, being the son of an Oxford squire. Such men need a few favours from fortune if they are to rise in the world, and the priest, it seemed, had been ill-used by fortune; but could he really have been the subject of so much envy, spite and wilful neglect as he made out?

'Why do you think your gifts have been so ill-rewarded?' Morton asked him.

'There is no respect for learning today. People are so doltish that even Abelard could not strike a spark from their dull wits.'

How little his flock must love this shepherd, Morton thought. Aloud, he said, 'I doubt that in any age men have succeeded who had no wish to please. As for Abelard, perhaps time lends a certain enchantment. He and the men who surrounded him spent their time arguing among themselves. Their discourses profit us little today.'

'Because we question nothing and so we believe nothing!' The priest had worked himself into a genuine passion. 'The priests mumble things they barely understand while men of noble birth talk and laugh at mass, even during the elevation.'

'Were they so much more serious in Abelard's time?' Morton asked drily. 'Even then, there may have been those who thought twice before putting their beliefs to the test, who shrank from giving their bodies to be burnt.'

The priest clasped his bony hands and a flush spread over his cheeks. He said in a low voice, 'You are right to rebuke me. I have ventured nothing.' He bowed his head.

A bitter, disappointed man, Morton thought, but one in whom conscience will always be stronger than ambition. Such men, if properly handled, can give useful service. Morton said, 'With the views you hold, you must surely be strong for King Henry, whose piety must commend him to you.'

Christopher Ormond looked down at his bony knuckles. His own interests would best be served by a Yorkist victory: he knew a man who had favours to expect of Richard, Duke of York, and who, in turn, owed a favour or two to Christopher Ormond. Had he said as much at this moment, Dr Morton might have passed out of his life. But Christopher Ormond disdained favours; he considered that his intellectual superiority should commend itself without any effort on his part. He said scornfully, 'I am no Yorkist.'

'And neither am I.' Morton smiled; he was at his most dangerous when cheerful. 'The King, as we all know, is not in the best of health; but Queen Margaret is a woman of such quality that nowhere is there her equal today.' He went on to praise Queen Margaret for her courage, intelligence and states-manship, imagining that Ormond would need persuasion to take note of any woman. In this he was mistaken. Women paid as little attention to Christopher Ormond as to one of the gargoyles beneath his church roof, but he was as ardent for love as any handsome gallant. It was not, however, for their courage or intelligence that he desired women, and so he listened un-moved as Dr Morton talked of Queen Margaret as though she were a man.

'I have the honour to serve those who serve Queen Margaret.' Morton was, at every stage of his career, aware of his position, its limits and strengths, and he never made the mistake of assuming authority that was not his. Ormond saw before him a man who understood power even if he did not yet possess it. He was impressed, and as a gesture of respect to Dr Morton, he declared himself to be strong for Queen Margaret.

Morton, well-satisfied, recollected his mission and said that he must depart without delay. Ormond, who was reluctant to part from this chance-met stranger, offered hospitality for the night; he looked at his guest hopefully, while fighting back a feeling of panic when he recollected how little food was avail-able, and most of it bad. Morton declined, but on the threshold he hesitated, the wind stirring his cloak. 'I wonder. . . . I have greatly enjoyed our discussion. It is important to me to be well-informed, and to this end I have sought out people like yourself—men of undoubted ability whose veracity and dis-cretion can be relied on—to send reports to me; in other words, to be my eyes and ears, and my nose as well, since I like to know not only what has happened but what is in the wind.'

'To what purpose should I report to you?' Ormond asked; then, as even to his ears this sounded churlish, he added, 'I ask in order to ensure that I may be of service to you.'

'I am writing a history of the times,' Morton said. 'And history is the story of man and his actions, is it not? So it is men and their actions which interest me primarily. If, at any time, there should be a particular issue which concerns me, I would communicate it to you.'

They talked for a few minutes and Morton told Ormond where to send his reports. It was only when Morton finally turned to leave that Ormond said, 'One thing I can tell you now. It is reported, by one who is usually reliable, that King Henry was surprised in his tent by Yorkist soldiers; and that the Earl of Warwick is escorting him to London, more in the manner of a prisoner than a king.'

Ormond watched Morton as he walked across the street to the inn. The sun had come out, but the wind was keen and smelt of rain. It was only when he turned into his house that he noticed the faint smell of burning. He went from room to room but found nothing to explain it. He must have gone to sleep puzzling about it, because he woke early in the morning recollecting an incident in his childhood.

When he was six he had spent a year with relatives near Kirkby Mallory. The dull monotony of their lives had irked him; but in the autumn there was an unexpected diversion. Each morning he asked, 'Is it today they are burning the priest? Why are they burning him?'

'Because he is a Lollard.'

When the great day came he was forbidden to go out because he was too young for such sights. He watched men pass the house carrying faggots and ran to tell his aunt, 'I must go! I have to go!'

'Must! Have!' she laughed.

'What is a Lollard?' he asked. '*Why* is he a Lollard?'

She did not answer him. Later, when she was not looking, he ran into the orchard, meaning to make his way into the town. But he took a path through a meadow and here he came across a rusty knife, an old coin, and a buckle from a man's shoe; he ran on, imagining himself a knight searching for treasure and came eventually to the river. The river ran fast, tumbling over boulders and he lay on his stomach and watched the trophies of the river borne by, a sack, a log like a monster with great branched head, a shirt wrested from some careless washer-woman, and a dead cat. He found a stick and made an oar of it and for a time he was a sailor venturing on an enchanted sea. Later, when he saw deer on the opposite bank, he became a hunter.

The moon was up by the time the truant came back through the meadow. As he came nearer the town, he noticed a smell of burning in the air and he imagined himself a tinker crouched over his fire as night fell. It had been a happy day.

2

The land had been long untended and violence flourished as the weeds grow in fields untended by the plough; there was no pattern in it and no one could tell how this state of affairs had come about or why. But the violence of December, 1460, was part of a deliberate design. Down the long line of the northern uplands, over moors where the red deer roamed, in dales cut deep into the hills and blocked on either side by impenetrable forests, little communication with the outside world was possible. There was only the one high road, bleak and often impassable in winter, and at the most three lower roads of varying serviceability. Isolation was a part of the lives of the people. But now they were vouchsafed some sense of belonging to a wider community. For there was a thread which linked hamlet to hamlet, village to village, and told a story of a kind. And there were signs which assured villagers still uncon-nected that they, too, would become a part of the design: it might be no more than a spiral of smoke against the dark winter sky, or, if they were fortunate, longer notice might be given by men in flight who had actually seen the flames and more besides. But some places, deep in narrow dales or sleeping in the hollow of a hill, had no warning.

In one such place, the wind, stirring amid the ashes, ruffled through piles of smoking cloth to the bone beneath; it surged lonely down the rough track which led to the manor house and found some resistance here for the walls were standing although the roof had gone. Beyond the manor, the church stood entire still, and in somewhat better condition than it had been heretofore since frantic hands had torn away the brambles thick around the porch. In the effort to gain sanctuary, the church had been better attended than at any time since its last incumbent left many years ago. But it had been to no purpose. The wind pushed at the door but met a resistance stronger than rust; blood had trickled beneath the door and collected on the one step, congealing at the edge of the pool, but darkly gleaming in the centre. For all its busy searching, the wind found nothing living in the church.

At dawn, the lad for whom moonlight had once lighted a path crept out from the shelter of the great raised tomb of the lords of the manor. The moon had proved a fickle friend, but he had managed well enough without its aid. He was a little thinner, for the last year had been hard, but he was no less enterprising. He picked his way purposefully among the bodies in the rough ground outside the church, bending sometimes to turn a shoulder and run a hand down where a trinket might lie between breasts, or searching in breeches, but it was a poor place and he found nothing.

'So what does Robin do now?' he asked aloud.

'How came Robin to be alive?'

The voice seemed to come from between his shoulder blades and when he tried to turn, he felt the prick of steel through his worn doublet.

'They all ran towards the church.' For once Robin Prithie could think of nothing better than the truth. 'I stayed in the open and kept out of sight. The soldiers had game enough and had no need to play hide and seek.'

'You have blood on your hands.'

The truth would not serve here. 'And who would not, seeing such piteous sights? I tried to tend their wounds, but it was no use.'

The steel moved from between Robin's shoulder blades. The man walked leisurely round and stared down at him, the sword pointing this time at his stomach. Robin saw a man of his own height and build dressed in the livery of the Earl of Northumberland.

'What are you doing here?' the man asked. 'By your speech, you don't belong in these parts.'

'My father was bailiff to Sir Geoffrey Warent of whom you may have heard.' The Earl of Northumberland's man had not heard of Sir Geoffrey Warent, which was a pity as it was the one part of Robin's story which could be verified. His father had been murdered by the Earl of Oxford's men, but Robin thought it wisest to name no names, so he said merely that his father had been set upon and murdered. 'And I have moved from place to place making a living as best I can,' he concluded pathetically.

'Following in the wake of Queen Margaret's army, robbing and stealing!' The man's lips curled contemptuously. 'I've a mind to serve you as these people have been served. Can you give me a reason why I should not?'

'The same reason that any of these poor souls would have given!' Robin retorted. 'I have no wish to die. Nor have I deserved to die. You, too, follow in the wake of the army. Does this prove that *you* rob and steal?'

'I do not follow the army!' The man had a great sense of his own importance and allowed himself to be distracted. 'I ride to Lord Stanley with messages from my master. I saw the smoke rising some distance away and hastened to discover the cause.'

Or waited until you judged it safe to come into the open, Robin thought: we are not so unlike, for all your splendid livery. He looked more closely at the man. They were indeed very alike, being of the same height and build. Robin was prepared to wager, however, that of the two he had the quicker wit. He made a move as though to walk away and the man poked the tip of the sword in his ribs. Robin looked beyond the man. His eyes widened so that they were like marbles which might roll out of their sockets at any moment; he croaked, 'They rise! Holy Mother of God, the dead rise!' The man, much alarmed by this performance, looked fearfully over his shoulder and Robin, catching at his leg, brought him crashing down. He had a jagged piece of flint ready to hand, but he did not need it because the man had split his head on the corner of the tomb-stone. Robin pushed the man's head down in the grass so that blood would not stain his clothing.

The business of changing clothes took longer than Robin had anticipated. One way and another, the last twenty-four hours had been very unpleasant and he felt sick and exhausted by the time the exchange was effected. He hoped the man's horse was near by since his own legs seemed unwilling to carry him. In this as in most things, for he was Fortune's child, he was lucky. The animal was tethered to a tree not far away; it was sweating and greatly agitated, not liking the smell of death any more than did Robin.

Robin, who had more patience with animals than with his fellow human beings, spent a little time calming the horse. When eventually he mounted he said, 'Now, we two need food and rest and I am hopeful we shall find both by the end of this day.' At least, the messenger of the Earl of Northumberland stood a better chance of hospitality than Robin Prithie, vaga-bond. Nevertheless, he was a little uneasy and hoped he had not changed his luck along with his clothes.

Many miles further south, in Foxlow, Christopher Ormond

was writing to Dr Morton, 'What news reaches us puts people in great fear. Queen Margaret has promised her Scottish troops that they can take their own reward and it is said she keeps her promises well; the country is laid waste and no one is spared. . . .'

3

Panic had not yet spread to the city of London. As the sun dipped low and the blue sky evened into pearl, people scurried along narrow streets and beggars drew tatters of clothing about their sores. Cold was the main concern on this particular evening when a messenger dismounted in the courtyard of the house where the Duchess of York was staying with her children.

Richard and George were sitting by the window in the hall when the messenger was brought to their mother. The window was open and the evening air was sharp. There were goose pimples on Richard's arm; he ran his fingers lightly over them and was nudged to be still by George. Light flickered as a taper was lit; the smell of wax drifted to them and words came to their ears. On the thirtieth of December, outside Sandal Castle in Yorkshire, some of their father's men had been attacked and instead of waiting for reinforcements, the Duke of York and the Earl of Salisbury had gone out to meet the enemy. The children glowed as the messenger described how valiantly their father had fought, but the Duchess cut short his tale.

'Yes, yes. Rehearse me no more details.' Her voice was dry. 'That they fought valiantly, I will accept without further proof. What has befallen them?'

'Both dead, my lady, fighting most gallantly. . . .'

The messenger would have stopped his tale there, but she sensed that there was more to be told and made him tell it. So she learnt that the head of the Duke of York had been impaled on Micklegate Bar in York, crowned with paper and straw.

Later, the children were formally told what already they had overheard. George, with the anger of the spoilt child, resentful of any denial of his rights whether large or trivial, spoke bravely of revenge and of how he would make the House of Lancaster pay for the ill done to his father. He was red in the face and his whole body puffed up with the enormity of his wrongs. Richard was silent, pale of face, lips pressed inwards; he was not built to swagger, being small in stature and of a rather frail appearance. His mother, more moved by what she took to be his mute acceptance than by his brother's bravado, laid her arm across his shoulders. Immediately the small body stiffened. The gesture was a mistake; the boy felt himself suspected of weakness. He was far from accepting what had happened and, possessing a vivid imagination, was able to visualise it only too well: a severed head crowned with paper and straw, a hideous picture never subsequently to leave the mind of this child who learnt his lessons well. As soon as he was able to do so without attracting attention to himself, he turned and made his way along the corridor; he moved steadily, one fist held against his mouth, carefully containing his horror like a splitting sack which burst apart the moment he was in the latrine. By the time he joined his brother in their bedchamber, he was composed again.

No one minded the children for the time being. Their mother was consumed by grief. She had borne the brunt of much trouble during her husband's lifetime and had done it gladly; but now that he was dead there was only the trouble left and no more joy of him. This night, she had little thought to spare for her children.

In their bedchamber, George, who felt that his performance had not been fully appreciated, gave an encore for the benefit of his brother. The two children felt no intimate grief for a father they scarcely knew; but they had a sense of the harm done to their line and they experienced a burning resentment, the rousing of the primaeval anger of the clan. To die in battle was an acceptable fate, but the ignominy of that head crowned with paper and straw was not to be borne! George trembled with fury and pronounced the punishments he would mete out when the perpetrators of this crime were at his mercy. Richard, being more frugal of his resources, contained his fury until such time as it might be profitably spent.

'Edward will see to it.' Richard spoke with assurance that this was an achievement well within Edward's capacity.

George said, 'Edward!' with a show of disdain, and stamped around the room, lunging with great ferocity at his own shadow, the performance being intended to convey that were he eighteen, and the Earl of March, no such calamity would have befallen his family. Richard watched uneasily, torn between affection for the handsome George who was his constant companion, and admiration for Edward who, being less well known, assumed godlike proportions.

'You do not need to think so much of Edward,' George said.

Richard looked away, awkward, but by no means irresolute. He absorbed ideas easily; but the mechanism of selection was remarkably well-developed and though he was so quiet, he was not easily influenced. But he was, after all, only eight and the night had brought many shocks. So after a time, he rather spoilt his obstinate stand for his brother Edward by yawning and pummelling one eye with a fist.

'The fault is,' George, too, was tiring, but still had energy enough to give his brother a history lesson, 'there are too many of these great lords. . . .'

George talked, enchanted by his own wisdom. Below the window, distant sounds came to their ears, hammering, the jingle of harness, the busy tramp of men coming and going. Much was in preparation, though for what purpose they did not know. Richard leant out of the window, but could see little except hurrying forms in torchlight. Immediately below the window, ivy grew from a crevice in the stone; momentarily distracted, he leant down to see if he could reach it, but his straining fingers dislodged only a handful of dust.

'You aren't listening,' George complained.

But Richard had no need to listen. He knew about the evils of the long protectorship, the decline of law and order as the great lords warred one with another, the weak-minded king not entirely to blame, for after so long a minority it would have been difficult for a strong man to wrest the reins from the hands of the power-greedy lords. These things had been talked of ever since Richard first opened his eyes on the world. The lesson was engraved on his mind: woe to that realm which has a child to its king.

At last, they went to bed. George, whose comfort meant a great deal to him, could so arrange his mind that things unpleasant should be put aside until morning. But Richard slept and woke and drifted sometimes half in and half out of sleep; and in this half-dreaming state voices came to him as men paused from their labours in the courtyard and talked.

'I'm old . . .' one of them said, and hawked prodigiously to prove it. 'I remember Harry the Fifth: I saw him once. Now, that was a man! Knew what he wanted and how to get it. That's the difference between him and men like the Duke.' He made haste to add, 'A fine man; oh, a very fine man was the Duke of York. But he didn't know how to get what he wanted. Honest, he was, and straightforward — too straightforward. He thought everyone was as honest as he was. He didn't understand strategy. There wasn't any need for him to be killed, charging off like that without waiting until he had all his men with him. No strategy.'

'Ah, maybe.' A younger voice. 'But while you're messing about with strategy someone steals up and cuts your throat! I reckon his mistake was, he never recognized his enemies until it was too late and they'd slipped through his fingers.' But I shall recognize my enemies, Richard thought, and he listened intently. 'If I'd been the Duke of York, do you know what I'd have done? I'd have got rid of men like Pembroke while I had the chance. I'd have struck them down in front of me the very first time I saw a gleam in their eyes I didn't much like.'

'You got to have cause. . . .'

'Oh no, you haven't, Grandad, don't you believe it! Not if you're a Duke you don't need to have cause. It's only the likes of you and me that has to have a good reason to show for cutting each other's throats. The Duke should have struck hard at the first sign of danger! A man's got to know when to stop talking and act.'

Later in the night, it was a woman's voice mumbling to herself, 'We shall all be murdered, oh Lord ha' mercy, they'll come and we shall all be murdered. . . .' The voice came from the corridor. Richard got out of bed and opened the door quietly. She was kneeling in front of a chest from which she was taking out linen and folding it, and all the time rocking to and fro and crying: an old, crumpled creature whom he had never seen before. He went back to bed and drew his knees up to his chin. As a result of his restlessness he had cold air for bedfellow and he could not prevent himself from shivering violently. He had heard people wailing that they were to be murdered often enough and this aroused no terror in him. But everything was muddled in his mind and sometimes he thought he heard that terrible cry 'Treason!' which had so disturbed his father and which he associated with all the ill that had befallen his family.

In the morning, the world had settled itself again. They were put to their studies as though nothing had happened. Weeks passed. February brought good news. Edward had defeated a Lancastrian army at Mortimer's Cross. But the fruits of this victory were squandered. Warwick tarried overlong in London and when eventually his forces met those of Queen Margaret at St Albans, he was defeated. He had taken King Henry with him, which was ill-advised, and had lost him to Queen Margaret, which was careless.

Warwick fled westward leaving London undefended as the Lancastrian horde approached. The citizens of London were known to look to themselves and be damned to everyone else, and the Duchess of York did not trust them to stand firm. She decided to send George and Richard to Burgundy where they would be safe from Queen Margaret. George, who liked London because it was so full of people, was downcast. Richard was not displeased. He felt suffocated in this city with its press of people, garrulous as monkeys, and its maze of narrow streets from which the foulness of the open sewers was never dispersed even in winter. He would be sorry to leave his mother but glad to quit London.

The voyage was represented to the boys as a great adventure and this they accepted all too readily. They were excited as children dressed up for a carnival when they donned the clothes of their servants' children, and they could barely contain their exuberance when they bade farewell to their mother. The Duchess, who had waved her men to battle without a sign of weakness, was almost overcome when she saw the young, excited faces uplifted to her. It was as though the grief she thought she had conquered had waited for this moment. She would have clutched these last treasures to her and refused to part with them had not the old mastiff come loping up, wagging his tail, and prepared to join in this strange frolic. George noisily berated the faithful creature for recognizing him, and the Duchess found relief in berating George in his turn.

'If you use that tone of voice, no disguise will be of help to you! If you cannot speak meekly, then learn from your brother here who at least knows when to hold his tongue.' She embraced Richard warmly. 'You are like your father, brave and staunch. Be always so.' She scarcely knew what she was saying, but Richard took her words seriously and imagined himself to have charge over George.

It was a bitterly cold evening when they set off and a fine drizzle was falling. The Lancastrians were already in the suburbs and there were those who would not scruple to ingratiate themselves with Queen Margaret by making her a present of the two young sons of the Duke of York. It was decided, therefore, that the boys should be conducted to the wharf on foot accompanied by only a few attendants.

The driving rain made it natural that they should shield their faces, but after a time naturalness began to pall on George. He felt that the adventure lacked excitement and it annoyed him that his presence should attract so little attention. He took to pantomiming secrecy, clutching his hood, plucking at Richard's sleeve, exclaiming, 'My goodness, that was a near thing!' and 'That gust of wind very nearly blew this hood right back!' and 'I had better walk on this side of you so that I can't be observed.'

'What about me?' Richard asked.

'No one will know you.'

No one appeared to know George, but he was behaving so oddly that attention was inevitably directed at the party. One of the attendants told him to quieten down, whereupon he turned about, bellowing, 'I am not to be spoken to like that!' A derisive cheer went up from men standing in the doorway of an inn. This piece of folly so infuriated Richard that he turned on his brother, kicked him in the backside, and told him to get on and not to be so stupid. Before the attendants could intervene, George had slapped Richard across the face. Richard was not much hurt, but the hood slipped back from his head and a man in the inn doorway shouted, 'There's a burning bush to go with that temper!'

After this, the attendants had no further trouble with their charges. George occupied the reminder of the walk in berating Richard. 'You should have had the sense to keep your hair covered.' He was deeply offended that it was Richard who had attracted the attention if only by the colour of his hair. Richard, more worried about the colour of his temper, accepted the tirade meekly.

By the time they were on the boat the wind was so strong that Richard had to turn his back to it in order to draw breath. George, forgetting his anger, turned his attention to one of the seamen.

'Does this wind never cease?' he shouted.

'Never.'

The thought of so much opposition from the elements was not pleasing to George and he continued to shout questions more because he refused to be silenced than because there was anything he particularly wanted to know.

'How long will the voyage last?'

The seaman began to talk of currents and of rocks to be negotiated, to say nothing of sea monsters which sometimes reared up to prevent the passage of a ship and of an island which was sometimes visible and sometimes faded away. Richard, sensing by his tone that the man did not know what he was talking about, turned away; but George, who liked a show of knowledge whether soundly based or otherwise, listened admiringly.

Richard huddled in his cloak. Waves broke over the ship and drenched him with spray which left a white crust on his cloak when it dried. He could taste salt on his lips. He looked up at the mast, which dipped and rose against a moving background of cloud. His eyes seemed nailed to the mast; he watched it dipping and rising, dipping and rising, dipping and rising, and soon he was very sick and continued so for the rest of the voyage.

Chapter 3

I

The Lancastrian army which Edward, Earl of March, had defeated at Mortimers Cross was led by the Earls of Pembroke and Wiltshire. Edward was merciful to the more humble of his enemies but not to their leaders. Jasper, Earl of Pembroke, in particular, had little to hope for from Edward: he was the bastard son of Harry the Fifth's Queen Catharine, and Edward would have welcomed the opportunity to cut a thread of that tangled skein. The Earl of Pembroke fled westwards. His father, Owen Tydder, failed to make good his escape. He was captured and beheaded in Hereford, refusing until the end to believe that anyone would commit so great an infamy as to sever from its body the head which had once lain in Queen Katherine's lap.

The news was conveyed to Margaret Beaufort who had been travelling to Brecknock with her son; she received it calmly, asking, 'And Jasper?'

'Fled to Pembroke Castle.'

She nodded her head, well-pleased. She had been little more than a child when she married Jasper's brother, the Earl of Richmond, and within a year he had left her a widow; but her loyalty to his family was strong. She was soon to wed again and had already decided that her son, Henry, should be brought up at Pembroke Castle. She had not anticipated, however, that the parting would come so suddenly.

'Why can't I stay with you?' the child asked when, heavy with sleep, he was summoned from his bed.

'Because you will be safer in Pembroke Castle.'

'Is Uncle Jasper coming with me?'

'He has gone already. He will be waiting for you there.' She hugged him and told him that he must be brave. He looked at her, solemn but tearless. He had never known his father and he had seen little of his grandfather. Those best known to him were his mother and his Uncle Jasper; now he was to set off on a journey without either of them.

'I think perhaps I won't go,' he said tentatively.

He set out early in the morning with a few trusted retainers. The Yorkist army was known to be not many miles away, so the small fugitive band kept to the hills. There was little to

distinguish the four men and the child from others who straggled
along the hill tracks, seeking shelter in that part of the country
still held by the Lancastrians. The ground was rough and at
times they had to dismount and lead their horses. It was a hard
journey for a grown man, severe for a child of four. He got
very dirty and wet, was often hungry and always uncomfortable; but he accepted this without making undue fuss. Henry
Tydder had already learnt to expect little of life.

In the brief sunlit hours, the folds of the hills were like the
full sleeves of a rich mantle, dark green inlaid with bronze,
with a gleam of stones caught here and there. They looked
deceptively smooth at the summit, but they widened out as the
party climbed and what, further down, had looked like a green
swathe proved to be a dense knot of brambles and bracken.
Late in the afternoon, the party stopped by a tarn, smooth as
glass and very cold. While the men struck camp, Henry was
left to his own devices. He amused himself wriggling on his
stomach through the undergrowth, pretending to be an animal
of some sort—not a monster, he had his imagination on too
tight a rein for that. After some growling and mewling, which
were the animal sounds most familiar to him, he tired of this
and, finding himself near the water, inched to the edge and
looked down. He beheld his own face, quite adequately re-
produced except for a rather long head. He was waggling the
egg-shaped head about slowly, and watching the image respond, when a stone plopped in the water; the face wavered
and broke apart. Henry looked up and saw a small, dark
man standing above him who was certainly not one of his own
party.

The man put a finger to his lips, then reaching his hand into
a leather bag attached to his waist, he drew out a small stone
and handed it to Henry. The action was accompanied by
words, softly spoken. The words made no sense to Henry, but
bribery has never needed words and Henry understood perfectly
that his silence had been bought. The stone was in fact a piece
of quartz which, when crushed, might reveal in its siftings a
trace of the riches beneath the earth's surface. But to the child
it was just a stone, pale and colourless. The bright-eyed tatter-
demalion who had given the stone was so different from anyone
whom Henry had ever met that it seemed possible he might be
one of the mountain folk of whom his nurse had told him, people
seldom seen in daylight and who had the habit of vanishing
before a stranger had the chance of a second look at them.
Henry blinked his eyes: the little dark man was still there and
quite made up for any disappointment occasioned by the

ordinariness of the stone. Henry's nurse had also told him that he should beware of strangers, but people came and went in Henry's life to such an extent that he adapted himself as well to strangers as to those who were supposed to be his friends. He much preferred this particular stranger to his attendants, who plainly regarded him as something of a nuisance. The dark man was as interested in Henry as Henry was in him; he squatted down and examined the material of Henry's clothes with wonder. As he fingered Henry's jerkin, he touched the chain of the locket which Henry wore round his neck. Henry pulled the locket free of the jerkin and the dark man gazed at its intricate workmanship in awe.

At this point, one of Henry's attendants called out, 'What's that brat up to now? He's very quiet.' Something that was no more than a shadow flickered past Henry's eyes and behind him the thorn bushes moved as though a light breeze had parted them. Then all was still and Henry was alone.

The attendant's passage to the tarn was noisy. 'What are you doing?' He glanced about him suspiciously and then gazed down into the water as though it could supply an answer. Henry found a heavy stone and threw it in the water; he watched with satisfaction while the attendant's face wavered and broke apart.

That night, when the party camped, the men huddled round the fire. Henry made no mention of his encounter, not only because he realized that it would not meet with approval, but because he liked secrets. The men, who were missing their women, laughed a lot and told bawdy stories. Then, as it grew colder, one of their number, a Welshman, sang a melancholy Celtic ballad. The child listened, rubbing his gift-stone in the palm of his hand. The voice of the singer seemed to be answered by strange echoes.

'How long are we going to be in these hills?' one of the men asked uneasily.

'In three days we shall come to a valley where my old aunt lives,' the Welshman answered. 'The people there will know where the Yorkists are.'

'Who carries news? We haven't seen anyone.'

'Maybe not, but we have been seen, make no mistake about that! These hills are inhabited by clansmen who know every move a stranger makes.'

The men glanced apprehensively over their shoulders. 'Do they cast spells?'

'I don't know about that; they are so handy with their axes they hardly need spells to deal with such as us.'

This did little to reassure his listeners. 'We have nothing with which to buy safe passage,' one man said.

'Buy!' The Welshman was angry. 'They are a proud, ancient people and they would not trade with Saxons. It would take many lifetimes for them to accept so much as a "good-day" from such as you.'

Henry put the gift-stone in his kerchief and knotted the kerchief securely.

The next two days the going grew rougher and they had to lead the horses much of the way. Only the child, humped on horseback, had any joy of it. He liked the lofty position; with stinging eyes and running nose, Henry Tydder bumped along, king of all the wilderness and carrying in his kerchief a gift-stone signifying his acceptance by a man of a proud and ancient race.

While the party was on the move, the little dark man did not appear. But once or twice in the evenings, when Henry wandered away to play on his own, the man came to him. He was very impressed with the locket, so Henry offered it to him. The gift was accepted with no sign of offended pride. Later, Henry gave the man a ring. In return, he acquired four more stones as uninteresting as the first one.

On the occasion of the giving of the ring, Henry was down by a stream which chattered noisily over huge boulders. One of the attendants came down to the stream hoping to catch fish for supper. The little dark man dodged behind one of the boulders at the water's edge. The attendant bent down to address Henry angrily, 'Haven't I told you not to wander away on your own?' The next moment his feet shot from beneath him and he went head-first into the stream. Henry viewed this performance with ecstatic delight; he rolled over and over, clutching his stomach and laughing until he could scarcely draw breath. But when he was ducked in the icy water himself he did not think it was so funny.

'He pushed me in the stream,' the attendant explained when he brought his streaming charge to the camp fire.

'Let him be,' one of the others said. 'If we don't hand him over fit and well, we'll have cause to regret it.'

Fish was eventually caught and cooked over the fire. After he had finished his portion, Henry went away, unwrapped his bundle, and counted his gift-stones, an expression of great contentment on his face.

The next day they reached the valley where the Welshman's aunt lived, and where she waited on them and fussed over the child. He stank abominably by this time so she picked him up and took him into the yard where she scrubbed him vigorously in a tub; he resisted this assault on his person with vehemence, but she stood no nonsense and smacked him soundly. Later, when the men were at supper, she talked to the Welshman in their own tongue. 'And has the child no kin?'

'His father died two months before he was born and his grandfather went to the block last month. His uncle has fled to Pembroke Castle where we hope to join him.'

'Ah, the poor little lad!'

The object of her pity squatted on the hearth shovelling gruel into his mouth, seemingly unmoved by his plight. A plain child, she thought him; and though years later she would relate that 'he was so beautiful it stopped your heart to look at him, and with something quite saintly about him, too!' now, she merely observed, 'He's a very messy eater, isn't he?'

There was no good news for them yet. Yorkist supporters had been reported not far away and they must move west without delay. The next morning, they told the child, 'One day's ride and you'll be there!' They had told him this each day to cheer him, and young though he was he had by now come to doubt the statement. But he did not protest at such duplicity; he was a patient child.

The land through which they were passing was green and gentle, threaded with small streams, and the men felt that now they had only the Yorkists to contend with, since this was not country that gave good cover for wandering clansmen. They stopped in the late afternoon to eat some of the food the woman had provided for them. After he had eaten, Henry opened his precious bundle and felt inside: the kerchief was torn and it contained only one stone. Henry's face crumpled with something more than misery. He had looked after his treasure with such care, and this was his reward! From the bottom of his outraged heart and at the top of his voice, Henry Tydder proclaimed to the heavens his fury at the injustice of this return for good stewardship. 'I lost my stones!' he screamed. 'I lost my stones!' He was not to be comforted and the journey continued to the accompaniment of his unforgiving protests.

'You've a long way to go yet,' they told him grimly, driven at last to the truth. 'A long way to go.'

At last he fell silent and slumped dejectedly on his mount, the one remaining stone held in his clenched fist.

2

While Henry Tydder was still in flight westwards, the battle of St Albans was fought and won by Queen Margaret's army, and the Earl of Warwick was put to flight. The Queen's progress south was, however, accompanied by such terrors that the citizens of London, their resolution wonderfully stiffened by fear, resisted her demands and held her army at the gates of London. Within a month, Christopher Ormond, who had been visiting relations in London, wrote to Dr John Morton:

'I have but recently returned from London. On the twenty eighth day of February, there was much excitement as it was said that advance parties of the armies of the Earl of Warwick and the Earl of March were arrived. There were men about with tales of a tremendous battle in which many had been killed. On the next day, I went to the Bridge where so many people were gathered that the shops could do no business, for customers could not move to make room for others. I was on the Bridge when the young Earl of March rode into the city. He looked about him from side to side as he rode, smiling in a way that people much liked, especially the women. The Earl of Warwick was there beside him. There was much rejoicing in the city that night and in some parts they burnt the barricades which had been put up in the streets, making bonfires and dancing around them, which displeased the shopkeepers whose premises were close by. The next day, as I was on my way to Budge Row, I was approached by a man who told me that a large crowd was gathering in St John's Fields; after he spoke to me I saw him speaking to a number of other people, and so I went to St John's Fields where there was a great press of people and all of them expecting something to happen but not knowing what. There were many soldiers and a platform had been erected; I saw several noblemen near the platform. Then one of the noble-men, I was too far away to be sure who it was but it might have been Lord Fauconberg, spoke to the crowd of the terrible things which had happened to the towns which had been taken by Queen Margaret's army, and of the terrors which the people of London had been spared by the bravery of the Earl of March. At this the crowd cheered mightily. Then he asked whether they still wanted to be ruled by a weak-minded king who was in the power of Queen Margaret, and they shouted "No" very loud. Then he asked if they wanted Edward, Earl of March, to be their King and they all shouted "Yes" louder still. Not content with this, he began to tell them the reasons why this Edward deserved to be king, and then he asked again who they wanted to be king and they thundered that they wanted King Edward.'

Morton never received this letter. Edward and Warwick,

wasting little time on ceremony, pursued the Lancastrian army and another battle was fought at Towton. It was a terrible defeat for the Lancastrians. After the battle Queen Margaret fled north with her son and sick husband. King Edward, on his journey south, paused at Grafton Regis.

Richard and George returned to England and saw their brother crowned king in June. The Yorkist cause prospered. In September Lord Herbert captured Pembroke Castle. Jasper, Earl of Pembroke, escaped and made his way to Britanny, but his four-year-old nephew was taken captive. Lord Herbert was rewarded with the grant of Pembroke Castle and he also acquired, for the payment of one thousand pounds, the custody and marriage of Henry Tydder.

Edward gave little thought to events at Pembroke Castle. He had more important matters which called for his attention. In late September, he was in Grafton Regis again, on a tour of a garden.

'From here it runs wild.' Elizabeth Woodville looked at the tangle of trees and shrubs disdainfully, holding her skirts about her like a prim maid instead of a widow woman and the mother of two sons.

'But I see there is a path over there,' Edward said, hoping to escape from the wide green lawns which allowed no privacy.

'It leads down to the place where the womere water runs,' she said. 'Shall we see if there is any sign of it now?'

'How could there be?' The womere water only ran at times when disaster was about to befall the country. 'It will be dry as a bone. Come! Let me prove it to you.'

The brittle twigs snapped beneath their feet and there was a hot, dusty smell from the ferns. Between the trees they had a glimpse of a small lake; the water had receded leaving the rushes high and dry surrounded by hard, cracked mud. It would indeed be a portent if the womere water gushed out in this place. Soon they came to a fallen tree trunk conveniently placed by the side of the path. Edward put out a hand to take Elizabeth's arm but she ducked beneath the overhanging branch of a tree, disturbing it by her passage and allowing it to swing back in his face.

'I am sorry,' she laughed.

'It will be my pleasure to make you show me just how sorry you are!'

But she knew this path well, else she would not have led him down it, and by now they had reached a bank which sloped steeply to the bed of a stream. The earth was bare and shifted beneath their feet so that they had to move cautiously. On the far side of the stream a great rock thrust up making the place dark.

'Bone dry,' Edward said with satisfaction.

'The womere water springs from there.' She pointed up at a crevice in the rock face. They stared up at it. A silver vein glimmered in the shadow.

'Not *quite* dry,' she said.

'But hardly gushing out.' He put an arm round her waist but she eased away from him and seated herself on a big boulder, spreading her skirts about her and folding her hands in her lap.

'You are a sorceress!' he said, bending over her.

'No. I have no magic, only a woman's gifts.'

'Those who are greatly gifted should be generous.'

'But not with their virtue.'

Her eyes met his; they were eyes that looked on life without illusion, but which as yet had seen more to make them merry than to arouse displeasure. The mouth was decisive; she would strike a hard bargain, but the slight fulness of the lower lip hinted that she would amply fulfil her part of it. The chin was nicely pointed so that one was not immediately conscious of its determination. At present, her femininity balanced her more formidable qualities.

'My parents will expect us to return in a minute,' she said.

'Why should they expect that?'

'Because they think that you have come to see them.'

'They could not think anything so unlikely. You are lying as usual.'

She remained quite calm, the folded hands emphasising her composure. Yet she was alert; the tilt of her head, the assured set of her shoulders, suggesting she was poised for whatever might be demanded of her.

'But it would be most improper were there any other reason for your visit.' She tilted her head back still further and looked up at the sky, musing on this. 'Especially as you are to be married soon.'

'Married?'

'They say that the Earl of Warwick plans for you to marry a French princess.'

'Does he?' Edward raised his eyebrows. 'I expect you are right. Warwick has plans for everything and everyone; it would be surprising if he had neglected to make plans for my marriage.'

'It has even been rumoured that you are already betrothed to the Lady Eleanor Butler.'

Edward turned his attention to the crevice in the rock, narrowing his eyes. 'I think you may be right. There is a little of that woe water dribbling out up there. How dismal!'

She saw that he was angry and that she must not provoke him further. This was a time when she was balanced between triumph and disaster and must keep her nerve. As they walked back Edward talked about his plans for hunting during the winter. He did not say whether he planned to hunt near Grafton Regis.

'This has been going on for five months!' Elizabeth's father, Lord Rivers, said when Edward had gone. 'Five months!' It was dangerous to stretch a man's patience so, and that man lustful and a king. Elizabeth put some more stitches in her embroidery. Her father looked out of the window at the clouds forming above the trees at the end of the garden. 'We shall have rain before the week is out,' he said dourly. He was superstitious and read omens in the quiver of a leaf when he was uneasy.

'We need rain,' Elizabeth said practically. What had she to fear from the elements? Had it not been snowing when King Edward stopped at the manor after the battle of Towton and saw her for the first time?

The father studied his daughter unhappily. He had seen her often enough over the years, but it had never been necessary to pay close attention to her until now when the family fortunes rested on her shoulders. Fortune was of considerable importance to the Woodville family, with its modest origins and lofty ambitions.

'You are too sure of yourself,' Lord Rivers said to Elizabeth. 'You have offended him so much he will never return. He will do as the Earl of Warwick wishes.'

'Do you know what he called me?' Elizabeth drew the thread between her teeth and snapped it in two. 'A sorceress!' She smiled, sure that her spells were stronger than those of the Earl of Warwick.

3

Whether the womere water ran or not, all was not well in Edward's kingdom. Robin Prithie rode through a countryside where woods and wasteland gradually encroached on land which had once been well-cultivated. He passed cottages almost completely covered with briars and brambles and sometimes a whole cluster of such places where a village had once been.

Even on the fringes of manorial estates, the land rotted and ran to waste. Old people in the inns where Robin passed a night told him that they could remember a time when the population of these parts had been much greater; there had been plenty of peasants to work the land; 'wages were low then and prices high,' an old miller said regretfully.

Robin paid little heed. He had troubles of his own to occupy his mind without bothering about the state of the country. It had been easy enough to deliver the Earl of Northumberland's message to Lord Stanley; but it was quite a different matter to deliver Lord Stanley's reply to the Earl of Northumberland. Robin had no great respect for noblemen and thought it possible that the Earl would not remember what his messenger had looked like when he last saw him; nevertheless, he was reluctant to put the Earl's memory to the test. So for nearly a year he had moved from place to place, never staying long enough anywhere for awkward questions to be asked. Eventually, however, he tired of this and one dark night contrived to change clothes with a drunken tinker. Then, for a time he worked at an inn, having ingratiated himself with the mistress of the establishment. This was in Yorkshire, and while he was there he sometimes saw the Earl of Warwick ride through the village on his way back to Middleham after a day's hunting. Warwick's party usually included boys who had been apprenticed to him and with them was the King's brother, Richard, recently created Duke of Gloucester.

Robin thought the north an uncommonly grim place and looked to a time when he would journey south again. To Richard, however, each day spent there was a delight. There had been a warmth and softness about Burgundy, an insidious charm which he had resisted. This country was harsher; it presented a challenge but not one so extreme that it could not be met: he liked to test his resources but had no taste for defeat. His loyalties were strong, he would love Middleham and this northern land always; and, being observant, he had already noted that what one loved, one possessed, so he thought of it as his land and regretted that the castle was not his, too.

In the autumn of 1462 the time came for Robin to journey south. He had made enemies as well as winning hearts at the inn. On his way he passed near the great castle of Middleham. Although he was sure that he could find employment there if he set his mind to it, he continued on his journey south. He thought how fortunate he was. He could go any which-way he chose and provided he kept his wits about him and let no man become his master for long, he'd keep his freedom and live well enough. The travelling life was the life for him. He sang as he rode. He was nineteen and Fortune's darling.

As Robin sang his song, Richard was jousting with Francis Lovell, watched by the Earl of Warwick and his two young daughters, Isabel and Anne. Richard and Francis felt themselves conquerors in a world new-minted for their delight, but the little girls had no such heroic vision of them. It was a bright day and the standard blew in a strong breeze, now stiff and straight, now twisting downwards, snakelike, now weaving back and forth so that the bright colours trembled before their eyes; it was boisterous, grew langorous, then wound itself into a frantic dance which slowed and became majestic. Behind the standard there was blue sky and a green band of hills in a great, sweeping semi-circle. A worthy setting for a great tournament. And what did they see but two boys bunched like frogs between their horses' ears!

'I think Francis will win,' Isabel said, feeling that participation would make the event more interesting.

'No, Richard will win,' Anne said.

Richard was the more assured horseman and his reactions were quicker; he pulled his horse up immediately he had passed his opponent so that he had turned and was ready to charge again while the more exuberant Francis thundered on, carried away by excitement in the sheer joy of the exercise.

'Francis rides the best, doesn't he?' Isabel appealed to her father.

'He rides well enough.' Warwick liked the boy's dash and vigour, but he regretted the fact that Francis seemed unaware that he was training for combat in which he might be killed.

'Oh, look!' Anne said. 'Richard is upon him and he is not ready!'

Richard had wasted no energy on bombast; no thunderous assault for him, only a precision which would one day become deadly.

'Remarkable!' Warwick muttered. He rode across to congratulate the boy who had now unseated his opponent. Before he could speak, however, Richard had taken off his helmet and dashed it on the ground.

'That . . .' he spluttered, pointing a shaking finger in the direction of his opponent, now remounting laboriously, 'That . . . is all I get . . . day after day. . . . How can I possibly test myself against that!' He was white-faced and spitting with rage.

A pity, Warwick thought, that so admirable a control should be destroyed by this spewing up of passion. 'You have much to learn yourself,' he said. 'Put on that helmet.'

The boy looked at him in surprise.

'You're dissatisfied,' Warwick said grimly. 'You shall have another bout.'

The lad was all to pieces now and the chance was that Francis Lovell, who had a more equitable disposition, would make a fool of him.

'Will Francis win this time?' Isabel asked her father.

'I think he may; and it will encourage him and teach young Richard a lesson.'

But it was Warwick who had to learn a lesson, for Francis might have saved himself the trouble of remounting he was so soon on the ground again. This time the fall was a heavy one. Richard's temper might cloud his reason, but on horseback it was an almost miraculous stimulant.

'That temper,' Warwick muttered, angry at his own lack of judgement, 'is surely of the Devil!'

The two little girls were taken back to the castle, and when evening came devil and victim must return also, sweat cooling on their brows as they rode from their exertions into the deep shadow of the keep. Isabel and Anne, lingering by a window in the gallery to catch the last of the day, watched them dismount and lead their horses into the courtyard. Richard, who seemed pleased with himself, looked up and called to them, 'Are you damsels in distress? Shall we rescue them, Francis, or leave them to their fate? What think you?'

The girls felt it was impudence to involve them in such nonsense and Anne, nose scarce above sill-level, piped disdainfully, 'Until you have mastered the art of the tournament, you hadn't better try anything more difficult.'

This very adult statement from so small a girl sobered her would-be rescuers.

'You'd have to climb out of the window, anyway,' Francis said. 'I don't suppose you could do that to save your life.'

'To save my life I certainly could,' she retorted. 'But not for a silly game.'

The two warriors turned their backs on the girls.

'Boys don't like being talked to like that,' Isabel said. 'You made them look foolish.'

'They *are* foolish.'

'But you mustn't let them see that you know it.'

'Why not, since it is so?'

'Oh, Anne, I pity your husband!'

'You're quite right to, if it means I have to puff him up and play silly games when I haven't a mind to. Ughh! I shall never do that willingly.'

'But don't you feel you want to go down to them and soothe them? I do. Particularly Francis. He has such a fair skin and it flamed so painfully when you were sharp with them.'

'What rubbish! And if I were to go down to either of them, it would be Richard. Richard at least knows how to fight.' She sounded very fierce for so small a child.

They continued to their chamber, arguing.

The boys had by now left their horses to the grooms. In the courtyard, shadow encroached and there was already a candle alight in an upper window. A smell of ale wafted from a grating, metal clattered on a stone floor and there was an angry exclamation followed by an explosion of laughter. The boys, alone now, hesitated, hovering between enmity and friendship. A moth flickered above their heads and Richard thrust out a hand and tried to catch it. Far beyond the castle walls, a night bird called, a flat, sad sound, dying away slowly. The boys looked around them, shifting uneasily from one foot to another, unused to being left alone. Francis picked at ivy growing in the armoury wall, it came away, powdering his hand with white dust; he rubbed his hand against his thigh and sighed, a heavy sigh which might have proclaimed the bitterness of defeat, or the fact that he was hungry, or that he must resign himself to some great deprivation the nature of which he could not have explained. Above them, the sky was ribbed with purple cloud and torchlight threw the shadow of bars across the courtyard. Richard put out his hands as though clutching at the bars and shouted, 'Let me out!' with a fine assumption of madness. Francis laughed.

'I wish we didn't have to go in so early,' Richard said regretfully.

Francis said, 'I was just thinking the same thing,' and the scales fell on friendship's side.

Chapter 4

I

In 1463 the womere water did not run, but there was water enough without that. Rain-swollen rivers burst their banks and villages were flooded. It was bad weather for ploughing. The peasants working on their lords' fields after Candlemas, urged on the oxen who could scarce drag the ploughs free of the mire. The oats were barely sown by the time the barley must be put in. The country folk prophesied a bad harvest with even more

dismal assurance than usual. Here and there, however, in spite
of the rain there were places which inexplicably remained dry.
There were tales of a pond in Sussex which had dried up
although the surrounding fields were sodden. Such phenomena
were known to herald disaster.

One person who might have done well to take note of these
ill-omens was the Earl of Warwick. Warwick thought of Edward
as a lad who owed everything to him and must continually
acknowledge his indebtedness. In fact, Edward was no longer a
stripling; his frame was big and powerful, and though still lean,
there was no doubting the muscular strength of his body and its
evident determination to develop quickly into full maturity. As
for gratitude, his was a more subtle mind than Warwick's, and
when he examined what it was that Warwick had done for him
one thought emerged with clarity: Warwick had put him on the
throne of England and there was little left that he could do for
him. In the matter of the restoration of power to the throne,
Warwick was an impediment.

When Warwick began to negotiate for Edward's marriage,
first to the daughter of Louis the Eleventh of France and, later,
to the daughter of the Count of Savoy, the only effect these
schemes had on Edward was to remind him that he must hunt
again in the neighbourhood of Grafton Regis. On the first day
of May, 1464, while pilgrims journeyed to shrines throughout
the land, Edward secretly married Elizabeth. It was not until
three months later, when his Council had met to hear details of
Warwick's negotiations with Savoy, that Edward announced
his marriage.

Warwick was stunned. After a time he appeared to make his
peace with Edward, but he was incapable of accepting the
dwindling of his power.

Warwick was not alone in his anger. Edward's mother, the
Duchess of York, when told of his marriage, disowned him in
words which she was later to regret. 'He is no son of Richard!'

'Not my father's son?' George, now Duke of Clarence and
with ambitions still unfulfilled, could scarcely credit what he
had heard, although he was willing to be persuaded.

'It is a way of saying things. I am angry. How do we know
what we say when we are angry?' She was still angry, but
aware of the need to control herself. 'I might as well have said
"He is no son of mine". You would have known what was
meant—that I disown him.'

'It has often been remarked how little he resembles my father.'
George went on working the matter over like dough. 'My father
was a small man, and not given to licentious pursuits.'

'Licentiousness is not unknown in the Plantagenets,' his mother said drily.

But it was not the arguments in favour of Edward's right to wear the sprig of brume with which George was concerned. 'I should like the truth about this.' He was as portentous as if truth had ever been his concern.

His mother regarded him coldly. In no circumstances would she have considered it her duty to have told him the truth on any subject if the truth was dangerous. She said, 'The suggestion that your brother is a bastard would be treason', which seemed to her more conclusive than any question of truth.

But George brooded on the fact that Edward was not made in his father's mould until the idea had quite set in his mind.

The rift between Edward and Warwick widened. A time would come when it would not be possible to owe allegiance to the one without offending the other. At Middleham, Richard had become aware of the need to make a choice. This time of learning to become a man had been sweet, and he owed much to Warwick. So it was with regret that he announced his decision to return to London. There followed a painful scene in which Warwick reminded Richard of the advantages which he had bestowed on him and the even greater advantages which he might confer on him in the future; at which point Richard saw fit to remind Warwick that the brother of the King has no need of a patron.

Richard sent word to Edward that he was on his way and when he eventually arrived at the Palace of West Minster he was impatient to see Edward and tell him what had passed between himself and Warwick. 'I will announce myself,' he said. He could hear the sound of music and a gust of wind carried the smell of roast meat to his nostrils. He realized that he was very hungry. He let his ear and nose lead him and came to the great hall.

The room was full of people and he saw no familiar faces. Two men standing near the door looked at him in amusement; they would have looked so at anyone who was not dressed in the height of fashion, but he thought their contempt more personal. Ever quick to accept an insult, he paused and studied their faces carefully, promising himself that when the opportunity presented itself, he would repay their incivility. One of the men, angered by this scrutiny, made a move as if to send him about his business, but the other put a hand on his arm and stayed him. Sober and sombre though the young Duke of Gloucester might be, the pride of rank was in his eye. The two men did not immediately continue their interrupted conversation, but watched as the slight figure made its way towards the centre of the room.

Richard attracted no particular attention from anyone else. He had hoped to find Edward at the centre of activity, but failing to do so he made his way to the far end of the hall and entered the corridor leading to the royal apartments. He had not gone far when he came upon his brother, who was being entertained by a bawdy tale told by a man whom Richard recognized as Lord Hastings. The two men were much amused. One should not come sober to such a scene, the participants appear incontinent, something less than men although they consider themselves never more manly. Edward inclined towards Hastings, laughter bubbling up in his throat; his skin was sweating, the bright eyes beginning to flood over with mirth, the cheeks to shake. It was as though laughter had loosed his features as lust his reason. Richard watched as the two men came together, heaving and clutching each other, clumsy as bemused bears. Over Hastings' shoulder, Edward saw his brother's face, so white and strained it seemed for a moment that it was a ghost come to haunt him. 'It cannot be!' Edward exclaimed. Hastings looked over his shoulder to see what frightful thing had put so abrupt an end to their jesting.

'But it *is* Dickon! You have indeed journeyed fast.' Edward held his arms wide and embraced his brother; then with one arm still round Richard's shoulder, he said, 'This lad has come from Middleham at great speed. I hope nothing ill has befallen our very dear cousin, Warwick.'

Hastings laughed; and he and Edward, who were both a little drunk, continued to laugh while Richard told his story. Richard felt awkward and humiliated. Worse was to come, for while they talked a door further down the corridor opened and Queen Elizabeth appeared accompanied by her brother, Anthony Woodville.

'My good Dickon here,' Edward roared in greeting, 'finds he can no longer stay in Middleham because Warwick loves us so little.'

Anthony Woodville said, 'One so young is to be congratulated on so much judgement.' He intended a compliment, but had a refined way of speaking which was quite foreign, and not pleasing to Richard.

'Such worth must be rewarded,' Edward said.

'Certainly he needs food after so long a journey,' the Queen said tartly.

Lord Hastings' eyes met those of Richard; Hastings was

amused by the Queen's quick jealousy and invited Richard to
be amused also. Richard turned his head away.

Richard was made much of by Edward, but later, in his
chamber, he thought of Hastings with loathing. Subsequent
events never completely altered that disastrous first impression.
Yet Hastings had qualities that might have commended him to
Richard. He had served Richard's father well, and now he was
very close to Edward. A loyal man. A good companion, too,
welcomed wherever he went. A master of the easy flow of talk,
he would stand, hand on a man's shoulder, the head laughingly
inclined. He was gay and bright as new steel, but no casual
jester; sometimes the head jerked back suddenly if something
displeased him and there was a flash of arrogance. He tended to
align himself with the old nobility. He did not like the Woodvilles, nor they him. He was too near Edward to be trusted by
them. He was too near Edward to endear himself to Richard.

As the months went by, Richard saw a side of his brother he
had not realized existed before. He had seen Edward, composed
and resourceful, at the conference table; he had seen him ride
out to battle, eager and undaunted; he had seen him uncon-
cerned in defeat. A hero. Heroes, of course, must eat and sleep,
drink and make love as other men; but that they should have a
talent for such pursuits to match, even to surpass, their military
prowess, was not to Richard's taste. First impressions are strong.
He could not believe that his brother had an immoderate
appetite for pleasure; this seemed to Richard to be something
grafted onto Edward's personality by his companions, and by
Hastings in particular. Hastings' talk was all of women, he
boasted of debauchery and Edward liked him for it. Richard
saw Hastings as the despoiler of his brother.

The summer was at its height and the heat in the narrow
London streets was more oppressive, the air more foetid than
Richard had remembered it on previous occasions. He longed
for the northern lands he had left. He even felt a traitorous
longing for the company of Warwick, whose view of life he
better understood than that of the men in whose company he
now found himself. During this time he saw much of his brother
George, Duke of Clarence, now approaching dazzling manhood
and concerned with marriage plans. George kept in contact
with Warwick and sought by alternate advice and raillery to
draw Richard to Warwick's camp.

'Why do you stay at court? Are you dazzled by these Woodvilles? Do you study to become like Anthony Woodville? I
hear he is reckoned second to none in a tournament though it
is said he has no real liking for a fight.'

'I certainly have no desire to be like him,' Richard retorted. Anthony Woodville played at all the things which Richard took seriously.

'Edward needs stronger men around him.' George turned from scorn to persuasion at which he was even less successful. 'Our cousin Warwick has ever been Edward's true friend, and with my help—and yours, were you but to look ahead—the crown would become strong again.'

The power would switch from the Woodvilles to the Nevilles; the crown would be no stronger. It was so blatant in George's mouth that a child could see it and Richard was not a child now. He stayed at Edward's court and Edward took note of him. The court was not everything to Edward. He had not yet lost his physique, his body was hard and his eye still bright; he had battles yet to fight and was aware of it. He saw beyond the gay circle of courtiers to a land of untamed forest and tangled vegetation which gradually encroached on pasture land, to a people grown used to misrule as to the ill-use of the land, a people as like to turn one way as another. It would require much ruthlessness and firmness of purpose to bring order to the realm and he did not see many of those who surrounded him in his hours of ease being of assistance to him in this task. But Richard had a more durable look. In 1464 he had made Richard commissioner for nine counties in the west and south-west, and now he set aside time to instruct his brother so that he should be able to carry out his duties effectively.

'Why?' Anthony Woodville mused when he was alone with his sister, the Queen. 'Why should he be so honoured?'

'You are not the only one to ask.' The Queen had recently given birth to a daughter, Elizabeth, and although Edward was delighted, the failure to produce a son made her quick to resent the fortunes of others.

Her brother, misunderstanding, said, 'Yes, I hear that George is beside himself with jealousy.'

'Oh, George!' Her mood lightened. George was liable to do foolish things when displeased and she saw no cause for dismay at the growing rift between him and Edward.

George did not disappoint Elizabeth's expectations. During the next few years he and Warwick became more estranged from the King. In July, 1469, he married Warwick's daughter, Isabel. The fact that Edward had not given his approval to the union was of little consequence, since Warwick and Clarence were now in open rebellion. Their purpose was to restore to the throne Henry the Sixth who, mad and frail, was imprisoned in the Tower. In August they met and defeated an

army led by Lord Herbert of Pembroke whom they subsequently
executed.

2

Henry Tydder was still living at Pembroke Castle. While the
Countess grieved for her dead husband, Henry walked on the
castle ramparts and wondered what would be his future now.
Would the Lancastrians come and take the castle and restore it
to his Uncle Jasper? He hoped so. Henry was twelve and he had
learnt not to invest his resources in others; he withdrew from
personal affection as a snail will withdraw its feelers into its
shell at the first hint of danger. So he did not long for his uncle
because he loved him as a man but because he was the most
permanent feature of his life and he had a need of permanency.

As Henry walked on the ramparts he looked at his kingdom.
Ever since he had ridden through the Welsh hills on his flight to
Pembroke, he had been in the habit of regarding that area which
his eyes could compass as his kingdom. It had started with a
range of barren hills: the view was hardly more promising now.
Mist curled over the woods and fields gradually isolating the
castle. He was king of the mist and rain today.

Days passed and Uncle Jasper did not return. A change of a
kind did, however, take place in Henry's life towards the
beginning of September. It was a fine, warm day and he had
gone riding with his tutor. The tutor talked volubly in a good-
natured attempt to provide the lonely lad with comradeship.
Henry, who was not a comradely lad, found this irksome. It was
a still day with an autumn haze blurring the landscape and
Henry gave way to a rash impulse. As they rode through a wood,
he stopped his horse at a point where the undergrowth had
almost obliterated the path. The tutor was riding ahead and
Henry waited until he had gone some little distance before he
called to him, 'Roper doesn't like the tangle. I'll take him
down the other path and meet you on the far side of the wood.'
There was no other path; he simply turned his horse about and
rode back the way he had come. When he reached the edge of
the wood, however, there were two tracks from which to choose
and he chose the one to the left. At first it seemed familiar, but
after a time the ground became stony and began to descend
sharply. 'I am going the wrong way,' he thought and reined in
his horse.

Insects droned in the bushes but even they seemed drowsy.
There was no other sound. In all his adventures he had never

before been completely alone. Prudence dictated a hasty retreat the way he had come. His horse, plagued by flies, twitched its ears and lashed its tail. 'This path is descending steeply and there is probably a stream down there,' Henry told Prudence. 'The horse is thirsty and I am very hot.' Also, there was a smell of wild thyme which filled him with a longing he could not explain but which urged him on. Soon, imprudence was rewarded by a glimmer of water below. The path was very steep now and Henry had to dismount and guide the horse down to the stream. The land rose high and densely wooded on the far side of the stream. Not a breath of air stirred. It was a strange, secret place. Henry let the horse drink while he sat on the bank and removed his boots. 'I am quite lost,' he thought as he dangled his feet in the water. He marvelled at his folly.

Soon, he heard the sound of stones moving and realized that someone else was riding down the path. It was not his tutor; his tutor would have had to dismount and lead his horse down. Horse and rider, when they emerged belonged so well together that Henry seemed to see a creature that was half man, half horse. The man-part called out to Henry:

'You, there! Where is Pembroke Castle, do you know?'

'I was wondering that myself,' Henry said.

'Then you're not much good to me, are you?' He sounded cheerful; it was obvious that being lost held no terrors for him. He dismounted and, sitting beside Henry, he, too, took off his boots and dangled his feet in the stream.

'Is that your horse there?' he asked Henry.

'Yes.'

'Nice bit of horseflesh. How did you come by it, steal it?'

Henry wondered whether it would be more interesting if he said he had stolen Roper, and while he was debating this, the stranger laughed and thumped him on the back. 'I might be able to sell it for you at a better price than you'd ever get.'

'What would I do without him?' Henry asked.

'What you usually do!' The stranger laughed and stretched himself out on the bank, his arms folded behind his head.

He had blue-black hair but his skin was surprisingly fair, pebbled with freckles across the bridge of the small, fine nose. The mouth was wide and confident, the eyes a light blue like spring water with only a dash of colour in them, and, in spite of their merriment, something of the water's coldness. The eyebrows were dark and heavy and curved upwards, giving a touch of the demonic to the face. Henry thought it was the most attractive face he had ever seen; not the face of someone to be trusted, but one that waived the question of trust and made it irrelevant.

'What is your name?' the man asked.

'Henry. What is yours?'

'Robin. Robin Goodfellow.'

'Robin Goodfellow?' Henry could tell from the way it was said that this was a joke, but could not see anything very funny about it; his folklore was limited to that of the Welsh people.

'Robin Goodfellow is a sprite,' the man said. 'Don't tell me you've never seen a sprite?'

Henry had to admit that he had not.

'Neither have I. And it's not good to see them. But I've heard them when I've been about at night.'

'What business are you about at night?' Henry asked.

'Business that belongs to the night.' He made a rueful grimace and sighed, 'Which is why I'm here, I suppose. I had to quit my master's service some months ago because there was trouble with a wench.' He looked at Henry to see how much interest he was arousing and then said, 'You haven't had a woman?'

'No.'

'How old are you?'

'Twelve.'

'I'd had several wenches by the time I was twelve.'

He began to tell Henry about his life.

'But now that you have nowhere to go, what will you do?' Henry asked when Robin brought his rambling history to its present conclusion.

'Nowhere to go! There's *every*where to go! I shall travel, spending a night here, a month there, perhaps a season in one place. But never as long as a year. One year follows another and that's the way a man gets snared as I've had cause to know.'

Henry was much impressed by Robin's audacity; it was a strange, but not unattractive idea, that a man might mount a horse and wander from place to place for the rest of his life.

'And talking of staying,' Robin said, 'this is no place to stay. I need food before the night is out and I shan't come by it here.'

Henry watched him putting on his boots. He liked the idea of this man riding away owing service to no man; yet something acquisitive in him made him say, 'I can find you food.'

'I want other things beside food, lad.'

'I can find you a place for the night.'

'I daresay, but there'd be some things missing that I'm much in need of.'

'You asked the way to Pembroke Castle. I can take you there.'

The man stopped, a boot in one hand. 'You can?' For the first time he looked closely at his companion. 'What would you know of Pembroke Castle?' he asked, jesting, yet already half-believing.

'I live there.'

Robin stared at him, and as he stared the boy seemed to change so that it would be absurd ever to have imagined he could belong anywhere else in this neighbourhood but to Pembroke Castle.

Henry went on, 'They will be grateful when I tell them that you found me and brought me safely back. If you wanted to spend a week, or a month, at the castle, I am sure they could find you work, since you know so much about horseflesh.'

Robin said, 'I mightn't mind a month of that.'

They mounted their horses and when they had climbed the steep hill, they found that the mist had cleared and in the distance they could see Pembroke Castle. As they rode towards it, Henry felt triumphant at bringing this trophy back with him. But when the castle loomed high and its shadow fell across the fields and the two riders, Henry was sad that this encounter, so strange and touched with magic, should resolve itself into a matter of servant and master instead of wanderer and chance-met youth.

Much later, when his tutor returned and asked him where he had been, Henry replied that he had been playing with the devil. As this was not well-received, he said, 'It was only a puppy devil.' After this, he found himself looking out for the devil's pup who was still at the castle after a week, and then a month, and then two months. After three months, Henry managed things so that Robin became his groom. Robin Goodfellow transformed himself readily into Robin Prithie, groom.

Chapter 5

I

Soon after the execution of Pembroke, King Edward was captured by Warwick and the Duke of Clarence. A few days later, the Queen's father, Earl Rivers, was captured and later beheaded outside the walls of Coventry. Edward was treated with wary respect by his captors and with patience and guile he managed for a brief spell to reassert his authority. But by

September 1470 he was again a fugitive. As he and Richard set
sail for Burgundy, Warwick sent word to the Constable of the
Tower that his prisoner was once more King Henry the Sixth.
They told Henry that he was to ride in triumphal procession
through the streets.

'Again?' he said.

They sat him on a horse and the people cheered and threw
caps in the air.

'How long?' he asked when they returned from the procession.
No one answered him. He looked out of the window. The day
was creeping slowly away, the long shadow of its skirts lingered
on the grass. 'How long, this time?' They thought him a fool,
but he was wiser than they.

Queen Margaret came to terms with Warwick. No other
course was open to her. She even assented to the marriage of
her son, Prince Edward, to Warwick's young daughter, Anne.
But she placed no trust in Warwick and delayed her return to
England.

In London, Elizabeth Woodville waited. She had given birth
to a son and looked forward to presenting the young Edward to
his father.

The months went by, January dwindled into February, and
still Margaret delayed. March came in without its usual bluster,
quietly, almost stealthily. At last the Queen began to make her
preparations, but she had delayed too long. On March 14th
Edward and Richard landed on the Yorkshire coast. George,
Duke of Clarence marched north, ostensibly to give battle; but
George, unnerved by Queen Margaret's delay, had begun to
think more fondly of his brothers. A meeting was arranged at
which he allowed Richard to persuade him to become reconciled
with Edward. There was a rumour that Warwick would be
offered a pardon if he submitted to Edward.

Warwick preferred to fight. The Earl of Oxford, one of
Warwick's most trusted commanders, was not impressed by this
decision. To him, Warwick now seemed no longer a heroic
figure, but an old war horse, slow on the turn, unable any longer
to manoeuvre with skill.

'Queen Margaret is on her way at last; and Jasper Tudor is
marching from Wales,' Oxford said. 'We should wait until our
forces are joined with theirs.'

'We have waited too long as it is,' Warwick answered.

It was spring and there was work to be done on the land; men
were drifting off, making their way home. His commanders
were at odds with one another; Oxford made it apparent that
he did not trust Montagu and the situation between them daily

grew worse. Warwick lacked the subtlety necessary to bind together these fraying threads. He did the thing he best understood. He moved south. On Easter Eve, while Queen Margaret was within a day's sailing of Weymouth, his army was camped near the town of Barnet.

It was a move which delighted King Edward. He had marched from London in the hope of forcing a battle before the arrival of Queen Margaret, and here was Warwick obligingly come to meet him! It was evening when he received news of the disposition of Warwick's forces. He decided that he would take up a position as close as possible to Warwick's army 'so that by morning, at first light, we can attack, and, by the grace of God, the business between us will be settled by noon.' He would take command of the centre and Hastings the left wing; to his brother, Richard, he entrusted the command of the right wing.

The air was damp and cobwebs of mist hung about as Edward's forces began to move towards the St Albans road, on either side of which Warwick's army was encamped. There was some activity from Warwick's artillery; but as the cannon fire was sporadic and overshot Edward's men it seemed likely that Warwick's commanders had little idea that the enemy was moving in so close. Richard had ordered his troops to move quietly so as not to give away their position. They dared not show any lights and the mist blurred their vision. It was a chancy business. From time to time a man stumbled and there was a clash of iron on stone. Any noise seemed to reverberate so loud it must be heard in heaven.

When as a child Richard had imagined himself in command, he had always visualized the opposing armies already assembled, neatly in place, like the figures in a puppet show when the curtains are pulled back. What commander would have chosen tonight's conditions to take up his position! Behind him, there was yet another clatter of steel and a great thrashing about as a horse stumbled into a ditch. Richard moved forward slowly, unable to see where he was going; he was shivering in the chill air and did not feel at all the decisive figure he had imagined would emerge on the great occasion of his first battle. Immediately ahead, lights danced momentarily as a rabbit scurried across the path. Then suddenly the mist parted and he had a clear view for some one hundred yards ahead. He saw that to his right, the trees seemed gradually to dwindle into nothingness. He hoped the nothingness would turn out to be a heath since it was on the heath that he was to camp. In Edward's tent there had been a map of the area drawn by a man who knew the lie of the land. It had seemed, looking at the clear lines on the map, that it must be a matter of minutes to reach the heath. But darkness and mist distorted the landscape and the road twisted and turned, quite unlike the straight line on the map. Richard could not even be sure that he was proceeding in the right direction. He fought back the horrid fear that he might lose his way and the battle as well. The mist had come down again; around him men grunted and swore and scrambled and the horses blew noisily, their harness jingling. They continued so for ten minutes which seemed an hour. Then the mist parted again and Richard saw the heath stretching away to his right. Impulsively, he bent down, felt the ground and tugged hard; as he stood up, rubbing the tuft between his fingers, he could not have believed a sprig of heather could have made him so happy. When all his men were assembled on the heath, one of his captains asked him, 'What do we do now, Dickon?'

'We wait.'

He spoke with calm assurance, but he was revising some of his notions about battles. The mist had damped down his excitement and blunted the fine edge of resolution; the blood itself seemed to have thinned. During the next few hours, he revised one or two ideas about himself. He learnt, for one thing, that he was not good at waiting. Years ago, when he was a child, he had heard a voice in the night saying that a man must know the moment to strike. He had always remembered this; it suited his temperament well. But now it seemed that there were times when it was not advisable to be so hot for action. When Edward assigned the right wing to him, he had brought himself to a pitch almost of ecstasy and must now sit out the night while ecstasy evaporated.

Dawn came at last, a poor thing, a mere paring away of the darkness leaving in its place an atmosphere as dense but of a lighter hue. Into this indifferent blanket, Edward's trumpeters hurled their urgent summons and in the distance Warwick's trumpets sounded. The cannon fire intensified. Richard commended his enterprise to God and ordered his men to advance. Advance they did, but met no resistance, although the ground showed a tendency to give way. Soon they were moving rapidly downhill while the clash of steel told them that men were engaged to their right. Richard realized that in the mist he had outflanked the enemy. To hurtle full tilt at the enemy had been his ambition, but now he must come upon him stealthily since his men had first to grope their way uphill, no easy matter to those in heavy armour. It seemed a bad mistake and Richard resolved to die honourably on the field of battle. When the lines were reformed, he again ordered the advance and, gripping his axe, charged recklessly forward. But the mistake had enabled him to take the left wing of Warwick's army by surprise and soon he found himself concerned with tactics rather than an honourable death.

Qualities were needed which he had not foreseen: however eagerly the spirit drove him forward, however the blood sang, a certain coolness must be retained, as though a chip of ice were lodged somewhere in his brain. Messengers came with news of how the battle went on other wings. He must listen and make decisions. But the messengers did not give the clear information he had expected to receive, they were confused and more often than not contradicted one another; it was impossible to form a picture of what was happening. He was blinkered by fog; the only reality was an area smaller than the tilting yard on which he had served his apprenticeship. For him, this must be the whole battlefield and he must fight as though victory depended on his defence of this small patch of ground. His troops were hard-pressed. But he decided to accept the blackest estimate of fortunes elsewhere — Hastings' wing was said to be broken — and resolved not to call on his brother to throw in reserves to aid him. It was a reckless decision, but he felt the better for it and fought with great heart thereafter.

The fog favoured no one and the messages which Warwick received were no less confused. A handful of panic-stricken men running from the field can give an impression that the whole wing of an army has been broken, just as the onslaught of a few rash spirits can appear to signal a formidable attack. Hastings' men misread the confused signs available to them and, not realizing the seriousness of their plight, fought on. The Duke of Exeter's men thought their plight was worse than it was and Warwick threw in his reserves to support the Duke.

In the mist men struck down their own comrades. The star of Oxford's banner was mistaken for the sun of Edward's banner. A messenger thundered up to Oxford crying, 'We are betrayed, my Lord!' He was supported by cries of 'Treason!' from men plunging desperately for safety. Oxford, who did not find it hard to believe ill of Montagu, fled. Warwick fought on. He had fought many battles and the discordant shrieks and groans, the wild neighs of horses, the shouted commands and counter commands, the boom of cannon and the clash of steel, the fierce oaths, and the prayers of the dying, orchestrated in his mind into something recognizable from which he could isolate those notes which carried the dominant theme. But the fog hampered him, and the withdrawal of Oxford and his men was a heavy blow.

Nevertheless, he rode among his men, rallying those who could see him and shouting lustily for the benefit of those who could not; and such was the power of his personality that he raised many a cheer from men who had sounder reason to curse him. When his own depleted ranks began to break he saw the need to retreat. As his horse carried him from the field, the retreat seemed no more and no less desperate than on other occasions. The heavy horse lumbered over rough ground and Warwick, tired, heavy-hearted, but by no means defeated, planned the next encounter, his mind muzzily mulling over the possibilities of new alliances. There was a group of men in pursuit and at a place strewn with thorny shrubs whiskered by fog, he must turn and fight, his mind still half-full of what would follow, where he would go, to whom he would turn first. He was at bay, but he had been at bay before, and even when he fell the situation seemed to him no different from other times. There was only a moment as the blood rushed out that he had the sense of himself flowing out with it, and it came to him with enormous surprise that this was a new situation; but before the idea could take shape in his mind, his spirit had outstripped it.

The news of Warwick's death was conveyed to Edward. He said, 'It was better thus.' Whether he felt this to be the best fate for his cousin, or the one which occasioned the least trouble to himself, was not clear.

Richard was slightly wounded, which was as it should be; he would have been sorry not to have sustained a wound in his first major battle. Exhausted, but triumphant, he rode among his men, praising them for their valour. He was rewarded by hearing one gnarled old warrior say, 'I'll follow him; he has the look of his father.' For the first time he realized that men would rally to his standard as a mark of personal esteem which had nothing to do with loyalty to the King. A part of Richard that was steady and sober would have liked to be indifferent to such regard; but a part of him that was none of these things delighted in it. He was at his beginning; all the jousting, the playing at combat, was behind him, he was involved in the real business of life and men had taken note of him.

2

Queen Margaret and her son, Prince Edward, landed in Weymouth and marched north to join forces with Jasper Tudor. As soon as the news of her movements reached Edward, he set out in pursuit. The armies met outside Tewkesbury on

May 4th. By the evening of that day, Queen Margaret was in flight, as yet unaware that her son was slain.

The fighting had overflowed into the country lanes and Christopher Ormond, riding from visiting a dying woman, was attacked, despite his protests that the battle was no concern of his. His horse was stolen and he was left lying in a ditch. He was sick and dizzy from a blow on the head and tried to bring his wandering wits to his service by composing a report to Dr Morton. 'At Tewkesbury . . . such terrible things . . . at Tewkesbury. . . .' He drifted into unconsciousness while Dr Morton, who had fought for Queen Margaret at Tewkesbury, was making good his escape.

A cool breeze woke Ormond. He looked up and saw the sky brilliant with stars. He closed his eyes and when next he opened them, he saw a face hovering above him.

'I feared you to be dead.' A young voice. 'And then there would be no one to help us.'

Ormond sat up and the world swayed and then settled itself. The speaker was a young woman but the rather flat face peeping from the cloak made her seem more like a little owl. 'Is there a place where we can shelter for the night? There is a house across the fields. If you could enquire for us. . . .'

'On whose behalf should I enquire?'

A voice behind Ormond said, 'Say simply that a small party of travellers has been delayed by the vile conditions of the roads and seeks shelter.' This voice had the iron ring of command; it had also an intonation that was not English. She was muffled in a cloak and the other women who were with her were no less reluctant to reveal their identities; but a better disguise than a cloak would be needed if Queen Margaret were to travel far unrecognized.

Ormond went to the house, which he recognized as Foxlow Priory, a small nunnery which he sometimes visited. He hammered loud and long before the window above the portal opened.

'We have the plague here,' the portress squeaked hopefully.

'Nonsense! Travellers are yonder, seeking shelter. Open this door immediately.'

After a few minutes the main door opened and Reverend Mother herself stood there; an old, unsteady creature who peered at Ormond and gave a little screech, 'Father!'

'You are to prepare a chamber for the lady and food for her and her attendants,' Ormond told her severely.

'But the soldiers are everywhere!' Reverend Mother spat through the gaps in her teeth. 'It is not safe. . . .'

'What is safety to such as you and me? I will bring the ladies here. Make your preparations.'

At the request of the Queen, Ormond attended the party while they ate the wretched food provided by the nuns. He gave her the information she required as to what route to take and what other houses of religion might give sanctuary if the need arose; but he swore he had no news of the battle. It was not for him to tell Queen Margaret of the death of her son.

The little owlet he had supposed to be a lady in waiting, but something said in conversation made him realize that this was the Earl of Warwick's daughter, Anne, wife of the dead Prince. She seemed little concerned with what went on around her, but sat looking out of the window. She was a delicate creature with small, fragile bones and a pale face, the skin traced with little blue veins and a hint of shadow beneath the eyes that was like the faintest bruise on a petal. But delicate though she undoubtedly was, the quality of her spirit showed in her eyes which had the detachment of a person striving to come to some kind of accommodation with suffering. The mouth was composed, the line of the jaw firm; only the quiver of a muscle in the left cheek prevented her achieving an expression of disdainful fortitude. Ormond recalled that Prince Edward had had the reputation of being a violent, immoderate young man. Poor child, he thought, how ill she must have been used, and what will become of her now? He felt an urge to reach out and touch her, his fingers itched to move; but he had no gift of healing and could only pity her.

He found it hard to sleep that night. He could not get the unfortunate girl out of his mind. It was usually only the young of birds and beasts that roused his pity; pity for a fellow human was a new experience. When he did sleep he had a bad dream. He dreamt that he was lying in this very room, in pain and great distress of mind. Evil forces threatened him. He shouted and the prioress came and bent over him; he saw not the present prioress but a much younger woman with a cold, resolute face. 'Where am I?' he screamed. She told him that he was at Foxlow Priory. In the shadows behind the prioress there was a nun with a face like a little owl; as he looked at her, her lips parted and terror bubbled out of her mouth like rainwater spurting from a gargoyle. The terror woke him. It was early morning. The room was bathed in soft light and smelt fresh and clean. He got up and went to the window. It was a fine, still morning, and there was a hawthorn in a glory of white just beneath the window. The tree seemed strangely luminous in this early light; its beauty was so extraordinary that Ormond had the feeling that he was glimpsing something beyond life. Had he not been so aware of his unworthiness, he would have thought he had had a vision. He stayed at the window, smelling the dew-wet blossom for some minutes. Then that other smell came to his nostrils; a smell of burning wood and tar and something else as well.

A few days later Queen Margaret and Anne were taken prisoner. In London, people in the streets shouted and cheered as King Edward rode by. But one old man, sitting hunched in a doorway, said, 'Which is it this time?' His companions berated him, but he merely snickered and said, 'King Edward, King Henry . . .' and made motions with his fingers as though plucking daisy petals.

King Edward was himself aware of the need to end this charade.

3

The spendthrift day burnt up its strength. The bars of light moved slowly down the wall until in the end there was nothing but a faint sheen on the inside of the bars themselves. Before they grew black, the moon came up and for a time silvered over the wall. Beyond the window, the night sounds of the city gradually quietened. The moon went down and the sky darkened; the stars went out one by one.

Water was dripping somewhere. This agitated the prisoner. He got up and crawled around, feeling the walls, exploring crevices with his fingers. He could not find the water and tiring of the search sat huddled in a corner, his knees drawn up to his chin. He could still hear the water dripping. After a while he heard something else; somewhere, a distance away yet, a door opened. Whoever came, came silently, no clanking of heavy boots, jangling of keys, exchange of crude pleasantries; his passage down the corridor was scarcely above the whisper of an indrawn breath. The visitor unlocked the door. He had the key to many doors. Although expected, he never ceased to surprise; in the case of the old king, the surprise was intense. As the fingers tightened around his throat, Henry felt the pull of life again. But the fingers were firm and sure of their purpose, releasing him from the bonds of time. He was running on a greensward; his arms were outstretched and there was joy. He strove to capture the memory; it danced and wavered down the years and he struggled towards it along a flaming crimson tunnel which crackled and roared in his ears and blinded his eyes with its brilliance until he and the memory were consumed.

Henry's body was borne to St Paul's with due ceremony. People shed tears as the bier passed, some because they thought he was a good man, others because it was customary so to do.

Edward looked forward to some peace now that the last hope of the House of Lancaster had been removed.

4

Some weeks later, a small band of men came to the Welsh coast to await the arrival of a boat at Tenby harbour. It was wiser not to go near a town or to the harbour until final arrangements had been made. One of their number went ahead, the rest waited in a small inlet on the rocky coast.

It was towards evening, a clear light but without much colour. Henry Tydder sat on a boulder while his Uncle Jasper talked to his companions. He looked around him, thinking wryly how cheerless he frequently found his surroundings. This place was like a great boneyard, as though the bones of all the people who ever lived here had been ribbed together to form a bulwark against an enemy which never wavered. The sound of the surf breaking above the concealed rocks was uninterrupted, like water boiling in Hell's cauldron. The sea drift made odd patterns, a forelock of green weed over a rock from which one encrusted shell peered gave a sense of a primitive face looking up from the pool. Henry bent forward so that his own face was momentarily reflected. He fumbled in his pocket, remembering the little dark man who had thrown a stone in a pool a long time ago. His fingers closed around his gift-stone.

Somewhere, round the next headland, out of sight, came the sound of children's voices, high-pitched and excited, then a scream; he could imagine them balanced on the sharp rocks, the seaweed oozing between their toes, slimy and treacherous. His arms, which had been wet up to the elbows, were drying in the wind, they felt soft; he licked his wrist and tasted salt. The children shouted again.

'Let us walk a little way,' he said to Robin Prithie who was standing beside him.

'What game do you think they are playing?' he asked as they walked towards the hidden children.

'Just pushing one another in the water.'

'No. There is some kind of chant to it. Listen.'

'The wind is too strong,' Robin said.

The water in the little pools between the rocks was becoming agitated as though anticipating its union with the advancing

sea. There was a spawn on the surface and on an impulse
Henry bent down and, cupping the water in his hands, drank;
it tasted foul and he spat it out hastily. Robin said, 'We'll have
better fare for you than that soon.' Overhead, a gull laughed
and wheeled screaming inland. The noise of the wind was
louder and sounded like tearing silk; Robin had to turn his
head to one side to speak because it was so strong. 'We'd better
not go any further.'

'Yes, you are right,' Henry said regretfully. 'Now I shall
never know what game they are playing.'

As they were talking, one of the children, who had scrambled
round the headland without their hearing him, emerged suddenly in front of them. He stopped, a ragged, bright-eyed boy,
more than a little surprised to come across strangers in this
place. For a moment they faced each other, hunter and hunted
brought unexpectedly face to face. No language existed between
them, but none was needed. Robin moved towards the boy, the
boy backed away, his eyes not leaving Robin's face. Henry
watched in astonishment, not at first understanding. The boy
eased from rock to rock with the agility of a cat, and Robin, no
less sure-footed, circled him like a wolf waiting the moment to
move in on its prey.

Henry called, 'What nonsense is this! Come back, Robin!'

He might as well have called a wolf to heel. Robin sprang
and had the ragged child by the throat. Henry was not agile,
but he had a good aim. He bent down and picked up a rock
which might have served David well enough in his dealings
with Goliath. As Robin bent forward, intent on smashing the
boy's head against a boulder, Henry hurled the rock and caught
his servant squarely between the shoulder blades. The boy was
free and scampering away. Henry picked his way carefully
towards the sorry heap that was Robin; he stood looking down
at him while Robin fought to get his breath back. They regarded
each other. There was something more than anger in Robin's
eyes. Henry said, 'I hope I haven't hurt you too much?' He was
apologetic but he continued to hold Robin's gaze until Robin
turned his head away. It took a little time for Robin to ease
himself painfully to his feet and he was still shaking when he
said, 'We'd have been wise to put an end to that game.'

'Why ever should we do that?' Henry asked gently.

'In case he betrays your presence here, of course.'

'And how would he know who I am?' Henry turned and
Robin walked beside him as they retraced their steps along the
beach.

'He may not know who you are, but he'll know your situation

is desperate. Do you imagine many strangers hang round this beach in the evening, or at any time, for that matter?' Robin was still short of breath, but he was mastering his temper. 'That boy knows something is afoot and it should have been into the sea with him.'

Henry held his gift-stone in the palm of his hand; he turned it with his fingers, it was very smooth and the motion of it against the palm of his hand was remarkably soothing. He walked for a while, turning the stone in his hand.

'How fierce you have become, Robin! Threatening to kill children on my behalf, something I would never have you do.'

'But I would do it. I would do anything to further your cause.'

'My cause?'

'You will be king, won't you?'

'Well, not immediately,' Henry said, cautiously examining the notion.

'But you will be one day.'

'And because I am to be king you would kill children for me?'

'I would do what is necessary. Perhaps you will remember that when you are king and grant me a favour.'

This was the first time that anyone had ever asked a favour of Henry and it made him think about the power that went with kingship. He was interested to know how he could exercise this power and he asked, 'What would you like me to grant you, Robin?'

'Why, I should like you to make me your emissary and then I could go from one city to another.'

Henry said, 'You always were a wanderer, weren't you?' But once, it had been the whole world that Robin dreamt of wandering while now his roving was to be confined to travelling between one city and another.

By the time they rejoined the party, the boulder on which Henry had been sitting was submerged and little spurts of foam reached beyond it and swirled round their ankles. 'I think we should go a little way up the cliff path,' Henry said. It would be a pity, having come so far, to be cut off by the tide. He was prepared to take risks if the stakes were high enough, but he was no lover of adventure for its own sake.

'You'll get more than your feet wet before this is out,' his uncle said grimly.

'Even so, I'll keep them dry while I can,' Henry retorted as he and Robin scrambled towards the rough cliff path.

'It won't be long now,' they assured him as the darkness

gathered round them. Henry did not need reassurance. The future was uncertain and kingship must wait, but one thing he had learnt about himself: he was a survivor. He intended to put all his wits to the end of remaining one.

Part Two

IN SUMMERTIME

'In summer time, when leaves grow green
And blossoms bedeck the tree
King Edward would a hunting ride
Some pastime for to see. . . .'

Chapter 6

I

To those who worked long hours on their lord's fields, the idea that a change of king should bring any change in their lives would have been greeted with scorn, had any such idea reached them. But they had no time for ideas. They worked, bore children who, it seemed, one day cried on their mothers' laps and the next were working beside them in the fields. They worked during the hours of light, in all weathers, were aware of changes of season and little else. Of the world beyond their fields, they knew nothing and cared less. Some, more enterprising, drifted away from the land and took service with one of the great lords. His world became their world, his writ was law. What the king wished or did not wish was of no account. And so it was over most of the country.

But in London, and other cities where the merchants were growing rich, it was different. A new king had indeed come to power and they had every hope that commerce would thrive. What others had won by foreign wars, King Edward the Fourth meant to achieve by foreign trade, and was prepared to pursue this end as adventurously as the great King Harry had waged his wars. He was as well-endowed to prosper such a cause as King Harry to lead an army. He had a splendid figure to show off fine materials, a good appetite for food and wine, his hospitality was lavish. A time of peace, justice and prosperity lay ahead. None believed this more strongly than Richard of Gloucester.

Richard had it in mind to influence his brother, George, in such a way that he would henceforth serve Edward with

unwavering loyalty. It was to this commendable end that in
company with his friend, Francis Lovell, he called on George
and his duchess at their London house.

'Anne is staying with us, as you know.' George made a
gesture which for him was unusually economic, introducing and
dismissing Anne in the one flick of the hand.

Anne kept her head bowed so that Richard's friendly greeting
was lost on her. Many years had passed since she and Richard
had last met. Richard had proved himself in battle, had
cultivated his mind, had had several women and was the father
of two bastard children. He regarded himself as a man of
considerable experience and expected to make an impression on
others. He was not content to be ignored. He asked Anne what
she thought of London. She appeared not to hear him and
seated herself at some distance from the rest of the party,
occupying herself with embroidery. Richard, who had intended
to speak to George of Edward's plans to bring wealth to the
crown, now found that it was more important to gain Anne's
attention. This did not please George and it embarrassed the
Duchess who scarcely knew what attitude to adopt, wanting to
be sisterly, yet anticipating that this would not please her
husband.

Anne's inheritance was considerable, and it was with this in
mind that George had taken her into his household. He had
little liking for her. This was apparent to Francis Lovell, but
Richard chose to be obtuse. He stood beside Anne and spoke
of her skill as a needlewoman, about which he knew nothing,
and then widened his subject to include other crafts about which
he knew rather more. George watched with evident dissatis-
faction and Francis Lovell endeavoured to engage Isabel in
general conversation. Anne continued with her needlework.
Had she paid Richard the attention he thought to be his due, he
would have been satisfied with the exchange of a few words.
Lack of encouragement, however, spurred him on mightily.
Francis Lovell thought he had never seen a man so excited by
so little. Since it was obvious that Anne did not wish to be
reminded of the time they had spent together at Middleham,
Richard began to talk of his foreign travels. He was not sorry
to have a chance to display his knowledge of music and art,
since he had few friends at court who shared his interests.

George now mounted his own hobby-horse and descanted
loudly to Francis on the problems attendant on being brother
to the King—so many duties, so little thanks. Francis, aware
that George was very easily offended nowadays, listened with
an appearance of sympathy. Isabel stared anxiously at her

sister. Anne, although saying little, was now regarding Richard. Isabel thought that her sister was rather too serious; men did not care for women to look at them quite so straight. But Richard seemed to gain inspiration. The harder Anne made his task, the more important it seemed to him to succeed with her. At last, he won his reward. Anne gave him a pretty smile and began to converse with him. What she said, Isabel did not know, but judging from Richard's expression it might well have been the most marvellous revelation. A pulse leapt in Isabel's throat. Something was happening here that should be stopped, but she was not an effective person and could not think what to do.

Fortunately, George was now occupied with something to do with his hounds which necessitated his leaning from the window and bellowing to a groom in the yard below. Isabel moved closer to Richard and Anne, wondering what it was that so held his attention. She was mystified to discover that all this excitement was occasioned by Anne's description of the Book of Hours which she had had from her mother. She was describing it with the animation with which Isabel might have spoken of a precious stone or a fine silk. Richard listened, his eyes exploring Anne's face. When she saw his expression, Isabel ceased to be mystified. She did not understand what was so marvellous about the Book of Hours, but she understood better than Anne a man's lust for possession.

'Dickon is much taken by your sister,' Francis Lovell said quietly. George was now so engrossed in the matter of the hounds that he was free to join Isabel.

'It won't please George,' she said wretchedly.

Lovell studied Anne. She did not use her features so busily as some women and perhaps because of this one was particularly conscious of the eyes. Now, while still regarding Dickon in a very straight way, the eyes expressed a great concern, as though they would draw the soul from his body. Dickon, for his part, seemed so vastly surprised that one might have supposed her specially created, that no woman before her had two eyes, a nose and a mouth!

'I swear I will not leave without you show it to me!' he was saying. Anne demurred.

'Dickon keeps himself occupied with Anne.' George had turned from the window at last.

'It is a matter of her Book of Hours,' Isabel said. 'He would like her to show it to him.'

'Then so she should.'

'I think she fears that he means to possess it.'

3

George laughed. 'Then she must make up her mind that he will have it. Make no mistake about that. He can be very determined. One way or another, she will have to part with her treasure.'

A few days after this meeting, Richard asked Edward for his consent to his marriage to Anne. George, infuriated that Richard's demands should advance so rapidly from the possession of a Book of Hours to the Neville estates, opposed the marriage vehemently. Richard's feelings were of the kind only to be strengthened by opposition. He meant to have Anne. He had known other women more obviously attractive, but in her quiet features he saw a promise of something that would meet his deepest needs. She was quiet, devout, of a serious mind; she would be tender and true. All these were admirable qualities, but would not alone have so greatly excited him. But she had an inner confidence which he did not possess and which seemed to him of inestimable value. She had an almost miraculous rightness, as though everything she said and did had the hallmark of perfection. Every movement, however slight, was finely executed; the words which passed her lips, unremarkable though they might be, were spoken with such precision they seemed new-minted for her use. She would be a source of strength on which he could draw. In return, she would make demands, she was fastidious and her standards of behaviour were high, though gentle she would not hesitate to rebuke him; but this only roused his desire to please her in all things. He would have her.

George imagined that Richard could be made to give her up. There was trouble with the Scots and Edward sent Richard north to put it down. George seized his opportunity.

One night, not long after Richard had left London, Isabel came running to her sister in great distress.

'Oh, my dear Anne, you are to go away! What are we to do? What are we to do?' She seemed ready to repeat this endlessly, with much hand-wringing and anguished snatching of breath.

'If I am to go, then I am to go.'

'How can you be so calm?' Isabel had risked her husband's displeasure by coming with the news so precipitately and felt that a more dramatic reception was warranted.

'It will make no difference if I am not calm,' Anne pointed out.

'It would relieve your feelings.'

'Where am I to go?' Anne showed no disposition to part with any feeling without first being able to measure what amount might be due.

'You are to go to a Mr Harbuckle, a merchant to whom George owes so much that the wretched man dare not refuse him anything in case he never receives payment. I gather that he needs a scullery maid.' Isabel exaggerated, making the worst of the arrangement because she was determined to wring some tears from her sister so that she might have the satisfaction of giving comfort.

'I see.' Anne remained motionless for a moment, her eyes narrowed as though she was trying very hard to see. Her face looked peaked with the strain of it. Isabel went to her and put her arms around her.

'It is because of this persistence of Richard's,' she said. 'As soon as he gives in, things will be better again.'

'You think he will give in?'

'George is very determined about this, and when he is determined he always has his way.' Isabel confronted her husband only in household affairs where his wishes were never questioned.

Anne turned away. 'I would like to make sure I take one or two things with me. Will you leave me.' When Isabel had left the room, Anne went about her business briskly, collecting a few personal effects including a heavy shawl in which she wrapped the Book of Hours. She then laid the shawl across her arm, pressing the book close, and waited.

If Richard loved her, he would come for her. For a time, he would suffer great distress but this would test his feeling for her; after her previous experience she had no mind to marry a man whose feeling for her was unproven. She lowered her head submissively when told formally of the arrangements which had been made for her future.

But it was not only Richard's determination which was to be tested. Mr Harbuckle was kind, and not a little embarrassed. He did the best he could for her and had put aside a room not much bigger than a cupboard for her use. There was a small, low window. 'So you will have air,' he said solicitously. The window overlooked the street and admitted evil vapours which nearly choked her. The noise was intolerable; people shouted all day and at night there were more sinister sounds. She lay with her fingers pressed over her ears until the stench so choked her that her own coughs drowned the noises in the street.

Mr Harbuckle remained considerate, and the rest of the household treated her with courtesy. It was the people in the street who most menaced her. She had not felt such hatred for her father's killers as she felt for this raucous mob who destroyed her peace by day and denied her sleep at night. For all her Christian piety, she would have been sorely tempted to pour boiling oil over them had she had any such remedy to hand. Worse than all this, was the racking cough. There were times when she fought for breath and, becoming panic-stricken, brought on an even worse paroxysm. She entertained the morbid fear that Richard would not find her alive. As there was no one for whose sake she must put on a brave face, she spent much time in solitary weeping.

She still believed that Richard would come, but was so dispirited that the thought brought her little joy. Only occasionally, when for a brief space it was quiet in the street, did she manage to comfort herself: in her mind, she again inhabited Middleham, saw the broad valley stretching beyond the castle walls, breathed good air into her lungs.

Richard, too, thought of Middleham as he journeyed south again. The estate had been bestowed on him; he planned to return to it when he and Anne were married. As soon as he arrived in London, he went to Clarence's house where he was informed that the Duke and Duchess were away, and that Anne had left there some weeks ago. No one knew her whereabouts. A meeting with George on his return proved no more helpful.

'I was prepared to make arrangements for her, to ensure that she was comfortably settled.' George spoke with every appearance of injured dignity. 'But it was taken out of my hands.'

'But you know where she is?' Richard persisted.

'No. Why should I?' He became petulant. 'It is all very well to turn to me now. You would not listen to me before, you swept my advice aside. . . .'

'Your advice! As I recall it was not given in the form of advice!'

'You recall nothing. No one pays any heed to me.' George's face was beginning to be marked by his grievances, his mind was entangled by them; it was doubtful whether he was really aware that he was lying to his brother.

Richard's face was impassive save for a slight tick beneath his right eye which afflicted him at times of strain. He said with a thin semblance of reasonableness, 'Come, you might as well tell me. I shall find her in any case.'

'How little you know of London!' George scoffed. 'Will you go from house to house, insisting on searching each room? You will make yourself a laughing stock.'

'She is in London, then. At least we make some progress.'

'I did not say so,' George blustered. 'I merely advised you not to make yourself foolish.'

'Pray give me more detailed advice. I promise to listen carefully.'

'I have nothing further to say.'

Now that Richard was angry he saw his brother more clearly than before. There was that in George's character which would always tend to play into his opponent's hands: he had a fatal lack of discretion. It was unlikely that his plan would have been formulated or executed with any degree of thoroughness; no doubt someone in his service could be persuaded to give information. Richard, who was nothing if not thorough, set his own servants to work and in a few hours he was informed of Anne's whereabouts.

Early that evening Anne heard people in the street scurrying in front of horsemen; she heard someone in the house call out, 'It's the Duke of Gloucester's men.' Eagerly, she knelt by the low window and saw Richard. At this angle, he looked little different from the boy who once at Middleham had called out to her and Isabel, 'Are you damsels in distress?' She watched him dismount. There would never be this distance between them again. She would like to have delayed him, to have fixed him there, unaware and undemanding, so that she could observe him without hindrance. And, for a moment, he did delay, turning to speak to a man beside him, making a show of authority. The other men were all taller than him. He is but a lad trying to make himself conspicuous, she thought; how ridiculous to have devised tests of his love! How often in the last few weeks she had envisaged this moment; yet now she felt no great surge of emotion, only a wry tenderness.

It was only when he disappeared from view that she realized she should have leant from the window to signal her presence. Now she was afraid lest he fail to find her. She ran out of the room and heard, far below, Mr Harbuckle's panic-stricken denials silenced by Dickon in an icy voice that was not that of a boy or any man she had known. She recoiled and turned back to the room, there to await this unpredictable stranger who had come to claim her. Soon, steps sounded on the stairs, the door was thrust open and she was in Richard's arms, shaking with a fear for which poor Mr Harbuckle was not responsible. Richard comforted her and held her tight so that she would understand that no one would ever dare to harm her again because she belonged to him. Imprisoned by his arms, Anne knew that more than duty would be demanded of this bargain. She gasped, 'I can't . . . I can't. . . .' He released her gently and she said, petulant with exhaustion, 'I have no strength. . . .'

'It is not far,' he assured her.

'Far?'

'I am taking you to St Martin Le Grand. You will remain

in sanctuary there until Edward gives his consent to our marriage.'

'St Martin Le Grand! I am to be shut up again, and still in London!' He looked down at her, hurt by her disappointment and a little afraid of her fragility. She sensed the ebbing of his vigour and said, 'Forgive me, I scarcely know what I am saying.'

'I don't like to see you so sad.' He was a lad again, despondent, the splendid rescue marred by his inability to perform some spectacular feat which would release her entirely.

'I am not sad!' She found there were a few grains of courage left which, with careful husbanding, would sustain her until they reached St Martin Le Grand. 'I am dazed with the wonder of being free and this has made me weak. I shall be glad to go if you will take me there now.'

As they rode towards St Martin Le Grand the last of the sun was smouldering in the west; it was already cooler and the dust had settled in the streets. People sat in doorways or shouted to each other as they closed the shutters of their shops for the night; they were no longer the raucous, boorish people Anne had found so frightening. Her unheroic lad had worked his miracle after all. As she looked about her, she saw the world sharp-edged and brilliant as though all her life until this moment had been spent waiting to emerge from a cold mist. She looked at Richard, riding quietly beside her; but either her eyes were not yet used to this radiant world, or he was too near, because she could not see him clearly.

'I am quite recovered,' she assured him when they parted; and then, seeing that this was not entirely to his liking, she expressed the quavering hope that they would soon be reunited. Her spirit was more stubborn than that of many a more robust person; but there would be time for him to discover her strength and now she made him a present of her weakness.

Richard made the journey to his own apartments slowly. In spite of the noise in the city, which had changed in character with the evening but was no less rumbustious, he felt at peace. On either side, the scrofulous hovels, touched with the first milky sheen of evening, had an air of enchantment, and the people, relaxing in their own noisy fashion, had a vibrance which made them almost beautiful. He made his way by the river, dun-coloured now, the reflections of the wooden buildings gradually dissolving. In the distance as the light thinned, the buildings of the city seemed to draw closer together, accommodating themselves to the oncoming night. He could almost understand, at this moment, why Edward liked London.

A few months later, Richard was less satisfied with life and London.

'You get me into trouble with Dickon,' Edward said jovially to George. 'When I represented to him your views about Anne's inheritance he became angry at the thought that I should attribute such base motives to him.'

'He is angry at the thought of foregoing anything which adds to his power. I tell you, he makes himself too great. It is something I can scarcely be expected to tolerate.'

'I begin to lose patience with both of them,' Edward confessed to Hastings. 'Richard maintains that it is Anne for whom he cares and not her inheritance, but at the same time he will not see her wronged, so this does not advance us very far.'

'Is it Anne he is determined to have or her estates?'

'I begin to believe that it is Anne.'

'Then perhaps he might consent to her being wronged just a little?'

Christmas came. Richard and Anne prayed that they might soon be together at Middleham, and George prayed that God would prosper his righteous cause.

A strange and wonderful thing happened at the beginning of January. This was the year 1472 when a brilliant star appeared in the south-east. At first, it rose at two o'clock, that darkest hour of the night when only fiends and those who do their work are abroad in the streets of cities, except for the watchmen. It was the watchmen who spoke of it, and then others, in towns and villages all over the land, looked out for it. The star moved westward and seemed to have a great hole in it from which flame flared out.

To Richard, it seemed that the star was an augury of future joy, and immediate events encouraged him in this belief. Edward offered George Warwick's lands and property, other than Middleham and one or two Yorkshire estates; he also said that the Great Chamberlainship of England would be surrendered to him by Richard. George eventually accepted this.

Richard and Anne were married with little ceremony. Soon after the marriage they went north, travelling for some time over a flat plain until in the distance they saw the hills massed strong and dark, and great spurs of rock thrust out towards them, covered with vast oak forest.

Richard rode in high spirits, looking forward eagerly to that moment when the valley opened out and there was Middleham; like a massive ship that would never veer in the teeth of the wind or bow to the sea's tumult, it thrust its towers into the sky, inflexible, built to outlive even its own purpose.

It was a fine day. As they came nearer, the brute strength of stone, the iron framework of a gate half-way up the castle wall, were more delicately rendered in the moat water. A breeze wrinkled the surface of the water and ripples of light flickered over the stone walls of the barbican. Anne, who had found the journey tiring, revived at the familiar sight. She looked at her husband, but at the moment he had thought for only one thing: Middleham was his. He rode towards it, totally absorbed in the pride of possession. She felt no resentment, it was only right that he should enjoy this moment alone. If she sensed that she herself was now numbered among his possessions, she did not resent this either, but felt instead only pity and a desire to protect this illusion as long as she should live. They crossed the drawbridge and passed from sunlight into the shade of the barbican.

Later, when they came together in their chamber, she drew from among her treasures her gift for him which was the Book of Hours.

'I give it with my love,' she said.

'Did you always mean me to have it?' He was more concerned with other proofs of love, but was diverted by the thought that she had withheld it only to please him the more.

'I believe I thought to show it to you one day.' It seemed to her it might be more precious being hard to come by. 'But I'm sure I had no idea of parting with it.'

'It will be my most valued possession,' he assured her, putting it lightly to one side and never imagining how heavy it would become in his hands.

They did not see the star while they were at Middleham. After fourteen days it had seemed to burn itself out. Then it appeared again, its course altered somewhat, but blazing more splendidly. Then it became pale and burnt more steadily, but gradually moving further and further away, until, as was recorded by a chronicler, it was no bigger than a hazel stick. On the twentieth day of February it had disappeared altogether and was not seen again.

2

By the spring, although the wonderful star had disappeared, it was still in men's minds. One young man tried to draw it. He produced a character something resembling a star on the parchment in front of him and added a flourish to it. Then he put his head against the full sleeve of his gown and gave a deep sigh that registered neither contentment nor resignation. When he raised his head, he saw that the sun shone on the lawn and so he had to hurry out to the garden to make the scene complete by his presence. He was fair-skinned and fair of face, with wide blue eyes which looked around as though amazed by a certain impudence in the objects his gaze encountered, questioning their right so to confront Henry Stafford, second Duke of Buckingham. He was nineteen, physically well-developed, but not mature. As he moved he gave the impression of being vividly aware of physical sensations but unable to harness them into anything which would give him pleasure. The desire for pleasure was in his face, but so was the certainty that he would not find it.

The reason for his frustration soon appeared at the window of the room he had just vacated. She might have been his mother; her manner suggested possession but no indulgence. She was, in fact, his wife. A vulgar hag, he thought, appraising her from this safe distance; avaricious, crafty, uncertain of her hold on anything and therefore never letting go—her claws even now gripped the window sill as though to emphasize her claim on the very masonry of the house. He reminded himself, feeling the spring breeze which had still some of winter's edge to it, of the circumstances of their marriage. At the age of twelve he had been the ward of Queen Elizabeth who had been free to dispose of him as she chose. She had shortly disposed of him in marriage to her sister. He was descended from Edward the Third: this creature he must call wife was infinitely beneath him. All these things he told himself as he walked across the lawn towards her, the breeze sharpening his senses and making him aware of matters within him which could not long remain unresolved.

'You have not written to my sister,' she screeched. She herself wrote constantly to her sister of the doings in her household, as though even the inspection of the linen was a task not to be undertaken without the prior knowledge of the Queen of England.

'I will write soon,' he said indolently.

'Letters do not get written on lawns that I have ever heard.'

He came slowly towards her, smiling, because she could hardly complain that he smiled at her. She sensed that he was growing out of her control, becoming somewhat large for captivity. She did not find the smile reassuring. 'I sometimes think he will be cruel,' she had confided recently to her sister. The only answer which the Queen had vouchsafed was, 'I daresay he may be.' He was one of the foremost lords in the land and as such he could be of service to Edward: Katherine must, if necessary, put up with a little inconvenience.

But inconvenience can last a lifetime. Katherine, gazing down from the window, felt a chill as she looked at that handsome face. The mouth was wide and the bright eyes were hungry, a rapacious creature! She trembled, and reminded herself that the spring was not yet out and she had perhaps not dressed wisely.

'My sister has done much for you,' she said. 'You would do well to remember that at all times.'

He stood beneath the window and laughed in her face. She clutched the sill even tighter. They had never before confronted each other so openly. 'Your sister, madam,' he spoke each word as though he had only now discovered a delight in words, 'has done much for *you*.'

He noted, not the unbecoming flush rising up her neck, but the cold fear in her eyes. That fear was in his nostrils, he tasted it in his mouth; nothing she could say or do would ever again have power to stay him now she had given him this taste for her fear. She leant forward, her gown slipping so that he had a glimpse of her small, mottled breasts. She ranted, her voice shrill, and he stood before her, momentarily satisfied. He was only beginning to understand this game, aware of the strength in the paw but not yet having developed the cunning of the predator.

Later, he wrote to the Queen. Elizabeth Woodville had owned him. When he was a child she had treated him as though he was an object which she could dispose of as she chose. Had he been threatened, hunted, maltreated, things might have gone better for him; he would have had a sense of the value which others put upon him, and pain and fear were things with which he could have come to terms. But he had been a pawn in a game the subtleties of which were beyond a child's comprehension. He had lived among people who had no sense of him as a person, with the result that he had very little sense of himself. Now, he wanted reparation. But this was not yet his time. The comet presaged well for Edward's reign, and although doubts might be cast upon Edward's parentage (and Buckingham had heard such doubts expressed) no one was presently disposed to question either his vigour or his will to rule. So, in spite of the spring torment in his veins, Buckingham must write courteously to Queen Elizabeth.

3

A few days before Christmas, some people claimed to see the star again, this time in the south-west. The Duke of Clarence, perhaps filled with seasonable religious fervour, maintained that it foretold the coming of another King.

Whatever might be the truth about the star, it was a fact that the following year, 1473, was not a good one. It started well enough with a fine, crisp spring. Richard of Gloucester's wife gave birth to a son who was given the name of Edward in honour of his uncle. But if Gloucester and his wife were happy — and they were reputed to be so happy one would have thought no other woman had ever borne her husband a son — all was not well in the realm.

After some rain in early May, June was fine and hotter than usual, and even the most pessimistic among the country folk began to talk of a good harvest. In July, it was hotter still; there had been no rain for over seven weeks, many of the streams were running dry and rivers were low. It grew yet hotter. By the end of July the land had a seared look and many river beds were bare as dried bones; a few could remember such arid desolation towards the end of August, but none so early as July. The workers in the field bore the mark of the heat, with dry, cracked lips and red, dust-rimmed eyes; they moved slowly and some dropped down in the fields while they worked and were found to be dead. Fever was prevalent and in some parts of the country people became ill with the bloody flux. Prayers were offered for rain, but no rain came.

On one very hot evening Christopher Ormond stood at the side door of his church. There had only been a few people in the church and now these had gone. Yet in other parts of the country the churches were full of people anxious to be forgiven for whatever sins had brought this dreadful drought upon the country. So why is my church empty? he asked as he looked down the dusty lane at the cluster of houses.

He had argued with the local squire, a stupid man with pretensions to learning who thought that Aristotle was still alive and living in Italy. Ormond could never resist the temptation to put down pretension. Unfortunately, the argument had ranged wide. The villagers would not be concerned with the details of the argument, but the one word 'heresy' would be enough to rouse their fears. But there was worse than that. He had defended a woman whom they said was a witch. He hated superstition. But she was a witch of a kind and as well as installing her in his house to serve on him, he had taken her to his bed. Some folk might say that the country was paying for the licentiousness of Edward's court, but hereabouts they blamed the drought on their priest.

Ormond turned back into the church. He hesitated at the rood screen, staring towards the altar where the candles burnt on either side of the cross. After a moment, he approached the altar and reaching forward, held one hand in the flame of the candle, palm downwards. There was a rustling sound and he spun round, his face contorted with fear and pain. The main door had been left open and wisps of straw skittered over the stone steps. Beyond, he could see the long grass moving against the deep blue evening sky. He walked slowly down the nave; his injured hand was cupped, palm upwards, in the other, it showed the marks of more than one burning. His spirit was strong and defiant, but his body was pitiably weak and as he turned to shut the heavy door behind him, he had to steel himself not to glance anxiously over his shoulder, and sweat trickled between his shoulder blades.

I *must* leave here, he thought. He walked slowly down the path, devising ways in which he might escape his fate. Then, in the distance, drumming on the baked earth, he heard horse's hooves. A solitary rider. He stopped, waiting. A robin, perched on the stone wall, also watched with bright interest. The rider was now in view. Although he had only met him once before, Ormond had no difficulty in recognizing Dr John Morton.

'Well met!' Morton greeted him. 'I am on my way to Chester and hoped to see you.' He was a little fuller in the face than when Ormond had last seen him but the eyes, although red-rimmed from dust and sun, were as sharply intelligent as ever.

'I had supposed you dead until I heard that you had been appointed Master of the Rolls,' Ormond said drily; and although he added that he was pleased, reproach lingered on the air.

The heat in Ormond's house was stifling and they sat outside in the yard to drink the ale which Ormond's woman brought to them. Morton was not in the least offended by Ormond's disapproval; he had no bad conscience. 'I went as far as most men in serving Queen Margaret and never deserted her while there was a cause for which to fight. But all that is ended now, and I am a man who must be of service to someone.' He was sincere in this; he had great gifts and he had used them as loyally as the next man. 'Who would benefit if I were to waste my gifts? Did not Christ Himself warn us that a man will be held accountable for the good use of his gifts?'

Beside him Ormond shifted his long limbs awkwardly. 'What gifts would one need in the service of King Edward?' he asked sourly. 'I was speaking recently to a kinswoman of mine, Ankarette Twynyho. She is maid to the Duchess of Clarence and hears much talk of the court life. She tells me that King Edward's attention is taken up with food and women, and that he surrounds himself by men of a similar mind, such as Lord Hastings, who is reputed to have relinquished his mistress, Jane Shore, to his royal master! If this is the way to please King Edward, how will you serve him?'

'There are other men of a very different stamp of whom Mistress Twynyho may not have told you: Richard of Gloucester, for example. He is somewhat uncomfortable company; a man of considerable wit but no great humour. He would be a bad enemy.' Morton paused for a moment, reflecting on Richard of Gloucester, and nodded his head. 'A bad enemy. But no one would accuse him of devoting himself entirely to pleasure.'

Ormond looked down into his mug of ale and waited for Morton to come to the point.

'There is one man, in particular, whose religious sensitivity is so exquisite that even you would be hard pressed to find fault. A man, moreover, with considerable pretension to learning.' (A man you do not much like, Ormond thought.) 'This man is in need of a secretary, the last being unable to meet his master's somewhat exacting requirements. I am in a position to put your name forward.'

'Am I to know his name?' Ormond asked dourly.

'Anthony Woodville, who is now Earl Rivers.'

'The Queen's brother.'

'But very different from the Queen. And, though you may have no great liking for the Woodvilles, this appointment would be more congenial than your present situation. For my part, it would give me pleasure to help you to advance in the world; and I confess that it is also in my own interests to be of service on this occasion.' He looked at Ormond in urbane good-humour. Ormond saw that this appointment would serve two purposes and that he would serve two masters; he would be Earl Rivers' secretary and Morton's spy. It was odious: yet he could not find the words which would enable him to refuse. Should he not also use his gifts?

'I will think about it,' he said; but the throbbing of his burnt hand told him he would not dare to refuse.

4

Anthony Woodville, Earl Rivers, was at this moment entertaining Lord Stanley at Grafton Regis. Lord Stanley had to admit that the Earl was a most cultured man and charming with it; but he was so damned knowledgeable that Lord Stanley was rather ashamed of his own lack of erudition and was forced to spend most of the time nodding agreement, while the Earl talked with great sincerity and most commendable humility of matters religious, broaching many topics which it had never even occurred to Lord Stanley to think about, let alone discuss. Lord Stanley was half-asleep when Rivers said, 'Where is one to put one's trust?'

The remark jolted Stanley into awareness. It was the state of the world around him which disturbed the Earl, but Stanley took the remark personally and said, 'No one could doubt *my* loyalty, I am thankful to say.' He was constantly vigilant in defence of his honour, it having been involved in so many transactions he must make it clear that he had never actually parted company with it. He was particularly sensitive at the present time. He was now married to Margaret Beaufort, the mother of Henry Tydder, and with Edward secure on the throne, this was hardly the time for a flirtation with the House of Lancaster, let alone a marriage.

'The King fully understands that his interests are well-served by this union which can only bring harmony between him and the one person who might otherwise have been the focus of intrigues against him,' he said ponderously.

Rivers allowed himself to be deflected from his contemplation of the world's ills. 'I hear that her son is now at the court of the Duke of Brittany and styling himself the Earl of Richmond.'

'A misguided youth but unlikely to pose a serious threat,' Stanley deflected the conversation from Henry Tydder. 'Edward's troubles come from nearer home. A Lancastrian parliament once declared Clarence heir to the throne after Queen Margaret's son, and since the prince is now dead, Clarence may well be mad enough to consider himself the rightful king.'

'Yes, yes.' The Earl bowed his head; a fine head, the hair beginning to recede a little from the forehead and slightly grizzled, but still thick and strong. 'I find more and more that life takes a turn I do not like. I have seriously contemplated retiring to a monastery.' His face assumed an expression of deep melancholy which was perhaps as much a reflection of his complex character as a response to the external ills of the times. 'I do not mock you. My intentions are most earnest.'

Lord Stanley was not impressed. He took Rivers to be a foolish dreamer who did not even know what was good for himself let alone the world. Stanley was free from that illusion of grandeur which goes beyond wealth and position and which had been the downfall of Warwick; he possessed no creative urge to alter the pattern of events but was prepared to study the patterns made by other men, seeking with infinite patience a way in which he could fit into the design with the most profit and least risk to himself. In the game which children play, where the one who is touched is singled out from the rest, he greatly excelled, twisting, turning, side-stepping, at times melting away on the periphery of the game, and somehow never being the one on whom the hand falls.

'Or does the world need men such as me?' Rivers mused. 'Should I remain where my influence can be felt?'

Stanley looked at him contemptuously. He doubted whether this man would be able to bear the burden of the world's need of him; there was an impression about him of strength going to waste. The room in which they were sitting was hot and outside the sun sparked up from cobblestones. Perhaps the heat affected him or he had drunk too much wine. Whatever the reason, as he looked at Rivers, Stanley had an oppressive feeling of doom. There seemed to be a darkness about Rivers; it hung like a cloak undispelled by the brightness of the sun or the lighter turn which their conversation subsequently took. Rivers wore his darkness seemingly without being aware of it. After some minutes of this, Stanley suggested a walk in the garden. 'You must take me to see this stream of yours.'

'It will be quite dry now,' Rivers answered. 'But my father was convinced that the womere water ran from a crevice in the rock, though I don't believe he ever saw it happen.'

The sun was going down between the trees when they set out. Even before they reached the stream they could hear the water running, but they were not prepared for what they saw. The water chuckled and gurgled as it spouted from the crevice in the rock and already the bare stones beneath were bespattered; as the sun's rays caught the bed of the stream it seemed as though the rock gushed blood. Lord Stanley crossed himself. Rivers drew back and put his hand across his eyes, shading them from something he had no stomach to contemplate.

In places all over the land the woe water ran hugely that autumn. In some places it ran full and troubled, which betokened battle, and in others it ran clear, which betokened

death and pestilence. Voices were heard crying from grave-
yards, 'Woe! Woe!'

Chapter 7

I

In the spring of 1474, a French nobleman visiting London
wrote to the Duke of Brittany. He felt very homesick and dis-
inclined to praise, and his digestion having been wrecked as a
result of a royal banquet his account of the life of the court was
particularly unfavourable.

'On my last visit,' he recalled, 'I was much impressed with
the King, but now find him somewhat changed. He lives in great
splendour and entertains most lavishly—the more I feel for his
own pleasure than for any great concern for his guests' comfort,
since it is assumed that all present share his immoderate delight
in food and drink. It is noticeable that he grows a trifle gross in
appearance. Louis de Gruuthuse is as ever very impressed, as
one might expect from one who has received some very fine
presents, including, I am told, a cup of gold garnished with
pearl.' The writer, not himself the recipient of royal gifts, went
on, 'For my part, I must confess I find some want of taste in all
this excess, nor is the company always to my liking. The King
is altogether too easy with people of very little birth. Indeed, it
is said of him that he much prefers such company and on this
visit I have been surprised to realize how ill the noble families
of the land have fared under King Edward. Some say it has been
his deliberate intention to destroy the nobility.

'This is an uncomfortable country, until recently torn with
civil strife and still with those ever ready to cause dissent, such
as the King's own brother, the Duke of Clarence. It is said that
the King's council favour a foreign war, believing that nothing
else will so occupy people's minds and dispose them to peace in
their own country. There is renewed talk of claiming the crown
of France or, at the least, of gaining possession of those provinces which England still regards as her own. The spirit of
Henry the Fifth seems to die very hard in this people. It is
rumoured the King would wish for a closer alliance with
Brittany, provided the Duke can be persuaded to surrender to
him the Earl of Richmond. . . .'

It is not comfortable to be a pawn, one can never be sure
when the player may decide that it would be to his advantage to

put one at risk. Duke Francis of Brittany had given Henry Tydder shelter and had treated him with warm regard, but Henry could never allow himself the luxury of gratitude.

'His stomach gave him trouble today,' Robin Prithie complained to one of the sewers. 'The meat was bad, I could have told him that! But he has made a list of all the people who came into his chamber and who waited on him at table during the last three days! The thing which distresses him most is that he dined with the Duke last night and cannot personally inspect every pot and pan in the kitchen because this would give too great offence to the Duke!'

Robin was now Henry's personal servant. He found the life tedious and had ceased to look to the time when Henry would be a king with favours to dispense. 'E'er that happens I shall be too old to enjoy my reward!' he had said sourly to the chambermaid with whom he slept. To the sewer, he said, 'I'd as soon have a dagger between my shoulder blades as ever again to check that there is no one hidden behind the arras, or standing behind a tree when he walks in the garden!' But he had no sooner said this than a messenger from the Duke arrived and he had to allay Henry's suspicions once more.

Henry was walking on the terrace with Philippe de Commynes, one of King Louis the Eleventh's councillors, who, on a visit to Duke Francis, had taken the opportunity to make the acquaintance of the young Earl of Richmond. Although Henry was not aware of it, Commynes had only that day informed Duke Francis that King Louis would take it much amiss should the Earl of Richmond be handed over to King Edward. The French king had no use for Henry save as a bargaining counter. 'In himself, he is of no importance.' Commynes, however, was impressed by Henry's knowledge of affairs in France, Brittany and Burgundy, and the astuteness of his comments. As Henry was also a good listener, Commynes thought him charming as well as gifted.

But to Robin Prithie, Henry had changed little over the last years. Familiarity had deadened Robin's interest and he failed either to see or to read the lines of character now lightly sketched on the young face. When the two men turned at Robin's approach, he delivered his message without observing Henry very closely. At seventeen, Henry was slim and pale and, in Robin's view, unremarkable.

'Do we know this man?' Henry asked when Robin told him that a messenger had arrived from Duke Francis.

Robin assured him that he had seen the man often in attendance on the Duke.

'Then I suppose I had better see him.'

When Robin departed, Henry said to Commynes, 'I dare trust no one here.'

'But it seems you trust your servant.' Commynes had not liked the servant.

'He has been with me a long time.' This did not make Robin trustworthy, but Henry liked to believe that it did. Robin was a talisman, like his gift stone.

The messenger brought a different kind of gift from Duke Francis. Henry, who had little to occupy his mind save his suspicions, received the gift with what to Commynes seemed an inexplicable lack of enthusiasm. Later, when Jasper Tudor joined them, he found Henry thoughtfully examining a small silver bowl studded with stones which flashed green and blue when he held it to the light. Henry fingered this tangible evidence of betrayal almost caressingly. 'The Duke sends me presents now.'

'A beautiful piece,' Jasper pronounced decisively, hoping to impress Commynes, who tended to behave as though only a Frenchman was a judge of good workmanship

'You think so?' Henry looked slyly at his uncle.

'You have found a flaw in it?' Jasper was mortified.

'No, no, I trust your judgement in these matters, my dear uncle. You tell me it is beautiful, and I accept it . . .' he put the bowl down and stepped back to gaze at it, '. . . as beautiful.' Commynes, who was a good judge of a performance, thought that the timing of this speech would have done credit to a player. Indeed, he had observed that there was much of the player about this interesting young man. He knew how to create an atmosphere of drama, but it irritated him when others did so and he then adopted the attitude that he was a plain man and could not stomach such antics. Now, he walked round the bowl, studying it from different angles, his head to one side. 'Well, well . . .' he said, as though humbly perplexed, slackening his features slightly so as to present an image of a very simple man.

'You do not like it?' Jasper asked impatiently. 'I am sure the Duke intended it as a token of his affection for you.'

Henry, who regarded the gesture as about as affectionate as the kiss of Judas, merely raised his eyebrows.

'I have news for you.' Jasper grew weary of the bowl and turned to Commynes. 'I have it on very good authority that an English army is even now embarking at Sandwich. Edward means to make war on France.'

'This army has been embarking for these past three months,

if rumour is to be believed,' Commynes said. 'And still it has not yet sailed.'

'I am also told,' Jasper was determined to be taken seriously, 'that in the north so many men have answered Richard of Gloucester's call that people are asking who will lead the army! Edward, you must know, has ever been slow to fight. And now it is said he has grown so lazy that he is content to leave the charge of military affairs to Gloucester, whose zeal no one can doubt.'

Henry said, 'I suppose it *is* valuable.' He had picked up the bowl and was now examining the stones with avid interest. 'Not priceless, of course. But then, I can never see what value can attach to an article which is beyond price.'

In the stables, Robin Prithie, who was not beyond price, was talking to a stranger.

2

Edward, bowing to popular demand and not averse to the diversion, asserted his claim to the crown of France. There was much talk of the exploits of Harry the Fifth and Parliament was persuaded to make a large grant. In July 1475, Edward landed in Calais. He had raised a fine army and, joining forces with the Duke of Burgundy, he marched towards St Quentin. King Louis the Eleventh, however, had no wish to fight and Edward, at heart, was more of a merchant adventurer than a soldier. So it soon came about that Edward's commanders, instead of discussing strategy, met to consider terms for a truce.

'On the field of battle, one prepares to fight a battle!' Richard of Gloucester was uncompromising.

Earl Rivers studied his finger nails, Lord Stanley picked his nose, Clarence whispered to the Marquis of Dorset and Dr Morton gazed blandly out of the window; the Earls of Northumberland and Pembroke looked owlishly at the King. Louis had offered 75,000 gold crowns to be paid at once and 50,000 crowns subsequently. This was a matter which merited the gravest concern. Edward could understand their feelings. 'Are we to fight when more can be gained by not fighting?' he asked. In his view, only a fool would exchange the certainty of such an income for the uncertain glory of victory in battle. He could see that he did not lack support for this view; only Hastings and Dickon had indicated that they were not in agreement. Hastings, he could deal with, but Dickon . . . Dickon was black as a thundercloud. And for what reason? He was now spitting out something about honour. Had honour been put above all things, none of those sitting around the table would be here today! Aloud, Edward said to his brother, 'You were willing enough to flee from England with me once, leaving honour to take care of itself. Why are you so reluctant now to leave a foreign country, not in flight, but. . . .'

'We had no choice but to flee before. But here, we have a great army, the men ready to fight. . . .'

'The men will grumble, no doubt.' They had had a long journey and some discomfort, and would now have no chance of plunder. 'But am I not sparing their lives? Will it not be thanks to me that they will return unscathed to wives and children? In time, they will be grateful.' He looked at Clarence and Northumberland, Morton, Dorset, Pembroke, Rivers. . . . They had a more immediate reason to be grateful, for they had all been offered pensions by Louis.

'What will people think if it is known that an English army can be bought off?' Richard persisted.

'Why, they will calculate whether they can afford it, I suppose.' Edward watched his brother's eyes narrow, the face grow still. What an intractable man this is! he thought. He was surprised to find himself observing Dickon as though he was a stranger. He shrugged off a moment's uneasiness and said lightly, 'Why be so eager to let blood, Dickon? Would it make the throne of England stronger if we lost a vast number of good men here in France? Would it provide money so that I need no longer beg for grants from Parliament? Would it make our merchants more successful, increase our trade?'

'A great deal of money has then been wasted in mounting this campaign,' Richard retorted.

The point was shrewdly made. Morton coughed and patted his lips. Edward smiled but his eyes were not amused. He turned deliberately to Lord Stanley. 'You have more years than some of us, my Lord, and can correct our rash enthusiasm with cool wisdom.'

Most of the men present, impatient to talk about the terms of the truce, looked hopefully to Stanley. But Earl Rivers looked at Richard, amused at his humiliation, and Richard saw the look and stored it in his mind. He scarcely heard Stanley reply, 'No one is more concerned than I with honour, but as I see it, the only person to lose his honour in this is King Louis.'

There was a murmur of agreement. Hastings glanced at Richard and made a wry grimace. The others were now talking of amending the terms suggested by Louis. Richard sat silent, nursing his anger.

A treaty was eventually signed, but Richard still refused to accept a pension.

'You do yourself no good by refusing to take tribute from Louis,' Edward warned. 'You will make an enemy of him and we need his friendship.'

'Perhaps you would have me emulate Lord Hastings,' Richard replied caustically, 'and refuse to acknowledge what is assigned to me, but allow it to be "put in my sleeve"!'

'You are unjust to Hastings. He expressed his doubts about the wisdom of the truce, as you well know.'

'And having done so, worked the harder to bring it about.'

'Because I wished it.'

Richard was silent. Edward looked at him. Familiarity had prevented him from seeing Richard clearly in recent years. Now, something sharpened his attention. Richard was staring beyond Edward with eyes that did not like what they saw; the lips were compressed. For all his forcefulness, there was at this moment an unexpected weakness in his face, a hint of the strain felt by a man of whom more may be asked than he is able to give. Edward drew back from speculation. He had no energy at this stage to reassess the value of so crucial a figure in the pattern of his life. He shrugged aside his momentary uneasiness and said, 'The country needs money, Dickon. And so do I. This money that Louis offers will keep me independent of parliament for the rest of my life. Think of that!'

But Richard could only think that it was not Edward's craft which had gained this treaty so much as his reputation as a lover of pleasure; Louis had known that he was dealing with a king who had no heart for war and much liking for ease. It would not have been so with my father, Richard thought.

3

If Edward had given up the idea of regaining the English provinces in France, he did not so easily renounce his claims to the person of the Earl of Richmond. Over the next two years his agents were active in the matter, until a time was reached when it seemed that his request must be granted.

Duke Francis of Brittany, in agony of mind and spirit, paced his room and sometimes, since he was a devout man, he knelt and prayed. Time passed. Day turned to night. No one could say his decision, when he reached a decision, had been taken lightly.

'God guide me,' Duke Francis prayed, passing the burden of decision to a higher authority.

Time and God, the economic needs of his duchy, and his own pressing desire for food, eventually combined to vouchsafe a decision to Duke Francis. 'I am convinced that it would be wrong, a very great wrong, to question the word of the King of England,' Duke Francis argued. 'And a refusal to comply with his request must seem to question his word; for what other reason could there be for a refusal to a request so reasonable and accompanied by assurances which reveal a most honourable and generous intent? The King promises that, on his return to England, the Earl of Richmond will be handsomely treated and provided with a marriage within the royal family. To refuse such a request would not only cause grave offence to the King, but would deprive the Earl of Richmond of great advantages. What, after all, can the future hold for this young man if he stays here (much though we love him) to compare with the opportunities which await him in his own country?'

'I shall have my life if I stay here.' Henry supplied the answer to the emissary who conveyed to him the Duke's decision.

'The Duke is completely assured that the King intends to treat you with the utmost generosity. . . .'

'But *I* am not assured.'

This was beside the point and the emissary continued to elaborate on his master's pious hopes for the future well-being of the Earl of Richmond.

'How seemed he to receive the news?' the Duke asked later.

'He received it well.' But the emissary had not enjoyed his task. This was not because he had fears for the young man's safety, he was not given to scruples of this kind. It was simply that his reception had not been what he had anticipated, and he did not like the unexpected; his success in life depended to a considerable degree on his ability to assess people and situations and a failure to do this was therefore disturbing. He had found Henry, Earl of Richmond, something of an enigma. The young man was but nineteen and had no particular grace of manner, nor did he bear himself with marked distinction; yet it could not be said that he was awkward, and though he spoke little he did not give the impression of being inarticulate so much as begrudging the use of too many words. The face was sharpish and belonged to an older man, the face of one who misses very little of what goes on around him and is not at a loss to interpret its meaning for himself. The pale blue eyes were shrewd; the mouth was thin with no fulness to the lips, but was not mean nor entirely lacking in humour. One would need to be well-prepared in one's dealing with this young man. The emissary said cautiously, 'When I say that he received the news well, I mean that he made no violent protestation. But he did say that he had not been well and had some doubts about undertaking the journey. . . .'

'The climate here does not suit his constitution,' Duke Francis said, and added hopefully, 'He will be better in his own country. Do you not think he will be better in his own country?'

'I have heard the climate there is very different.' He had, in fact, heard quite the reverse, but one was hardly likely to be called to account for inexactitude about the English climate.

'If he is really ill, then of course he shouldn't travel,' the Duke said uneasily.

'No doubt Lavigny, who is still with him, will report to you on the arrangements made for his departure and on the state of his health.'

The Duke said, 'Ah, yes,' but he still looked unhappy.

His unhappiness was shared by Henry himself. 'Well or ill, they mean to bundle me into the next world without delay,' he said to his uncle. 'But try to convince them that I must have at least an hour's rest to gather my strength for this journey.'

After his uncle had departed, Henry wrote a letter to his friend, Pierre Landois, who was the Duke's treasurer and a man of influence with the Duke. Henry was not gifted with great powers of persuasion, nor was it in him to make a strong emotional appeal; but he was good at using the facts at his disposal to the maximum advantage. He wrote:

'There is only one person whose word is to be trusted in this matter of the wisdom of my returning to England, and that is my mother. I have only recently had from her a message warning me in the most compelling terms that the King intends my life, and has said in the hearing of several people at court that he means to lay his hands on "the only imp now left of Henry the Sixth's brood". '

He had not, in fact, heard from his mother for some time; but Edward had indeed made some such remark as that now attributed to him and Henry had stored it away in his mind ready for use should the occasion arise. It brought his brief note to a not insignificant climax. He did not enlarge on it; he had never been given to excess. He despatched the letter by a messenger who seemed to him the least unreliable of those at his disposal. Then he lay on the bed where he remained staring at the ceiling and praying for a bad road and a wild sea—he thought it incautious to go beyond these moderate requests, since flood or earthquake might well do Edward's work for him.

His uncle and three others were to accompany him. Robin, who had reasons of his own for wishing to return to England, begged to join the party.

'I have never been far from you, my Lord, since first we came here.'

'There is little advantage in being with me now.'

'Where you go, I would go.'

'You are a fool,' Henry said. 'But I have a need of fools, so you shall come with me.'

When the time came for him to leave, Henry refused food, and was careful to stumble twice on the stairs in the sight of those who might be asked to report on the circumstances of his departure. He was determined that there should be nothing done on this occasion which would lighten the conscience of Duke Francis.

Lavigny later reported that 'he was very pale and walked unsteadily but he made no protests and his manner was gentle and resigned.'

He was far from resigned. In the view that he took of his situation, resignation of such an order would be a submission to death. Rash gestures, however, would gain him nothing. He was not a believer in turning to confront one's fate head-on; at least, not until all else had failed. And if he were to escape, where could he hide? On either side of the track along which they rode was moorland, bleak, inhospitable country offering no shelter for the body or comfort for the spirit. He looked at Robin who rode beside him.

'In all your adventures, Robin, you must have been in more desperate situations than this. Tell me how you escaped from them.'

'I don't recall a situation the like of this one.' He seemed in poor spirits.

So, Henry thought wryly, even my friendly sprite has little advice to offer me! I must fend for myself, it seems.

As he looked across the moors, desolate in the level light of evening, Henry was conscious of a great loneliness. He had a long way to go and he would always be alone. Just for a moment, he saw what he had previously been careful not to see, a puny, slightly ridiculous figure, with a poor straggle of supporters and no wealth, not the proud rose of Lancaster but a briar in a hedgerow. He felt small and unequal to the demands which life would make of him. But the briar has a vicious prickle, as anyone who has tried to pluck its rose must know. After a time,

Henry's spirit revived, and as it revived, so his body drooped and he presented a pitiable figure. The ambassadors of the English king conferred among themselves and agreed that it would be advisable to take the journey in easy stages. There were several villages on the fringe of the moorland, and they decided to make a number of stops for refreshment and the greater ease of their prize whom they were anxious to deliver in good condition.

The people, however, were no more welcoming than their country. The first village to which they came was a dour place, with men sitting hunched against the walls of their hovels talking among themselves. As the party approached, one very old man who, in spite of his rags, had an unmistakable air of dominion, greeted them with mock obsequiousness, bowing very low and muttering asides which were obviously obscene and aroused the raucous laughter of his companions. There was nothing good-natured in this display, it was menacing and primitive. These were a malevolent people who nursed a fierce hatred of strangers. There were no strangers in the village, a glance at the upturned faces gave proof of this; there was something closer than resemblance of kith and kin, one model had served them all but instead of being perfected with repetition had, in the younger generation, deteriorated into hideous grossness. Here, if ever, the dark forces gathered.

They had stopped outside a low, shambling building, dark as the pit inside, but bearing a sign which pronounced it an inn, or whatever was the equivalent in this uncouth place. As Henry crossed the threshold, he stumbled and fell on the floor which was covered with filthy straw and the droppings of animals. The stench very nearly made him sick. The Englishmen bent over him. Henry yielded his body to the floor as though he would bury himself in its loathsome depths; they were unable to raise him. While they shouted orders to others to come to their aid, Henry began to babble some of the strange words he had heard in childhood in the Welsh hills. The King's men thought he must be speaking in the language of these parts and kept asking suspiciously, 'What is it that he says?'

'I don't know what he says.' Jasper, hastily summoned, was genuinely alarmed and this greatly enhanced the authority of Henry's performance. 'He is possessed.'

One of the King's men crossed himself; the other, more prosaic, said, 'He has a fever. I have heard men talk such nonsense in a fever.'

The villagers, however, believed Henry to be possessed by spirits foreign to their own particular demons. They ordered the party out of the inn. There was much shouting and threatening, and the wrath of Duke Francis, the King of England, the Pope, and God Himself, was called down upon the villagers; but these were rude men not to be bound by any law other than their own and the strangers were forced to quit the inn. Henry recovered sufficiently to allow himself to be supported to a bench by the side of the building.

The Englishmen regarded him sourly, wondering, no doubt, why it could be of such importance to their king to obtain possession of so miserable a creature, although years later one of them was to recall 'with what quiet courage and dignity he did comport himself' on this occasion.

While they were wondering what to do, Robin approached them. 'If you leave this to me,' he said, 'I will see that he accompanies you.'

'What is your name?' one of the men asked.

'Robin Prithie.'

'If you can help us, you shan't be forgotten, Robin Prithie.'

It was on the tip of Robin's tongue to say that he had already been enlisted in King Edward's service, but as he had done little to justify the payment he had so far received, he thought better of it and devoted himself to his present task.

After half an hour of gentle persuasion, Henry consented to continue his journey, but made such heavy-going of it, swaying this way and that, and sometimes rising in the saddle to shout wild words at some phantom he swore accompanied them always a little ahead on the road, that they halted for the night earlier than they had intended. The small town where they stayed was somewhat less barbarous than the village, but even so the accommodation available was squalid. Henry's fever became worse and as he was apparently suffering from hallucinations a priest was sent for. Henry and the priest conversed, the one in Breton and the other in his own eccentric Welsh, while the onlookers stood uneasily by. The priest, a sly, obdurate peasant, was not prepared to admit ignorance of Henry's condition and pronounced him to be in a fit. Several remedies were suggested, but as these were rather extreme, and as Henry seemed suddenly to have become quieter, it was decided that it would be better for him to be treated in England.

They set off early in the morning, by now a somewhat anxious party. When they had been on the way for some time, Henry said to the man who rode beside him, 'Were you asked to deliver me alive to your master?'

'Of course.'

'I doubt if you will do that.'

'As soon as you get to St Malo you shall rest awhile,' Robin assured him. 'You will be better then.'

'It warns us!' Henry rose in the saddle and pointed excitedly ahead. 'See, it comes to warn us against this road!'

'There is nothing there.' But the light on the moors played strange tricks, and Robin could have sworn that an eerie light flickered above the deep green grass ahead and some way to their right.

'I have seen such a light as that before,' Henry said truthfully, for he had seen it hovering above bogs in Wales. 'It is a sign of evil. I have known men ride out towards it and never return.'

'It is not directly in our path,' Robin muttered. But for the sake of Henry's soul, and perhaps for his own, he persuaded their escorts that the party should halt for several hours when they reached the next village. It was late afternoon when they set out again.

They had now travelled a night and a day and were but three miles from St Malo. The wind had salt on it, the stunted trees and bracken bent to it and pointed its passage inland. It was getting dark and the moon was up in a cold, clear sky. Henry felt the air on his throbbing face and was glad of its sharp sting. He wanted to live: life had not offered him much, but he had acquired a taste for it. He believed in his power to survive, but he knew that he must pass through a time of agony and doubt when the last flicker of hope would seem to be extinguished. He was like a child who has been assured that a story ends well and yet is racked with terror at the fear of what might be.

The stone walls of St Malo rose dark against the skyline, and then, as they came nearer, they were silvered with moonlight; Henry watched, unbelieving, as the walls grew higher and higher until the moment came when he must pass beneath them. He could not believe that this was happening to him, that he was being carried remorselessly into the stone heart of a fortress from which there could be no escape. He experienced the same feeling of outrage he had had when as a child of four he had discovered that the stones he had so diligently hoarded had fallen out of his kerchief. He had asked little enough of life, taken few risks, indulged no rash fantasies; he had not arrogantly challenged his fate nor made great demands for himself; he had been patient, long-suffering, frugal of his emotions, had conserved his energy and disciplined his mind, had avoided all bodily excesses. If ever a man had husbanded his resources and made good use of every talent God gave him, he was that man! It was not right that he should be so ill-rewarded. The small-minded meanness of life overcame him. Now, as a grown man, he could not put back his head and bellow his rage to the indifferent stars; but fall into a fever he could and did. He let all control slip, the fever opened out for him and he passed through into the centre of it; it closed around him, keeping him safe within a wall of fire which none should penetrate.

'I told you we should not have come thus far.' The Englishmen began to quarrel among themselves. It was agreed that the party must lodge that night in St Malo and that the best physician must be summoned. Henry tossed and turned, dreaming he was riding round and round an arena of fire, trying to find a way through the flames. Occasionally, the dream lost its impetus and he heard voices. Once, a man was saying that King Edward would be angry at the delay. How impatient people were to despatch others! A wait of a few hours, a day, what was that to King Edward? How could it be compared to the luxury of another day of life? The fever carried him soaring away again out of the range of people as greedy and ruthless as King Edward. Foolish. It came into his brain, sharp as a needle, that this way of killing off anyone whom one regarded as a threat was foolish, something belonging to a system which had worked its way out, there were other more effective ways. . . . He saw this with tremendous clarity as though it had been cut in glass on his mind, and the next moment it had gone and his thoughts were muddled and incoherent. He roared away again. Then, something jerked him out of the dream. New voices. Different rhythms of speech. No longer men who knew each other well whispering among themselves; dialogue, back and forth, the two parties clearly distinguished. Interesting. Wished he could have stayed long enough to find out. . . . But he was away again, riding that monstrous circuit of flame.

They came in the dark, he tried to fight them but he was too weak; he tried to cry for help, but they muffled his face, nearly stifling him. They carried him down narrow stone stairs, he knew that they were narrow and stone because as he struggled and thrashed about he smashed his fist against the wall, grazed his cheek and had the taste of blood in his mouth. He tried to pray but the wrong words, terrible blasphemies, came to his lips. He could see nothing, he was half-strangled and in great fear and pain. The wickedness of it, this ignominious bundling of a man into eternity!

'In here,' one of them said. 'In here with him.'

They laid him down and he clung to one of them, pulling him forward so that the face was close to his own. It was Robin. He groaned, 'Oh Robin, Robin, Robin!'

'Tell him he is safe,' Jasper commanded.

'You are safe,' Robin said.

Henry lay back on something that was soft and yielding as a wave of the sea; he floated up and down, up and down, thinking how wonderful it was to be safe. Then the wave reminded him of something and he said to Robin, 'The children! We'll go round the headland and see what games the children play.'

Someone tried to intervene, but he clung to Robin. 'They are singing. Listen, Robin, the children are singing. Sing me the song, Robin. The children's song.'

Robin sang and Henry floated out of the reach of the shore.

After a time, however, he seemed to grow heavier and the wave steadied and became remarkably hard. He was aware of pain all over his body. He heard someone say, 'The fever is leaving him now.' He opened his eyes and found that he was lying on the floor, wrapped in a blanket; the room was small and seemed to be full of well-intentioned people. His uncle Jasper bent over him and spoke slowly and clearly as to a child.

'The Duke has decided that it would be advisable for you to remain in Brittany after all. As your condition necessitated so many interruptions on our journey it was possible for your good friend, Pierre Landois, to get here in time to convey this message to King Edward's men. He is with them now. We thought it prudent to remove you to this place in case they are unable to accept the decision calmly; and a hard task it was, with you shouting and struggling all the while! Now you had better rest and compose yourself for your return.'

Henry closed his eyes, his fingers still holding the blanket, rubbing it gently between thumb and forefinger. It had a coarse, but not unpleasant, smell.

Duke Francis received Henry back with lavish protestations of affection and remorse. Henry, enfeebled by fever, was spared the necessity of responding with a similar outburst of emotion; but he contrived to look so pitiful, woebegone, and yet withal to display such a pathetic dignity, that the Duke was all the more touched and swore to protect him so long 'as I, Duke Francis, shall live.'

'We must hope he will live long,' Henry remarked drily to his uncle when they were alone together. 'But I doubt he is to be trusted even in this.'

'He saved your life,' his uncle said.

'Having first endangered it.'

'It would be well to bear no resentment since at present he is your only benefactor.'

'Oh, I bear no resentment,' Henry answered equably. 'I merely note that he is not to be trusted.'

He was no lover of his fellow men, but he was no hater, either. And he needed friends. This was but the first of many attempts to return him to his own country. It had whetted his appetite for the enterprise and he looked to a time when he might have more say as to how it should be accomplished.

Chapter 8

I

Anne, Duchess of Gloucester, sat at a window in Warwick Castle. It was January of 1477. She was alone with her brother-in-law, the Duke of Clarence. It was a forbidding day, grey, with a dark, implacable sky. She said, 'It will be dark early today.'

George regarded her with dislike. Her tone seemed to him to suggest that this early coming of the dark was a phenomenon peculiar to Warwick Castle.

'In winter in the north, I am scarce aware of the light,' he retorted.

She looked at him, lips parted as though to speak, and then forbore. George thought that forbearance in a woman was the very devil; submissiveness was quite another thing, but this was not a submissive woman. He was in a particularly sensitive condition, aware of animosity even where none existed, and therefore acutely conscious of his sister-in-law's disapproval. He began to stride about the room. His wife had died in childbirth only three weeks ago. 'But three days short of our Saviour's birth!' The infant son had not long outlived her. George proclaimed his grief as though it was a personal injury for which some miscreant must be brought to justice.

'But what justice is there? My brother is concerned only with pleasure, he is so besotted by Jane Shore that he thinks of nothing else, while affairs go from bad to worse.'

Anne, noticing how quickly his mind moved from his grief to his grievances, did not reply. George, to whom silence was always hostile, grew more angry. His features were heavier now, and a colour that was always in his cheeks and a slight loosening of the lines of the mouth, hinted at excessive drinking. His thick hair had receded at the temples and as it retreated seemed to have pared away the superficial charm, revealing a face that was resentful and scheming. His anger did not effect that fusing of energy and passion which made Richard's outbursts so deadly, but seemed to scatter his resources so that he was unable to bring his mind to bear on any one thing for long. Now, he was proclaiming inexplicably, 'I tell you, there are things I have seen. Oh, I am not blind! I see these things, I know their meaning. There are those would do me great evil. . . .'

The light in the room had been growing dim for some time. A servant came with a taper; perhaps the man heard these last words, but whatever the reason, his hand trembled and he made a clumsy business of lighting the candles. A tremor of fear passed from one person to another. When the servant had gone, Anne said quietly, 'Of what are you speaking?'

'I know that people with evil powers have been introduced into my household. You don't believe me? Yet my wife is dead, and my son, too.'

She sat motionless, pools of shadow making her cheeks look gaunt so that she seemed momentarily a much older person.

'They killed your father,' he said, standing above her, looking down. 'And now your sister. Have you no feeling for your own kin?'

'You cannot think. . . .' She shrank back, disliking his nearness as much as his words; he was physically repellent to her. 'No, that is surely not possible.'

'Do not forget that I was declared next in succession to the throne after the son of Henry the Sixth, and that since his death I stand in Edward's way. Yes, yes, yes!' He tossed his head back, his hands clenched in petulant anger as he saw that she still did not believe him. 'I stand in his way, I tell you.'

'Edward would not spill his own blood.'

'He is no blood of mine.' He had said this before and on each occasion it had heralded an outbreak of violence and ill-considered action.

Anne was spared the necessity of responding by the arrival of her husband. Richard had grave news. The Duke of Burgundy had been killed during the siege of Nancy on the fifth of January. Richard said, 'This is a heavy blow.' The Duke had been a strong, if erratic ally, and his death was a breach in England's defence.

Later, when they were alone in their chamber, Richard told Anne, 'The Queen has plans for her brother, Earl Rivers, to marry Mary of Burgundy. Her ambition for her family knows no satisfying.'

Anne was already in bed, but his resentment kept him prowling round the room. She watched him, thinking that his energy might be put to better purpose at this moment.

'If Edward consents to such a marriage, it will not please George,' she said.

'Why should George be especially displeased?' Something in her tone warned Richard that they were on a familiar battle-ground, and one on which she had proved to have the sharper weapons. 'It does not please *me*, either. Rivers is a man for whom I have no liking.'

'George means to marry Mary himself.' She settled herself comfortably against the pillows. 'I saw it in his face when you told him that the Duke of Burgundy was dead.'

'How mercilessly you examine us,' he protested. 'When we are out of humour we shall have to keep our faces turned from you.'

'George was in humour. He was delighted, like a little boy who has found a treasure and only keeps quiet for fear it is taken from him.'

'What fantasies you weave!' He spoke lightly, but the set of his mouth betrayed the obstinacy of the man who does not mean to see something which is unpleasant to him.

'Oh Richard, Richard, you are loyal to a fault, my dearest!' His loyalties put down roots deeper than reason; were they ever to be torn up, what a bloody business that would be!

He looked at her, his resentment tempered by concern for her health. Her sister's death must, he supposed, have brought back many unpleasant memories in which George himself played no small part, and during their stay here she had become very strained although she had not complained. As always when her face became thinner, her eyes seemed unnaturally enlarged. He came to the bed and said anxiously, 'What is it? Are you not well?'

'It is *you* who are not well!' She drew him down beside her and laid her cheek against his. 'Can you not see how they will twist and tear you, these brothers of yours? My dearest, *why* will you not see? You would not go into battle so ill-prepared.'

'I can only see that you are out of spirits.' He took her hand; it was cold and the wrist was thin, but the bones were unexpectedly large, giving an impression of strength rather than frailty. 'We shall be leaving here tomorrow. When we return to Middleham, you will be better.'

She laughed because she invariably became merry whenever he talked of her health. 'Not until we return to Middleham? Am I to remain uncomforted so long? Come! You can coax me better than that!'

But he was preoccupied and it was she who must coax until he was roused and his energy flowed into her. Long after he was finished, she lay awake, breathing gently now while his gift spiralled lazily in her body. Her body was like a strange house

which she had inherited and in which she moved about with a
sense of discovery, aware of another woman, a strange, passionate creature who had lain hidden deep in darkness and would
never have stirred had not Richard forced a way through to her.
Had he had any idea of the wonders he was still to perform when
he rescued her from Master Harbuckle's house? She turned her
head and saw her knight frowning in his sleep, his mouth
slightly open.

'Richard?'

He made a protesting snuffle and turned away, burying his
face in the pillow. She smiled and let him sleep.

2

Ankarette Twynyho's maid had been to the Fair. She put
the articles which she had purchased on the kitchen table,
pepper, onions, sugar, ginger. . . . Ankarette watched, paying
more attention to the maid than to Christopher Ormond who
had come to see how she had settled in her new cottage, and
also to impress her with his lately-acquired importance. The
kitchen door was open. Dust and pieces of straw swirled in the
yard. It was one of those agitated April days when the wind
can leave nothing alone; the maid's face burned where it had
caught her across the cheekbones. She was attractive in a
coarse way.

Ormond said, 'Should Rivers marry Mary of Burgundy, I
may not be in England for long. Burgundy is a country I should
very much like. . . .'

'You've forgotten the cinammon,' Ankarette said to the maid.

'There wasn't any cinammon.'

'There's always cinammon.'

'There wasn't this time.'

Outside, trees swayed against a pale lemon sky and nearer to
hand clothing on a line billowed out, dancing this way and that
as though it had come to clownish life. The wind was raw, it was
a cruel time, the spring.

'She always liked a touch of cinammon,' Ankarette crooned.

She is going to spend the rest of her life talking about the
Duchess, Ormond thought, instead of enjoying her retirement.

'Three hours before she died, she said to me, "Apple tart
and cinammon, 'Karette. . . ." '

The rooks were gathering in the trees, their harsh cawing
drowning all other bird song. The maid listened to Ankarette,
arms folded across her breasts, rocking gently to and fro,

4

thinking that this was an evening that stirred one up, all this wind. . . .

When at last the maid had been sent to get apples from the loft, Ormond had a chance to talk to his aunt.

'Earl Rivers is responsible for the education of the young princes and I have sometimes given lessons to Prince Edward. . . .'

'Earl Rivers is a Woodville,' she said dismissively. 'They're not well-thought of, the Woodvilles.' She was not prepared to recognize that anything of importance had ever happened outside the Clarence household.

The maid was leisurely hauling herself up the steps to the loft. An old hen was scrabbling about in the yard, pecking diligently but ineffectually for grain. Ormond watched the maid; the wind parted her hair at the nape of her neck. It was no use trying to talk to Ankarette; it had been a mistake to make this journey. He watched the maid come slowly down the steps, carrying a basket heaped with apples. A noise of which he had been half aware now became more definite.

'Horses!' he exclaimed. 'Fancy, more than one horseman riding this way!' His voice conveyed his contempt for the dull life which Ankarette now lived. They both listened while the distant drumming became more distinct and metallic. 'Fancy, Ankarette,' Ormond said with heavy humour, 'A fair and several horsemen riding by! And all in the one day.'

'There is plenty to do here for those who are willing,' she said touchily.

But the horsemen were not riding by. Suddenly, they were there in the yard, four or five men, all well-mounted. Ormond and Ankarette, talking in the kitchen, were in the shadow and the men could not see them; one of them said to the maid, 'Where is your mistress?'

Ormond moved abruptly towards Ankarette, knocking over a stool. He took her by the arm. 'What's the matter, what are you doing?' she asked querulously. As he looked at her, he saw her as he had known her when he was younger, plump and rosy, wearing a yellow kirtle. She had always been kind to him.

Then the men were in the kitchen and Ormond was pushed roughly against the wall. He saw Ankarette slung over the shoulder of one of the men, her hair was wild and she was screaming. 'Don't let them . . . don't let them. . . .' Her eyes seemed to stare right out of her head as though they were willing her body over these men's shoulders into Ormond's safe-keeping. He pulled at the man nearest to her, caught him off-balance and brought him to the ground. He grabbed a warming pan and belaboured the man with it as he fell. The other men rushed out. There was the sound of horses' hooves. Ankarette was still screaming. Ormond went out into the yard. The maid was huddled on the steps to the loft, crying. Gradually, the screams and the beat of the horses' hooves died away and only the barking of dogs and the distant complaint of cattle told of the intruders' passage. The old hen crept out from the shadows and pecked around to see whether this disturbance had produced any grain.

Ormond went back to the house. He was trembling. Something stirred in him, not the wind, but something as old as the wind. The man whom he had knocked down was easing himself up, still very befuddled. The warming pan was a few feet away from him. Ormond picked it up. The man looked at him and Ormond swung it with all his might, hitting the man between the eyes; he hit him many times until he was no longer recognizable as a man.

Ormond looked about the kitchen. He thought, 'I have killed a man.' The table was up-turned and there were bits of pastry all over the floor. He opened the pantry door. There was pigeon pie left over from yesterday; he picked it up and sat on the edge of the up-turned table, eating ravenously. After a time, he was conscious of movement out in the yard. The maid had come to the door and was gazing in, her face white as flour. Ormond wiped pastry from his lips.

'You'd best go away from here,' he said. 'Your mistress won't come back.'

3

'How often do I trouble you, my lord?' Queen Elizabeth asked.

It was a formidable opening, betokening much trouble, and Edward, who had eaten well, had no stomach for argument. As others tried to repeat their triumphs in the lists when their greatness had passed, so Edward expected of his stomach gastronomic feats to which his digestion was no longer equal. His pleasures taxed him now. Some of his amiability had gone, he was often angry for no reason, and even when he was gay, irritation was there at the back of his eyes, waiting its moment. But he was still in control and now he mastered his annoyance. If there was one person whom he had learnt to respect, it was his wife.

Elizabeth Woodville had thrown off youthful pretensions as

though they had been an encumbrance. That air she had had of being aware of the pattern of her life and resolved to make the most of it, which had been rather daunting in a young woman, had found true expression in her middle years. She was a woman who would strike a hard bargain and abide by the consequences.

Edward, who had had many proofs of her reliability in the matter of bargains, said warily, 'If you have troubles, I hope I can help to resolve them. My own troubles, I must deal with as I think best.'

'And how do you think it best to deal with this latest outrage committed by your brother George?'

He shrugged his shoulders. 'I have found that it pays to ignore George.' He walked to the window, hoping to dismiss the subject. April sunlight probed the room and outside the wind frisked across the grass and ruffled the feathers of swans, one of which was tapping with its beak on the kitchen grating.

'And *how* has it paid?' Elizabeth demanded relentlessly. 'When Warwick rose against you, *who* was at his side?—George! When you were taken captive outside Nottingham, it was George and Warwick who held you prisoner at Pontefract.'

'But not for long,' Edward recalled, smiling at the imperious swan.

'Nor was it for long that he was reconciled with you! By March, he and Warwick were stirring trouble in Lincolnshire, and with the purpose of putting George on the throne! They fled to France whence they invaded England. Again, he was reconciled with you—being no more capable of loyalty to Warwick than to any man. In fact, so eager in your support did he become that at Tewkesbury he despatched Queen Margaret's son as he fled the battle, for all that he cried out for mercy. Did he recall then, as he does so frequently now, that the Lancastrians had named him next in succession to the throne after Prince Edward? Little wonder he showed the young man no mercy!'

'These are but rumours.'

A young man had come out of the kitchen, using the swans as an excuse to turn his back momentarily on pots and pans. How fine it was to be young in this green season of the year, and how ugly everything else was! He looked at Elizabeth, who was saying:

'And is it a rumour that he took this woman, Ankarette Twynyho, who served the Duchess, had her charged and condemned for poisoning the Duchess, and that she was hanged last week? People are murmuring that if the King's brother can behave in this manner, there is no such thing as the King's justice, and every great lord will have his own justice as it was in the old days.'

'How well you are versed in this matter.' Edward sounded more indolent than ever, a sign of danger with him. 'Can it be that your good brother, Lord Rivers, has reported in as much detail to you as to me?' He turned reluctantly from the window.

She ignored this reference to the campaign now being waged by members of her family, but sensing that his patience was wearing thin she attacked on another front.

'It is for you and your good that I speak so. I think you cannot doubt my concern for you. Indeed, the proofs are not far to find! At court they laugh at my forbearance with Mistress Shore. Yet I have suffered this — nay, not even suffered it, but submitted gladly and with high good-humour! Can you deny that? Have you ever had sighs and reproaches from me?'

Edward counter-attacked, 'I married you because I could have you no other way, but it was the wisest thing I ever did, as I have proclaimed many times.'

'And the wisest thing you can do now,' she had no intention of being disarmed by sentiment, 'is to put your brother where he can do no more harm. If you will not do it for me, then you must do it for the sake of your son.'

There was silence. Then he said, in a different voice, low, and surprised as though she had cheated by introducing this new element into her old grievance, 'My son?'

'George has spread rumours that you are illegitimate. Perhaps you think this is of little consequence since he makes so many wild remarks. But if you were to die before George, can you not see what would happen? Your son would never come to the throne.'

Edward turned from her to the window again. 'I intend to live a long time yet,' he said lightly. The sunlight fell across his face, bright, but austere, lacking summer's warmth; it inspected Edward's features critically, noting the bloated cheeks, mottled and veined with wine, the reddened eyes, the tinge of purple on the lips. Edward winced and turned his head slightly, and by way of punishment for this evasion, it thumbed grimy shadows beneath each eye. Elizabeth, who was watching, had a glimpse of a man who was sick and aware of it. She experienced a sense that something inconceivable was happening; and, at the same time, there was the recognition of having arrived at some dreaded part of a journey, the stark landscape long anticipated, yet still coming upon her unawares. She cried out, no longer calculating the effect of words and actions, but stretching out her arms from the abyss into which she had inadvertently stumbled. 'My love! You must take care for us, you must, you *must*!'

This agonized appeal, and the reversion to a former intimacy, seemed singularly inappropriate to Edward. He was embarrassed and irritated.

'Of course this cannot continue, nor will it, I assure you!' He was now brusquely in charge of himself and the situation. 'But George is important enough in his own eyes without we encourage him by ravings as lunatic as his own.'

She stared at him, her eyes dull as though she had not taken in what he was saying. He had never seen her when she seemed so discomposed; there was a time when he would have been grateful for such weakness. But not now. He took his leave of her, striding out purposefully as though going immediately to put to rights this nonsense of Clarence's.

In fact, however, he had not yet decided how best to deal with Clarence and, because her words still echoed unpleasantly in his ears, he went instead to the children's chamber.

It was the hour when the older boy, who was six and a half, should have been receiving instruction from the chaplain (Edward had laid down strict rules for his son's conduct, being as anxious for his spiritual well-being as he had been careless of his own) but he found both children play-acting in the company of a harassed nurse. The older boy was draped in an embroidered cloth and had a crudely made crown upon his head about which he was now complaining peevishly.

'It's heavy. I'm not going to wear it. We'll pretend I'm wearing it.'

The younger child, more determined a player for all his youth, would have no truck with this kind of pretence and maintained stoutly, 'If you don't wear it, *I* will.'

'You can't, because you aren't king.'

'But you don't want it.'

'It's mine, whether I want it or not!'

Unconvinced by this argument, the younger boy lunged at the crown and, failing to get it, pummelled his brother, his face becoming crimson with temper. The nurse intervened and dragged the contestants apart. While she quieted the younger boy, the older one rubbed his forehead and grumbled, 'It's made a dent, I can feel it!' He then perceived his father, standing in the doorway, and hastily replaced the crown on his head, but further back so that it resembled a badly adjusted halo.

The nurse, no less embarrassed than her charge, stood back while the father greeted his children. It had been poor weather lately and the children had not been out and were therefore fractious and difficult to handle; but she was sorry she had given way to the chaplain's suggestion that they should play at a time when Prince Edward should have been receiving instruction. Their father, however, did not seem annoyed, and he now resolved the dispute over the crown by taking off the gold girdle which he wore round his waist and draping it sash-like across the younger boy's shoulder. 'All will be well now,' the nurse thought grimly, 'until he's expected to part with it. *Then* his father will see!' She considered that the father spoilt his sons vastly, being in the habit of playing with them in a way she had never encountered in any of the other great households in which she had served. When these periods of play, sometimes quite rough, were finished, it took hours to quiet the excited children.

On this occasion Edward did not stay long, the younger boy early developing a coughing fit which he was wont to do when over-excited. While she comforted him, the nurse took possession of the girdle without his realizing it.

'I see you are here alone,' Edward said to her. 'The Princes should be attended throughout the day. I thought such arrange-ments had been made.'

'The man who was here was sick.' He suffered from an inflammation of the bowels, but it seemed to her that he had best explain this for himself.

'In any case, it is time something more detailed was laid down to govern Prince Edward's day, else he will grow idle. I will speak to Lord Rivers about this.'

On leaving the children's chamber Edward made his way to the chapel. He had meant to spend a few quiet moments ordering his thoughts before God, an exercise in which he did not often indulge. Something quite different happened. There was some loose plaster around the window frame and the wall was damp. The smell which came to Edward's nostrils, however, was of dirty clothing faintly tinged with stale urine. The years performed one of those extraordinary somersaults they were wont to do now that as much time lay behind him as ahead. When he was a young man he had come into this chapel and found that frail, mad king, kneeling in prayer. Later, relating the incident to a friend, he had made a joke about the odour of holiness. He crossed himself.

Most of his life, Edward had been a stranger to sombre thoughts; but lately, as his digestion grew worse, he had been afflicted with fits of melancholy. At such times, it was much in his mind that many of the present evils of the realm had their origin in the long minority of Henry the Sixth. He would not be alone in thinking thus. Were he to die suddenly, the people would have no stomach for another boy king. Undoubtedly, there would be contenders for the throne, and who would have a stronger claim than George, Duke of Clarence, already named as heir by the Lancastrians? Now, as he knelt where Henry the Sixth had once knelt, it came into Edward's mind that his own son might meet the same fate as that unworldly fool. It could not be! But how could he be sure of that since, when he signed Henry's death warrant, he had himself proved that such things can be?

4

Edward replied in kind to the affair of Ankarette Twynyho. One of George's trusted retainers, Thomas Burdett, was condemned and hanged for treasonable writing and attempting to procure the King's death by necromancy. George would acknowledge no comparison between his treatment of Ankarette Twynyho and Edward's cynical despatch of Thomas Burdett. So outraged was he that he interrupted a council meeting at West Minster to protest Burdett's innocence.

One incident followed another; each speech made in private by the main contestants was carried from one person to another by spies and gossips. To Richard of Gloucester it was reported how 'the Duke of Clarence not only repeats that the King is a bastard, but furthermore that his marriage with Queen Elizabeth is not legal because of a previous contract.'

At this stage, King Louis thought it entertaining to join in the game and let it be known to Edward that George had planned to marry Mary of Burgundy in order to seize the throne of England. By June, the need to teach George a lesson had resulted in his confinement in the Tower.

The following January when Edward's son, the young Duke of York, was married, George was still in the Tower. For some, this cast a shadow over the festivities, but Prince Edward had other problems. He wanted to know why, since he was the elder and heir to the throne, his brother should be married before him. 'He's only four,' he had protested to his attendant. 'Only *just* four!'

The attendant laughed and said to Dr Ormond, the Prince's tutor, 'At the ripe age of seven! A proper son of his father!' Dr Ormond looked disapproving and said nothing.

This was one of the lessons you learnt early in life, Prince Edward realized. It was all right during instruction with the chaplain or the tutor to ask questions; but when it came to the things that really mattered to you, it was very hard to get a sensible reply.

As the wedding banquet at last came to a close, young Edward stood in the great hall pessimistically assessing the potential to answer questions sensibly of the three men who were with him. His Uncle Richard and the Duke of Buckingham had escorted the young bride to the wedding banquet and had then paid some attention to Prince Edward, but had now forgotten him, although Uncle Richard had one hand resting lightly on his shoulder. They had been joined by Lord Howard. These were not men in whose company Prince Edward had spent much time and he was apprehensive, being a child who preferred the familiar even when it was not particularly pleasing. He was, however, greatly interested in the Duke of Buckingham. Edward hoped that when he grew up he might seem as important as the Duke and he watched carefully to see how it was done. Buckingham stood legs apart, head and shoulders braced back, and every so often he rearranged his cloak, swinging it across his shoulders with a flourish that made Prince Edward think he was going to perform some spectacular feat, although usually he just changed his weight from one foot to the other. He did not speak much, Uncle Richard and Lord Howard were doing most of the talking; but he listened with wonderful vivacity, making himself so much a part of what was said that Prince Edward was sure he had thought of everything before either of the other two men.

As for Lord Howard . . . Prince Edward moved closer to his uncle who gave his shoulder a little shake and went on talking without registering any other interest in his nephew. Lord Howard was a wholly frightening person, big and dark and terribly fierce. His skin was coarse and swarthy and, though by no means inscrutable, his strongly carved features were somewhat slow to express his changes of mood. All of which gave the boy the impression that his face was made of something less yielding than flesh. In speech and manner he lacked the refinement of the courtiers to whose stylish airs Prince Edward was accustomed. It worried Prince Edward if people did not conform to the accustomed pattern of behaviour; if he had had his way people would have been like as peas in a pod. As it was, people represented a series of traps, each sprung differently so that in negotiating them you never seemed wholly to escape injury of one kind or another. Prince Edward looked round the room, seeking in vain for someone to reassure him. Oh, for one kind face among these splendid men!

'That's a miserable face to wear at your brother's wedding banquet!' His misery had been noticed by Lord Howard. 'Perhaps he's hungry. Didn't you eat when you had the chance? Too busy watching what was going on, I suppose.' To Edward's dismay he was led away from his uncle and the important Duke of Buckingham, his arm in the grip of this burly barbarian who now thrust a way through the crowded room and instructed a servant to bring a few tasty morsels for the Prince. Edward was too sick with apprehension to swallow, but fortunately by the time the servant arrived with a dish of fruit and nuts, Howard had again been joined by Uncle Richard and the Duke of Buckingham and Edward and his supposed hunger was forgotten. The Duke of Buckingham was talking about the mummers who had played for the King and his guests the previous week. Uncle Richard said, in the tone of one who puts paid to the pleasure of others, that he had no stomach for such entertainments at this time. The three men suddenly became very serious, and Howard said mysteriously, 'I never knew a man better able to make enemies.' While they engaged in a conversation of ever-increasing obscurity, Prince Edward passed the plate of food to an attendant.

The snow which had been falling earlier in the day had stopped and it was very cold now; Edward saw ice on the window pane. There was a bitter draught cutting across the stone floor and his feet were frozen. Then fingers tightened on his shoulder and he forgot about the cold. He looked up, terrified that the disposal of the food had been noticed. But it was his uncle whose hand was on his shoulder, and whoever had done something wrong, it wasn't Prince Edward. His uncle was looking at the Duke of Buckingham who was saying, 'He took it particularly ill that the King, while refusing consent to his marriage with Mary of Burgundy, should support the claims of Lord Rivers. . . .'

'Lord Rivers!' Uncle Richard spat out the words.

'It is said that the Queen pressed this very strongly.' The Duke of Buckingham's voice was as important as his manner and Edward was sorry when his new hero was brusquely interrupted by the grim Howard.

'Whatever is said, it is of no consequence now, since it seems the lady hasn't a mind to marry either of them.'

'It is of some consequence to my brother, who now finds himself arraigned for the treason of hoping for what, it seems, was not begrudged Lord Rivers!'

'And for much else besides, Dickon.'

'But nothing he has done recently compares with his earlier

follies, all of which were forgiven. Why act now when there is less to forgive?'

'One person is the more injured this time. You know the rumours he has set afoot as well as I do.' Howard growled this reply so low his voice seemed to come from somewhere in his stomach rather than his throat.

'On the contrary, I know very little. It's only in London where so much attention is paid to gossip and rumour. . . .'

Howard said, 'It's no use, Dickon. Parliament meets to try him tomorrow and nothing you can say can prevent that—or anything that follows. And best say no more now.' He spoke the last sentence in a changed voice, quiet and abrupt. Turning his head, Prince Edward saw Lord Stanley approaching them. His face was flushed and unlike the others he seemed in a very merry mood. He had apparently heard the mention of Clarence's name, because he began to speak of him at once. Although Lord Howard tried to stop him, Lord Stanley went on talking, laughing loudly and slopping wine from his glass.

'You know what he said to me once? He said, "If I had the choosing of my end, I'd be drowned in a butt of malmsey!" Very good that, I thought. At least it would enable him to die as he had lived!'

Lord Howard said, 'Careful!'

There was silence. All the rest of the room continued to jostle with noise, but here it was cold and still. Then Lord Howard moved forward and took Lord Stanley by the arm. 'The wine is talking too loud,' he said, and he led Lord Stanley, who was no longer laughing, away. The Duke of Buckingham had moved back a step and he was looking at Uncle Richard as though he had never seen him before instead of having looked at him for the last half-hour at least. Uncle Richard did indeed look very strange; against his red hair, his face was a lemon colour and his mouth was very thin and Edward could see that the lips were chafed. He had been told that his uncle sometimes flew into great rages, but as he associated rage with a lot of noise Edward assumed that whatever had made his uncle so rigid must be a kind of sickness. He was very frightened and began to tremble.

Then, with that unreason which is a part of adult behaviour, Uncle Richard suddenly became aware of him. 'You are very quiet,' he said. 'What is the matter?'

Edward, tired and close to tears, said hoarsely, 'Why is my brother married before me?'

Uncle Richard studied him thoughtfully for a moment, then he bent down and said gently, 'You are not married yet because we have to find someone much more important for you to marry. Do you understand?'

Edward understood perfectly, and the relief was so great that he forgot all the unpleasant things that had been happening and was filled with simple joy.

Later, as his attendant led him away to his chamber, he heard Lord Stanley grumbling, '. . . can't take the mildest joke. . . .'

'Jokes about Clarence are out of season,' Lord Howard said.

The door into the palace yard was open, people were leaving; there was the sound of snow crunched beneath heavy boots and the jingle of harness. Edward could see the roof of the opposite wing of the building; the layer of snow was blue and fitted close and snug as thatch. Impulsively, he ran forward and in spite of the protests of his attendant, stood on the threshold. 'Come away from that door!' the attendant was alarmed as though the night air harboured murderous intent. There were a lot of stars, very bright and near. The discomfort of stinging cold on his cheeks, of which Edward would have complained miserably on a less magical evening, now only sharpened his pleasure.

'Can I go and watch them leave?' he asked eagerly.

'Of course not. It would be the death of you with that chest.'

'No, no, it wouldn't, really it wouldn't. I'd only stay a minute, just long enough to crunch the snow.'

'Plenty of time for that,' the attendant said.

They always said that, but it wasn't true. The next time, it was 'You're too old for that, now.' There never was a time when things were just right for you to do what you wanted to do.

Even over the drapes round the bed, he couldn't get his way. 'I don't want them pulled tonight,' he said. 'Then I can lie and look at the snow.'

But the drapes were pulled, and he was cut off from that magical world; the heavy material soon stifled every breath of that sharp, clear air.

Chapter 9

I

Parliament found Clarence guilty of treason and he was condemned to death. By what means he met his death, few knew, but Stanley's joke gave rise to the rumour that he was drowned in a butt of malmsey.

Richard of Gloucester founded two colleges where prayers

would be offered for members of his family and for the souls of their departed brethren. Over the next five years, Richard spent much of his time in the north and saw little of his brother, the King. He put his absence from court down to the press of duty. 'Also, the climate here suits me better,' he said to his friend Viscount Lovell.

In the far north, the country was grimmer than Richard's beloved Yorkshire. On the wild heights, over desolate tracts, the wall the Romans built still stood guard against the ancient enemy. It was a country where man must always be vigilant, the eye straining in the twilight, the ear alert in the dark night. This suited Richard; he was a vigilant person. There would never be rest here, never a time when a man would walk easily. This was something to which he could accustom himself. He was not a man who looked for ease or would have known what to do with it had he found it.

The fortifications must be kept in repair. He saw to it. It was something beyond duty; there was a sense of inheritance, a stewardship for which he would be held accountable. He liked particularly to watch new work in progress. The stone itself drew a response from him: it was hard, durable, unrelenting, all of which he found admirable, but at times it was speckled with darting shafts of light by that rare northern sunlight which sparked his own brilliance.

'This is the life for Dickon, he thrives wonderfully in this bleak soil!' Lovell remarked wryly after he had accompanied Richard on a tour of inspection, albeit a little reluctantly for he preferred a softer climate. 'I think Dickon would not much like it were the Scots to turn their swords into ploughshares.'

But Richard had other achievements. The Bishop of Durham could have wished him more concerned with warlike pursuits. He told Dr Morton, who had now become Bishop of Ely, 'The Duke of Gloucester has instructed that all fishgarths be removed from rivers in his estates, and I am invited to follow his enlightened example!' The Bishop's full lips drooped; he was wont to dine well on the salmon trapped in his fishgarths and saw no reason why he should be deprived of his privilege in order to meet the demands of the common people. 'The Duke of Gloucester,' he said privately to the Bishop of Ely, 'is now so rich and powerful he can afford to sacrifice a few salmon in order to win popularity.' Publicly, the Bishop promised to consider the request.

Few shared the Bishop's jaundiced view. 'Never have we been so justly ruled,' was the verdict of the aldermen of the City of York, not a little influenced by the fact that the Duke was always prepared to use his authority to further the interests of the City.

When he went in procession to York Minster, his secretary, John Kendall, thought that his master now had a nobility and dedication of the highest order, the austere simplicity of the saint. 'I have seen that look on the face of men on their way to the stake,' he breathed.

His companion, more cynical, replied, 'Aye, and on the faces of those who sent them there.'

But even this cynic must concede that, whichever way you judged him, Richard, Duke of Gloucester, had become very impressive. As he walked up the aisle, he looked over the heads of the people to some authority which lay beyond of whose judgement he appeared to have no fear. He was now balanced at the supreme moment of his life, utterly sure of himself and his purpose, equal to the tasks set upon him which demanded sufficient of him to still ambition and discipline his restless energy. His wife walked beside him; she was thinner but had a gaiety of spirit which seemed to increase as she grew more frail as though this very precariousness of existence was a source of positive joy. Even their young son, about whom they had had many anxieties, had at this time a fitful bloom in his cheeks. There was about the family an aura of happiness, piercing in its intensity. The bells rang out, one joyful explosion after another. This was in June of 1482.

2

In London, in April 1483, the bells rang a muffled peal.

Three days before, King Edward had been out hunting. On his return, he said, 'I think I have caught a chill.' He tossed the reins to a groom and walked away. Now he was dead and the bells rang a muffled peal.

Part III

THE LAND WHERE THE CHILD IS KING

'Woe is that realm that hath a child to their King'

Chapter 10

I

It was April and the air keen, there was little warmth in the pale sunlight, so it was estimated that the body would keep for a few days.

'But I wouldn't risk it beyond the week-end,' Lord Stanley said to Lord Hastings.

The body of King Edward lay upon a board, naked save for a cloth laid across his loins. Such of the lords spiritual and temporal as could be quickly assembled had been invited to the Palace of West Minster to view the body. Lord Stanley and Lord Hastings, having done this, left the Palace together. They looked thoughtful; there were other questions to be considered besides the time the body would endure in a good condition.

Stanley squinted in the sunlight, sandy eyelashes brushing his puckered cheeks. 'I never expected this,' he said peevishly.

Hastings said, 'No one did.' At least they were all at a disadvantage.

'Last thing he said to me before he took to his bed was that he had lost his appetite,' Stanley said. 'After that, he didn't seem to bother. Extraordinary.'

In the streets people stood about, some ostentatiously prayed, a few women cried, but mostly the people stared up at the faces of the noblemen who rode by in the naïve expectation of seeing marks of grief. But death is a busy time for those who are left, and never more so than when a king dies. Even Hastings, genuinely bereft, put grief to one side until there was time for it. 'They say the Queen is too overcome to leave her chamber,' he said.

Stanley did not reply. Already there was a need to watch one's words, and no one knew better than Stanley how to keep his own counsel. His face was tired and the mouth sagged as though he had received cause for complaint. This constant need to reappraise one's position was beginning to wear him down; he wasn't young any more and he would have been content to see his days out in Edward's service. It was damnable that his allegiance should be so ill-rewarded. 'In the end, he didn't even seem to try,' he muttered. 'He just let go of life.'

Two grubby-faced urchins squatting in a doorway watched the men as they rode by. 'They looked sick, you see, didn't they look sick?' one said to the other triumphantly. 'I told you, didn't I tell you? They cut him open and take out the bowels.' He made a graphic movement with his fingers accompanied by an unpleasant sucking of saliva between his teeth which made a sound like rending calico.

'But they say he's going to lie there for a week!' the other boy protested; he had gone pale beneath the grime and this made his face the colour of bad liver. 'They couldn't cut him open and leave him for a week.'

'They left old Harry Gymes hanging longer than a week!'

'Harry Gymes!' The sick face turned in the direction of the Palace of West Minster, awed at the company in which Harry Gymes, one-time highway robber, must now find himself.

It was evening when the last of the lords spiritual and temporal had satisfied themselves that the King was indeed dead and that no violence had been done him. The body had then to be purged (though not yet disembowelled) and prepared for the morning when, covered in cloth of gold, and with a sceptre placed in the right hand, it would be brought into the chapel where masses would be sung.

At night, by the light of candles, Edward was as well watched over as ever in his life. On the watch list for the first night appeared the names of Lords Howard and Hastings among others. Lord Howard had but lately arrived in the city and there was information which Hastings could give him.

'The Queen is no longer one of the executors. This will not please her.' Hastings lowered his head and muttered a prayer as the Queen's son by her first husband, the Marquis of Dorset, moved forward to kneel before the bier. Hastings and Dorset had little liking the one for the other, but in the emotion aroused by the King's brief illness they had embraced and sworn to forget their rivalry. The emotion had been short-lived and the vow would not long survive it.

'There is one other change,' Hastings said, turning again to Howard. 'He has named the Duke of Gloucester as Protector.'

Howard said 'aah!' in a non-committal tone. He liked

Hastings well enough; he was no prude and did not condemn Hastings for his debaucheries, his own reputation did not stand high with some people who called him a buccaneer. But there was strength in Howard's bold, dark face. He was a man to be trusted, a good man to have at your side in a fight. Hastings hadn't this kind of strength. He had been loyal to Edward because he loved the man; but now Howard could sense him feeling his way, as unsure of himself as of others. Henceforth, he would be guided by ambition. What else remained to him? Howard moved away.

That night, the noblemen present did not form into groups, there was still a semblance of men performing a vigil. The candlelight flickered, shadows danced on the wall. One of the guard watched a spider climbing the side of the bier: from the expression on his ox-like face it was doubtful whether he derived the same inspiration from the spectacle as had that great opponent of the early Plantagenets. Lord Richard Grey found he was kneeling on a crack in the stone floor and tried to re-adjust his position while keeping his face set in lines of deep melancholy which he thought suited to the occasion and to his delicate good looks. Behind him, Lord Etchard, who had bladder trouble, fretfully drew his robe about his abdomen. The room was very cold and damp rose from the ground. The Marquis of Dorset, his head bowed, thought that now that Edward was dead he would be free to seek out Mistress Jane Shore.

On the Wednesday of the following week, the body was moved to the abbey, Lord Howard bearing the King's banner. After the mass the great procession of lords set out for Windsor, the King's body carried on a chair covered with black velvet and draped with black cloth of gold with a cross of white cloth of gold upon it.

The first night was spent at Syon. It meant three nights away from London at least. Hastings was unable to conceal his impatience. 'I have sent a messenger to Gloucester,' he told Lord Howard. 'The Queen has not informed him of the King's death. I doubt that she has been so tardy in sending to Lord Rivers at Ludlow.' The boy King, Edward the Fifth, was at Ludlow.

'When will your messenger reach Gloucester?' Howard asked.

'He should be there by now. But that is a week's delay.'

Meanwhile, there remained the ceremony in the newly-erected chapel of St George at Windsor, which was followed by a watch kept by the lords, knights, esquires of the body, and the next day there was the mass of Our Lady sung by the Bishop of Durham, the mass of the Trinity sung by the Bishop of Lincoln, and the mass of requiem sung by the Archbishop of York.

The chapel, so recently built, was bright and richly decorated, but many of their lordships' black robes were old; furthermore, it had rained during the procession to the chapel. The smell of mould and damp mingled and it was as though several hundred old dogs had gathered here together. One or two of the aged lords looked as though they were weighed down by thoughts of mortality. Hastings, who expected to live a long time yet, was concerned with more immediate matters. When would Gloucester come, and how many men would he bring with him? Now was the time for a display of strength. Would he realize that?

2

An April shower, rain heavy against the window, great globular tears running fast.

'Get you to London,' Hastings had said to Gloucester. His message bore all the signs of panic. The second messenger brought even more urgent demands, advising Richard to come in strength and to make sure he secured the person of the young King. It was a time to think clearly.

Richard had sent to Earl Rivers in Ludlow, a reasonably worded request for information as to the route which the young King would follow on his journey to London. No answer had been received. He shivered and crossed himself, not an act of piety for his dead brother, but an instinctive wish to preserve himself from the evil which now distorted the natural world. He could hear his secretary pacing about in the corridor. He had told him that no one was to disturb him. No doubt the man considered, as did all the others who now waited on his word, that he was planning his future course of action.

A great gust of wind and rain buffeted the window and for a moment everything beyond broke up into unrecognizable fragments; it seemed impossible that walls, tower and barbican gate should ever assemble themselves again in any meaningful pattern.

Pattern was destroyed anyway, the centrepiece had gone. He had waited in here for a sign and had been vouchsafed a vision of chaos. The chaos was tangible. Some of it was trickling down the wall beneath the window and forming a puddle on the floor. He crossed himself again, lest the chaos should invade his own person. Already it had made a preliminary foray. He could not think clearly. His mind insisted on relating to a higher authority by which his actions would be judged and eventually rewarded. He was deeply religious, but it was secular authority which he sought. He accepted the death of a brother, but not the demise of ultimate authority.

He stood, one hand fingering the brooch on his doublet. His face betrayed no dramatic signs of strain; a slight frown drew his brows together, his eyes were bemused. He might have been trying to remember something recently related to him, the elusiveness of which irritated and disturbed him because it indicated a failing in his powers of concentration. To those who knew him as a man of sharp wit and formidable energy, resolute if sometimes rash in action, it would have seemed that he was bewitched. If this was so his wife, now entering the room, did something to break that spell.

'I said no one was to enter!' He was angry at being caught at a moment when he was so little able to command himself.

'You have delayed too long,' she replied. 'Edward has been dead for over a week.' She imagined that excessive grief had paralysed his will to act. She had never thought that Edward's influence was a good one, and that he should continue to exert it after death was not to be borne. 'When I am dead I hope you will not linger over me like this.'

She made these references to her death from time to time as though she was rehearsing it. She tried not to play on Richard's emotions because she loved him, but sometimes it gave her a pleasure which she could not resist. Today, however, she had good reason to be cruel. Someone must goad him to act.

'You should be in London by now,' she said. 'You are the Protector. If you do not go, then someone must represent you there. I shall go. I do not like London, it will kill me one day; but I shall go. I should not dream of staying here when there is such need to be in London.'

In spite of the frailty of her appearance, which was enhanced by the sombre clothes which mourning necessitated, the ferocious strength of her determination demanded she be taken seriously. As a child she had frightened her nurse, not by anything she actually did but by her ability to suggest that nothing would be beyond her should she set her will to do it. Her husband was dazed by her. He put his hands over his face, cupping them over nose and eyes like a mask; he drew a long, deep breath. Something tingled at the back of his nose. He sneezed violently. All things considered, something of an anti-climax. He sneezed again. When he opened his eyes tiny spots of light danced before him as though a fire-cracker had gone off in his brain. The terrible inertia was over. His mind was sharp and clear; and beyond the window he could see that a great blue wedge had been cut in the grey sky.

He made his preparations quickly. Those who had grumbled at his delay had little cause to grumble on that account now. Hastings had warned him that Earl Rivers was travelling with a large escort. 'I shall travel faster with a few men,' Richard said.

There was no more irresolution. Yet during that strange up-heaval which followed the news of Edward's death, something had happened. The world had settled down after the tremor much as before, but something was missing. It would take him by surprise sometimes and he would look round, trying to think what it could be.

Events crowded upon him. On the day that he set out from Middleham a messenger arrived. 'What ill news does Hastings send this time?' he commented, grimly amused as he saw the rider from a distance. But the colours were not those of Lord Hastings. The messenger was from the Duke of Buckingham, who offered his loyal service and hoped to join the Protector on the route to London.

The rain had ceased by the time Richard set out with his party, but it was still misty and the hills and sky ran together like the landscape in a badly smudged painting. Richard rode frowning, as though displeased by the messiness of Nature. There was a lot to think about and most of it unpleasant. Earl Rivers had sent word that he would be leaving Ludlow with the young King on April 24th and it had been agreed that Richard would join them at Northampton so that they could make the progress to London together. Reports had come in since then that Rivers was making some speed on his journey, and that he was travelling with a considerably larger force than was necessary merely to convey the young King to London. What-ever Rivers' intentions, they could hardly be construed as friendly. As Richard urged his horse up a steep, stony path an old resentment throbbed and seemed to communicate itself to the animal who thrashed about, his hooves dislodging the stones. Richard listened to the clatter of the stones, one striking another until it seemed that to his left, somewhere in that misty territory, the whole hillside was on the move. He slowed his pace. It would mightily please those in London who awaited the arrival of Rivers and the young King were the Protector to make a false move in this precipitous place.

The path led to high moorland. Below, the mist still hung thick and yellow in the valley, and it seemed to Richard that it smelt foul as the breath of an unclean spirit. But ahead, the swathes of mist grew gossamer thin and finally dissolved; the air was cleansed of all impurity and they could see their path clear and straight as an arrow pointing them towards the south. Richard, riding along the spine of England, felt free of the dark spirit which had invaded and impeded him during the past days. He recalled that he was shortly to join forces with Buckingham. How good it was that there were still loyal men who offered their service immediately and without question! Buckingham's gesture was the more splendid for being unexpected; the people from whom much is expected so often fail. This gesture was all gold. It was timely, too. The Dukes of Gloucester and Buckingham would be a formidable combination. As he rode across the wild, soaring moorland, Richard experienced a surge of hope. But years in the service of Edward had made him a lonely man and a wary one, and soon he became suspicious of his own hopes and cautiously reminded himself that the Duke of Buckingham was descended from Edward the Third, and men of such lineage tend to ambition. Even so, when the next day he arrived at Northampton and Buckingham was not there, his disappointment was sharp. Worse was to come, for he soon learnt that Rivers and the young King had already passed through Northampton and were reported to be encamped at Stony Stratford.

'So?' Richard appeared to take the news quietly, and repaired to the inn where it had been arranged that he and Buckingham would spend the night. But to his secretary, John Kendall, he voiced his unease. 'The Lord Rivers is in great haste; the Duke of Buckingham delays. What think you of this?'

'I think that the Duke of Buckingham has had far to travel,' Kendall replied soberly.

'And Lord Rivers must as easily be excused in that he had not so far to travel?'

Kendall, who was standing by the window, said, 'He comes in person to make his excuses, if I mistake not the colours of these men.'

Richard joined him by the window and saw that he was right. Rivers, however, had arrived too late. The time for excuses was past. There was in Richard's character an element of rashness which led him to favour attack when diplomacy might have served him better. Now he was ready for a clash with Rivers, and it was irksome to find that instead he must listen to the man's explanations about the difficulty of quartering troops in Northampton and the great advantage, which he was unable to specify, of quartering them in Stony Stratford.

'You must be hungry after so much exertion,' Richard cut him short and sent a servant to bring food and wine. When they sat down to dine together, he picked up his flask of wine and leant forward; he was laughing and seemed to have shed all the restraint which had been apparent in his manner when he first greeted Rivers. Torchlight flickered across his face, making something extravagant and a little grotesque of its impish gaiety, a gaiety which the bright eyes invited Rivers to share. Rivers raised his flask to return Richard's salute. He seemed bemused by this unexpected vivacity in a man he had deemed unduly sober.

'This is well met indeed, for I must confess I was afraid you intended to press on to London without me. Yes, yes! I assure you!' He treated Rivers' protest with amusement as though they both knew it to be an empty gesture. 'I know that the Queen, your sister, has no liking for me and I had it in mind that she had exhorted you to make all haste without me.'

'As you see, this was not so,' Rivers answered uneasily.

'I see at least that you have not complied.' Richard flung himself back, tilting his chair; he was restless but still seemed in a good humour. 'I am very glad to find you here; because I shall need to examine your stewardship and, I am sure, to compliment you upon it.'

'My stewardship?'

'You have for some time been in charge of my nephew. He must have learnt much from you.'

Richard's face was in shadow now. Rivers, a natural actor, began to assert himself. 'I take no credit.' He made a light movement of one hand as though bidding credit stand aside. 'He is a studious boy.'

'Studious? Oh, I feel you should take some credit for that.'

'And pious.'

'Studious *and* pious! The realm will indeed be well-served by this youth. He has learnt something of the affairs of the state, no doubt?'

'As much as befits a boy. . . .'

'Who at any time may find himself a king?'

'It was very sudden. We none of us. . . .'

'As long as there is nothing to be unlearnt.' Richard swung forward into the light, elbows on the table, chin propped on clenched fists. He smiled at Rivers, one eyebrow raised. 'What, for example, have you taught him about me?'

'You are his uncle. . . .'

'He would have known that without your teaching.'

The eyes were extraordinarily compelling. They convinced

Rivers that he was indeed guilty of something, though he knew not what. He protested, 'I assumed that, as the boy's uncle, you would have had the opportunity to teach him anything you wished.'

For some seconds the two men sat staring at each other; then Richard laughed and, leaning forward, shook Rivers' shoulder. 'I have had no such opportunity, as well you know!' He sat back, seemingly in good humour again. 'But this will now be remedied so we will talk about it no more. Come, the food gets cold. I am hungry, if you are not! Tell me, while we eat, what news you have from London, for I am sure you are better informed than I.'

Rivers favoured him with a long, melancholy dissertation on his weariness with London and the intrigues of the court; all of which he expressed so fastidiously that Richard, who might well have agreed with some of his sentiments, found himself wondering what place could possibly satisfy a man of such exquisite sensibilities. As Rivers talked of the wonders he had seen on his pilgrimages and how they had made him dissatisfied with the life of a courtier, the door behind him opened. Richard raised his eyes to meet those of the man who stood there. Rivers, imagining that a servant had come with more wine, continued to extol the glories of St John of Compostella while Richard, Duke of Gloucester, and Henry, Duke of Buckingham, looked into each other's eyes and understood one another a deal better than they would have done had words been demanded of either at that moment. By the time Buckingham and Rivers had greeted each other, and the three men were seated at table, it was as though Buckingham was a player in a scene long-rehearsed between himself and Gloucester. The stage was now his and he filled it magnificently.

'They tell me you were unable to accommodate your party here,' he jested with Rivers. 'You must travel in great splendour.'

'These are uneasy times.' Rivers' thoughts were now much with St John of Compostella, else he would surely have minded his words more. 'There must be many who are not pleased at the prospect of another long minority. We must look to the safety of the young King.'

'Indeed,' Richard acknowledged with mock gravity, 'this will ever be my purpose.'

'And those who have long memories will surely recall how during the minority of our late but little lamented Henry the Sixth the country was bedevilled by the weakness of those in power; and none weaker than the man *then* named as

Protector.' Buckingham looked at Rivers. 'We are more fortunate because the affairs of the state will be in firm hands. Do
you not agree with me?'

While Buckingham behaved in a lively and provocative
manner which made it obvious that he enjoyed challenging
Rivers, he also made it apparent that in his view the authority
of Gloucester was beyond challenge, a thing as little subject to
chance or change as the rising of the sun in the east. His broad,
fair face glowed as though, sitting here opposite Gloucester, he
felt the touch of that same sun.

Rivers did not seem to find the prospect of a long protectorship any more pleasing than a long minority. Perhaps to make
up for his lack of fervour, or perhaps because he was singularly
unable to assess his situation, he said, 'I have no liking for these
matters and shall be glad to relinquish my authority over the
young King.'

'I may be able to assist you in this,' Richard murmured. In
the flickering light Buckingham's eyes glinted merrily.

'I had thought I might go on a pilgrimage to the Holy
Land.'

'Our thoughts could scarcely be more in accord,' Richard
said drily.

'I swear life is almost too easy for a man such as you!'
Buckingham exclaimed. 'You have no ambition and intrigue
must, therefore, be unknown to you; your tastes are austere,' he
re-charged Rivers' glass, 'your desire's so stern you would prefer
to mortify the flesh rather than to satisfy its lusts. Your very
presence is a rebuke to such as I, who have enjoyed the food
which you have tonight eaten with the utmost reluctance. Your
purity condemns my weakness, you make my faults the blacker.
This is not kind. Rather than go on a pilgrimage, I think you
should do penance for so shaming lesser men by your virtue.'

'I have been no stranger to vice,' Rivers assured him a trifle
querulously. He began to recount incidents from his past to
show that whatever else he might be, he was no prude.

It was after midnight when he left them. They watched him
ride away, the sparks flying round his horse's hooves.

'Who is this man?' Buckingham said. 'Is he a soldier, a
scholar, an artist, a religious? It seems he scarcely knows himself! You seek his counsel and he will give you an account of
the binding of a book; you look to him for stern judgement, he
will be exquisite; he dines well, yet when you seek him as a
companion he will fast! You talk to him of purity and he
becomes bawdy. Above all, when you look for him at your side
in danger, you will find him lost in meditation.'

'He should not be denied the opportunity for meditation.' Richard turned away from the window to where a group of their more trusted followers awaited them. 'I shall give him much to think on.'

'But beware!' Buckingham joined the group, dominating it by the liveliness of his personality as much as by virtue of his rank. 'If he meditates for long it is extraordinary how his thoughts turn from things holy to schemes of a baser kind.'

'What think you?' Richard turned to Kendall, whose judgement of men he respected.

'I doubt that you have much to fear from Lord Rivers. He is the kind of man who would never be resolute for fear of being thought rash.'

'Aye, that may well be so,' Buckingham intervened. 'I too doubt whether on his own he is capable of action. The danger lies in his joining forces with those who can put him to good use.'

'Is such a man good for any purpose?' Richard looked at Buckingham.

'He has young Edward's confidence. I hear much of this for, whether I wish it or not, I have my wife's confidence and have to listen to endless talk about the Queen and her brothers. And if one thing is certain, it is that it will take more to wean the young King from Rivers than ever it took to take him from his mother's breast.'

Buckingham did not seek to temper his dislike of Rivers with a pretence of reasonableness; but he spoke with a passionate conviction which was irresistible. Richard, watching him as he argued, thought that here was a man who had qualities which he himself did not possess; together, they would be eloquent, zealous, wise and resolute. He could have stormed London, there was something so wild in the air that night! The fate of Rivers seemed unimportant and Richard ended the talk abruptly by announcing that Rivers was to be arrested in the morning. Buckingham applauded. This was his first cause and he was resolved to give himself to it with all his heart. To Richard, it was the only cause. They were close to each other at this time.

Although Richard agreed to see Rivers the next morning, nothing that the Earl could say was of any avail. Richard knew that he was fighting for his own survival and a strong gesture was needed to show the Queen that the Protector had every intention of assuming power.

The first who must learn this lesson was the young King, who now awaited them at Stony Stratford. The boy greeted his uncle and the Duke of Buckingham quietly, his pale, thin face looking chilled in the spiteful April wind. He asked repeatedly after Rivers and did not seem much comforted when it was explained to him that from hence he would be guided by his uncle.

'A poor, queasy boy,' Buckingham said.

'No doubt he will grow stronger,' Richard replied somewhat brusquely, being reminded of his own delicate son.

As they set out for London, Richard settled himself more easily in the saddle. He had taken a step of some consequence but had no regrets; whatever else might one day lie on his conscience, it would not be the fate of Rivers. This was no time for temporizing when he who moved first might gain all. He began to discuss plans for the future with Buckingham.

'Hastings grows impatient and fears conspiracy.'

'Hastings has done you good service.' Buckingham's voice lacked its customary enthusiasm.

Richard said, 'I need friends in London. Things have never gone well for me there.' He had no illusion that the man who had been so close to Edward would serve his brother as faithfully: whatever Hastings' feelings for Edward had been, they were not of the kind which can be transferred to another. Nevertheless, he owed much to Hastings and must put his doubts aside for the time being.

3

Two pigeons on the ridge of the stable roof were performing an elaborate courtship. It was a surprisingly intricate ritual and Henry, Earl of Richmond, observed it thoughtfully because he had nothing else to do at that moment. The footwork seemed to follow a pattern, three steps forward, a bow of the head, three steps forward, another bow, then a return to the original position; while the female perched with downcast head, her beady eyes fixed on a patch of moss a pecking distance away. Finally, goaded by this lack of interest, the male jumped up and perched on her back, a manoeuvre which she accepted with complete unconcern. This, however, appeared not to be the consummation, for the male then returned to his original position and began to step neatly forward again, while his chosen partner raised her head and gazed towards a distant birch tree. Henry said over his shoulder to Robin Prithie, who had come in bearing a tray, 'Even the pigeons know that something strange is abroad.'

'Something strange?'

'It is spring.' Henry turned from the window, amused by the

concern in Robin's voice. 'That season about which the poets have so much to say. The drumming in the blood. . . .'

'Why, yes . . .' Robin seemed unable to pick up the thread of Henry's discourse. Yet who, Henry thought, should know more of spring than my spritely Robin, this devil-may-care green shoot, this wicked thrust that prises open the clenched bud, that cuts the knotted weeds and plays havoc with the stagnant water? Even now, in this dull room, the light singled him out and quivered around him as he moved to set the tray down on the table. Henry seated himself and picked up the knife, then paused, the knife poised above the plate. 'I think that perhaps the coming of spring should be celebrated in some small way.' He wondered whether he should send for wine; last week the wine had given him stomach ache and he had drunk water since then, but the water often had a bad effect and did not taste as pleasant as the wine.

'You should indeed celebrate!' Robin was as fussed as a nurse whose charge shows signs of becoming petulant. 'Will you but eat this now, and I will see that you are provided with more substantial fare tonight. With roast ox and venison, perhaps salmon. . . .'

Roast ox *and* venison! Henry felt his stomach distend. Robin was talking about pigeon and swan now. He knew that Henry was not apt to gorge himself, yet there was no humour in his manner. Some lack of nerve prompted this agitated chatter. Henry put the knife down slowly; he felt as though a great hole had been opened in his body and that although he was surprised, he had nevertheless always known that one day this would happen. He stared at the fish. He had not eaten any of it; yet his body told him he had already suffered a terrible injury. He pushed at the fish with the point of his knife; out of the corner of his eye he saw that Robin, who had now become silent, was watching him closely. Beyond, the ripple of water in sunlight was reflected on the stone arch of the window, like gentle, mellow flames of light. I have never trusted him Henry thought, so why is the pain so bad? Is there some indulgence more dangerous than trust which I have unwittingly permitted myself? He speared a piece of fish and saw a flash of relief light up Robin's face.

'And you will bring me roast ox and venison tonight?' he asked softly.

'Roast ox and venison! Did I say that?' Robin laughed.

'And pigeon and salmon. Indeed, we are celebrating!'

'My wits must have been wandering.'

They both laughed. Then Henry extended the knife with the

speared fish towards Robin. The liveliness drained from the impudent face, leaving it dun-coloured and unwholesome.

'I have already tasted it.' Robin's mouth was so dry he could scarcely speak.

'I am not concerned about poison.' In truth, Henry cared so little he was tempted to eat rather than make the effort to speak lightly. 'But that fish we had last week did not agree with me. I should like to know if this is the same; you remember, we commented that it was uncommonly oily. An unmistakable flavour.'

Robin's tongue flicked across his dry lips. 'I had forgotten.' His voice was shaking. 'It *is* the same, I particularly noticed the flavour. I had forgotten . . . I will take it away.'

There was silence. Henry looked at him and Robin stared at the knife with the piece of fish on it as at a sword pointed at his stomach.

Henry said, 'Yes. Take it away.' He put the knife down on the plate. Robin moved forward, his head bent, and reached for the plate; a hand came down and gripped his wrist. Robin fell clumsily to his knees. Henry was not a strong man, but the grip on the wrist made Robin moan with pain. Henry looked at the dark head with its strong, black curls and it seemed that it was he and not Robin who was moaning. But moaning is a ritual lamentation: this pain needed tongues of fire. Henry's face was grey, its withered lips parted slightly; as he twisted Robin's wrist so Robin began to scream and when the wrist was broken he screamed the more unrestrainedly so that he who had given so little at least now gave to Henry the sound of his own pain. It was only when the door was flung open by his uncle that Henry let go of Robin.

'Dear God, what has happened?' Jasper summoned others to his aid.

'I don't like the fish.' Henry turned his ravaged face from them. 'Send him about his business and see that he finds something more to my liking this evening.'

Robin was dragged half-senseless from the room.

Henry was not given to violence and this scene would at any other time have aroused some concern; but Jasper had news which could not wait the telling. 'King Edward is dead.'

Henry said, 'Is he indeed.' He laid his hand on his thigh, clenching and unclenching it to relieve the cramp in his fingers.

They crowded around him. The room seemed full of people bearing down on him, saying that if he did this and that, he might one day be King of England. He who had ridden with the Welshmen past hooded mountain peaks, who one summer afternoon had come upon Robin Goodfellow riding out of the mist, he might, they said, be King of England. It seemed a very little thing. When he couldn't bear their talk any longer, he said, 'That fish. . . .' He pressed a hand to his stomach. '. . . it is burning inside me. . . .'

'I thought you hadn't eaten any of it,' his uncle said sharply.

'A little. . . .' He closed his eyes. 'I ate a little, but not enough. . . .' He got heavily to his feet and then, registering at last the full extent of their dismay, added, 'not enough to do me any harm.'

'This worrying about food will do you harm!' his uncle said angrily.

'Edward died of over-eating, so you have just told me.' Henry recovered himself because he saw that he must. 'A fate I an unlikely to suffer.'

'The important fact is that Edward is dead,' Jasper snapped.

'And his son?' Henry turned on him, spitting words out angrily to the surprise of the onlookers who had never seen him show anything but respect for his uncle. 'How old is the young Edward? Eleven? And am I to expect that he, too, will shortly die of a surfeit of good food and wine? If not, what profits it me that Edward is dead?' He turned and walked away, the sleeve of his gown catching the remaining dishes on the table and sweeping them to the floor. 'What cause have I for rejoicing?'

'There are many in England who will not be pleased by the prospect of a long minority.'

'Why should they look to me in their displeasure?'

'When they are dissatisfied with the Yorkists, they will look to the House of Lancaster.'

'And when the House of Lancaster no longer pleases them, they will turn again to the House of York. No!' He held up a hand as his uncle began to speak. 'No!' He faced them, standing at a distance which something in his manner warned that none should seek to lessen. 'This game that they play with kings does not please me. Before I take part in this game, I shall need to be very sure that it is worth the winning.'

'While you remain here what can you hope to gain?'

'Gain? It is for others to lose. I can wait.'

'And while you are waiting. . . .'

'I shall be well-informed while I am waiting.'

'There is a limit to what my spies can do,' Jasper said dourly.

'But I have spies, too; did you know that? One of them has just tried to poison me.'

At first they were disbelieving, but the authority of his manner finally convinced them. Then they must have it that

Robin should first be put to the torture and then disposed of.

'No, no, no,' Henry answered wearily. 'It is unwise to ill-use enemies. There are too many.'

'This is madness!'

Henry shook his head. 'One must accept one's enemies. Once they are known, they can be turned to some account. This young man has his uses. I have not eaten the food he has prepared for me; but he shall eat the food *I* prepare for him.'

And so, Robin was fed with such tales about Henry's movements as it was deemed expedient should reach the ears of Henry's enemies and confuse them.

Henry had learnt his lesson. He would never again be surprised by the treachery of his fellow men, though he would sometimes grow weary of it.

Chapter 11

I

The noise of the wagons rolling over the cobbled London street drowned the voice of the crier. People shouted angrily and waved clenched fists, although few of them knew what they were angry about. This did not please Christopher Ormond who liked to establish good cause for his anger. 'What does he say?' he demanded of the man standing next to him.

'He says the armour of those wagons belonged to Lord Rivers. Lord Rivers meant to have himself crowned King, only the Duke of Gloucester put a stop to that.'

Ormond was really angry now but kept silent, telling himself that it would serve no purpose to make public protestation. 'I should merely gratify my own passion,' he thought; though, in fact, it was fear of punishment that kept him silent.

The last of the wagons was passing. Ormond had a good view, having climbed onto the low roof of the stables adjoining The Cock Tavern. He watched the bend in the road. Already he could hear the sound of horses' hooves and the angry cries had turned to cheering. Into the narrow street rode the young King attired in blue, riding a rather dour horse, and flanked by the Dukes of Gloucester and Buckingham in black on somewhat more lively mounts. The boy King looked from side to side as though afraid the people might press in upon him, while his dark-clad companions talked across him, the Duke of Buckingham pointing to The Cock Tavern as though recalling something

of interest associated with it. The Duke of Gloucester, seemingly unimpressed by his handsome companion's tale, leant
across to speak to the boy who thereupon, still looking at
the people as though he feared them, held up his hand in stiff
acknowledgement of their clamour. The boy's face glistened
white as lard in the sunlight. The people cheered as wildly as
though there was something miraculous about this sickly boy.

The street was full of men and horses now as the black-clad
followers of the Dukes of Gloucester and Buckingham rode by,
hard men, unused to London, not rating its people very high.
There was not much cheering now, the Londoners saving their
breath for the arrival of their own men. Ormond turned away
and began to push his way to the back of the roof where there
were steps leading down to the courtyard of the inn. 'Don't you
want to see the rest of the procession?' A man caught his arm.
'See! Here they come!' He pointed to the plum-coloured robes
of the burgesses of the city. Ormond took no heed, but
clambered down the steps into the shadowed courtyard. To his
left there was a narrow alleyway which ran along the backs of
the buildings flanking the street. Here he was near the Thames
and had he been a Londoner would have known by the smell
that the river was at low tide.

In the distance he could see a wharf with boatmen idling in
the sun, not having much custom on this festive day. Nearby,
there was a big house with a garden running down to the river.
Ormond had come to London in the hope of seeing John
Morton, now Bishop of Ely. What influence he had with the
Protector, Ormond did not know, but he meant to urge him to
intercede on behalf of Earl Rivers. Ormond thought the Earl
a man of little sense, but he was cultured and, so far as Ormond
could judge, sincere in his religious beliefs if not a profound
thinker. Such men were few and Ormond, who so constantly
complained of the general corruption, felt he had little choice
but to plead the Earl's cause. It was unlikely, however, that he
would be able to see Morton today, even if he could find where
he was lodged. So he must look for lodgings for himself. He
walked towards the big house and sat in the shade of the garden
wall to eat the bread and cheese which he had brought with him.
The tide was on the turn now and a light breeze was stirring.
He was glad to rest here awhile. He was tired and slept after he
had finished eating. Gradually, the light faded and the breeze
grew sharper. Ormond woke to the sound of water lapping
gently against the timber of the wharf. As he looked at the
darkening river, he was conscious of sadness welling up within
him. His sense of justice, always strong, had been roused by

Earl Rivers' plight, but Ormond seldom felt sad for adult men and women, most of whom, in his opinion, were in large part responsible for the ills which befell them. It was the boy King for whom he felt sad. He had not liked seeing the youthful figure flanked by those black-clad men.

There was mist rising from the opposite bank of the river where the ground was marshy and at first he did not see the boat. It made little noise; whoever rowed touched the water stealthily as though afraid to disturb it. A few yards out from the wharf the mist lifted and the boat nosed out of it, long and dark. The rower was resting on his oars; water lapped against the side of the boat but there was little other sound as it drifted in. Ormond was seized by a sudden dread of death. A man was standing in the prow with a lantern and behind him other figures crouched low. Death did not usually travel in company; nevertheless, Ormond crossed himself and pressed close against the wall. At the wharf, the man with the lantern leapt ashore and stood swinging the light from side to side as he looked around him. Then he put it down and began to tie up the boat. Three other people clambered ashore. They had cloaks muffled around them and did not speak until one of them tripped over Ormond's foot as he crouched against the wall. A hand caught hold of him roughly and the man with the lantern came and held the light so that they could see him.

'As like as not he's harmless, but we'll take no chances.' Hands grabbed Ormond and began to drag him towards the river. Another voice said, 'Let him be! I want no priest's curse on me; I've trouble enough in store without that.' The speaker affected a jauntiness that failed to mask his unease. 'Let him go. And, Father, since I've saved your life, say a prayer this night for Robin Prithie.'

But Ormond had other things to think about. In his heart, he believed that Rivers' cause was already lost and he had decided that when he saw Morton he would plead his own cause; for what was to become of him when Rivers was dead?

2

A few weeks later, in a house not far from West Minster, Robin Prithie sat writing by candlelight. First, he must report on affairs in London to his master. Later, he would seek an opportunity to report on his master's affairs to such as might be suitably appreciative.

'Queen Elizabeth Woodville and her children have fled to West Minster and taken sanctuary in the abbey. The Duke of

Gloucester is now proclaimed Protector and he has given great honour to the Duke of Buckingham and this has displeased many, including Lord Hastings.' He thought it politic to begin with those acts of the Duke of Gloucester which had caused displeasure, and this was certainly the foremost of them. 'I have been about the town in the taverns and heard much talk of plots; in particular are named Lord Stanley and John Morton, the Bishop of Ely. And it is rumoured that Jane Shore is now Lord Hastings' mistress and that she will have him reconciled to Queen Elizabeth Woodville.' Robin wrote this with some misgivings, for the idea that there should be any sympathy between a man's wife and his mistress seemed strange and not pleasing to him.

'The date of the coronation has again been postponed and it is said that even when the King is crowned, the Protector will continue to rule until he comes of age. The Protector is much seen riding about the city, and whereas at one time he was little recognized, now a cry goes up as soon as he appears—"Here's Dickon!"' He thought of adding that while some people did not like the Protector because he was a hard man and from the north, others were saying that such a man was needed to keep the great lords from starting to war among themselves again; but he doubted whether his master wanted to hear praise of the Protector and left this out. It was of no importance that he omitted it, for others reported more fully to Henry, who was interested to learn all he could about the Protector's efforts to maintain peace in the realm; if ever he came to the throne the maintenance of peace would be his aim and he was as content to learn from another man's achievements as from his mistakes.

Robin wrote finally, 'There is much talk of where the King will take up residence, some say the Palace of West Minster and others that he should remain at the Bishop of London's Palace; I have heard the Tower mentioned, and even Crosby's Place so that the Protector can keep his eye on the young King.'

The letter finished, Robin sat crouched over the table, massaging the misshapen bone in his left hand while he made his plans. One of the men who had met him on his arrival in London had warned him of the need to be on his guard at all times. 'For there are those who would dearly like to have news from one who knows the Earl of Richmond's mind.' Robin had protested that not even the torture would make him betray his master's secrets; but he had enquired who the men were 'so that I may be particularly careful should I encounter any of them.' This information was supplied with a readiness which might have given a shrewder man pause for thought.

5

Robin was particularly attracted to a certain Osbert Scouser who was a clerk in the service of the Duke of Buckingham. The Duke of Buckingham had all the attributes which Robin deemed necessary in a man who has far to go.

The future residence of the young King was a matter of concern to the members of the Protector's Council, and to none more so than the Duke of Buckingham, who thought he should be concerned in all matters.

'I say it should be the Tower.' He put the suggestion in the first instance to his wife; not because he valued her judgement but because he knew she would be angered by the proposal.

'He should be with his mother,' she protested.

'He could scarcely go into sanctuary, and she will not come out, so how can he be with her?'

She looked at him resentfully, biting her upper lip with pointed yellow teeth. He was very powerful now and this suited her ill, she aged with every honour set upon him. But in spite of his increasing power, he was still not sure of his own role and tried out first one part, then another: the warrior impatient for action, the statesman whose keen wit is as dangerous a weapon as his sword, the elegant debator who can capture men's hearts, these diverse people roamed around in his imagination barely acknowledging one another's presence. All three tended to desert him in exchanges with his wife.

'In any case, it would not be advisable for Edward to be with his mother,' he said. 'Indeed, this is one of the reasons why I consider it particularly important he should be in the Tower where he will be well away from her influence.'

She poked at a boil on the side of her nose, her eyes watching him malevolently.

'It is he who must rule, not his mother.' He paced about the room, energetic but aimless. 'Is this not so? Or do you fear, as I must confess I begin to, that he has been made unfit to rule?'

Alarm flickered in her eyes. She repeated 'Unfit to rule . . .' tonelessly as though any inflection might be dangerous.

'I mean that he has had bad advice.' He meant to taunt her about the fate of her brother, Earl Rivers. It was to plead for her brother's life that she had insisted on coming to London. On this occasion, however, instead of becoming agitated, Katherine's alarm died down. Buckingham noticed the slight slackening of her shoulders; he was not perceptive, but he had an animal awareness and he pounced now. 'What did you think that I meant?'

She made a movement as if to turn away, but he caught her

by the shoulders. 'Have you heard the rumours which I have heard?'

'I don't listen to rumour,' she spat at him, momentarily recovering her old temper.

'Perhaps in this case you have no need to listen to rumour? Is that it?' His fingers pressed painfully to the bones of her shoulders. 'You *know* the truth, is that it?'

'Truth?'

'That King Edward was wed before he took your sister to wife.'

'It was nothing.' The pain in her shoulders put everything else out of mind. 'And a long time ago.'

'You knew of a previous contract?' He stepped back, releasing her. He had not really believed the rumours which he had heard and had only intended to torment her.

'I know nothing of the sort.' She tried to recover the situation. 'But I remember something being said, a long time ago, and my sister making light of it. Can you imagine that Edward would have contracted a secret marriage? He was much too astute for that!'

'Indeed? When he kept his marriage to your sister secret for some time?'

'That was different.' There were special circumstances governing the affairs of her family and any failure to recognize this caused her great offence.

Buckingham turned away. He had started this to annoy her, but now she no longer had his attention. He stood by the window looking down into the courtyard, conscious of something stirring within him that was new and exciting. 'What was it Clarence said?' he mused. 'That Edward was no son of the Duke of York?'

'Clarence said anything that came into his head because he wanted to cause trouble,' she said scornfully.

'Was his mother not supposed to have said this very thing when she heard about Edward's marriage?'

'To spite my sister she would have said anything. They were all jealous of my sister. They hated her.'

'And she is no mean hater, either. Dickon has always held that she was responsible for Clarence's death.'

'Clarence was a fool. No one took anything that Clarence said seriously!'

'Except Edward, who had him put to death.'

'Lies!' she resorted to vehemence. 'Lies and rumour! Always lies and rumour!'

'Rumour doesn't rise out of the air. There is no rumour surrounding *my* birth.'

'You are not the King.'

'But it seems my claim to the throne might be as strong as young Edward's.' He made the comment idly; but it pleased him and he allowed it to dwell in his mind. She warmed his pleasure with her anger.

'*Your* claim to the throne! What claim have you? You trace your family back to the youngest son of Edward the Third. Everyone traces his family back to Edward the Third. It is nothing. He had all those sons, and then John of Gaunt with his wives and his mistress and all those children legitimized. It was monstrous.' John of Gaunt's marriage to Catherine Swynford was a matter she would argue as passionately as if it were in her power to reverse the event; Buckingham had no mind to listen to her on this subject now. Nevertheless, he had gained more than he had ever expected from an exchange with his wife.

Katherine, left alone, transferred her anger with John of Gaunt to its proper source. 'God save England if you are to have the running of it!' she shouted. 'Can't run your own estates, never look at your account books, don't take any care for your tenants, and can't tell a good steward from a bad.' She stamped her foot and screamed, 'God save England, I say!'

Buckingham put his view strongly that the young King should be resident in the Tower. There were good precedents for the King to take up residence there and ample state apartments were available; it seemed a sensible suggestion and so, on a May day of fitful sun and showers, the young King rode to the Tower.

He was pleased to have somewhere of his own; it made him feel more like a King, a sensation which had been sadly lacking so far. Now, he sat astride his horse and looked about him with cautious interest. In the distance, he had his first glimpse of the Tower. It was rather squat in comparison with some of the great castles of the Marches, but it compared favourably enough with the Bishop's Palace. As he drew nearer, it seemed to grow more massive and he felt reassured by its clumsy strength. In front of it, grass sparkled after the rain and beyond he could see the thin blue band of the river; a few rooks cawed in the trees. He thought that perhaps he might do well enough here.

He enjoyed inspecting the state apartments. The pleasure-loving father had seen to it that his sons lived modestly, and the apartments seemed luxurious to young Edward. There was much to which he must attend and by the end of the day he was exhausted and confused. He had dreaded the moment when the drapes were drawn around his bed and he was alone in this strange place, but in fact he fell asleep almost immediately and did not wake until morning.

It was in the morning that he began to wonder what he was to do from now on. Hitherto, others had planned his time for him and had done it so thoroughly that every minute was accounted for. Was there someone who did this for the King, or was the King supposed to dispose of his own time? Before, there had always been someone to provide answers. Now there was no one except his Uncle Richard, whom his mother had told him he could not trust. But all the people whom he was supposed to trust had been taken from him, so what was he to do? It was very difficult and he didn't like difficulty.

He embarked on the morning with misgivings. The earlier part went much as most days in his life had gone. When he was dressed a chaplain came to him to sing mattins, he went to hear mass, and he had breakfast. It was immediately after breakfast that the first difficulty arose. The dishes had been cleared from the table; he could see two stewards moving about at the far end of the room, and nearby his attendant was in close conversation with the chamberlain. One of the stewards glanced in his direction and looked away again. Perhaps there is something I should be doing, he thought; they will judge me weak and stupid if I fail to do it. Edward had spent much time with his uncle, Earl Rivers, whose handling of ceremonial was so impeccable that court life became a dance in which never a wrong move is made. Edward had not imagined the ceremonial had to be thought about, it had seemed to him that everyone involuntarily performed his appointed role. Now, things had gone badly out of joint. Not for the first time, but perhaps more profoundly than before, he mourned the loss of his uncle. What was he to do? At the thought of leaving the security of the table a wave of panic seized him. What was life in this place to be like if the problem of rising from table could create such difficulty? He got up. The steward looked at him again, but neither the attendant nor the chamberlain paid any attention to him. Was it possible that here, in this crude, strong building, there was a way of life quite different from the exquisite dance Earl Rivers had contrived for him? He felt an overwhelming loneliness as he began to walk slowly across the hall towards an antechamber at the far end. What was he to do when he reached the antechamber? Out of the corner of his eye he saw that the attendant had broken away from the chamberlain and was now following him.

In the antechamber there were two tall chairs and a table; on the table books were laid out. He remembered with a rush of relief so violent he could have cried out that a priest was coming this morning to instruct him. He said to the attendant, 'I will wait here until the priest comes.' There was an arras on the wall which depicted a warrior on horseback looking very fierce and waving an axe to cleave a way through people who quailed beneath him. Edward studied the arras while he waited. When the priest arrived he was surprised to find that he knew him. It was Dr Ormond who had been secretary to Earl Rivers. In the past, he had sometimes given lessons to Edward.

Edward said warmly, 'I am so glad to see you,' although hitherto he had never liked this sour-faced man. 'Has my uncle, Lord Rivers, arranged for you to be here with me, and will I see him soon?'

The relief in the boy's voice made Ormond wince. He said austerely, 'It was Dr Morton, the Bishop of Ely, who recommended that I should instruct you.'

They sat at the table. Edward remembered that Dr Ormond was respected as a man of learning. Edward was himself well-versed in many subjects and foreign visitors had been impressed by the fine quality of his mind. Since Ormond was the only person in this strange place whose worth was known, Edward was anxious to acquit himself well in the priest's eyes. He sought about in his mind for a subject which would display to advantage his learning and his piety. Eventually he said, cutting across Ormond's discourse, 'Tell me, Dr Ormond, what think you of this printing machine? What will be the outcome of it?'

Ormond regarded questions as an impertinence and invariably dealt with them by making the questioner appear stupid. 'What can any man of learning have to fear from books?' he said acidly. 'What can any man of learning have to fear from anything which widens the boundaries of knowledge?'

Edward was disconcerted. To him, learning was precious because it gave inner sustenance—like good food, only without the disadvantage of indigestion. There was something reckless about Ormond's statement which startled him.

'But suppose it were to come that translations of the Bible into English were to be printed.' He took refuge in a subject on which there could be no two views: the existing Lollard translation was in his mind. 'Such books might get into the wrong hands. . . .'

'What has the truth to fear?' Ormond asked austerely.

Edward was nonplussed. He said, 'It is men like you, Dr Ormond, whom I think of as guardians of the truth, and I would prefer it always to remain so.'

'You must be the guardian of your own truth,' Ormond

retorted. He did not think whether this statement was wise, he merely intended to teach the young King not to interrupt again.

Edward was crushed by this appalling statement and remained subdued for the rest of their time together. Later, he spoke of it to his attendant, and the attendant repeated the remark to the chamberlain. And there, for the time being, it rested.

3

About the time that the young King moved to the Tower, Anne came to Crosby's Place. Richard had sent asking her to join him and she had responded at once, sensing the urgency of his need. She travelled south through country where life was harsh, robbery and murder still common; but a land no longer lawless. Edward the Fourth had given personal authority to the King's Peace and the King's Writ ran throughout the land. But misrule was too near, the country needed years to grow used to order. One night, in a remote valley, Anne dined with a Justice of the Peace. This man had performed his duties scrupulously, secure in the power of the King behind him. Now, he was afraid. For the folk in this wild place, order had no past; when they gathered round the fire at night their stories were of massacre and blood feuds. Lawlessness would spread here as the forest encroaches on clearances if strong measures are not taken to hold the ground which has been won. He did not speak of this to Anne, but the fear was in his face as though already he smelt the predators, saw the bright eyes glinting in the dark beyond the window.

Anne made few other stops on her journey. An observer, seeing her face, calm and resolute, might have judged her eager for her first glimpse of London. It was almost dark when she passed through Aldgate and flares had been lit in the narrow city streets although there were still a few sunset streaks in the western sky. The day had been hot and breathless and the city was like a great cauldron which has retained the odours of everything good and bad which has been brewed in it. Darkness came like a lid pressing down on the cauldron. Inn doors stood open; people crouched in doorways gasping for the first cool breath of evening. From balconies, faces, distorted in flickering torchlight, hung over the street grotesque as gargoyles awaiting some malign event. Anne wanted to turn her head away but could not; a power beyond her will forced her to take in every detail of this lurid scene.

When she arrived at Crosby's Place Richard was away attending an urgent meeting of his Council, but his concern for her comfort was apparent. Their bed-chamber was small, by no means the best bed-chamber, but it was at the rear of the house, away from the clamour of the city. Anne thanked the servants and dismissed them as soon as possible. When the sound of their feet had died away, it was blessedly quiet. Through an open window came a freshness, faint and unidentifiable, yet familiar, evoking other scenes than this; somewhere near at hand there must be a flowering shrub with a scent that was just sharp enough to cut the languid air. She went to the window and leant out, but could not see it. As she reached down, one hand probing the wall, there came a distant cry, at once harsh and plaintive. Perhaps it was only the cry of a night bird on the marshes on the far bank of the river; yet it was of Death that she thought. She drew back from the window lest he should be waiting below in the shadow. 'Oh God,' she prayed, 'I am weak and cowardly, and though I do not complain to others, Thou knowest how I complain to myself. Forgive me this weakness and do not answer my constant longing for rest; but have regard to the needs of Thy servant, Richard, my dear lord, and for his sake let me not be taken from him. Renew my ebbing strength; kindle my dull spirit.'

It was agony to look to a time when she would no longer be able to comfort Richard. He needed her as the plough needs the earth. She wondered what she could offer, what sacrifice she could make to the watcher in the shadow. Chill came the thought that she would give her son. Even him.

'This will not do, these thoughts are too dark!' she chided herself. And then, 'Now that I am in London I must not hide away in here.' She went out of the room. A maid was hovering in the corridor, uncertain what her mistress expected of her.

'And what do you think of this great city?' Anne asked her.

'Not near so fine as York, to my mind,' the woman replied.

At the end of the corridor there was a window overlooking the courtyard and now there came the sound of horses' hooves on the cobblestones. Anne hurried to the window in time to see Richard ride into the yard. He reined in the horse and looked up, his eyes searching the windows, and just for a moment this was not Crosby's Place, but Master Harbuckle's house, and it was all to be done again. How sweet that moment, and how small had been her response! She had held back, keeping some of her feeling in reserve, measuring it out to him. She was better rehearsed now. She leant from the window and let joy spill out into the warm night.

He came to her quickly and took her in his arms; her body seemed all bone, yet he asked, 'It will not make you ill to be in London?' as though illness were still some distance away.

She gathered all her store of gaiety together; the eyes became enormous in the fragile face. 'It makes me ill to be apart from you.'

She was as impatient as he for love and made no plea for gentleness but with eager moaning welcomed the urgent thrust which pierced the darkness and held them so close even Death could not come between them. Her body was a pulsing crimson spiral through which some wanton creature was dragged down, clawing and screaming, to the place where ecstasy and agony are one. Then, even that creature was swept away, she had no being but was part of a tide drifting in timeless bliss. Oh, if *this* was what Death offered. . . . 'What is it?' She came to herself with a shuddering start to find not Death but an alarmed husband reared above her. Richard looked shocked by her wildness as though he had found a stranger in his bed. He is like a child, she thought wearily, who asks for the sun and is frightened when he burns his fingers. She wiped the sweat from his forehead and drew his head gently to her breast. 'Did you not know how much I loved you?' she chided gently, and stroked his head as though he was child instead of lover. At last when some measure of peace came to them, she said, 'I shall grow fat now I am with you.' And he believed because he must believe.

Afterwards, when they were apart, Richard told Anne the latest news. As he talked he paced the room. She saw that an angry spirit possessed him.

'We meet in Council,' he said, 'and then Hastings and Morton go away to councils of their own. If I am to hold them together, I must persuade, conciliate, say this to this one, and that to that one, spend precious hours playing the one off against the other. I am not skilled at such games even if I had the stomach for them.' The scorn in his voice made it apparent that he had little respect for such skill. 'If there are people whose loyalty is in doubt, the sooner it is out the better.'

'But Hastings sent for you. Can his loyalty be in doubt?'

'Jane Shore has become his mistress and she will have him reconciled with Elizabeth Woodville. I have this on Buckingham's authority.'

'And Howard?' Anne knew little of Buckingham and would

not put trust in a stranger; but Lord Howard was a man whose
worth was known and proved. 'What does he say?'

'He, too, doubts Hastings, though he thinks Morton is the
more dangerous.'

'And Lord Stanley?'

'Stanley's health is a sure guide to my fortunes, and for this
he will always be of value.' Richard laughed for the first time.
'If Stanley is well, then I know all goes well with me. If he
becomes sick and talks of returning to his estates, then I know
an ill-wind blows for me. At present, he complains the heat
loosens his bowels, but he still eats well.'

'How long can this state of affairs continue?'

He did not reply. She searched his face but found no answer
there. The anger had drained away and he looked tired and
unexpectedly irresolute. Yet he must know, she thought, that
he, and not this child, must rule.

Chapter 12

I

On June 10th, Richard sent for aid to the North where his
strength had always lain. He spoke of plots against him and of
those who would take his life. The recipients of his appeals
must have imagined the atmosphere in the capital to be tense,
with men alert to danger at each step they took.

Yet, as often happens, those nearest danger became accustomed to it, treated it familiarly and were sometimes more
concerned with trivial matters. On June 13th, when members of
Richard's Council met in the White Tower, Lord Stanley was
complaining of the heat; and Howard, who sat next to him,
thought that to hear Stanley talk one might suppose there to be
no place but Cheshire where a man might hope to find a
temperate climate. Hastings wanted the business of the coronation settled, it was the delay over this which had first aroused
his suspicions of the Protector; but though he wanted the matter
settled, he hoped it would not be discussed at length today, else
he would never get to Mistress Shore. The heat affected him
in other ways than Lord Stanley and he was not in the habit
of practising self-denial.

John Morton, Bishop of Ely, was not one to deny self, either.
He was ambitious and not a man to be troubled by the crowing
of a cock. But he knew, better than most, that there is a time to

act and a time to wait. He did not judge the time for action to be ripe; so now, he turned a tranquil gaze to the window and meditated on the King whom he could see exercising with two attendants on the grass. Young Edward was a rather puny figure, and Morton was sufficiently able to wish for a more effective master. The sun sparked on stone, and Morton wondered about Henry of Richmond, the sharpness of whose mind had impressed those who had seen him recently.

While Morton was taking a long view, beyond the figure of the young King, the winding river, and the distant fields, the door of the room had been closed by an usher. The Archbishop of York, a frail and fussy man, frowned his displeasure at the richness of the Duke of Buckingham's robes. 'Preens himself like a peacock, and yesterday he scarcely existed!' Hastings, also looking at the Duke, reflected that never before had a man been rewarded so far beyond his worth. 'There is scarce any matter in which he is not inexperienced,' he thought scornfully. It was damned hot! Sweat pricked like thorns over his body.

The Protector, who seemed unaffected by the heat, said that he had called his Council together because of certain matters which concerned them all. He spoke quietly, almost monotonously, and Stanley thought, 'I shall go to sleep if he goes on like this.' The Protector said that reports had reached him which he had not at first believed. Buckingham, red lips pursed, listened with the owlish gravity of a man who hears things which are not displeasing to him. Hastings, watching Buckingham, thought, 'They are planning to postpone the coronation again. Well, they won't get away with it.' He looked round the room, counting those on whose support he could rely, the Archbishop, Morton, Stanley. . . .

'. . . to conspire against the government is not a matter which can be tolerated. . . .'

'Conspiracy is a strong word,' Hastings intervened, having done his arithmetic and found the answer to his satisfaction. 'We have no proof of a conspiracy so far as I am aware.'

Buckingham flashed in at this point to say that Hastings and his friends were accused of plotting against the Protector. Hastings, who had not expected such a direct attack, dismissed the accusation contemptuously. 'Was it not I who sent to the Duke of Gloucester entreating him to take the young King from Lord Rivers and make all haste to London? Is this the action of a conspirator? If so, the word must have acquired new meaning.'

'On which of your actions would you wish to be judged, my lord?' Buckingham's condescending tone was nicely calculated to rouse Hastings' quick pride. 'When the Woodvilles sought to impose their influence on events, you did indeed send messages to the Duke of Gloucester urging him to come with all speed and every show of force.'

My God! Hastings fumed to himself, anyone would think the man a justice and I some poor miscreant, he has such a conceit of himself.

'And when the Duke of Gloucester came, not as you had envisaged, with an army of two thousand, but with a modest force of three hundred, this does nothing to assure you of his peaceful intent. You turn again. And now it is the Woodvilles that you favour. There is no pleasing you. Can it be that it is not the arrangements for the coronation which concern you, but the fact that you had hoped your own future to be better advanced?'

'It is rather the advancement of others which concerns me.' Hastings was eager to teach Buckingham a lesson. 'For I see only trouble ahead for a man whose power far outstrips both his ability and his practical experience of the affairs of state!'

He was speaking of Buckingham, but Buckingham was quick to put another interpretation on his words. 'Matters could not be in more experienced hands than the Lord Protector's,' he rebuked smoothly. 'This "concern" of yours gives us some unease.'

'Your "unease" is without foundation.' Hastings was as hot as Buckingham was cool. 'My one desire is to see King Edward's son crowned. It was for that purpose I sent for the Duke of Gloucester when it seemed to me things moved too fast here.'

'And now?'

'I stand where I always stood on this. I have a duty to the late King.'

'As have we all.'

'None more so than I. I was closer to him than any other man, I knew his mind. . . .'

The Protector stiffened, but did not speak. It was Buckingham who intervened again. 'You, my lord! You but kept him company in debauchery.'

'I served him well!' There was no doubting Hastings' sincerity and a shutter came down over the Protector's face. 'I served him not for any honours he bestowed upon me, but for what he was. . . .'

'For what he became after he fell to carousing with you.' The Protector's voice was level, his face expressionless.

'You must not boast of your loyalty in the presence of my

Lord Protector.' Buckingham was quick to make the comparison. 'The service he rendered to his brother over the years surpasses all.'

'And his rewards have matched his service.' Hastings thrust in the opening made for him.

There was an uneasy stir. Stanley's eyes flicked sideways to the still figure of the Protector; whatever he saw made him flinch and he bowed his head. Morton's mouth had gone awry as though something set his teeth on edge. Even Buckingham stayed whatever words were on his lips.

'You . . . presume . . . to judge me?' The Protector's lips twitched so that it was difficult to get words past them. 'You . . . question *my* loyalty?'

'Loyalty!' Hastings threw the word back in Richard of Gloucester's face. 'I know nothing of *loyalty*. I loved the man!'

Many times Hastings had laughed at the young Richard of Gloucester who must always measure himself against other men in order to demonstrate that his was the greater loyalty. He had not realized until this moment that the mockery must be paid for. Now, one glance at the waxen face told him the time for settlement had come. He must rouse support or perish. Whatever else he lacked, it was not courage, so he made his bid.

'I say that yours was a loyalty amply rewarded. E'er you were twenty, the North was yours, such power did Edward invest in you, and afterwards left you free to do as you thought best. And this because he thought you kept the North for him.'

'And did I not keep it for him?'

'You served the North so well, my lord, that the people in those regions thought it was you who ruled the land. And think so still.'

Howard cried, 'In God's name, man! Be silent.'

But Stanley was wavering, there was care for his Cheshire estates in the glance he directed at the Protector. At the first hint of weakness, Stanley would close in behind Hastings.

'And where does it end?' Hastings cried. 'I ask you all, can you not see where this man's ambition leads him? The North will rise for him.'

The Archbishop laid a hand, wrinkled as a chicken's claw, on the table. Stanley's hand was in the folds of his robe. Morton had his eyes on the door. Richard said, 'My ambition is to carry out my brother's bidding. As Protector. . . . .'

'In three days King Edward the Fifth will be crowned. Is that not the plan, or has yet another cause for delay been discovered?'

'You are saying?' Richard sounded quite calm now.

'That it is not your intention young Edward should ever take the throne!'

'TREASON!'

Richard's fist crashed on the table. He crouched above it, so still he scarcely breathed. To each man around the table it seemed the Protector's eyes looked directly into his. They sat, not daring to move a muscle; it was as though they were afraid that by some magic those eyes would winkle out any treacherous thought and impale it for all to see. Richard had struck at the moment when the waverers most needed time. Now, when even thought was petrified, he said, 'Choose, now!'

'We are with you, my lord,' Howard spoke and meant it with all his heart.

Stanley passed his tongue across his lips; moisture gathered in the Archbishop's weak eyes and trickled unheeded down his cheeks; Morton counted the beats of his heart: they did not look at Hastings nor did they ever look upon him again. The door to the chamber was thrust open and armed men rushed in. The Protector said, 'Take him away; he is guilty of treason.' When they had hustled Hastings out, he straightened up and put one hand to his side. He stood for a moment or so thus, his upper lip caught in his teeth, breathing fast. Then he said, as though it was of little account, that Stanley, the Archbishop, and Morton were to be detained.

In under half-an-hour, Hastings, scarce cooled from the heat of his anger, stretched his neck to receive the axe. Even at the last this agreeable man could hardly believe what was happening to him. When he saw the improvised block, he laughed and asked if they meant to scare him with this rough piece of carpentry.

A messenger went to the Protector and told him it was over. He received no answer.

Later, Buckingham went to the Protector. 'It was magnificently done!' He regarded himself as a good judge of a performance and was a little surprised to see how ill this one was now sustained. Richard looked sick as though some pain had come upon him; there was a film of sweat on his brow and the lines around eyes and mouth were sharply etched. The power which so short a time ago had dominated his companions, had gone from him. The clouded eyes looked puzzled, even a little hurt. He said in that dry, toneless voice which seemed intended deliberately to confuse his hearers so that one hardly knew whether he spoke seriously or in jest, 'It was not only Hastings who lost his head.'

Buckingham said uneasily, 'Come, Dickon, you are tired. Things will seem different in the morning.'

Richard raised his eyebrows. 'For Hastings?'

Buckingham stared at him; for a moment the unpleasant idea occurred to him that he might have cast his lot with the wrong man. He said, 'You must not let anyone see this weakness. If Gloucester doubts himself, what hope that anyone else will believe?'

'Actions count for nothing.' Richard looked down, moving the ring on his little finger back and forth, back and forth. The jewel caught the last light of the sun and flashed. He closed his eyes as though the little spark hurt them. 'If I was judged by my actions, I would have no reason to fear. But here, men judge by whispers, at each change in the direction of the wind they change their allegiance. . . .'

'It has ever been so.'

'He talked of my rewards! When Edward quarrelled with Warwick, I left Middleham, where I was happy. What reward had I then? I hated his court, but I bore with it for his sake. When he was taken at Nottingham, did I not raise men to his side? When he fled to Honfleur was I not with him? What danger was there that I did not share with him? And in later years, I heard it said that he left too much to me, stayed at court while I fought his wars. . . .'

He went on talking, fanning the spark of an anger that refused to be rekindled.

2

'He was my father's friend,' the young King said to Ormond.

'But your uncle's enemy,' Ormond replied, though he doubted that Hastings had ever found time to be any man's enemy. For a man who was so amiable, Hastings had met a strange end.

It did not surprise Edward that Hastings should be disliked. He had constantly made jokes which Edward did not understand, and had made him feel foolish; whereas his Uncle Richard, in his rather awesome way, had treated him as a person to be taken seriously. But it was one thing to dislike a person, another to cut off his head. Hastings' end seemed undeserved, and the manner of it did not accord with Edward's understanding of his Uncle Richard; for whatever others might say of his uncle, he had always seemed to Edward to be sober and less given to excess than the other men who surrounded his father. In fact, if anyone was to lose his head, Edward would have thought it more likely that the volatile Hastings would have had his uncle's head. Edward liked time to form his opinions of people, and was now panicked by the need to make a rapid revision.

Ormond did not know what went on in the boy's mind; but he was aware of the panic. He felt very unhappy as he looked at Edward. Ormond prided himself on being a man of reason; but God, who has his own reasons, never spoke to Ormond's mind but attacked him in the pit of his stomach. The boy is too much in the company of adults and strangers, he thought, he badly needs the companionship of another child: if his brother were here, he might be better. Ormond spoke of this to the chamberlain in the hope that the suggestion might eventually be passed to the Protector.

Others, more powerful than Ormond, advocated this course and for different reasons, and soon afterwards Elizabeth Woodville was persuaded to let her nine-year-old son leave the sanctuary of the Abbey and join his brother in the Tower. The death of Hastings and the arrest of Morton and Lord Stanley had convinced her that there were few to further her cause. She was also mindful that no decision had yet been reached about the fate of her brother, Earl Rivers, and hoped that by compliance she might win a reprieve for him. 'Though I fear it is too late for that,' she said to her daughter, Elizabeth. 'This "conspiracy" of which they make so much presents them with a chance to rid themselves of him while feeling runs high.' She understood very well the way in which men's minds work when they seek power for themselves.

Her daughter, less resigned to this, asked, 'Are all men so cruel?' Elizabeth, at seventeen, was a soft, dimpled creature whose cheerful countenance gave little hint as to how much, if any, of her mother's strength of character she might have inherited.

'A kingdom crumbles beneath the hand of a kindly man,' her mother retorted. 'Look what happened to us when that holy fool, Henry the Sixth, reigned.'

'But can a man not be strong *and* merciful? I would like to think it might be so.' Elizabeth spoke gently; yet there was that in her tone which suggested that, wanting it, she would have it so.

Soon after this conversation took place Earl Rivers was executed. He had already reconciled himself to this fate and seemed not sad to leave a life in which he had never found his way with any great certainty.

Lord Stanley was more fortunate; he was released and reinstated as a member of the Protector's Council: Richard needed his weathercock. John Morton, Bishop of Ely, was dealt with leniently; at Buckingham's request he was held in the Duke's castle at Brecknock where he was treated with consideration. Morton had been more tolerant than some of Buckingham's rise to power and Buckingham was not ill-disposed to him.

The men who had opposed Richard had been silenced. Now strange rumours began to circulate and Dr Ormond felt no lightening of his spirits when he saw the two Princes playing together on the dappled grass outside the Tower. God gnawed at his stomach. He contrived to send a message to Morton at Brecknock. 'I fear for the Princes.' Morton, however, had too much need to fear for himself to spare a thought for the young Princes whose youth would protect them from the worst evils. Morton had the shrewdest head in the kingdom and was determined to keep it on his shoulders.

3

Richard prayed.

He was always more than conscientious in his devotions and would not have embarked on any enterprise without first seeking God's blessing. The blessing had never so far been withheld. His cause was just; he was, after all, a Plantagenet and a scion of the House of York: it was enough.

Until now. Now, he found he had to elaborate, to remind God that from birth his path had been clearly marked out for him, to draw attention to the unswerving devotion with which he had followed that path to this point. Surely he could not turn aside now. To let the throne go to a boy who would lose all they had gained would be to make worthless the sacrifice of his father and all the nameless people who had fought and died for the House of York because they believed its cause to be right. There had been too many deaths to turn aside now.

This weakness over Hastings was the Devil's work. He wrestled with the Devil who cunningly explored some cleft in Richard's nature which the present crisis had exposed and through which seeped terrible doubts. To doubt at such a time was madness. For him, it was the throne or extinction. He equated his own survival with the good of the realm. England needed a strong king. For England's sake, he fought the devil of doubt with all his strength.

Gradually, as the days of June passed, his prayers were

answered, the doubts were dispelled. One day, when he had talked with his mother in her home at Baynard's Castle, he walked afterwards in the garden by the river. His mother was angry about rumours which had come to her and she accused Richard of lacking all consideration for her. But when he asked what rumours she had heard, she only answered, 'Terrible things!' When he asked if the rumours had any truth in them, she cried out, 'Would that your father were here! He would never have let such things come to pass.'

'Would my father be happy to see another child on the throne?'

'No, of course not. But then it would never have come to pass had he been here.' She looked at Richard contemptuously, as though his father would have resolved such a situation without inconvenience to anyone. It was plain he would get no sense out of her. It was not that her mind was wandering, but that she believed there are times when sense is best avoided.

'Do not come to me with your questions,' she said when he left her. 'I am old and have fought my battles. This is a matter for you.'

He looked at the river winding past the clutter of buildings away towards the green fields of West Minster. The very quietness of the scene made him feel dizzy. Life had moved like a runaway horse since Edward died, and he had gone with it; it is often wise to let a runaway use up its energy, but the rider must have a cool head. His head was in a turmoil. Now, looking at the river which seemed to shake and shudder as though he was flashing past it, he cried out, 'THIS MUST STOP!'

It did stop. For a moment, it was as though everything stopped—the busy commerce of the city, the creaking of a boat at its moorings, the chatter of birds in the trees, even his own heart-beat—all stopped. A ray of sunlight glanced off the river and sparked into his eyes so that the visual world dissolved in brilliant white light. Then, as he stood breathless and blinded, there came a great surging as if the sea swept inland; he felt its force strike his chest, heard its roar in his ears, felt himself lifted and borne aloft by its mighty impetus, so that he seemed to be stretched out above the city and the distant fields; he soared up and up and they grew smaller, closing in together, so that he could hold them in his arms. He knew this was a vision and that it meant God had entrusted the care of the realm to him. When all was calm again, every cranny and crevice of his being had been washed free of doubt. From that moment all things affirmed his purpose in the most miraculous fashion; as he rode about the streets, in every face that turned to him he read the will of the people.

But he knew that the common people are contrary. If they are given what they want too suddenly they will stampede and turn from the giver in mindless panic; if they have to wait too long, they will lose interest, for they are as easily distracted as children. While he pondered his next move, Buckingham brought to him the Bishop of Bath and Wells, a man with a strange tale to tell. Bishop Stillington made a long business of the telling; but, in brief, what he had to say was that King Edward, when he was twenty-one, had entered into a marriage contract with Lady Eleanor Butler, the daughter of the Earl of Shrewsbury. His subsequent marriage to Elizabeth Woodville was, therefore, bigamous.

'And the witnesses?' Richard asked.

There were, it seemed, no witnesses other than Bishop Stillington, death having inconsiderately carried off the people concerned including Lady Eleanor herself.

'And you yourself have kept quiet as the dead,' Richard said, watching Stillington's face.

'With good reason, my lord. I told the story to the Duke of Clarence and the Duke was dead soon afterwards; I was myself put in prison for no very specific reason.'

There were other explanations for Edward's final loss of patience with Clarence, but Richard was satisfied with the one now offered. It suited his purpose to accept it, but there was nothing cynical in his attitude. A man does not commit his cause to God and then quarrel with the means of furthering it which God puts at his disposal.

The next day, Richard and Buckingham, with their supporters, went to Paul's Cross to hear Friar Ralph Shaa preach.

So, too, went Robin Prithie, who afterwards wrote to his master describing what there took place.

'All the rumours which have been whispered abroad lately were stated roundly to be facts this morning by Friar Shaa, who started by praising the Duke of Gloucester so that one might think no other man in the whole realm to be of legitimate birth.' On re-reading this, it occurred to Robin that jests of this nature might not be welcome to his master, so he deleted the last part of the sentence and wrote instead, 'who extolled the Duke of Gloucester's virtues.' As bastardy was the nub of the matter, the report began to present difficulties. He wondered how Henry would respond to Shaa's text, 'Bastard slips shall not inherit.' He decided to leave this out, and after much writing and re-writing confined himself to the simple statement that as it had been discovered that King Edward had been contracted to another when he wed Elizabeth Woodville the children of their marriage were illegitimate and Richard of Gloucester was therefore the rightful heir to the throne.

'While this went on,' he concluded, 'there was much whispering and exclaiming and shaking of sage heads; but the Protector sat still as a statue, looking stern and grave. People around me seemed much impressed by him, as though to sit a horse quietly for half-an-hour were a mark of exceptional virtue.'

Henry, Earl of Richmond, did not receive the letter for some weeks, and all he said when he read it was, 'Bastards those children may be; but no man will sit easy on the throne while they live to attract any who have a grievance.'

4

London was alive as an enormous cheese with maggots crawling all over it. From all sides, people converged and headed towards the river. Excitement leapt like flames from one person to another; it licked high into the sky where the masts of foreign ships were swarming with sailors eager to see this new pageant the people of London were staging. To the right rose the wall of Baynard's Castle and here the people stopped and looked about them. Many exalted personages were gathered here, noblemen and priests and dignitaries of the city. Small boys were lifted onto shoulders so that they could have a sight of them. A cripple with a withered leg tried to thrust his way through the crowd, shouting, 'Let me through to Him, let me through!' thinking Christ had come again and he might be cured; he did this at every great event, remembering what had happened to Bartimaeus as a result of his persistence. Even the gulls were excited, sweeping low over the heads of commoners and nobles alike and spattering more than one brilliant cloak. Boys climbed trees and walls, and a young girl sent a big, scarlet ball soaring into the sky.

A murmur at the front of the crowd sent ripples of sound back so that everyone exclaimed 'Aaah!' though many did not know why. Then, beneath the battlements there appeared a gloriously apparelled figure, variously described as the Duke of Buckingham, Lord Howard, the Marquis of Dorset and, by a very old man who could not possibly see anything, the King-maker returned to earth. This man, although his voice could not be heard by many, contrived nevertheless to suggest most eloquently by the movement of head, shoulders and wonderfully generous hands, that he had great treasure to bestow on the people. The people became impatient and began to shout, demanding to receive at once the riches he promised them. The man held his arms aloft and then let them drop and with them all his glory, which fell like a mantle beneath the feet of the man who now came forward from the shadow of a doorway high in the wall.

There was no doubt as to who this figure was, for all around people began to cry, 'Dickon! Dickon!' This, however, was no strutting peacock eager to display his exotic plumage for the crowd's approval. He stood before them quietly, a small, gaunt man in a dark robe. Yet, by his very stillness, he held the attention of the great crowd spread out below him. They cheered and waved and shouted, but he did not move, only stood contemplating their strenuous activity as though measuring its worth. He was the guardian of the treasure: was it possible he would deny it to the people? They shouted louder and louder. At last, he relented and raised an arm; he turned his head slowly from one side to the other so that they should all see his face and he theirs. A moment later, he had withdrawn. There was only the stone of the battlement, rosy in the morning sunlight.

All around people began to shout, 'King Richard! King Richard! King Richard!'

In the White Tower, Edward sat on the edge of his bed and talked with his younger brother.

'What will happen to us?' the young boy asked.

'The people will rise and put me on the throne.' Edward spoke firmly, but not loudly for it was as well to be discreet until rescue came.

'How will they rise?' his brother asked.

'I don't know. But our mother will see to it.'

The younger boy pushed his fist against his mouth; even so, tears gushed over his knuckles.

Edward looked at the table which was heaped with fruit and delicacies which their uncle, who was now King Richard the Third, had sent to them. He would like to have swept the tray to the floor in a grand gesture of defiance, but lacked the courage. Also, he badly needed comfort and since none other was offered he went to the table and ate greedily, stuffing food in his mouth in a way which was quite alien to him.

Part IV

THE WINTER OF OUR DISCONTENT

Chapter 13

I

'Richard, by the grace of God, King of England and of France and lord of Ireland, straitly chargeth and commandeth, under pain of death, that no manner of person, of what estate, degree of condition soever he be, for old or new quarrel, rancour or malice, make any challenge or affray, nor rob or despoil any person, nor break any sanctuary, whereby his peace shall be broken, or any sedition or disturbance of his said peace shall happen, within this his city of London. . . .

And to the intent that peace and tranquillity among his people may be rather kept . . . our said sovereign lord straitly chargeth and commandeth that every man be in his lodgings by ten of the clock in the night, and that no person other than such that his highness hath licensed or shall license within the franchise of the said city or in places thereunto nigh adjoining, bear any manner of weapon . . . under pain of forfeiture and losing of the same and imprisonment of him or them that so offendeth, to endure at the King's pleasure.'

It was after ten now and few seemed inclined to risk the King's displeasure. Had he not given them as fine a display as could ever be provided in the whole wide world? What could rival the splendour of the English court arrayed in velvet, cloth of gold, and satin, in brilliant hues of purple, scarlet, blue and gold? Even those greybeards who tended always to remember life being so much more extreme in the past—the winters colder, the summers hotter, wars more bloody and men more godly, and spectacles the like of which would never be seen again—even these old people were staggered by the brilliance of King Richard and his Queen.

Now, safely in their lodgings by ten o'clock of the night, the

King's obedient subjects basked in the afterglow of these golden coronation days. There were few, in this merchant city, who disapproved of such a display of riches: a coronation is a time for a country to show its resources to the world. From one open window voices floated into the street and were heard by two men who were walking by.

A man's voice said, 'On the showing of his coronation King Richard means to be a right royal king, and that is how it should be! A strong king is what we need.'

'I'll give him six months.' An old man's voice this, querulous. 'Six months to prove how strong he is!'

'And if he doesn't satisfy you after six months, will you change him for the lad in the Tower? You think *he'd* be a strong king, do you?'

'How splendid the Duke of Buckingham looked!' A woman's voice intervened. 'There was no one to compare with him, save the King, of course.'

'And his Duchess not with him! I heard from one of his clerks that she has to ask her lord's permission before she dares venture out of her chamber these days, let alone attend a coronation.'

The two men, who had paused to listen, walked on. They walked with assurance because they were abroad lawfully; but Robin Prithie bent his head and kept the collar of his cloak up about his face because he did not want to be recognized. There were few in London who knew him, but life could play mean tricks on a man and he was not taking any chances. In spite of his precautions, or perhaps because fear adds a certain spice to life, he was enjoying himself. It was no part of the job which had been assigned to him to keep the Duke of Buckingham informed of his master's intentions; yet, here he was on the way to see the Duke himself, and mightily excited by this double game he was playing. He, too, had been impressed by the splendour of the Duke at the coronation, although he had heard men mutter that such splendour would be Buckingham's undoing. 'Would he rival the King?' Robin thought the Duke might well rival the King, but saw no reason why it should be his undoing.

Buckingham received Robin alone. Such privacy was exceptional, and Robin preened himself, imagining that the Duke was showing consideration for him since he risked much by serving two masters. He looked at the handsome face. It was the first time he had been close to the Duke so he was not aware that over the past weeks the face had changed as though a sculptor had put the final touches to his work, slightly flattening the nose so that the nostrils splayed, and fleshing the upper lip. These two small touches had set the seal of character on the whole face. Robin, who thought neither greed nor sensuality out of place, was nevertheless surprised that such a man should be sensitive to the danger in which Robin had placed himself; it was always Robin's weakness to see himself in the centre of the picture. Buckingham had reasons of his own for seeing Robin alone and had made sure that no servant was within sight or sound of them. Treachery must have a beginning; although Buckingham served but one master, there was something tainted in the curiosity he now displayed.

'This Henry Tydder, or Tudor, has proclaimed himself the Earl of Richmond. What new honour will he seek to confer upon himself?'

'He says he has no ambition,' Robin replied. 'To any who would be ambitious on his behalf, I am to say that he is most anxious to live in peace and sees no profit for him in a return to England. To any who may try to persuade him, he begs that they should not endanger their lives on his behalf since he cannot hope to reward their misplaced loyalty. He is on the most excellent terms with Duke Francis and has become so much attached to the country in which he now lives that it would grieve him ever to leave it.' As Buckingham's eyes grew wider, so Robin continued ever more gravely; it was a performance which both men enjoyed. 'He is, moreover, of a religious disposition and thinks little of the affairs of this world. In fact, he is resolved to devote the rest of his life to the service of God.'

'And if God were to call him to His service in England? What then?'

'He is very pious. I doubt he would resist such a call.'

'I have heard he is a coward; that he has never been tried in battle and will never willingly put himself to the test.'

'Most certainly he is a coward,' Robin assented. 'When he thought Duke Francis intended to hand him over to King Edward the Fourth, he went quite out of his mind.'

'Yet there are those who praise his patience and forbearance, who speak of him as a wise man, and a good judge of men and affairs.'

'It's of little use being a good judge of men if you don't reward them well for their service to you.' Robin allowed his personal feelings to show, and Buckingham, who had been wondering how much this man could be trusted, was reassured. In a conspiracy, a man with a grievance is likely to be more reliable than a man of honour whom conscience may render unpredictable.

'I have heard he is generous,' Buckingham said.

'Generous! He is exceeding mean. A mean, harsh man.'

'But patient and forbearing withal, so I am told.' Buckingham was amused.

'Yes, perhaps.'

'And pious?'

'Most certainly.'

'And a coward, and no doubt a fool on horseback? Come! You must know him rather better than this. I warrant any servant of mine could give a better rendering of my character.' In this Buckingham was entirely right, although it would be some time before he discovered how ill he was liked by his servants. 'Tell me what you know of the Earl of Richmond,' he pressed Robin.

Henry was a boy when Robin met him, and then he became a lad, and now he was a man of twenty-six. But this was hardly what Buckingham expected to hear. What then? Robin thought of the boy whom he had met one misty afternoon to whom he had recounted exaggerated stories of his own exploits and who had seemed to believe all that he was told. Lately, Robin had come to realize that the child was not as naive as he had seemed, and had grown into a man who had behaved with remarkable duplicity to his servant, Robin. But these were not the things which Buckingham wanted to her.

'My Lord,' he said, '*your* servants see in you what it is right that they should see. They see that you dazzle those around you; when you sit at table you feed better than anyone else in the land (he was shrewd enough to recall that this had been said of that other Kingmaker, Warwick); and when you go hunting, there is none to surpass you. In war, you are terrible.' Buckingham made a movement of impatience with his hand, but his eyes were not displeased. 'It is not so with my master. He does few of the things which men have a right to expect of him, and so it is difficult for me to answer you. He is more concerned with the cost of his clothes than their quality. He likes music above all things and I have seen him close to tears, especially when he listens to the flute, while the call of the hunting horn leaves him unmoved. The French ambassador has said it is better to go well-fed to his table because he cares more for disputation than food. Once, when he was a boy, I told him the story of a famous battle, and all he said was, "It seems a very chancy way of getting rid of enemies." '

Buckingham paused by the window to ponder this re-mark which evidenced shrewd practicality rather than un-worldly piety. Perhaps Henry had grown more ethereal as

he put on years, but this is not usually the way of a man.
'When you have more to tell me, send word,' he said.

2

Henry, Earl of Richmond, intoned, 'I come to right the
wrongs which Richard has committed.' He stood up straight and
made a noble gesture; he had always enjoyed a little play-
acting. His audience was not much amused. Henry shrugged
his shoulders, letting fall the mantle of kingship. 'And these
children? How am I supposed to right this particular wrong?
Am I to restore young Edward to the throne? Don't shake your
head so impatiently, my good uncle. It bears some thought. If
this wrong is not righted, am I not in danger of finding Richard's
action justified?'

'The young King is ailing, so it is reported.' Jasper Tudor was
always ready to credit reports of the illness of those who stood
in his way.

Henry said, 'Well, well, well, well! How events do join
themselves to my cause!' He was sceptical and intended to
remain so until he had better reason for rejoicing. This was an
uncertain time for him. He had felt a chill of fear when he
heard of Edward's death. He had got used to Edward's tactics,
but he had no idea of the methods Richard the Third might
employ to rid himself of Margaret of Beaufort's imp. He was
older now and tired of being a pawn. Nevertheless, he would
let them all think they could play with him until he was ready
to play his own game. It would take patience and courage, but
where would he be now without these qualities? They were the
necessities of his life. He was sure that in the end he would win.
God, who had brought him safely so far, undoubtedly intended
him to be king. But it would be foolish not to take precautions:
God, Henry was sure, had very little time for fools.

He stopped striding about the room and held his arms out
wide to his uncle. 'We will assume young Edward dead. What
of his brother? Am I to serve him?' He regarded his uncle
earnestly as though waiting instructions. 'And there are
daughters, too, are there not?'

'The daughters are a different matter.'

'Oh?'

'Elizabeth is seventeen and not yet married.'

'And?'

'Why, we will graft the red rose to the white rose.'

'God knows what that would produce,' Henry said sombrely.

'Peace.'

'Mmmh, peace or a bed of thorns!' Henry turned away, his face glum. After a moment, he said querulously, 'You have not answered me. Am I to serve young Edward or his brother?'

'Of course not. The people call on you to take the throne.'

'Because Richard has usurped it? *I* am to be usurper in his place, is that what the people want?'

They assured him that the problem of the young Princes would be solved.

'I am glad to hear it,' he replied. 'For I shall make no move until it *is* solved.'

He was well aware, if his uncle was not, that at this moment the people, far from calling on him, were scarce aware of his existence. A lot of work needed to be done before he would be advised to declare himself. It was this, as much as the problem of the Princes, which concerned him. It was, however, his comments regarding the Princes which were best remembered by one or two of his listeners.

3

The crown had left a weal on Richard's forehead, it was still visible today, a faint red mark like a burn. He was the thirteenth Plantagenet (he did not count young Edward) to wear the crown and regarded it as his inalienable right as had those other kings who had ruled by right of heredity or by right of conquest; all linked by Plantagenet blood and sharing the same passionate belief in their right to wear the crown. He felt both humble and proud and was determined to be the greatest of all the Plantagenet kings. He who tries for less has no right to rule.

Ideas great and small tumbled into his mind in bewildering disarray: he would bring order and justice to the realm; he would take strong measures to suppress local tyranny and abuse; he would improve the system of empanelling jurors; he would reform the laws concerning the conveying of land; and he would abolish the King's own right to exact money from his subjects by means of benevolences; above all, he would create a Council of the North which would bring lasting peace to that troubled land he loved so well. His heart was filled with a passionate desire to serve England and its people. He prayed earnestly for God's help and guidance, and while he prayed he rubbed his forefinger along the weal on his forehead where the crown had marked him. It was one of his weaknesses that he concerned himself too much with detail so that it was not enough to vow to improve the jury system by ensuring that only persons of good name and fame should be empanelled, but he must go on to think about what freehold land a man of good name and fame might be expected to hold. He felt his head would burst with the pressure of ideas before ever he could bring them to fruition. The trouble with being a king is that one has less, and not more, time for ruling. First, the king must show himself to the people throughout the country. His royal progress, which would begin next week, would take many months; it was important and he looked forward to it, yet he begrudged the time.

There were other considerations, the thought of which now darkened his mind. Yesterday he and his wife, Anne, had been to see his nephews in the Tower.

Edward was nervous and kept probing his jaw; when he was not doing this he held his jaw cupped in one hand as though it would otherwise fall out of place. The jaw was red and swollen; the rest of the boy's face was like a wet, grey dough. He looked unwholesome and Richard thought, 'This is no kin of mine!'

The younger boy, although by nature the livelier of the two, looked all the while to his brother for a lead as though he had no will of his own.

'Have you the toothache?' Anne asked Edward, trying to keep the sharpness from her voice; she was impatient of her own sickness and doubly so when she saw it mirrored in others.

Edward shook his head, sullen as well as sick. The younger boy momentarily transferred his eyes to Anne without turning his head; the eyes travelled down the length of her gown from the cloth of gold trimming at the neck to the tips of her shoes pointing out from the hem of the skirt, and back again, to rest momentarily on her face. His eyes registered that intense hostility which only children are prepared to display unmasked.

'How long have you had the swelling?' Richard asked, wondering if it was contagious.

'I don't remember.' Edward moved his jaw with difficulty, either because it was stiff or because he did not wish to be communicative, it was difficult to tell which.

'I will send my doctor to you.' Richard tried to make it sound as though he was giving the boy something which no one else would have thought to offer him.

Edward said, 'Thank you, Sire.'

Anne said, 'And I will send you some grapes.'

The younger boy's mouth twitched in a sneer. She could have struck him. The coronation had taken a heavy toll of her and she had not the strength for too many complications in her life now. All her resources of love were centred on Richard, she had no concern to spare for others. The children aroused nothing in her but anger for being in the way; she would have been as angry with her own son had he tried to tug at her weary heart at this time.

Richard said, 'This is an oppressive place.' He leant towards Edward. When Edward was a child at court he had taken him by the hand and tried to reassure him; he remembered the childish fingers gripping his hand, holding to someone known and safe. He wanted to win the boy's trust again. 'I myself dislike London,' he said. 'I am never easy here. It would be better for you to be far away from London. . . .' He broke off.

Edward's dull eyes had brightened, but it was fear that brought them to life. Richard, looking into those eyes was as shocked as if some terrible obscenity had been revealed to him. His face went red, and then slowly drained of colour. Anne, looking at him, stretched out a hand and held it poised just above his sleeve, not daring to touch him. Edward sat transfixed by terror, but the younger boy, quicker and more alert, jumped up and whirled out of the room. As he ran down the corridor he shouted to someone whom he recognized and it was the urgency of his cries that brought Richard to himself.

'We waste our time here.'

He and Anne went out of the Princes' chamber. At the end of the corridor, in the half-light, they could see the younger boy huddled close against the robe of a priest. Richard walked slowly towards the man who remained still, one hand on the boy's shoulder.

'Have you charge of these children?' he asked the priest, a gaunt man with a sardonic face that spoke more of concourse with the Devil than God. The priest bowed his head.

'What is your name?'

'Dr Christopher Ormond, Sire.'

'Who appointed you?'

'The Bishop of Ely.'

'The Bishop of Ely!' Richard exclaimed, thinking that it was a mistake that any appointment of Morton's should have continued in contact with the Princes. He said to the priest, 'Your charges do you little credit! They suffer from nightmares and start at shadows.'

The man gazed down at the boy huddled beside him; there was no humility in his face and Richard, looking at him intently, had that same impression of something evil which he had so recently glimpsed in Edward's eyes. Here, perhaps, was the source of that evil. He would have this man investigated.

'Take the child back to his chamber and leave him there,' he commanded the priest. 'I will see that he is attended to.'

He and Anne watched while the priest walked quietly with the boy to his chamber; he went inside and stayed perhaps for only as little as three minutes, but long enough to make Richard the more suspicious.

'I have seen that man before.' Anne searched her memory but failed to identify Ormond, just as Ormond himself saw no connection between the haggard Queen and the little owlet fugitive whom he had once pitied.

'He has some hold over the children,' Richard said to Anne. 'They will be better once they are away from him.'

But the sense of evil was not so easily dispelled. That night he dreamt that his nephews were dead and he cried and tried to revive them and woke crying for his own dear son.

The day following, Buckingham came to him wanting instructions about arrangements for the Princes while Richard was on his progress; Buckingham was now Constable of England and seemed to feel that this made him responsible for everything that happened in the realm.

'Edward is not well,' Richard said. 'And neither is it well that he should be seen so often. The sight of him and his brother aggravates an already inflamed condition in the people of this city.'

'I see.'

'What do you see?' He looked at Buckingham with eyes that were dark and not friendly.

Buckingham said, 'Why, simply that your nephew is not well.'

Richard continued to stare at him. Then he said, 'He has some childish ailment from which he will no doubt recover. Perhaps I will move him to the north where the atmosphere will be better for him.' It was not possible to guess what was going on in his mind, but it was apparent he was uneasy. He said wearily, 'We will not talk any more of this.'

'But others will talk, are talking in fact. . . .'

Richard said, 'I will not talk of this now.' He was angry. 'I have much to do.' Presumably as evidence of this, he left the room.

So, Buckingham thought, he has taken no decision; his uneasiness and ill-temper were proof of that. It was not easy to guess what his eventual action might be. Buckingham stood by the window, not trying to guess. One thing was certain, whichever way things went and whatever path he himself might take, nothing could be resolved while the Princes lived.

Richard was angered by his nephews. He was angered

because their eyes told him he had earned their fear. He knew that to delay a decision regarding their future was to endanger their lives; yet he delayed and let strange thoughts hover on the fringe of his mind and at night he dreamt again that the children were dead. And so it went on.

Buckingham watched and waited. The day came when on the morrow Richard would set out on his progress. There were other matters to discuss beside the Princes.

Buckingham had been made Constable of England and Great Chamberlain and was promised considerable grants of land. Richard had raised him high. But others had also been given great power, in particular John Howard, now Duke of Norfolk, and Henry Percy, Duke of Northumberland. Buckingham was liked by neither of these men. Norfolk was too close to Richard to be criticised openly, but Buckingham took it upon himself to warn Richard of Henry Percy.

'You have made him Warden of the Scots Marches; yet he shows little pleasure at having been raised to such great power.'

'Nothing would ever please a Percy,' Richard smiled. 'And as for being "raised to such great power", I have no doubt he would remind you that it is only the restoration of a small part of the power once vested in his ancestors.'

Percy, had he chosen to speak, would have gone further than that. He would have said that nothing would please a Percy while a king sat on the throne who exercised any power over the North, which he considered to be as much the inheritance of the Percys as Richard regarded the throne as the inheritance of the Plantagenets. Percy, however, had departed north having said very little, and Richard had more immediate problems to deal with, namely the government in London while he was on his progress. John Russell, the Bishop of Lincoln, now the Chancellor, was to be in charge of the group of councillors who would stay behind in London.

Buckingham begrudged Russell this power, not because he wanted it for himself, but because power granted to any other man diminished him. Richard had valued him above all others and had rewarded him accordingly. But the old loyalties had struck deep roots and already Buckingham was aware that there was an understanding between Richard and men like Norfolk and Lovell which needed no words or fine gestures. Buckingham stood outside this harmonious circle. He was as uneasy as a spoilt child who can only assess his value by the worth of the gifts bestowed upon him and who, therefore, demands a never-ending supply of gifts. He could even be jealous of Stanley, who was to accompany Richard on his progress.

'Do you think it wise to have Stanley at your side?'

Richard laughed, 'Better at my side than behind my back!'

Buckingham toyed with a ring on his finger, his dissatisfied mind flitting here and there. Presently he said, 'It is Stanley's wife to whom you should look. I hear she is in touch with her son, the so-called Earl of Richmond, exhorting him to declare against you.' He had no certain knowledge of this but was prompted by a desire to talk about the Earl of Richmond who increasingly occupied his thought.

Richard shrugged his shoulders. 'It would be unlikely were it not the case, knowing the determined character of Margaret Beaufort.'

'And her son?'

'You think that Henry Tudor intends to invade the country in order to restore my nephew to the throne? It could be so; certainly he has reason to be sympathetic to bastards.'

Buckingham had not intended to raise the issue of the Princes again, but now Richard himself had spoken of them he said, 'If it is not Henry Tudor, it will be someone else e'er long. They have only to show themselves practising archery on the Green, or looking from a window, to attract interest. And that interest will soon stir someone to mischief.'

Richard said slowly, 'I have been thinking about them. I do not intend that they should remain behind while I am out of London. It would be wiser for them to be transferred to Pontefract.'

'Pontefract has an evil reputation.'

The two men looked at each other. Buckingham thought of Richard the Second who had met Death at Pontefract; it was hard to tell what Richard the Third was thinking, his face was inscrutable. 'Then this will be an opportunity to amend that reputation,' he said quietly. His eyes held Buckingham's, dark and still. He, too, has Death in his mind, Buckingham thought. Richard looked away. He said, 'The arrangements I leave to you.' There was silence in the room. Afterwards, when he looked back on that scene, Richard would maintain that he regretted not having given Buckingham explicit instructions. Yet in that silence he was as close to Buckingham as he had ever been.

Soon after this, the two men parted. Buckingham, going out into the night air, felt the wind gentle against his face and marvelled how providence will suddenly throw a gift to a man. He was not the man to refuse a gift.

So Richard went on his progress and Buckingham was left in London. Life had lost its savour, it was flat and stale. He was at the beginning of his power yet there was nothing ahead of him. As he rode through the city he found people bustling about their business just as before. It was amazing the way the common people went on with their mundane lives as though great events were quite irrelevant to them. Buckingham would not normally have noticed this, but now he was so empty that alien thoughts filled his emptiness. They came in bewildering succession, these thoughts, like a charade played out within him by a troop of players, rascally characters, some of them.

Gradually, he became aware of the plots and counter-plots being hatched in the city, whose people were not so uncaring of great events as he had thought. It was like a heart-beat sounding again, a pulse bringing him back to life. He could not have enough of rumour and would take it from any who proffered it.

Buckingham used the rumours as an excuse for discussing Richard with other powerful men. He was interested in assessing the strength of Richard's position. There was no questioning the loyalty of men like Norfolk and Lovell; but others might be less unwavering in their allegiance. Russell, Bishop of Lincoln, and now Chancellor, had served Edward the Fourth well, but the example of Hastings and Morton showed that those who had served Edward were not necessarily friends of Richard.

'How little one can rely on the people of London,' Buckingham said to Russell. 'Already there are rumours abroad that treachery is planned.'

The Chancellor, a man with an invariably benevolent smile and bright, shrewd eyes which missed little, said gently, 'There were the same rumours in Edward's reign. It does no harm. As long as rumours are allowed to circulate we all know what is happening.'

Buckingham, who only thought men dangerous if they showed their steel, said, 'Do you think the Londoners will support Richard as they supported Edward?'

'They didn't always support Edward.' Russell was beaming now, his fingers steepled under his chin as he recalled the situation in those days. 'They only supported him at the end, when he owed so many of them money they would have lost all hope of repayment had he been defeated.'

'And Richard? Does this apply to him?'

'Hardly!' Russell was gently disapproving, as though rebuking a dull pupil. 'He is concerned with justice and good government. He doesn't understand yet that they have to be paid for; Edward always provided the money and Richard thought it grew on trees. But he'll learn. He'll never be as artful as his brother, but he's no fool. Given time, he'll learn.'

Had that 'given time' had a sinister ring? Russell's bright eyes were without guile.

Time, Buckingham thought: years stretching ahead while Richard masters the tedious business of financing his tedious reforms! It was not a future that appealed to Buckingham, or one in which he saw a place for himself.

Russell did not see a place for Buckingham either: an unstable man who would shine brightly for a short while and then fizzle out like a spent firecracker. This was another lesson Richard would have to learn.

Buckingham, having gained little from his talk with Russell, was soon to find a man who could offer something better than rumour. Robin Prithie came to him with a new and rather more likely tale to tell. It was said on good authority that the Earl of Richmond was reluctant to move while the young Princes lived. As he listened, Buckingham felt energy flow back into his body; he could have embraced the rapscallion who stood before him. How foolish to have imagined it was all over, this business of kingmaking! The future was his: Richard had provided him with the key and Henry Tudor bade him use it.

Late that afternoon, he went to see Sir Robert Brackenbury, the Constable of the Tower, and took the opportunity to talk to the young Princes. Their meal had been provided in their chamber. Edward, who ate very slowly, was still at table. The younger boy was standing by the window moving pieces about on a chess board and making nonsense of any game which had been set up. The two children regarded Buckingham warily, as they regarded all visitors now.

'Well, now, what is this!' Buckingham strode across to the chess table. He knew little about the game but had never allowed himself to be daunted by lack of knowledge.

'It isn't anything,' the young boy said indifferently. 'Dr Ormond set the pieces, but he is not allowed to see us any more, so it doesn't matter.'

'Did you like Dr Ormond?' Buckingham asked.

'Yes.' The boy replied so wretchedly one might have thought him desolated by the loss of Ormond; whereas the desolation lay in the fact of having no one to like save the unattractive Ormond.

'You may see him again soon,' Buckingham improvised. 'As you know, you are to move from here and he will be waiting for you at Pontefract.'

The boy looked at Buckingham doubtfully, biting his thumb nail. At the table, Edward had put down his knife and was staring at Buckingham. Buckingham moved away from the

chess table and gave his attention to Edward. He talked about
the arrangements for the move and the advantages of life at
Pontefract. His nature was such that once embarked on any
discourse be believed what he was saying, and was now so taken
up with winning the children's approval to the move that he
quite forgot that they would never reach Pontefract. Edward
was still chewing some meat. As Buckingham talked, the boy
moved his jaw in an awkward, brutish fashion and gravy ran
down the side of his mouth. The jaw was swollen and this
distorted his face unpleasantly. Depression dulled his eyes, and
to Buckingham it seemed that the last spark of intelligence had
flickered and died. He was shocked and thought there was
something monstrous about the boy. The younger boy, still
standing by the window, was at present without blemish; but
how soon would it be before this evil marked him, too? As
Buckingham talked to the children, the last of his compunction
ran out with the dwindling daylight.

He went to see Sir Robert Brackenbury to tell him of the
move. Brackenbury, a blunt, thick-set Yorkshireman, appeared
not to have noticed anything monstrous about either of his
charges, and even spoke of them with rough affection.

'I wouldn't want any bairns of mine cooped up here,' he
said. 'I'll be glad to see them go. They'll fare much better up
north.' He shared the view of all Yorkshiremen that the south
was a treacherous place and that a man could only be expected
to thrive in a bleak landscape with a bitter climate. Buckingham
was not disposed to argue with him. He talked briefly about the
arrangements for the move and then left the Tower.

It was a murky evening with a grey mist curling up from the
river; Buckingham felt a sickness in the air that nothing would
cleanse until they were rid of this bestial thing. He felt justified,
his mission purified. He had needed this certainty and it had
been vouchsafed him. As usual, feeling ran away with him, and
he saw himself as taking on the mantle of the saviour who grants
release from evil, who protects by his strength. Richard needed
him, Henry Tudor needed him; who knew but that one day
England might need him?

Chapter 14

I

There were pilgrims on their way out of London; they were
singing, this being the beginning of their journey and their

spirits high. The roads were not safe for the lone wayfarer and people usually banded together, so as well as the pilgrims the cavalcade included merchants, clerks, jugglers, a bear-baiter, scholars and stone-masons. It was a fine day and for one reason or another most of the company were in a hopeful frame of mind. Robin Prithie, however, had small reason for hope.

The Duke of Buckingham, who had been well-pleased to receive the information which Robin brought to him, had revealed another side of his character on their last encounter. It was only by the chance slip of a foot that Robin was with the pilgrims on this high summer day.

'You will be rewarded,' Buckingham had assured Robin when they last met. The Duke's manner had changed. As soon as Robin entered the little room where the Duke always received him, he was conscious of a change in temperature. The room was like a vault, yet the sun shone and through the open window came the sound of bees, drowsy with heat. The cold was inside the room. Buckingham was studying a roll of parchment on the table in front of him, he did not look up immediately and when eventually he glanced at Robin, only the eyes moved; Robin saw that the frost had been at them. Buckingham listened to Robin and asked a few questions, but those eyes which previously had watched Robin's face so avidly, now had no real concern with him and the occasional smile was only a crack in the ice.

From the far side of a green lawn, near the stables, children who should have been otherwise employed were playing, their excited voices piping a round. Robin wished profoundly that he was out there with the children, and perhaps this thought communicated itself to Buckingham. He stopped talking and for a few seconds it was so quiet that the room seemed full of the children's nonsense. Then Buckingham crossed the room and closed the window. The idea sidled into Robin's mind that the Duke wished the Princes might be silenced as easily. Then, as Buckingham turned to face into the room, his eyes met Robin's and Robin realized that murder was indeed on his mind. At this moment, the two men understood each other too well for Robin's good. It was then that Buckingham said, not bothering to cloak his meaning, 'You will be rewarded.'

Buckingham summoned two of his retainers to escort Robin and to give him his reward. They were strong, thick-set men and needed to be so, Robin reflected grimly, else the weapons they carried must surely have weighed them down. He was relieved to see that they were leading him towards the door by which he had entered. At least he was not to be done to death here and now. When they came out into the sunshine, he said, 'If you leave me here, I'll find my own way out through the stables yonder.'

'And forgo your reward?'

'I have no thought of reward,' Robin assured them. 'It is enough to be of service to so noble a lord as your master.'

There was silence while they walked across the lawn and the men digested this sentiment; from their expressions and heavy breathing it seemed to lie like lead on their chests. They came to a gate in a high brick wall and one of the men produced a key and unlocked the gate beyond which was another high brick wall; the thin alley between the two walls led towards the river where Robin could see the sun glinting on water and a small rowing boat chafing at a stake. The tide was flowing towards the Great Bridge.

'It will be safer for you to leave by the river today,' one of the men said.

The brick walls came to an end where a willow bowed over the water. Robin, not usually given to admiring Nature's effects, felt his heart contract with wonder at such effortless grace. This evening, when the first cool breath came off the river, the willow would shiver gratefully, while he. . . . He was staggered by the monstrous impropriety of it all; but by the time they came to the river's edge he was thinking calmly, 'It will be wiser to go with them in the boat. I can't be worse off on the river than here on firm ground where a man can more easily wield a weapon.' There was a lot of traffic on the river and it would surely be too cynical, even for the powerful Buckingham, to have a man murdered by his retainers in full view of so many gaping citizens. But then Robin remembered how fast the current ran, and how little chance a man would have were he unfortunate enough to go overboard, especially near the Great Bridge.

By now, one of the men was in the boat and had motioned Robin to join him. Robin put one foot over the side of the boat and then his other foot slipped on wet stone; forgetting everything else in an attempt to regain his balance, he grabbed frantically at the man standing beside him. They swayed drunkenly, Robin clutching at his companion as though nothing more was at stake than saving himself a wetting. The man tried to free himself, and while he had his mouth wide open cursing Robin, they both pitched forward into the river.

The man in the boat shouted, 'Stop him! Stop him!' but his companion had his lungs too full of water to heed him. The little boat was swinging round aimlessly and Robin, blinking water from his eyes, saw that one of the oars was floating out towards the centre of the river. He followed it; indeed he had little choice for already the tide carried him. The man in the boat was shouting, 'Stop him! Stop him!' He might have saved himself the trouble and let Robin do his own drowning, but he was in too much of a panic to leave anything to chance. Men rowing a boat loaded with pigs and poultry lent their voices to his, and several small craft manoeuvred towards Robin; but he was carried away from them towards the centre of the river. His 'rescue' was effected by one of the crew of a big barge who threw a rope to him.

'Bring him back here!' Buckingham's retainer called as Robin was hauled aboard the barge. The cry was faint, but it was taken up by voices in boats nearer and came clearly enough to Robin's ears when he had drummed the water from them. The men standing around him, however, appeared smitten by deafness. The barge was on its way to the docks beyond the Great Bridge and they were anxious to shoot the Bridge before the current became too strong. Delay would mean that they would have to wait another tide.

Now the situation seemed very much brighter. Fate, as usual, had looked after Robin Prithie; Buckingham's men would undoubtedly keep watch for him at the gates leading out of the city and the river represented the best way of escape. At the docks he would get aboard a ship for France and all would be well. He leant his elbows on the rail and looked towards that eighth wonder of the world, that floating city, the Great Bridge, without fear that he would be sucked into the torrent beneath it. Fate, however, was in capricious mood. The men on the barge had had second thoughts and now decided that it would not be wise to take him beyond the city walls. For a moment he thought that they, too, planned to throw him overboard, but instead they hailed one of the watermen and told him to put Robin ashore at a wharf near Queenhithe.

Ten minutes later Robin was shivering in a narrow alley at the back of a warehouse. He wondered how this had happened to him. When he was young people had said how 'knowing' he was, and he had cultivated this talent, as talents should be cultivated. Whoever would have thought knowing could lead to this? It wasn't how he used his knowledge that mattered, whether he was discreet or untrustworthy was immaterial, it was the knowing that was his doom. There was nothing he could do since he could not unknow it. He was caught in a trap he had not foreseen when he began to trade in knowledge.

And what knowledge! Even in his miserable state, and little given as he was to thinking of others, he spared a prayer for the Princes, but forgot them when ahead he saw an inn of the kind frequented by beggars and ruffians which might provide an answer to one of his problems. His clothes, though wet, were of good cloth and he was able to exchange them for the robes of a nun who had but lately died in this place while giving birth to a child. She must have been a big woman for the robe was long and the girdle had to be drawn tight to enable Robin to walk; but this was no bad thing, since it restricted his gait to one more appropriate to a woman.

Soon he was on his way and now Fortune favoured her darling once more. As he came into Budge Row he saw a slow straggle of men and women coming from the direction of St Paul's and on enquiry learnt that they were pilgrims on their way to a shrine at a distant place which they would not reach for many weeks. What more natural than that a nun, seeking an excuse to adventure beyond the priory walls, should form one of this humble company?

The pilgrims wound their way to the Great Bridge, singing as they went, and Robin walked well to the centre, his head bowed. As he had feared, Buckingham's men were waiting at the gates; they stopped the pilgrims and asked questions of the man they took to be the leader, although no one man could know the business of all the diverse people gathered here. Their examination of the pilgrims was cursory and the cavalcade was soon inching its way across the Bridge. There was quite a forest of heads on the poles decorating the Drawbridge Gate, some with hair and beards remarkably well-groomed while others looked as though they were left over from King Edward the Fourth's days. When he was young, Robin had laughed at such sights, saying if a man was fool enough to be caught he deserved what came to him. But now, wits not so nimble, nor so fleet of foot, these spectacles became more distasteful. He took no last look at the city when they had safely crossed the Bridge.

He was not the only fugitive in that company. Robin had seen death in Buckingham's eyes: Christopher Ormond had seen it in King Richard's eyes and his own death at that. How strange that he whose aspect was so forbidding should have been undone because a frightened child had run to him for protection! He kept his head low and rode hunched on his horse. The men at the Bridge were not looking for him—King Richard's men did their master better service than this and he would not have escaped them—but they were a reminder of the need to be careful. So, too, were the heads. He heeded their warning, but it was his hand not his neck which itched and he felt flames licking up from the hot stones.

It was dark by the time the pilgrims reached their first stop at a town in a narrow valley with houses built so haphazard on the hill slopes it seemed that at any moment they must fold up and come tumbling down on the inn, itself a precarious-looking structure in half-timber and white-washed plaster. They ate in a big hall already crowded with other travellers, very hot and clamorous. Ormond, not usually sociable, kept close to the other pilgrims. It would be wise to remain with them during the first two or three stops in case men came searching the inns. When he felt he was safe, he would set out for Brecknock and there try to get word to John Morton. Morton was Buckingham's prisoner, but it was reported that he was living in conditions which were not uncomfortable and Ormond thought there was a chance that he might be allowed to receive visitors.

When they had eaten, the pilgrims departed to the sleeping quarters. The women's quarters were in a long, low building little better than a lazar house in Robin's view. It was a long time since he had been so uncomfortably lodged; not, to be precise, since that journey to St. Malo when Henry Tudor was all but taken by King Edward the Fourth's men. How might life have turned out for Robin had that adventure ended differently? Overlooking the fact that he had first attempted to poison his master, and was now in trouble as a result of trying to sell information to Buckingham, he blamed Henry for his recent woes. The broken wrist which had never mended properly ached as a reminder of Henry's spite.

The heat was stifling and it was over an hour before the other occupants of the room settled down. When they were quiet, Robin went outside, hoping to steal a horse. There were few people about now but a light burnt high in the church, like an evil eye looking down on the little town.

2

Now, when he least wanted it, how belief surged up, how it began to curl around Ormond! He was in the winter of life and if he played his hand well and Morton eventually came back into power, advancement might lie ahead of him; his last days would then be honourable, to say nothing of comfortable. This was no time to find himself negotiating the testing ground of belief. It was cold in the church, which was surprising when one considered what a hot day it had been. He would have to break his vigil and go outside again; something, he didn't think it was compassion, had loosened his bowels.

Man is small, helpless, he thought in uncharacteristically humble mood as he squatted looking up at the dark hills massed above the town. What can such as I do for princes in danger? Could I say: I have seen them playing on the green, merry as children should be, yet bearing the mark of those who are doomed like the children the fairies spirit away because they are too lovely for mortal life? That would rightly be dismissed as superstitious rubbish. Added to which, these children were not lovely; apart from being princes, and standing in the way of a throne, they were unremarkable. But that was no consolation, their very plainness only made their fate harder to bear. 'I have done all I can,' he told himself. 'At least, all that it was wise for me to do.'

Nevertheless, he returned to the church. It was after midnight now; he would stay here and make intercession for them until the dawn came and he must be on his way.

Before it was quite dark, the children had had their effects packed and had been told to wait in their chamber until the men came to take them on their journey.

'You are going north,' Brackenbury told them. 'You will like that.'

'We shall not like it,' Edward said firmly. 'We want to stay here and be near our mother.'

It was the worst argument he could have put to Brackenbury who was not entirely happy about what was happening. Brackenbury would have been hard put to it to have explained his disquiet. He knew that Richard had at one time spoken of putting the children in charge of the Earl of Lincoln, and moving them to Sheriff Hutton. There was nothing untoward in the decision that they should be sent north. Perhaps it was Buckingham's repeated insistence that this was the will of the King which rang false in Brackenbury's ears. Buckingham liked power and it was more usual for him to assume responsibilities that were not his than to take shelter in the King's authority. Edward's remark about his mother, however, served to remind Brackenbury that there were good and sufficient reasons for removing the princes from London.

The starlings were in flight, like ashes born before the wind. Colour was draining from the sky, one gash of pink, the rest grey. Was there no one, no one among these grim, gaunt men whose heart could be touched? What change had come about since the days when they had romped with their father and quarrelled as to who should play the King? When had life been wrung dry of love? Where was their mother, why did she not come to them? So many questions: no answers.

Edward said, 'We should pray. Our Lord Jesus will protect us from harm.'

They knelt on the floor, hand in hand, and Edward prayed while his brother stared up at the bars at the window. There were swifts swooping round the battlements, later there were bats; and, in the last level light before it was quite dark, a white owl glided by on silent wings. Still Edward prayed.

The younger boy said, 'My knees are hurting.' He was kneeling on a crack and could not bear it another minute whatever might happen to him in another hour. He got up and rubbed vigorously at one knee. 'Look, it's got a furrow in it!'

There were footsteps in the corridor. It was a relief that the time of waiting was over and they felt a lightening of their spirits as they were mounted and the horses clattered across the yard. Some little flicker of exitement, a feeling of embarking on an adventure, spurted into brief life when they left the city behind. They passed a wayside gibbet and the young boy thought he would like to be a robber and live in very wild country where there was no one to tell him what he might and might not do. Edward imagined he was setting out on a crusade.

At first, the night was bright and stars came right down round the edge of the fields. A group of vagabonds, who tomorrow would harrow town dwellers with a story of how they had not eaten for many days, feasted round a fire. Further on, a lantern swung from side to side and soon they passed a peasant singing drunkenly as he made his uneven way to his village. The village when reached was a cluster of cottages surrounding a church and manor house. Edward wondered what it would be like to live in one of those cottages so snugly hunched into the earth. The fancy, bringing him nearer home than the crusade, left him disquieted, so that he noted with misgivings that ahead the country grew wilder. The road ran along the edge of a wood. Soon it began to climb steadily. On the skyline a stag stood sentinel guarding the pass into his territory; it put its head back, but no sound came and after a few moments it turned and trotted into the wood. Soon after this, the moon went down. One of the men said it was a black night, and another man agreed that it was indeed. They could tell that they were moving out of the shelter of the trees because there was a smell of fern and bracken and the wind had become desolate.

'We are on the moor,' the man who appeared to be in charge said. He reined in his horse. 'We will rest here.'

'A strange place to rest,' Edward thought.

'You go ahead and make sure we are awaited. We will follow more slowly.' The men to whom he spoke rode off as though the devil was at their heels; only one other man remained.

Edward's mind was cold as ice. He thought: they will wait until the others are out of earshot. He slid quietly from his horse and pulled his brother down beside him. Then the ice broke and terror surged up. 'Run!' he urged. 'Run to the woods!'

In that darkness they would have done better to have gone to earth, but terror drove them stumbling forward with shaking limbs over ground on which they made no more headway than if it had been treacle. Their pursuers, who had paused to grab a lantern, could hear them thrashing about in the heather. Edward ran, dragging his brother with him. The effort to keep ahead of terror was too much; it was a relief when the men came close. He flung his arms round his brother and bore him to the ground; he lay on top of him as the men stood over them. In the tiny pause that followed he felt the terror would cleave him in two. But when it happened, it was such a little thing; after all that fuss, such a little thing, just a blow in the back, nothing to have been so frightened about. His father slapped him on the back and shouted, 'You shall have my cloak, Edward. Look how fine you are!' It was warm and dark, his fingers scrabbled at it, trying to pull it from his face, but it was too heavy. He coughed and nurse said, '*And* again! Let's have it all up.' He wanted his mother, she was there somewhere beyond the cloak; his fingers stretched out, but he couldn't, couldn't quite. . . .

The men dug a shallow grave in a small clearing in the wood. They worked by the light of the lantern and this attracted many creatures who came to stare just beyond the ring of light. They buried the children at first light and not a cock did crow.

3

On his progress a King must show himself to the people so that they can see with what wisdom and benevolence they will be governed.

'If King Richard be as good at doing as he be at promising, then we have a right good King and no mistaking.' This remark, overheard in an inn at Reading, well summed-up the impression which the King had made in the towns through which he had passed on his progress. The people had yet to be won; but they were well-disposed to the new King and prepared to give him a fair trial. They marked his piety, respected his love of learning, and agreed such attributes would do no harm provided they did not distract him from his avowed intention of bringing law and order to the realm and dealing with the complaints of the poor (by whom they took him to mean themselves). They also enjoyed the festivities put on for his benefit and were relieved when he modestly refused the sums of money offered to him. This gesture greatly diverted Henry, Earl of Richmond, when it was later reported to him. 'For myself,' he said gravely, 'I had rather not so offend the people.'

Richard, however, was much in earnest. He offered what he intended to fulfil; most important of all, he offered himself in the sure knowledge that no one was better fitted to rule than he.

After visiting Reading and Oxford, he was well-content by the time he reached Minster Lovell where he stayed with his friend Viscount Lovell. It was here, on a hot, sultry day, that he was joined by Buckingham who had ridden straight from London on his way to his Castle in Brecknock. A little less than three months had passed since their meeting at Northampton. They had accomplished much together in that time and had now been apart but a few days; yet as they greeted each other some warmth was lacking. Perhaps it is that early friendships seldom need renewing whereas the friendships formed in later years can scarce stand a separation. Whatever the reason, Richard was not at first disposed to talk in private with Buckingham. That countenance which had glowed with such unalloyed enthusiasm now seemed tarnished by the London air; the eyes stored rumour, the lips were impatient to spill out news of dissension. As though warding off some deeper evil that he saw in that face, Richard began to talk of his plans to Lovell and his companions.

'The country has had too much of strife. We must put this behind us. Many of our poorer subjects, through no fault of their own, have lost goods and property, and these must be compensated.' His concern for the poor had not prevented him spending lavishly on his attire and Buckingham's eyes dwelt enviously on the cloth of gold robe with its beautiful collar encrusted with gems and pearls. 'We must set an example to those lords who are not of our mind and who continue to abuse the people. I am told, for example, that the goods of people charged with felony are often seized before conviction. . . .'

'You will have to take your time, Dickon,' Lovell warned, knowing that persuasion was not one of Richard's gifts, and doubting the wisdom of some of the more far-reaching of the proposed reforms.

Buckingham reflected grimly that all the common people wanted was a strong king. Show a man your mailed fist and he will respect it!

'Time is something one cannot take for granted.' Richard had always been impatient and now was increasingly inclined to live as though each day was his last. The energy he had displayed on his progress had already worn out Lord Stanley, who had taken to his bed with a stomach ailment and begged to be excused the morrow's celebrations in Gloucester.

William Herbert, who was acting as Richard's secretary in the absence of John Kendall, now brought a letter for signature. As Buckingham watched the lighted taper applied to the sealing wax something inside himself seemed to melt and flow hot through his veins. Only three months ago, it had been Richard, Duke of Gloucester, and Henry, Duke of Buckingham. But now. . . . He thought how the name 'Richard' appended to a document could confer honour on a city, send a man to the scaffold, detain another at his pleasure, ransack the coffers of the wealthy, set an army on the march. . . . A wave of burning nausea came over him as the pen scratched on the parchment; he could not bear that 'Richard' should have so much more power than 'Henry'. He moved to the window alcove. It had begun to rain, warm summer rain falling in great drops on the sun-baked earth. A few small birds fluttered about excitedly.

'And what news do you bring us?'

Richard was speaking to him. Buckingham turned to him with an effort and said hoarsely, 'News for your ears, alone.'

Richard raised his eyebrows, not pleased; he had no appetite for bad news at this time. He found another matter on which to instruct Herbert and then must add a note in his own hand to a letter already written. His mood was incalculable and Buckingham, who seldom thought ahead, wished he had prepared himself better for this meeting.

When they were alone in a little room off the hall normally used by the clerks, Richard said, 'And now, what is this dread news that you have to impart? Is Mistress Shore not confined in Newgate, Elizabeth Woodville not in sanctuary at West Minster?' His tone was amused, but he made it plain that he was in no mood to listen to idle rumour and would not be grateful to the bearer of serious news of conspiracy.

Buckingham, left with no choice but to displease, said, 'The Princes, Sire.'

Richard said, 'Ah, yes,' as though he was summoning

half-forgotten figures from a distant past. 'I proposed to send them to Sheriff Hutton in the charge of my nephew, the Earl of Lincoln, was not that it?'

'You proposed to send them to Pontefract and left the arrangements to me.'

'Ah, well.' Richard looked at him with some reserve. 'I have changed my mind.'

Buckingham watched a pool of water collecting on the window ledge. The rain was coming down heavily now, darkening the room.

Richard said, 'You do not approve of this proposal?'

'You will never be secure while they live, any more than your brother was secure while Henry the Sixth lived. I speak, not to please you, Sire, but being prepared to risk your displeasure because I have such great concern for you.'

'And my brother's other children? His daughters. Am I to do away with them, also? For if I do not, then may I not be endangered by the Princess Elizabeth? No! This matter must be allowed to rest on the issue of their illegitimacy, not on the disappearance of the whole brood! If you have lost your sense of proportion, at least keep your sense of humour.' He was in doubtful humour himself and there was no little malice now directed at Buckingham; the man who had been raised high must be taught that there was a point beyond which he might not presume. 'Would you have me spend my time inventing reasons for their disappearance one by one? How many daughters are there . . . let me see, three, four. . . . What arrant nonsense! I have better work to do. And when it is done the people will give me their loyalty because they see that I am a good and just ruler.' He rapped the table sharply with his knuckles to emphasize this.

Buckingham said, 'It was not of goodness and justice that we talked that day at Northampton when we had to put a stop to Rivers' ambitions.'

'What is that to us now?'

'To me it is everything!' Feeling always came spontaneously to Buckingham when he needed it; now it surged up and he spoke as one deeply moved. 'We were so at one on that occasion speech was scarce needed between us; we looked in each other's eyes and read a common purpose there. We were not poets, visionaries, judges, but men who saw their situation clearly and knew what must be done. We were strong and resolute.'

Richard said, 'So are we still. Tell me your news.' His voice was soft, but his eyes said, 'Beware!'

Buckingham, who was now intensely eager to recapture that

lost identity of interest, felt himself betrayed by this cool, dispassionate stranger. He held his head high and answered, 'When we last spoke of the Princes you left matters in my hands. Did you think I would not act, when all our understanding has been proved in action?'

'So, you acted. Well?'

'You asked that the Princes should be transferred to Pontefract. I took you at your word, as I have ever done.'

'And?'

'They set out for Pontefract, three nights ago.' Buckingham had had little idea up to this moment what he would say, but the words came readily enough, so readily that while he spoke he believed. 'It seemed better to me that they should travel at night, their movements unobserved by any who might wish to harm them. They were accompanied by a small party of men who were recommended to me by Sir James Tyrrell, who serves you well. On my way here, however, I received disturbing news. Two of these men, both of whom should even now be proceeding with the Princes, were seen in London by one of my most trusted men who had reason to be searching an inn near the docks. I sent a messenger with orders that they be taken into custody, and I also sent word to the Chancellor. Then I came here to inform you as speedily as I could.' When he stopped speaking he could feel a pulse thudding in his throat.

Richard watched Buckingham, his face impassive, three fingers of his right hand pressed lightly against his lips. Eventually he said: 'You think some harm may have befallen the children?'

'I fear so.'

'Why? What could it profit such men to harm the Princes? Unless they seek an early grave, for such will be their fate should this prove true.' He still spoke quietly but his face was white, his eyes ominously bright.

'It is said that the Earl of Richmond has let it be known that he will make no move while the Princes live.'

'It is said! It is said!' Richard mimicked, then struck the table with the flat of his hand so that it shuddered beneath the assault. 'The murmurings of a man of little consequence in Brittany do not dispose of Princes! Who plotted their death *here*? Who?'

'We do not know that they are dead.'

Richard turned away. 'Yet we talk as though we know it. Would we had been more careful in our speech, you and I.' The anger seemed suddenly to have drained away as though something which was necessary to sustain it was lacking. After a moment, he said, 'Perchance they had an accident, or one of them fell ill? These men but rode to find help.'

'I am afraid it is worse than that. My tale is half-told. It seems that the route which the party took was not the route to Pontefract.'

Richard stared at him; and Buckingham, his resentful pride roused by the distrust in Richard's eyes, boldly met stare for stare. Richard burst out, 'It is their mother! This is another of her wicked schemes. She means to challenge me even now.'

'I have always said this was a danger, while they lived.'

'You have been so concerned with it you have lost your judgement.' Richard's anger flared up again. 'But for your hasty action they would still be safe in the Tower. You have been in such haste to bundle them out of London you may well have bundled them out of life!'

'Dickon, believe me, all that I have done, I have done for you. I looked in your heart and saw what was written there.'

'You go too far! No one, no one can know such things!' The reply, which came unbidden to his lips, was so worded as to suggest that there are things too dark for knowledge; confused, he put his hand across his eyes and so did not see the look of triumph on Buckingham's face. When he was more composed, he said drily, 'Who else knows of this?'

'That they are gone from the Tower, Brackenbury knows; and, as I said, I sent word to the Chancellor.'

Richard began to pace the room which was small for such exercise. 'If one of them was ill, the party may well have had to change its route; perhaps we despair too soon. But some action we must take so that all shall know how deep is our concern.'

He called Lovell, who seemed not to know what to make of the matter. The news had come at an inconvenient time and none of them was disposed to look too far ahead. Eventually, Richard sent instructions to the Chancellor:

'Right Reverend father in God, right trusty and well-beloved, We greet you well, and whereas we understand that certain persons have taken upon themselves. . . .'

He thought for a moment, not wishing to be specific, and then continued:

'. . . an enterprise as we doubt not that you have heard, are now apprehended, we desire that our Council shall try them and proceed to the due execution of our laws. . . .'

After the letter was signed and despatched he talked long with Lovell. Should they send men to follow the route to

Pontefract, gathering what information they could? What value was this, if the party had not gone by this route? Also, 'If we do this, we make that public which it is wisest to keep private,' Richard said. 'At best, we appear foolish, at worst, villainous.' They decided to wait until they had received news from the Chancellor and Brackenbury.

It was early evening and the rain had stopped at last. Richard walked in the garden. The sun had come out and beyond the formal lawn the meadows steamed. A blackbird was singing. Richard was filled with an intense yearning that all might be well with the children. The lawn shimmered with little drops of light. He remembered seeing grass like this after rain in his childhood, and since then there had never been time to look at such sights again. Suddenly, yearning carried his senses away and he flung himself down on the grass and licked it as though he thought he might gather some part of its wonder and purity to himself. After a time, perhaps a few seconds, though it seemed much longer, he recovered and got hastily to his feet, brushing down his cloak and carefully wiping his face. 'We may well have good news tomorrow,' he muttered. 'For who could wish to kill these children?' He remained walking round the garden for some time, trying to calm himself. When the dusk came, however, it brought a feeling of despair so strong that he was driven indoors to seek out Buckingham.

'You were right to remind me of how we joined together in such great undertakings.' Now it was he who strove to rekindle their friendship. 'You must understand that, if I seem to have little time, it is because I must turn to good account all our past enterprise and boldness. If I seem distant, or am unaccountably cold in my response to you, it is because I must now bend everything to fashion the future that we dreamt of, that we made possible between us. In fact, dear friend, I am most loyal to you when I seem most removed.'

That *we* made possible, Buckingham thought; but it is *you* who are the King. Aloud, he said, 'I will indeed remember this.'

The next day he rode to Gloucester with Richard and there they parted cordially.

Chapter 15

I

The news of the death of the Princes had not yet reached Brittany. It was with the death of an older king that the Earl

of Richmond and his friends were concerned. King Louis of
France was dying and seemed determined to stir up as much
mischief as possible in the short time left to him. The Earl of
Richmond offered as good an opportunity as any for making
trouble in England, and so Louis pestered Duke Francis to give
him custody of the Earl. Duke Francis, now intermittently
insane, appealed to the King of England for men and arms.

'The result of all this death-bed bargaining will be to make
life unsafe for me here without in any way furthering my
cause.' Henry had a cause to lose now, and was the more angry
that it should be prejudiced by an artificial quarrel between a
dying king and a deranged duke.

It seemed perverse, to say the least, that while France and
Brittany were in decline, England should flourish. The King of
England, so reports said, was everywhere welcomed and fêted;
one of his bishops had written, 'I never liked the conditions of
any prince so well as his; God hath sent him to us for the weal
of us all.' When he reached York (by which time, Henry thought
wryly, he must be well on the way to being canonized) his
reception was overwhelming, and on the occasion of the in-
vestiture of his ailing son as Prince of Wales, the people of York
seemed determined to demonstrate that here in the north King
Richard was securely enthroned in the hearts of his people. All
of which made dismal tidings for Henry.

Then there was the ever-present question of the Princess
Elizabeth. Would King Richard arrange a marriage for her to
ensure that this prize did not fall into the hands of the Earl of
Richmond? Henry, who in Richard's place would certainly
have made such an arrangement, found himself divided on the
subject of Princess Elizabeth. He did not want to marry her,
but could not bear the thought that she should be given to anyone else. Women, apart from his mother, had played but a
small part in Henry's life; he trusted them no more than men
and understood them rather less. If God could have found
some other instrument for the creation of man, Henry would
have been well pleased. Nevertheless, he saw the importance of
Elizabeth, and when Jasper, in what was becoming a favourite
phrase, said, 'The white rose shall be grafted onto the stem of
the red rose,' Henry no longer protested, but asked:

'What is she like?'

'A beautiful young girl, so I am told.'

'And had you been told otherwise, you would not have said,'
Henry retorted. 'But 'tis no matter; ugly or beautiful, I shall
have to wed her.'

As there was some way to go before this happened, he tried

to put her out of his mind; but she crept back again and frequently caught him unawares.

2

In Brecknock, John Morton was gradually reversing the roles of prisoner and guardian and, in the course of long and earnest discussions, was well on the way to taking captive the Duke of Buckingham. The Duke admitted that he repented his espousal of the cause of Richard the Third, whom he now saw as an ambitious and evil man, quite unworthy to sit on the throne of England. The question then arose as to who was worthy to sit on that throne. It was evident to Morton that the Duke saw himself as the most worthy and he used all his considerable cunning to prevent Buckingham from putting his ambition into words, knowing that once Buckingham had declared himself his vanity would not allow him to withdraw. Gently, patiently, as befits a good priest, Morton led the Duke away from the path of temptation. His main argument was that the people who could effectively oppose Richard were the Lancastrians and they would only rally to the cause of a true scion of the House of Lancaster.

Buckingham, in cunning no match for Morton, eventually wavered and remarked that he had for some time been sympathetic to the cause of the Earl of Richmond. Morton, having removed his man from temptation, then began the task of fitting him to his appointed role, for in the Kingdom all have a place.

'Already there are many small fires smouldering,' he said. 'The name of the great Duke of Buckingham will set the country ablaze from Kent to Pembroke.'

Buckingham found this imagery to his liking. Once such a fire was started, might it not be beyond the power of Henry, Earl of Richmond, to damp it down when he landed, a stranger more acquainted with life in Brittany than in Wales or England? 'I will light this fire and see what happens,' Buckingham thought. 'Whichever way things go, I shall not be the loser.'

Once reconciled to his role as firelighter, he was impatient to act, but Morton stayed him. 'Fires may be smouldering, but how are they to be set ablaze?' The name of the great Duke of Buckingham was not, it seemed, quite enough. 'People are weary of fighting. Something stronger than mere discontent is needed to turn them against Richard. You yourself have discovered that he is an ambitious man, but ambition is hardly a fault in a king.' He steepled his fingers and looked at

Buckingham. 'But there are crimes which people do not forgive.'

'The murder of children is more grievous a crime than any,' Buckingham said heavily.

'Ah, yes,' Morton sighed.

'Richard wanted the Princes out of the way,' Buckingham continued.

Morton tapped a thumbnail against his front teeth.

Buckingham said, 'He made . . . certain arrangements . . . before he left London; the children, I fear, are dead.' He paused. 'This is painful to me. . . .'

Morton made a fastidious gesture with one hand. 'We need not speak of it, save to consider how best the matter can be related to the common people. It is our intention that they should know the kind of man who now sits upon the throne; to this worthy end it is permissible that we should construct a story which will be short and straightforward, allowing of no confusion in their simple minds.'

The construction of such a story did not take long. The telling would take longer and here Morton had unexpected news for Buckingham.

'You are not the only bearer of this sad tale. Before you returned here I had already been warned of the matter by a priest, Dr Christopher Ormond. He had reason to believe that King Richard planned the death of the children and will, therefore, recount your story well since he will be convinced of its truth. If you agree, we will talk to him. I should tell you, however, that he is of a rather contrary nature. It will be best that we do not appear to instruct him, but rather that we allow him to find his own way to our conclusions.'

He had been wise to give this warning, for, as he had anticipated, Buckingham and Ormond soon discovered that they had no liking one for the other.

'I want you to tell my Lord Buckingham what you have told me,' Morton said.

Ormond's face was grey and he looked a sick man. He spoke monotonously. 'For a time I instructed the young Princes in the Tower. But I did not please King Richard. One day,' he raised his eyes to Buckingham's cold blue eyes, 'looking into King Richard's eyes, as I now look in yours, I saw murder there. And he knew that I saw. He soon had me dismissed and before he could take any other steps against me I fled from London.' He looked sombrely at Morton. 'I came here to the one man I admired and respected above all others.'

'And, alas, I did not believe you,' Morton said softly. 'The story was too horrible. But now I know better.'

'The story is not now so horrible?'

'Ten times more horrible now that I must believe it.'

Then why do I not see ten times more horror in your face? Ormond wondered.

Buckingham, growing impatient, said, 'The children were smothered while they slept. I have this on good authority.'

'Then I am too late.' Ormond closed his eyes.

Morton said quietly, 'You were too late to save them, but their deaths must now be avenged and in this it is possible that you have a part to play. But no. . . .' He shook his head. 'King Richard dismissed you, and this means that you have cause to fear him. You have taken enough risks already.'

Buckingham's impatience was palpable. Ormond realized that these two were concerned only with exploiting the situation to the full. What chance had the children ever had when all men of power were glad of their deaths?

'. . . the world must know of such things. . . .' Morton was saying.

So, Ormond thought, I am to be your tool and go from place to place telling of this terrible deed so that all shall know what manner of man King Richard is; yet you, my masters, are you any better than him?

'You will do this?' Buckingham had had enough of this taciturn priest. 'Such service will be well-rewarded.'

'No.' Ormond shook his head.

Buckingham moved sharply, but Morton checked him. He had formed his judgement of this man a long time ago and when eventually Ormond spoke again he was pleased to realize that he had not been mistaken.

'I shall not do this for reward,' Ormond said heavily. 'But because I cannot do otherwise. Were I to keep this secret concealed, it would rot within me. For my own sake, I must spread my sickness around the countryside.'

3

Jasper Tudor said, 'In a year, the throne of England will be yours!' He was exultant. Letters had been received from the Countess of Richmond and from Robin Prithie each telling in its own way of the death of the children.

Henry felt a thrill of pleasure, sharp, immediate, unusual for him. He noted the reactions of those around him. These children had, in life, made small claim on men's hearts, but now what passions of love, tenderness and burning indignation they aroused! And if these men, some of whom were hard and cynical, talked like this, how much more would the common people be moved by such infamy? Then it would be woe to any man whose hands were stained by the blood of these innocents. As he listened, it occurred to him that his own fierce joy had been occasioned by the murder of the two children. He thought, 'This is not seemly,' and was anxious to correct an impression which might have awkward repercussions.

'We will not speak of the death of these children today,' he interrupted the eager talk. Faces turned to him in surprise, as he had intended that they should. He wanted those present to remember that the news of the Princes' death had given him no pleasure. He said, 'I would be alone,' and departed to sit in the courtyard where they might observe him, alone and sorrowful of countenance.

Work had recently been carried out on a new wing of the building and the masons had left behind a large block of stone which provided an ideal seat on which to muse. It was mid-day and the sun cast no shadows. In the centre of the courtyard a small fountain erratically squirted jets of water. It was a peaceful scene; yet for all that it was so peaceful and the air unseasonably soft and warm, Henry shivered when the spray fell on him.

He had come out here ostensibly to think of the young Princes and found that he was in fact doing so. He believed in examining the situations with which he was faced so that he might learn from them. Had he not learnt his lessons well he might not be sitting here now. 'I have survived,' he thought. 'God has brought me to manhood so that I shall be remembered for my life and not for the manner of my death.' But in spite of this comforting assurance, he found himself remembering how he had been hunted over bleak Welsh hills and desolate moors in Brittany; he felt again the choking fear as the pursuers closed in on him. But he had known good fortune, too. There had been times when he had asked for mercy and had found it. He hoped he would always remember this, that a time would never come when necessity pressed so hard that he would forget mercy. He shivered as the cold spray fell on him.

From the long gallery came the sound of a flute. Music was known to please him and no doubt one of his musicians had been instructed to soothe him into a more reasonable frame of mind. He listened and after a time he began to weep, which was not his habit. There had been a time when he had not understood that it could ever be thought necessary to kill children. But now, although he deplored it, he understood, and it was as much for that understanding, as for the pity of it, that he wept.

When the weeping ceased and there was only the music of the flute, he said to himself, 'Well now! I had not meant to take sorrow this far when I came out here!'

4

'The Duke of Buckingham will lead your cause!' The land stirred at the words and brought forth men from Kent and Surrey, from Devon and Dorset, from the Welsh Marches: surely the greatest army the land had ever seen. Buckingham gazed from the battlements of his castle in Brecknock as though he expected to see a vast human tide flowing towards him.

It was not so, of course; these were a stealthy people, if you so much as turned your head away they dissolved into the mist. There was mist a-plenty today; it curled up from the river bank and hung thick in the valley. Autumn. They must strike soon while there was still movement in the rivers, some warmth in men's hearts. Who wants to fight in winter? He had written to Henry, Earl of Richmond, urging him to invade without delay. What a long way he had travelled since his wife instructed him to write gracefully to Queen Elizabeth!

He watched a buzzard soar leisurely overhead. So, too, my fortune soars, he thought. A flash of sunlight gladdened his heart. Further away, in open scrubland, a cloud of small birds rose suddenly from a knot of thorns, but he took no notice of their agitated clamour. Nor did he look towards the dark hills to the west. Here the air was clear of mist, but it was not from this direction that he expected men to flock to his army. The lowland people said that demons lived in those hills and that no man dared venture into them.

On this October morning, however, three men looked down on the castle from the nearest of those demon-haunted hills. They were little dark men on little squat horses sitting so still one might have thought them asleep. But they knew better than Buckingham the movements of his bailiffs, the number of men recruited, whence they came and how equipped. Their eyes caught the wink of sun on steel, they heard horses' hooves dislodging stones, and the uprush of startled birds told of the passage of men. At night they smelt the smoke of camp fires. They knew all the comings and goings in this country, just as others of their race had marked the progress of the men who had brought the child, Henry Tydder, across the mountains over twenty years ago.

At night they lit no tell-tale fire, but softly they sang the mournful ballads of their people recording days of great glory in these hills. In the morning they thought of a time when the mountains shook with anger and the rivers flowed blood-red, a time neither past nor future, but *their* time.

In the castle, Buckingham received reports from his stewards and was satisfied that the human tide was flowing his way; nevertheless, he emphasized that every man who could bear arms was to be brought in, 'let none hold back.'

Even while Buckingham was talking a great gale was sweeping through Crosby's Place in London. The men at work on alterations gazed aghast at the Duke of Norfolk and wondered what bad workmanship had driven the Duke into such a temper. He shouted orders to the men with him and cursed at any who got in his way as he strode through the building, his face as lowering as the leaden sky.

'I said that arch wasn't ever meant to support that weight,' one of the masons said, 'Didn't I say that?'

'There'll be terrible trouble if that's what's happened,' the other mason said, and added admiringly, 'He's a bonny fierce man.'

The Duke strode past followed by several scampering attendants; they went into the yard, mounted their horses and rode away. The dust swirled about for a time and then settled.

'What was that all about, then?' the first mason asked, disappointed that such violence should pass by and leave the world so tamely unchanged.

The masons' apprentice, who had been hovering about in the courtyard where he had no business to be, now came back full of excitement. 'They sent word to the Duke that there's an army marching on London!'

'They may have sent word to the Duke,' the first mason replied forbiddingly, 'But they'd hardly have told you, would they?'

'It's true! "Men from Kent", they said. I heard them.'

'Oh, Kent!' The two masons exchanged looks compounded of scorn and resignation and turned back to their work.

The boy watched them for a while, then he said, 'Do you know what? Before he rode away, the Duke said, "If it had to happen, better now." And he smiled!'

Scotch it now, Norfolk thought, while the rumour is still new and undigested; a few malcontents may rush into action, but most Englishmen like time to make up their minds. They hadn't been given that time and this was a mistake; but who would expect wise judgement from Buckingham? The Duke of Norfolk had reason to smile. He enjoyed action. Once arrived at West

Minster he despatched a messenger to King Richard who was now on his way to Lincoln. Norfolk had already taken some pains to ensure that there would be no insurrection in his own country of East Anglia; now it remained to deal with the men of Kent. He would have smiled still more broadly had he known that these men, impatient as they ever were, had come too early to the fight, thus jeopardizing their cause.

The messenger rode north. The sun had started its long winter journey; it was pale by day but blood-red when it set as though each night it drew to itself more and more of the earth's warmth. The nights were sharply cold. He was glad when he reached Lincoln just before noon. There was no difficulty in finding where the King was housed, all Lincoln knew the answer. John Russell, Lord Chancellor and Bishop of Lincoln, was now in London, but he had ensured that the reception accorded to the King should not fall short of that given him by the northern towns. The King and his household had just dined when the messenger arrived.

Richard said, 'Dear God, no!' very quietly when he was informed of Buckingham's treachery. He bowed his head and whispered, 'Oh no!' His face was twisted with nausea.

The messenger did not know what to make of this, it seemed an odd way for a king to behave. But no sooner had this thought crossed his mind than the King drew himself up and began to rap out orders which took his bemused clerks by surprise. Soon summonses were being inscribed calling men to arms from all parts of the kingdom. The instructions were given with such rapidity and lucidity one might have thought the King had been waiting this event for some time and was glad to find it upon him. This, the messenger thought, was the way for a king to behave!

While all this activity was going on, Lord Stanley hovered by the window, scratching his behind and musing on the ruthlessness of women. The Earl of Richmond was rumoured to be assembling a fleet and a look-out was to be kept for his ships. There seemed no reason to doubt that Stanley's wife, the Countess of Richmond, had been active in this enterprise; that she should so arrange matters that insurrection should break out while Lord Stanley was accompanying the King showed scant concern for her husband's well-being.

'You look sick. I trust, my lord, you are *not* sick!' Richard had despatched the last of the messengers and was now regarding Stanley with amusement as though he could read his thoughts.

'I am sick for you, Sire,' Stanley said.

'For myself, I had rather you were not sick.' He was still amused, but the signs of danger were there; Stanley had seen that strange merriment in his eyes before and knew how quickly it could give way to temper.

'Sire, I and all the men I can muster are entirely at your disposal.'

Richard regarded him as though he was a personal possession whose value to its owner was in some doubt. Lord Stanley looked dejected; but then the deep furrows of his brow and the pouches beneath the bloodshot eyes gave him a look of perpetual dejection. The pallor of the face was new, however, as were the beads of sweat along the hairline and above the upper lip. Richard nodded his head, satisfied that there was some use left in this dyspeptic old bloodhound.

'With such support, how can we fail?' he said lightly. 'For you can muster . . . ten thousand men?'

'You make mock of me,' Stanley said hopefully.

'It has been said that your son, Lord Strange, could raise such a number.'

'The wild talk of a young man.'

'Certainly he talks wildly.'

There was a rumour that Lord Strange was raising men to fight for Buckingham; never had Lord Stanley thought himself so unfortunate in his family.

'At any rate, *you* will do well, I am sure.' Richard dismissed Stanley and watched him walk away. 'I have shown much mercy to that man and little good it has done me,' he said drily to his secretary, John Kendall. 'Yet, see what wonders fear can work! There goes a man as determined as any to further my cause.'

He worked for the rest of the day, calculating, planning, studying the reports which had so far been received, driving himself and others to exhaustion. Then, suddenly, at twilight, all his energy drained from him; he barely managed to sign the last document John Kendall put before him. Beyond the window the sun had faded, but it was not yet dark enough for candle-light to be effective. This time that is neither dark nor day is more dangerous than midnight, he thought; for at midnight we know what to expect and can arm ourselves against it; but who can fight the emptiness of this bloodless hour when the world's heart ceases to beat? Oh Buckingham, Buckingham, there is more than treason here! He walked round the room, going from one of his clerks to the other, but could find nothing to fill his mind. He went back to the window. This wing of the build-ing stood on a small promontory, jutting out like the bow of a ship over the town. It was darker now. Beyond the walls of the city the forest had already swallowed up the daylight. Something fluttered at the edge of his mind, beyond the reach of reason.

In the street immediately below there was a commotion of a common enough kind when an arrest has been made; two men were dragging a woman, the crowd pelting her with any refuse which came to hand. He grasped at this distraction as at a staff held out to him from the darkness. He called Kendall to him and said, 'Send one of my men to find out what she has done.' He watched as one of his yeomen strode into the fray, conscious that he acted on the King's authority and eager to make others aware of it. Of those present, the woman seemed the least impressed; while the men argued she looked about her in a haughty manner which went oddly with her ragged clothes and was yet convincing. A woman who practised the black arts, perhaps? As Richard gazed down, he felt himself possessed of something rank and vile.

His man returned and reported that the woman had been arrested for speaking treason.

'Treason!' What alliance of Fortune and the Devil had brought her here to speak treason beneath his window at such a moment? He shivered. Yet such 'chances' are to be accepted by all save the coward; so, he said, 'I will see her and hear what treason she speaks.'

'She shall be brought here, Sire.'

But dark things are for dark places. Richard said, 'And rehearsed on the way as to what she shall say? No. Do you know where the jail is?'

'Yes, Sire.'

'Then you shall conduct me there, quietly, after the curfew has sounded.' He saw the excitement in the man's face and added, 'And you will not speak of this to anyone?'

'No, Sire.'

'Nor make mysterious statements which excite curiosity.'

The man said, 'No, Sire' more soberly.

Richard waited for the curfew impatiently, feeling himself imprisoned here in this place where everything had been prepared for his comfort. The room was full of people whose purpose it was to beguile the evening for him with food and wine, music and conversation. How was he to escape them? 'I can command anything,' he thought, 'yet I must lie and deceive in order to win a few hours alone.' He joked that Lord Stanley's 'sickness' must have infected him. He would retire early and on no account was he to be disturbed. 'For I have disturbance enough in my stomach.'

Later, as he was conducted through the dark streets of the town, his stomach was indeed disturbed. He felt strangely apprehensive and drew the dark anonymous cloak about him. There was only one man on duty when they reached the jail and he was truculent. 'If I let in everyone who came here saying he was the King, where would I be?' Richard held out his hand. Perhaps it was the manner in which the gesture was made, as much as the ring, which convinced the jailer that it would be wise to give this man the benefit of any doubts he might still have. There was a room kept for the private examination of prisoners, well away from other rooms, and thither he conducted the King before he went to fetch the woman.

A torch flared in the corridor; Richard bade the man stand it in the room so that he could see her clearly. Water trickled down the walls and the floor was slimy with filth. There was a high window in the outer wall which let in the noises of the street and the smell of human ordure with a piquant dash of entrails of fish. There was smoke in the air, too. Bonfires had been lit and the citizens danced around them, celebrating the King's visit.

One citizen, however, was not in festive mood. He could hear her jeering as she was led down the passage, 'The King here! I saw him yesterday all dressed up like the King o' the May. One whiff of this place would kill such as him!'

The jailer thrust her into the room. She was a thin, sinewy creature with a mass of tangled hair from which sharp eyes stared at Richard like an animal peering from a thicket. She said, 'The King, is it?'

The jailer said uneasily, 'She's mad. We've had her here before.'

Richard said, 'Leave us.'

The jailer's footsteps receded and then it was quiet save for the trickling of water and the scuffling of rats in the corner. Outside a church bell began to chime the hour and bells all over the city joined in. Richard waited, counting the chimes and watching the woman. She remained quite still, studying Richard, her eyes narrowed. Suddenly, she said imperiously, 'Well, speak man, are you the King or not? If you're an impostor, you'll pay for it. This King thinks no price too high for the throne.'

Some obscene thing he had glimpsed once before but had managed to escape stared out from the woman's eyes. She *is* a witch, he thought; it is madness to have commerce with her. But the trap was set and it was too late now for escape. He asked, 'And what price will the King demand of me if I am an impostor?'

'Why, your death, what else? He killed his own nephews so he'd hardly think twice of killing you.'

Her voice was strong and resonant. How long had he been summoned by this knell? Faint at first, then louder, it had tolled through his dreams, and as he rode from one town to another, he had heard it and known it was drawing him nearer and nearer to a place at which he must one day arrive. Yet even now, he protested, 'They are not dead!'

'Smothered as they slept!'

'Who told you these wicked lies?'

'Them as know.'

'Then you know murderers!'

'I have known murderers,' she said indifferently. 'Highwaymen, robbers, all dead now. But they will not hang the King on the roadside, nor hack out his bowels while he still lives to burn them beneath his nose.'

He put his hands to his face willing that this thing should not be. But when dark things begin to take shape, when dread words are spoken, then must the strong man not cravenly seek to turn aside, but boldly stand and defend himself. Before God, I will state my case, he thought, and he said, 'Who told you this story?'

'A priest.'

'A priest! I know that man. I read murder in his eyes. In *his* eyes, not mine. I have a son of my own whom I love dearly. How could I harm these innocents?'

Her shoulders twitched. 'Someone did.'

'But not I!'

'You men are all the same,' she spat. 'When things don't turn out the way you like, you shout "it wasn't me!" '

'But I loved them. When they were children I was good uncle to them. It was their mother who poisoned their minds against me. If it hadn't been for her they would have trusted me still; they would have come to me with their fears and I would have protected them.'

'You, not their mother! Never their mother!' The creature began to rock to and fro clutching at her breasts and moaning. Now the evil is most potent, Richard thought, and he spoke loudly and firmly.

'It was indeed their mother! That wicked woman corrupted my brother and now she has destroyed her own sons by her scheming. She should have trusted me.'

The creature moved her lips as though trying to spew something out, her tongue became rigid, the breath whined in her throat. She began to shiver; soon the shivering convulsed her so that she had no control over muscles and limbs. Surely, the evil that has tormented me is being taken from me, Richard thought, it is passing into this woman.

'What harm have I ever done these children?' He had thought this was a subject too dark for words, but now the words began to come. 'It was no light burden I took from Edward, but one he could never have borne . . . it was not to satisfy ambition that I seized the throne, it was for the people, that they might not be thrown back into another age of misrule. . . .' The woman fell to the floor, vomiting, her fingers scratching at the cracks in the stone. 'How could I have stood by and seen this happen? I, a grown man, strong and with years of government to school me for the role of King, how could I have watched a child stagger beneath such a load, have abandoned him to those who would have broken him ere ever he came to manhood?' Gradually the squalid room was being transformed; every stone in the wet walls glistened, the slimy floor was silvered over. 'In generations yet unknown men would curse at the very mention of my name had I turned aside from my duty.'

Gradually, the woman's shuddering ceased and she lay still. Richard said, 'As God is my witness, I speak the truth, and in the light of this truth may my actions be judged.' The moonlight, slanting through the window, marked the woman's body with the shadow of iron bars. Richard felt cool and clean. When he left he said to the jailer, 'You say you have had this woman here before; whatever her offence was then, she shall be charged with the same again. There will be no more talk of treason.'

In the morning he heard the bells ring as the city gates were opened; he stood at the window of his chamber and heard the market come alive as the stall-keepers put out their produce and, far in the distance, the singing of a goatherd taking his beasts out to crop the lean fields at the edge of the forest. Later, he went to Mass and thanked God for purging him of evil.

He set about the business of the day with confidence. He knew he was a better soldier than any of those ranged against him and he felt the old itch for battle. Only the thought of Buckingham unsteadied him and after Kendall had penned a letter to the Chancellor asking him to send the Great Seal, Richard appended a note in his own hand, '. . . . Here, loved be God, is all well and truly determined, and for to resist the malice of him that had best cause to be true, the Duke of Buckingham, the most untrue creature living; whom with God's grace we shall not be long till that we will be in those parts, and subdue his malice. We assure you there was never false traitor better purveyed for, as this bearer Gloucester shall show you.'

'And that priest,' he said, as an after-thought. 'He must be found and silenced.'

5

Buckingham's blood thrilled and his quicksilver spirits soared as he rode out from the shadow of the barbican into the bright sunlight. There was not to be much sunlight from now on, but he wasn't to know that.

The King is a pawn; it is the hand that moves the pawn that rules. Buckingham looked down at his own hands on the reins. So, too, he thought, had that other Kingmaker ridden out to war. But Buckingham was mistaken, for the great Earl of Warwick would have taken more note of his men, dealing harshly with the poor-spirited and slovenly, making sure they did not remain to infect the whole. Buckingham glanced from side to side as he rode, but as he held his head high he saw little but the line of the mountains giving way to softer hills and the river winding through the valley. He did not note that the river was high even for this time of the year, but he did say to Bishop Morton who rode beside him, 'See how fast the river runs.' His tone was one of satisfaction that Nature should swell its forces to meet his own.

The place where Nature and Buckingham's forces actually met was at the first river crossing. But before then the rear of his army had been attacked by riders who came swooping down from the hills only to disappear as soon as the soldiers had marshalled themselves to deal with the attack. The first attack was as irritating as the buzzing of flies; but when it became apparent that these attacks were to be a recurring feature of the march, men began to thrash about, maddened as if stung by hornets.

Buckingham was maddened when he realized that it was impossible to cross the river at the place where they must do so in order to head east. They had to follow its winding course, travelling for many miles in the wrong direction, before they came to a place where they could make the crossing. By this time the sun had been sucked down between the mountains and it was raining steadily.

It had been hoped that more Welshmen would join them en route, but thanks to the demons from the hills the army was cut off from Wales. Worse still, Buckingham could no longer communicate with his own castle.

He was preoccupied with rain and flood. Morton, hunched sodden and grim on his horse, reflected that to pit one's strength against wind and rain avails a man little; it would have been better to turn about and deal with these wild men from the hills. After they crossed the river they were soon held up again because the path was blocked by a landslide and they had to wait while men cleared a passage. Morton looked at what remained visible of the landscape, dark brutish hills and valleys insubstantial as a twist of broken thread. This place was ideal for quick raids by men who knew the territory and merged with the vegetation so that you couldn't see them until they were on top of you. Anyone who wanted to bring an army through land such as this would be well-advised to make sure the inhabitants supported his cause. Morton looked at Buckingham's bedraggled banner. When I come here again, he thought, it will be under another banner. In the meantime, he hunched his chin down in his cloak and passed the time planning at what point it would be best to break away from this mismanaged expedition. Certainly not now. It was safer to travel in company of any kind, however demoralized, until comparatively civilized country was reached.

Others of Buckingham's company had the same thought. His men did not begin to desert in large numbers until they were in the gentler country of Herefordshire. A few days more and the Duke of Buckingham was himself in flight.

King Richard could congratulate himself on conquering without having the bother of fighting. The rebels of Kent and Surrey, hard-pressed by the Duke of Norfolk, had abandoned their attempt on London; and by the end of October Richard had reached Salisbury without encountering any resistance. All that he needed to secure his position was to take the Earl of Richmond prisoner. 'Not that he troubles me, he is scarce to be taken seriously. But I, too, must be allowed some whimsicality, and it is my whim that he be taken.' Accordingly instructions were given that should Henry's ships be sighted, those on shore should give the appearance of welcoming him.

Duke Francis, in one of his more lucid moments, had been generous to Henry and had drifted off into insanity before he was disposed to change his mind, leaving Henry with a gift of 10,000 crowns as well as ships and men. The weather was less favourable to Henry's enterprise, hampering his ships so that his departure was delayed and buffeting them with high winds and huge seas so that they were scattered. When Henry had his first sight of the coast of Dorset, there was only one other ship with him.

'There are men lined up on that beach,' the captain said to

7

Henry, who could see that for himself. The tiny figures waved and gesticulated and over the water came the faint sound of cheering.

Henry scratched the side of his nose. 'I have little stomach to be taken prisoner now,' he said. After his tempestuous voyage he had little stomach to be proclaimed king either. Nevertheless, he despatched men in a small boat and in due course they returned saying that his cause had triumphed and his loyal supporters waited to escort him to London. Henry gazed thoughtfully at what he could see of his loyal supporters. The boat rocked and pitched for the sea was far from calm still; Henry felt a deep unease in his stomach. It was a long time since he had waited on a rock-strewn coast for a boat to carry him away to safety. Robin had been beside him then. Must one always look for treachery? The green land beckoned him, the sand was golden and looked firm; behind him there was nothing but heaving grey-green water and, over the rim of that desolate horizon, Brittany and the weariness of having it all to do again. He had waited so long for this moment, was he to be cheated of it now? He groaned in spirit, tempted as seldom before to gamble everything, but his senses warned him against the welcome now being crudely enacted on that golden shore.

'If we have had this tremendous victory, then all along the coast I shall receive news of it,' he said at last. 'I can as well travel from Plymouth as from here.'

'I think Plymouth is much further,' he was cautiously informed.

'Is it indeed?' he said dispiritedly. 'Well, that is a risk I *am* prepared to take.'

Shortly after this he received news that his cause had foundered. He felt more broken than at any time in his life. Fortunately, he could feign seasickness so that the men with him should not see how badly he had taken this blow. 'God,' he thought wretchedly, 'you try me too hard! This man who has done such evil things triumphs, while your good servant, Henry, must crawl on his belly back to Brittany, 10,000 crowns the worse, and begin all over again this wretched business of begging for money, men, and ships. I have never been able to afford pride, but even I tire sometimes of humiliation.'

A hand gripped his shoulder and turning round he saw an old man who had been with him for a long time now; the old man gazed at him with eyes full of pity, and behind him, Henry could see others looking at him. Their sympathy was well-meant, but he knew that he must not accept it.

'Why are you all so disconsolate?' he rebuked. 'I have good

cause to thank God and so have all of you. We must thank Him for this miraculous deliverance which has proved how He guards us from the snares of our enemies, and intends our cause to prosper. Were this not so we should by now be captives on our way to London.' He looked at their faces to see if there were any would add, 'instead of returning in great ignominy to Brittany.' But he saw that their faces reflected his own apparent assurance. They will only feel ignominy if I show it to them, he realized; that being so, I must remember that if I cannot afford pride, neither can I afford ignominy.

If King Richard and Henry Tudor could find cause to thank God for watching over them, the Duke of Buckingham had no such comfort. He saw only the works of the Devil in his sudden fall from the dazzling heights of power to the wretchedness of shelter in one of his tenant's homes. He had never learnt, as Richard and Henry had learnt, to deal with the rightabouts of fortune. His situation was desperate but he still refused to believe it and managed to convince himself that he could be reconciled with Richard just as Warwick had been reconciled with King Edward. His moods fluctuated between periods of despair when he would sit for hours staring at the wall opposite and moments of wild excitement when he thought of how Richard would forgive him and he would fall at his feet, crying for joy. Tears gushed down his cheeks as he pictured the scene. It was very exhausting and made him hungry. Arrogantly he insisted on more food than the household could supply. Perhaps the family tired of this, or perhaps others noticed that they were living rather better than usual. In a few days Buckingham was found and taken captive to Salisbury.

He confessed to all the charges put to him; he seemed to feel that the more complete his confession the more completely would he be forgiven. He spoke with that boyish frankness which was a part of his charm; his one concern was that nothing should be left unrepented. When he was sentenced he seemed amazed as though it was he whose trust had been betrayed.

'I will speak to the King,' he said. 'I have things for his ear alone.'

Even when the priest came to him at the end, he still said, 'There is no need of this. The King will see me.' As they led him to the scaffold, he screamed, 'You will be punished if you do not take me to the King. I tell you, he WILL see me!'

Richard had no intention of seeing him. There was too much blood between them. Buckingham was beheaded in the market place at Salisbury on the second of November.

Chapter 16

I

The brown hillsides and the copper and gold leaves of trees signalled the hard times ahead with no hopeful green shoots to delight the eye and no fresh food to fill the belly. By Martinmas, the cattle would be slaughtered and from then to late spring there would be only salt meat and a little butter or milk.

'I hated Martinmas when I was a child; you wouldn't think that, would you, a farmer's daughter like me?'

Ormond waited while the old woman talked. He was lodging with her son who was the sheriff and a distant relative of John Morton.

'There was a white cherry in the orchard,' the old woman said, while Ormond listened, waiting his opportunity. 'It was said that some years it blossomed red and this betokened war; but I thought it blossomed red because the earth was saturated with blood after Martinmas and the tree sucked it up. I had this vision of the ground running red with blood. . . .'

'Your tree must have blossomed red this year.' Ormond did not think he would have a better opportunity than this. He told his story. Although he had told it many times by now, the hearers were always new and this gave it freshness. He had wondered if this old woman was too concerned with the past to care very much about breath so lately stifled, but as he talked he saw that this was not the case. She was horrified, and eager to share her horror. He had found the bearer of his tale in this village and must now move on.

'You have not slept and you have hardly eaten,' they protested when he left. He said that he had pressing business to which he must attend. He was long past sleep by now.

He rode past fields where the oxen pulled the plough and birds hovered above the furrow as the seeds were sown. Further on, he passed fields which were running to wilderness because there were no men to work the land. He came to a village where no one stirred and the houses crumbled into the grass; here, the Black Death had struck in days long before he was born. His horse stumbled, picking its way over the broken stones, and the wind soughed, hungry for something else to wear and break down.

2

'The Countess of Richmond to be stripped of her titles and her lands to be given to her husband! Is this punishment?' The Princess Elizabeth did not reply since it was obvious that her mother intended to supply the answer herself. 'And not only is Lord Stanley to have her lands, but he is created Constable of England in place of Buckingham. What does King Richard think to gain by such folly? Or is he mad, like Henry the Sixth, and forgives for the love of it! He cannot be fool enough to imagine that generosity will win Lord Stanley's affections; Lord Stanley is so perfidious as to be beyond price.'

Princess Elizabeth gazed out of the window, making little secret of the fact that she was bored. At seventeen she had reached an age when even the most good-natured girl finds her mother excessively irritating.

'You are never to trust the Countess of Richmond,' her mother said sharply, aware that she was losing not only her daughter's attention but her habit of filial obedience. 'For all her saintliness, Margaret Beaufort is the most ambitious of all women.' It was the saintliness she could not forgive. 'That pious woman will sacrifice anyone to put her son on the throne, as we have cause to know.'

Princess Elizabeth's jaw set mutinously. She mourned the death of her two young brothers but resented the way in which they were introduced into a conversation whenever her mother wanted to shame her into attention. Her mother talked all day; she had little else to do since she had been forced to exchange the sumptuous royal apartments for confinement in the Abbey. Life had been pared away to the meagre bone of existence. Small wonder that she was ruthless in the exercise of what little power remained to her. Her daughter was reminded at every hour of the day how well-informed her mother was on any subject one might care to name. Elizabeth could not be frivolous, but her mother must be more so. A comment on the brevity of a man's doublet would inevitably give rise to recollections that when she was young the amorous courtier wore his doublet so short it did not conceal the privy parts. At such times, Princess Elizabeth was afraid she would be bored with talk of seduction ere ever she suffered it.

'. . . privy. . . .' Dame Elizabeth said. Princess Elizabeth, surprised into attention, found that her mother was accusing Margaret Beaufort of being privy to the death of the two princes. Princess Elizabeth bit her lip. When she thought of her brothers the world grew so dark that she could hardly bear it. Nor could she bear to think how time was wasting away her life so that at seventeen she had had no other taste of pleasure than to contemplate the brevity of a man's doublet, and even in this she was, it seemed, denied the delights which had been available to her mother. Her hands clenched on the window sill in an agony of mingled grief and frustration.

'Is he attractive?' she asked her mother, thinking of Margaret Beaufort's son.

'Lord Stanley? Where are your eyes, girl, you've seen him! All arse and a bag of wind.' She continued talking about Margaret Beaufort whom she hated because she was free to plot and scheme, which were the only interesting things left to an intelligent woman of mature years; and who had a son through whom she hoped one day to rule the land, just as she, Elizabeth, would have ruled had her son survived. 'I have no quarrel with ambition,' she said. 'Only let it be open, unashamed, not secret, prim-lipped. It is whey-faced creatures like this who commit the greatest crimes.'

Princess Elizabeth continued to gaze out of the window; the sun had come out and her young breasts ached. When her mother showed signs of putting Margaret Beaufort to rest for the day, she said, 'And her son, this Henry Tudor, what is he like?'

'An idle, paltry creature who fawns on the Duke of Brittany for his very existence! A man who has done nothing and knows nothing. A straw king he would make!'

A straw king, Princess Elizabeth sighed; well, that was better than all arse and a bag of wind.

'Life,' her mother said, aware of her daughter's mood though not of her thoughts, 'is not all honey, my child.'

But my life will be happy, Elizabeth thought; it will be happy because I WILL have it so!

3

The womere water ran throughout the country. It welled up from the ground like a running sore oozing through the common meadows. In the village of Foxlow in Gloucestershire the reeve's wife heard the babe in her womb begin to cry. This was Martinmas and a busy time for country folk. The cattle must be slaughtered and the meat salted; it wasn't a time when men wanted to be involved in woe of any kind. The stranger who now rode out of the village had found scant welcome here.

It was towards evening. The outline of distant hills had lost its sharpness although the houses in the village stood out clearly in the blue-grey twilight. The moon was small and a little out of shape and only one star ventured near it. A querulous wind blew the branches of the trees this way and that and swirled dust in the face of the tired rider. There was a stream which divided the priory grounds from the common land. Christopher Ormond stopped and looked across the stream at the priory. He had decided that if he arrived here before vespers he would go on to the nearby town, some ten miles away. But the dwindling light told him it was nearer compline than vespers.

Before he set his horse across the stream, he reined in and looked back the way he had come. The village was hidden behind a bank of trees and there was no sign of human habitation, no homely inn or comforting smoke rising from a fire. A lonely place. The soil was poor and thorns and small trees bore witness to some loss of heart in those who strove to cultivate this land. 'I might be looking back on the whole of my life,' Ormond thought. Well, it was late in the day for self-pity. Even so, he asked, 'Where did I go wrong?' It wasn't an idle question, he was going to need the answer soon if he was ever to have it. Fear kept him constant company now. It was not to descant upon a life ill-spent that he had paused beside the stream, but to listen. For days now as he had ridden he had fancied that he heard the drumming of horses' hooves close behind him, but whenever he turned to face his pursuers there was no one there. Now, there was only the restlessness of the wind and the distant lowing of cattle. He closed his eyes, waiting for relief to come. The horse moved uneasily beneath him. He steadied it, stroking gently until he felt the taut muscles relax. 'I can soothe you, but not myself,' he said. He turned the horse into the stream.

'I was priest at Foxlow, many years ago, when Dame Alice was prioress,' he said when he was with the prioress. 'I used to come here often.'

At first, the prioress thought that curiosity had brought Dr Ormond back here. 'He wants to know what changes I have brought about since Dame Alice died.' On close inspection, however, she decided that the Devil had driven him, there was such a darkness about this gaunt, ill-favoured man.

'You may stay here as long as you like,' she said kindly.

'You would rue that offer were I to accept it.'

The prioress, young and self-assured, was not impressed by his sombre tone. Ormond cried out passionately, 'I have a sickness. I have been spreading my sickness around the country and now I have brought it to you.' He leant towards her and she drew back, unable to conceal her distaste. 'If you do not want to be contaminated, you must turn me away.'

'We will see about this in the morning.' She spoke coolly, displeased by this ranting.

In the morning, Ormond was quite out of his mind. The prioress, hastily summoned, bent over him. He stared up at the cold, resolute face. 'Where am I?' he screamed. She told him that he was at Foxlow Priory. 'I had a bad dream,' he said confusedly. For a moment, he was quiet, then he said, 'When I was a young man I had such wonderful dreams. I dreamt I would bring back the age of Abelard. But God doesn't love proud people, so don't you be proud; and whatever you do, don't go whoring after learning. God loves a fool. Make me a fool, God; take my mind away.' Behind the prioress stood the youngest nun, round eyes staring from a flat, owlish face. Ormond suddenly beat his fist between his eyes and cried out, 'Take my brains away, tear them out!'

They had to take hold of his hands to prevent him from digging the nails into his eyes. When he was exhausted and ceased to struggle, they bandaged his fingers together.

It was three weeks after his arrival that a man came to the priory to take Ormond away. The portress to whom he spoke hastily summoned the cellaress who fetched the prioress. The man had a red face threaded with purple veins and eyes small as currants. He breathed heavily while he looked about him. In an alcove to his right the Virgin clasped her child; her face, illuminated by a candle, gazed down with a small, seraphic smile which seemed to make the man uncomfortable. He tried guile, which ill became him. 'Dr Ormond be troubled in mind and I be sent to take him. . . .' Destination presented difficulty and he finished lamely, 'where he will be safe.'

'He is safe here,' the prioress said.

Something moved in the shadows on the staircase. The man and the three nuns had their backs to the staircase and could not see Ormond's scarecrow figure.

'Sheriff sent me to take him,' the man told the prioress resentfully.

'The Sheriff has no authority here.'

The man rubbed a hand round his jowls wondering how to talk to such a foolish creature. 'I can't tell Sheriff that!'

Ormond spoke from the stairs. 'Then tell him that I have been granted sanctuary here.'

The Sheriff's man spun round. 'You've to come with me. Sheriff will have me split in two if I go back without you.' His hand went to his sword.

Ormond spoke in a terrible voice. 'If you draw a weapon in this house, God will strike you dead where you stand.'

The man removed his hand from his weapon in order to cross himself. His predicament, menaced by an ever-present God and an absent sheriff, was one of great difficulty. He looked from one to the other of the nuns. They were frightened but used to immobilizing their features and in the muted light the little white faces seemed inhuman as turnips. In the alcove, the light from the candle flickered in a draught; the Virgin's eyes grew dark. The man turned and stumbled down the corridor. The prioress said to the portress, 'Make sure that he leaves.'

Ormond collapsed on the stairs, his head bowed to his knees. The prioress breathed a long sigh. 'What *have* you done?'

He told her his story. 'I should have told you before, but I was too sick.' He is still sick, she thought, looking down at his thin, ill-made body; a sick old man whose diseased brain has surely conjured up this grim fantasy. But what of the King? This new, unknown King would not be pleased by this fantasy. His wrath would fall on them all. She felt it quiver in the air even now. The cellaress was moaning, 'What will become of us?' The prioress sent her about her business.

Ormond suddenly hauled himself to his feet and lurched down the stairs; he fell clumsily on his knees before the prioress, gabbling, 'I pray you will not deliver me up to them. I am not ready for death, I haven't lived a good life. I am not worthy.' He crouched before her, panting with fear and talking for all the world as though the martyr's crown was to be his. Certainly, he was not worthy; the prioress was surprised that the question of worthiness should ever have occurred to him. His fingers plucked at her robe. 'I am at your mercy.'

'We are all at God's mercy,' she rebuked him, firmly shaking free her robe.

In the distance, the bell was ringing for Nones. The prioress walked thoughtfully towards the chapel.

4

Richard took two decisions with regard to the fate of the young Princes and then put the matter behind him. The men who had been arrested in London pleaded that they were innocent of the crime, having fled when they realized what was intended. They were persuaded, however, to locate the place where the children had been slain. 'While these innocents lie in such a place I shall know no peace,' Richard thought; and being anxious for peace he instructed his Master of the Royal Henchmen, Sir James Tyrrell, a man whom he had long known and trusted, to arrange for the pathetic remains to be reclaimed and conveyed secretly to the Tower where they were to be lodged in a place of concealment until in a kinder time they could be buried with the honour due to them. The same need for secrecy prevailed in the case of the priest, Ormond. He was in sanctuary and Richard was prepared to play a waiting game. When the man came to trial he thought it better that the charge should not relate to the Princes. 'The people murmur still,' he said to Lovell who well understood his mind. 'Murmurings, however can be silenced easily enough and often die away from lack of nourishment. But publish this news throughout the country and who can tell when the reverberations will cease? It is too soon, there is too much to be done, to allow for this distraction.'

He bent his mind and will to the work to be done, and during the next few months he devoted himself to measures aimed at bringing justice to the realm and, most dear to his heart, peace to the north. It would take time to translate his ideas into statute and institution, but he was now confident that time would be vouchsafed to him. The country was more settled. Those who had fought for Buckingham, or risen for Henry Tudor, or rebelled for the sake of rebellion, made their way to their homes grumbling that it would be a long time afore they took arms again!

Robin Prithie fell in with some of these men. They would walk together for a time but Robin could not keep up with them. Once he had had no difficulty in keeping himself alive on the road; but years as another man's servant had unfitted him for being his own master.

In the pale November light Robin's face seemed smaller, compressed by cold, the features drawn together by discomfort. His breath whistled through the gaps in his teeth. He had done a lot of walking, trying to keep clear of Buckingham's men. In the end he had come close to Buckingham himself, for he had seen him executed in Salisbury. 'Now, here's a thing!' he thought as he saw the Duke's head fall. 'First this man is for King Richard, and then he is for the Earl of Richmond, and where does it all lead?' He had never been given to philosophical enquiry, but he came near to it as he limped from one hamlet to another, begging and stealing and doing a bit of tinkering when all else failed. The Duke of Buckingham had come to a sorry end, and perhaps something was to be learnt from that. Did people who didn't turn and turn-about fare any better? When he was a lad he had had two great gifts, a fine body and a quick wit. So many paths had been open to him then he had scarce known which to follow, nor did it seem to matter for every way was sweet. But at some time, without his realizing what was happening, he had been cheated of his inheritance. Other men, plodding stolidly like great yoked oxen, had grown prosperous ploughing a single furrow. Robin had neither their fortune nor their strength; his body had become soft and could not be relied on when conditions were harsh. He had but the one gift now, his wit.

So, he asked himself, as he trudged along the road, who am I to serve? The vagrant life was too tough for him and before winter came he must turn back to the only trade he knew. Either he must convince Henry of Richmond that he had information which would be of value to him; or he must convince someone else that he could obtain information of value about Henry. His shoes must have the deciding of it, and they voted for London and someone else.

So, to London he went, and in three weeks 'someone else' had clothed and equipped him and he was on his way to Brittany. He had lost weight and the thick curls were grizzled. He hoped this would convince his master that his faithful servant, Robin, had suffered much in his cause. The more he thought about it, the more true he felt it to be; he was so touched by his loyalty that his eyes filled with tears. It was seven months since he had seen Henry and seemed much longer. He enlivened the journey by imagining the reunion of a Gaveston returning to his Edward. King's favourite was a part he would play well: was it possible that Henry might one day be king?

Things had changed in Brittany. Henry moved about with even greater freedom and numbered his followers in hundreds. It wasn't as easy to gain audience with him as once it had been. 'It seems to me he must already be king by the way you behave,' Robin said impudently as he was handed from one dignitary to another. 'In which case, there is little reason for me to see him since I thought to help him gain a throne.'

By the time he was brought into Henry's presence he had warmed to his part and immediately prostrated himself on the floor. No hand was stretched out to raise him. His heart pumped at the exertion but had time to slow to its normal beat before a voice, cool and amused, said, 'The English climate does not seem to have agreed with you, Rob, it has turned you quite grey. Let's hope it suits me better.'

Robin looked up to see whence came this voice. There were

four men in the small chamber, three standing back a little, their faces pinched with irritation and contempt. The fourth man stood in front of Robin, tall, slim, and young in years, but with that kind of face which never knows a summer. The narrow grey eyes were shrewd, but not ungenerous; nor was the wide, thin-lipped mouth ungenerous; in fact, the face had resolved to be tolerant of life's little failures of whom Robin Prithie was undoubtedly one. There were limits to tolerance, however: this king would have no Gaveston.

Robin, who had thrown down his pride in the expectation that it would soon be gathered up, began to feel very foolish; he raised himself to one knee, but receiving no encouragement to proceed further balanced there as best he might.

'And what news do you bring me?' Henry asked agreeably.

Robin would like to have said that he had news for Henry's ear alone, but there was something about that face which warned against making extravagant claims which could not be met. He said instead, 'The people wait for you impatiently.'

'They will have to learn patience,' Henry said. 'It is a great virtue.'

'I have letters for you.' He had been provided with letters from men who promised what they had no intention of giving and he now wished he had weighted them and dropped them into the sea.

For the first time Henry held out his hand. He took the letters and dismissed Robin. The men with Henry all began to talk at once, each saying in his own way that Robin Prithie was not to be trusted. Henry nodded. 'You see how wise I was to use him? Had these letters come to me by anyone else, we should have wasted much time over them, whereas now we know who our enemies are.' He laughed about it and would not be serious. 'So long as we know we cannot trust him, he can cause us little harm and may do much good. Those who do good involuntarily often have more to commend them than those who make it their business to be helpful.' He could not bear to squander life, to let it slip through his fingers unused.

'This is nonsense,' Jasper said to him later when he tackled him on the subject.

'Oh, everything is nonsense!' Henry's mood had changed and he had become pettish. 'What else is there but nonsense?' He drummed his fists on the window sill, staring out at the bruised purple sky as though he feared the coming rain would wash away the last trace of reason from the earth. Every day that passed now helped Richard to establish himself on the throne and there were times when Henry found the tediousness of waiting in Brittany hard to bear. When his patience was not being tried, there was Duke Francis to try his nerves. Repeated attempts to get rid of Henry had made the Duke aware of his value; but now that his mind was failing the Duke sometimes evinced a regrettable desire to get rid of his valuables. 'It was all right giving him shelter when he was a cub,' he had mumbled to Pierre Landois. 'But now there's a whole pack, roaming about wherever they please.'

The vagaries of Duke Francis, however, were as nothing to compare with the agonies inflicted on Henry by the Princess Elizabeth. The women whom Henry took to his bed as and when the need arose troubled him little and he would have been hard put to it to have remembered them subsequently. But no ardent lover was ever so tormented as was Henry by the inconstancy of the Princess Elizabeth who, by one report was still held virginal in sanctuary, by another was given as a reward to one of Richard's lowliest supporters, and by yet another was pledged to a Spanish nobleman. The situation became so bad that by Christmas he must declare his right to her, and on Christmas morning in Rennes Cathedral in a ceremony so moving that the actual marriage rites seemed an irrelevance, Henry pledged himself to marry the Princess and thus to unite on one stem the white and the red rose.

Among those who knelt and did their King and his unseen betrothed homage was the Marquis of Dorset, half-brother to Elizabeth. As he knelt, he studied Henry's intent white face. He recalled his half-sister as a smiling, golden-haired lass as full of joy as a sunbeam and reflected that the House of Lancaster had more to gain by this marriage than the House of York.

5

It was achingly cold. There were icicles on the walls of Foxlow Priory. The square of sky framed in the window of the chapel was blanched as were the faces of the nuns. It had snowed a little yesterday, but not enough to relieve the intense cold. The villagers had raided the priory's store of kindling and all that remained was a stack of logs in the empty strangers' stable which must be kept to light the kitchen stove so that once a day they could have hot soup. They had been under siege for several weeks now and must go sparingly with their stock of food. The priory, which for many of them had been a shelter, was now a prison.

The cold preyed on their minds. Then, because of the cold,

they began to think of fire. They thought about the dancing flames, the reflection on the walls, the gradual warmth stirring in the limbs; after a time, they began to see something in the fire which at first looked like a very long log, but which they eventually realized was an empty stake around which the flames roared wasting their radiant warmth and power. It did not take long for the nuns to decide that the stake was waiting for a body which they could supply.

'He is a bad priest,' they murmured among themselves. 'Why should we be punished for his sins?'

The prioress argued with them, using the weapon of her intellect; but the one power which these weak women appeared able to resist was the power of the intellect. The old cook answered the prioress by throwing pots and pans about the kitchen and vowing she would do no more work. Her face had changed, the years in the priory had peeled away as though they had never been and the prioress was confronted by the face of a peasant, stupid, sly, obstinate. 'I know your kind,' she shouted. 'You mean to be a saint if it kills us all!'

The prioress' control held for another week. Then, one morning after the nuns had sung Lauds and were on their way back to the dorter, the youngest nun had a vision. She became rigid, blocking the doorway to the dorter. It was the worst possible time for such a thing to happen, the darkest, coldest hour of the night and the nuns longing to get back to their beds for what little comfort remained to them before dawn. The young nun, however, was quite rigid and there was no moving her. The doorway in which she stood so arrestingly led from the chapel to the dorter so that the nuns were forced to remain in the chapel. The prioress had already departed to her chamber. While they huddled together debating their predicament, the young nun began to speak in a strange high voice using words which none of them could understand. Gradually, her voice rose to a wolf-like howl and her lips were flecked with spittle. After making frantic snatching movements at the air, she began to tear off her gown and the nuns realized that this visitation was of the Devil; one of them sped towards the prioress' chamber while the older nuns wisely covered their faces and prostrated themselves on the floor. By the time the prioress arrived, two of the younger nuns were letting their heads roll back and were making inarticulate gargling sounds.

Ormond had been listening to the sounds for some time. His room was on the far side of the cloisters, but in this still, icy air the tormented howls vibrated in every chamber, stable and store and beyond the outer walls. He went out into the cloisters, walking carefully so as not to slip on the icy stones. When he entered the chapel the prioress was laying about with a whip but the blows only increased the nun's excitement. Ormond strode across to the demented creature, who was gyrating with arms held above her head. As he looked at her he saw that her little breasts stood out like unripe apples and he thought, 'Why, she is only a child!' And he felt the pity he had always felt for young, helpless things, unfledged birds, motherless ewes left out in the cold, abandoned children. . . . Terror bubbled from her lips like rainwater spurting from a gargoyle; it was just as he had dreamt of her many years ago. Then he had not understood what he must do; but now. . . . He laid his hands on her shoulders. '*I* am your devil,' he said. She drew breath for a scream but only managed a hiccup whereupon she clapped a hand to her mouth; over the splayed fingers her eyes stared at Ormond, wild and wide, but not without intelligence. He felt a current begin to flow through him as something he had stored away deep moved at last in his body. He said, 'It is I who have brought evil into this house. But I am going away. I promise that tomorrow all will be well and you will live here in peace.' He was not confident about this since he himself had never known peace; yet as his hands held the young creature's shoulders, there seemed to flow from them the fragrance of Balsam of Gilead on a sunny day with the light breeze stirring the ancient, healing trees. He was intensely surprised.

The young nun looked about her and said childishly, 'My robe is torn . . . and my shift!'

The prioress put an arm about her. 'You are all right now; everything is all right. Come. . . .'

By the evening, Ormond had gone. The nuns came quietly to compline; the prioress could not complain of any lack of devotion. The air was so still one might hear a feather fall.

In spite of cold nights smelling of frost and the hectic bluster of the wind, spring would not delay its coming and daffodils thrust green shoots through the hard earth. Soon the grass would start to grow again in the pastures. Winter dies hard though and foodstocks were low; life was dull and monotonous. Perhaps even now there was a child asking, eager for an event, 'Is it today they are burning the priest? What has he done?'

It had taken Ormond a long time to realize what he had done. He had assumed he would be tried for treason and was puzzled by some of the questions put to him which seemed irrelevant.

'When you were priest at Foxlow, did you not take a woman who was accused of witchcraft to be your servant?'

'I had forgotten,' he said, surprised.

'And the witch, Ankarette Twynyho? Have you forgotten her, too?'

'She was not a witch,' he answered angrily.

They brought forward a plump matron whom Ormond did not recognize; she said that she had been Ankarette Twynyho's maid and had seen Ormond kill one of the Duke of Clarence's men. 'Do you deny this?'

'No,' Ormond answered indifferently. 'I have worse things than that to repent.'

'And when you were tutor to Prince Edward. . . .' Ah, now we come to the nub of the matter, Ormond thought. But the man was talking of a conversation about the printing of the Bible. Ormond began to be uneasy.

'And when the young Prince very properly said that it was men such as you, the priests of God, who should be the guardians of the truth, did you not reply "You must be the guardian of your own truth"? What meant you by that, Dr Ormond?'

'Why, that he must guard the treasures of his mind.'

Their faces, which had seemed so unintelligent, had become as sharply evil as the gargoyles which laughed down from the roof gutters of the little church at Foxlow. He stared at them fascinated. The lips of the nearest gargoyle moved.

'Do you remember talking about this question with Sir Geoffrey Warent at Foxlow Hall? No? Let me refresh your memory. Sir Geoffrey said, "Will we have masons and carpenters reading books? We can't tell but what one day it might even spread to the peasants. They'll be going to a book for instruction rather than a priest." And you replied that you looked forward to a time when all men would be trusted with the holy mysteries and there would be no need for priest, bishop, or pope. Later, you referred to the writings of Wyclif. . . .'

So, it was as a Lollard that he was to be condemned! It had never occurred to Ormond that he would be called upon to die for a belief; even though men counted that belief heresy, he knew that he was still unworthy of such a death. When he was back in his cell, he prayed, 'Oh God, thou knowest my life has been devoid of charity. I sheltered a woman who was charged with witchcraft, but I took my pleasure of her. I tried to find help for the young Princes because their plight was thrust upon me. And those healing hands. . . . I did not know what they were doing, they were not my hands! All my life my good deeds have been done accidentally while I was thinking of something else. I am not worthy of this death.'

As the days went by, his mind, of which he had been so proud, began to betray him and spiralled beyond his control. When eventually he was led to the stake, he called out to the crowd, 'You do not know what you do. This is blasphemy.'

There was a big crowd in the market place and soldiers were clearing a passage for men carrying faggots; a man with a torch thrust the flame threateningly towards a tinker who was trying to steal some of the tools which had been laid down by the men who built the bonfire. 'Be off unless you want your beard singed!' he cried. The upper rooms of inns and houses were crowded with spectators. A woman was shouting to two boys who were scaling the roof of the White Hart Inn, warning them not to interfere with the lines of washing strung across the narrow street leading off the market square. At first, the fire burnt slowly and faggots were dipped in barrels of tar and forked onto the flames.

Two friars had stopped to watch the burning and one said to the other, 'A Lollard, so they say.'

'There can't be any Lollards left to burn!' the second friar protested.

'Heresy dies hard. Perhaps we have the last of them here.'

As the flames began to lick his shirt, Ormond shrieked, 'Lord, I am not worthy!'

A breeze was blowing now, stirring the washing and fanning the faces of the crowd with hot fumes. Smoke dimmed the brightness of the bunch of grapes which hung above the inn sign.

'If that is the last of the Lollards, then it's a bad end for them,' the second friar commented as Ormond shrieked for mercy. Although the friar had no love for the Lollards, he needed them to make a good end.

More tar-soaked faggots were forked onto the fire and suddenly the flames soared. Now Ormond was a sheet of flame. The breeze was stronger. It filled the shirts and hose on the washing line and Ormond, gazing at them, saw his own poor body dancing there in grotesque agony; he watched while the bits and pieces of his body jerked and twisted, writhed and turned and gradually lost all human semblance. The flames formed like petals around his spirit, and when he could no longer see beyond the rim of the petals, there was stillness in the centre of the flower.

The sudden quiet of the burning man surprised the two friars. One said, 'They don't feel the pain after a time.'

'Is that so?'

'Yes, that's the reason. They don't feel the pain.'

Chapter 17

*

'The willows are coming out all along the river bank,'
Princess Elizabeth said. 'It is beautiful, beautiful!' She leant
far out of the window as though she might breast the buoyant
air and fly away from the Palace of West Minster, beyond the
willows and the river. 'There is a scent of something . . . what
can it be?' She closed her eyes and inhaled deeply. Behind her
in the room her younger sisters made no answer, but one of
them sniffled. Elizabeth remained leaning out of the window,
not daring to let them see her face because she was so happy;
even if the willows hadn't been green, if there had been no
scent carried on the spring air, she would still have been
happy.

'I hope our mother is not sad,' her younger sister said
unsteadily.

Elizabeth glanced briefly towards the buildings of West
Minster Abbey; her joy at being freed from sanctuary was so
great that she could not squeeze out a drop of sadness at the
thought that perhaps her mother was even now standing at one
of the windows in the Abbot's parlour. She did, however, say
'poor mother' and then, deplorably, found herself laughing for
no reason at all. It was unfortunate that at this moment King
Richard should cross the courtyard and look up at her window.
He said, 'A delightful morning.'

Cecily hissed, 'Ask HIM what the scent is, why don't you?'

'It would be more delightful were our mother with us,'
Elizabeth said haughtily.

He put his head on one side, studying her face and assuming
a judicious air. 'No, I don't think the picture would be improved
by your mother's presence.'

Behind her, Elizabeth could hear her sisters making kittenish
spitting noises. She knew that she should withdraw but was
afraid to offend him and ashamed of herself for being afraid.

Richard said, 'If you are unhappy about your mother,
perhaps you can persuade her to join you? She knows that I
should be willing to extend my hospitality to her.'

Elizabeth said, 'I will speak to her.'

'I am indebted to you.' He made her a fine bow and walked
away laughing.

The other girls crept to the window to get a look at him and
were faintly disappointed to see a man, handsomely dressed, but

in all other respects much as other men, having the one body with the usual attachments. Their mother's attitude to this man had varied so much that the girls had no idea how they should regard him. Her last words when they left the sanctuary of the Abbey had been that he would do them no harm, but that they should not trust him. They stared unhappily into the now empty courtyard while Elizabeth paced up and down the room. Only a few moments ago, she had felt light-hearted and free as a bird; but her Uncle Richard's appearance had reminded her that she had but crossed from one building to another and as she walked round the room which seemed very dark after the bright light at the window, the dreadful thought occurred to her that life might be like this, a succession of dim rooms one opening into another.

'You're frightened of him,' the youngest sister accused tremulously.

'Mother would never have agreed to put us in his care if there was any need for fear,' Elizabeth said.

'Why doesn't she come here, too?' Cecily asked.

'Because she thinks she is better off where she is. And that we are better off here. Don't question her decision. She knows what is best for us.'

They stood looking down dejectedly; something more than words was needed and Elizabeth went to them and put her arms around them. 'As long as we're together, nothing can happen to us.' The warm physical embrace gave the comfort they needed. Elizabeth felt like a mother bird spreading her wings about her chicks.

'You will never leave us, will you?' Cecily asked.

Elizabeth replied, 'Never!' and they all chanted, 'Together for ever and ever!' It was a vow which none of them believed would be fulfilled but which at this moment each needed to make.

The two younger girls went back to their needlework. The sharp-scented breeze stirred in the room, but when Elizabeth went to the window she saw the enclosing buildings more clearly than the trees and the distant river. The sun was bright in the courtyard; then a shadow came from nowhere and glided between an archway and over the cobbled courtyard. Elizabeth glanced up, but the bird, if bird it was, had disappeared: it seemed to have taken with it the innocence of the day.

'I will ask my Uncle what has happened to my brothers,' she thought. 'I will know from his reply whether he is to be feared or not.'

The sun climbed higher into the sky and the light no longer

slanted in at the south-facing windows of the Palace of West
Minster; but one dust-speckled beam fell across the table in
the Abbot's parlour at which Elizabeth Woodville sat writing to
her son, the Marquis of Dorset.

'I have entrusted Elizabeth and her sisters to King Richard's
care,' she wrote. 'It seemed wiser to do so, since if I refused I
should but have kept Elizabeth for the Tudor to marry.' She
wanted her son at home, it irked her that he should be serving
Margaret Beaufort's son. 'I am convinced that Richard would
reward you well were you to return. He has need of men of
ability and the sense to realize it.' She paused, contemplating
the sunbeam and wondering whether to say that she, too, had
need of him. It was a fatal pause; she had placed her hand on
the table and the sunbeam caught the ruby ring on her little
finger. Light fractured into tiny splinters which pierced her
flesh. 'Edward!' She had not been able to recall his face since
he died but now, for a second, she saw him as he had been when
he called on her at Grafton Regis, laughing, 'They believe me
to be out hunting—and what a hunt it will be!' She bent forward
groaning, glad that she had sent her maid away; the girl would
have thought she had been taken by a fit, for how else could
one explain such behaviour in an ageing woman with a wrinkled
disfigured body?

The letter did not get written that day and when it was
eventually sent it did little good. The Marquis of Dorset
deserted Henry of Richmond, but was caught before he set
sail for England. Henry had the trouble of persuading him to
reconsider his decision; he could ill-afford to be seen to lose so
notable a supporter at this time. The task was not to his taste,
but as fortune had never pandered to his taste he undertook the
unsavoury business efficiently and without fuss.

Although Henry usually appeared calm, he had a temper
which he was not always able to control. When he was told that
Elizabeth Woodville had consigned her daughters to Richard's
keeping, he shouted, 'Was ever woman so unwomanly! I shall
not forget how this mother has dealt with her daughter.'

The daughter now spent much time in company with Richard
and his queen. To Anne, who was ill, it seemed that Elizabeth
shone like the brightest star in the sky. 'What pain life has in
store for you,' she would think. Then, recognizing that envy
directed such thoughts, she would say to herself, 'Whatever
happens to this child, she will survive; she would be radiant on
a dunghill.'

Elizabeth was fascinated by Anne. At first, seeing that face
and body were now pared to the bone, Elizabeth had felt

protective towards her aunt, and it had come as a surprise to realize that such a frail vessel could contain so tough a spirit. The mind, too, was sharp as a pair of shears and even Richard was not safe from its snips. Once, when he talked passionately about a king needing the love of the people because he could only rule with their consent, she interrupted him to ask, 'Is it marriage you are contemplating, or a love affair?' He was reduced to silence.

Only a saint, Elizabeth thought, could wield such power over such a man. And if Anne was a saint, then surely Richard could not be wholly evil?

'How can a woman be sure a man is worthy of her love?' she asked Anne.

'If you are going to keep that kind of account, the matter will never be put to the test,' Anne said crisply.

'But I long to meet a man I can respect in all things.'

'You'll go to your grave a virgin, then.'

'But how can I love someone who is not worthy of my love?' Elizabeth's lips trembled because she knew how pompous she sounded, and yet it mattered so much.

Anne's mood softened and she took Elizabeth's hand. 'Whoever you marry, you must love him,' she said urgently. 'If he is not quite what you would have him be, you must not mind, you must love what he is. You are made to love and it would greatly injure you not to do so.'

'But I can't love without cause!'

'Oh, my dear, the seed is within *you* and it is you who must nourish it. The man will be too busy with all the important things men do.'

'Has this been so for you?' Elizabeth asked.

'I was very fortunate.'

Elizabeth was dismayed that she had spoken in the past, and she knelt beside her and said warmly, 'I love you more than I will ever love any man.'

Anne shook her head. 'That, were it true, would be a great waste.' She looked down at Elizabeth's young, flushed face and said fretfully, 'What can one say to you?' She ran a finger thoughtfully over her pale, dry lips. 'Whoever you marry, there will be some good in him. Think only of the good. Others will make his faults their business.'

'I may go into a nunnery,' Elizabeth said, dejected. 'I think I should find it easier to love God than a man.'

She did not, however, have much time to dwell on such thoughts. It did not need the flag straining from the standard to mark the King's presence at the Palace of West Minster, the very air was charged with it, and Elizabeth in common with every servant, clerk and courtier felt that the universal pulse had quickened. He who snatches a crown must lose no time in showing himself worthy of his trophy and to this end Richard worked tirelessly. His energy was formidable. He was zealous in all things, whether making plans for his council of the north, discoursing earnestly with his bishops, or talking into the early hours of the morning with foreign travellers and wearying them with questions ranging from the affairs of princes to the quality of a local wine. He was lavish with his gifts, generous to friend and adversary alike, passionate in his protestations of love for the common people, most earnest in prayer. To Elizabeth, his brilliance seemed dazzling, the world his sunflower. If one thing is certain, she thought, it is that Henry Tudor will never come to claim me now.

Others thought differently. There were rumours that Henry Tudor would soon land in England. Richard decided that Nottingham was better placed than London to be his headquarters. A great hush seemed to fall on the Palace of West Minster after he and Anne rode north in the middle of March.

Richard was well-received wherever he stopped on the journey and this pleased him. He never tired of hearing his praises sung and at night he would repeat flattery which at one time he would have dismissed with contempt. After a while, Anne would turn her head away and say, 'I must sleep if I am to accompany you tomorrow. I have not your strength.'

When the morning came she would still be exhausted. The exhaustion discoloured life. There was nothing to which she could look forward with pleasure; she could think of no change in her condition or that of the world which would give her joy. Once, when she was alone in her chamber, a blackbird came and perched on a tree outside the window and chided her for her weakness, repeating his message over and over again. When at last he flew away, he seemed to have chanted some ease into her and she managed to greet her husband with her old gaiety of spirit.

A few days later they came to Nottingham. Richard looked up at the castle, dour and majestic on its great rock, as though measuring his own strength against it. Anne, riding from the bright sunlight into the shadow of its walls, felt the chill of death. Within three weeks of their arrival, the news was brought to them that their son had died.

It was for the mother that their friends most feared thinking that the frail body must break under the strain of her grief. Richard, however, was seized by a madness which seemed beyond grief. At first he appeared incapable of understanding what had happened, and then, when realization could not longer be delayed, he shouted wildly, 'God! You have deceived me!' The onlookers were horrified by this blasphemy.

Anne put grief aside to combat the strange disorder which troubled her husband. After his terrible outburst he was quiet during the day, but at night he was afraid to sleep and when he found himself drifting away he would start up, crying out that God had purged him of evil so why was he still punished? Then he would be frightened by his own words and tell her that they must pray together.

'What should we pray?' she asked.

'That God, who knows all things, will cleanse men's hearts so that they cease to impute evil to me. I am innocent, God knows I am innocent! Pray that I be honoured and respected.'

When they had prayed she would hold him close and try to soothe him. She ordered the servants away from their chamber, fearing that if any heard him they would suspect that he was mad. At last, he became calmer and slept at night. But now, when she turned to her own grief, she found that it had dried up. Everything in her seemed dry as a river bed in a drought. She lay in bed, looking at her husband, and wondering how long she would have the strength to love and protect him.

The news of the death of Richard's son eventually reached Henry Tudor's camp. These had been dispiriting days for Henry and his followers and the news that Richard had no heir put them in good heart. The news reached Robin Prithie in the stables. The man who saw himself as King's favourite had been treated harshly on his return; Henry had other personal servants now and Robin was one of the grooms. His fall was noted by others for the servants were as aware of the importance of position as were their masters. Had this been England and not a foreign country, Robin swore he would not have stayed to endure such humiliation. When he heard of the death of Richard's son, he did not rejoice for Henry but thought sourly, 'Now King Richard cannot afford to ignore my master; and once he turns his attention to him, he will soon make an end of him.' Robin had a high opinion of King Richard's efficiency in such matters.

Spring turned to summer and in June Robin had proof that he had been right about Richard's intentions. Henry was staying in Vannes and many people came to see him there for the Tudor was now of some importance. One visitor was a merchant on his way to London. What business he had with Henry, Robin did not know, but one day this man approached Robin to make enquiries about his horse which would have been better directed to the saddler. A few moments' conversation and it became apparent that the man's business was neither with Henry Tudor nor the saddler; he had instructions for Robin Prithie.

'King Richard is negotiating an alliance with the Bretons and he will insist that any agreement is dependent on Henry Tudor being put in safe custody. It is important the Tudor does not escape before the terms of such "custody" are agreed. You are to report on his movements. Instructions will be sent to you but in an emergency you must yourself ensure that he does not leave the country.'

'But how can I do that?' Robin glanced about uneasily; he could see two of the other grooms at the far end of the yard but they appeared to be absorbed in conversation. 'I am not close to him as once I was and he is well protected.'

'Should he try to leave the country he is unlikely to signal his departure by travelling with a large party. He will, therefore, have little protection.'

'You are asking me to kill him?'

'He must not leave the country. Those are your instructions.' He had been speaking quietly but now raised his voice angrily. 'Well, if it is the business of the saddler why didn't you say so in the first place instead of wasting my time?' He turned to one of the other grooms who had drawn near. 'Have you nothing to do but idle about? I would have no grooms of mine so ill-employed. Take me to the saddler.'

Robin watched the two men walk away. He felt old and unsure of himself and he cursed the day that he met Henry Tudor. What would life have offered him had he not encountered that goblin child whom he had sought to enchant while all the time the web was wound around Robin Prithie? He had been a rogue when he met Henry, but he had been his own man. Now, he had served so many people to each of whom he had been a different Robin, that he scarcely knew who he was.

In the days that followed this meeting with the merchant, he kept as close a watch as was possible on Henry. Sometimes, when he looked at his destroyer's calm face, madness welled up in him and he wanted to rush at Henry and demand to be given back his life. In this mood, he had little compunction at the thought of killing Henry. Whatever harm he had done this man, it had been repaid a thousand times.

It did not occur to him, he was now so full of hatred, that he might try to regain Henry's confidence by warning him of his danger. The warning came, however, but from another source.

John Morton, who was now in Flanders, was kept well-informed of King Richard's activities and as soon as he heard of the threat to Henry he despatched a messenger to warn him.

Henry held council. All eyes observed him carefully. There were those among the men now gathered together who had misgivings about this young man who had never fought a battle.

Jasper Tudor said, 'Unless we act quickly, King Richard may succeed where King Edward failed. We cannot hope for a second change of heart on Duke Francis' part.'

'What do you suggest?' Henry asked. 'Whatever we do, we can be sure that already we are watched.'

'Then those who watch must not see signs of preparation. You must go to France, but with only a few men.'

'And those I leave behind?'

'We must hope that King Louis will agree to admit them subsequently and that Duke Francis will not in the meantime take his revenge on them.'

Henry considered this calmly and then said, 'I have over three hundred loyal men here in Vannes; if I abandon them and things go ill for them, I shall lose not only their support but my good name.'

Jasper nodded. 'If you escape you *will* abandon those you leave behind; if you stay and are taken prisoner, you will have abandoned your cause.'

Henry studied his thumb nail. If he was to take the throne he must one day engage in a battle in which he would risk his life and many of his supporters would lose theirs. 'What is your plan?' he asked. 'I assume that none of you are intending to remain behind?'

'We shall leave before you. Fortunately, Duke Francis is at this moment staying near the French border, so it will be possible to disguise our intention. It is well known that King Richard and Duke Francis are negotiating. So what more natural than that you should send those whom you trust the most to represent your case to the Duke? The fact that you yourself are not of the party will lull suspicion since we would be unlikely to make our escape while you remain behind.'

'But that, in fact, is what you will do?'

'At a certain point we shall wander off our route and with any luck we shall cross into Anjou before the alarm is raised. In the meantime. . . .'

'In the meantime, I shall have made my own arrangements and I shall be in Anjou a few days later.' Henry made it clear that discussion was at an end; he wished each man well and said how he longed to be reunited with him. In spite of the warmth of his words, there was no doubt that he was eager for their departure. 'A hard king he'll make,' one of them said with dour respect as they left.

Henry could not so summarily dismiss his uncle. 'Have no fear for me,' he said. 'If there is one part in which I have some experience, it is that of the fox, and by now I play it very well.' He looked suddenly tired and sighed dejectedly, 'All my poor fools will have to be left behind; I shall be sad if I do not see them again.'

'Never mind about your fools,' Jasper said sharply. 'But be sure that whichever servants you take with you, Robin Prithie is not among them.'

Two days later when Henry set out to make a local visit he took only five servants with him and Robin Prithie was one of them. Henry hoped that the inclusion in the party of the man whose job it was to betray him might confuse his enemies and win him a little travelling time. Before he left, he rehearsed details of the journey with one of the servants, Duncan, a Scotsman.

When they set out two servants rode in front of Henry and two behind and Robin rode beside him. Robin felt uneasy and this feeling by no means diminished as they rode from under the walls of the old town. They would be in sight of the walls for a long time and must proceed without any show of haste. Henry rode with his hands slack on the reins, looking about him and commenting on the birds and other features of the countryside in which, to Robin's knowledge, he had shown little interest before. The country was flat and provided little shelter for man or beast; Robin felt that not only the people of Vannes, but every peasant in the fields, must know that on this morning Robin Prithie had set out in Henry Tudor's company. Among those people must be some who would ask why he had given no warning of Henry's departure. 'In an emergency, I was instructed to kill,' Robin thought, 'but how am I to know whether this is an emergency?' The men who rode in front were strangers to him, but he knew the two Scotsmen who rode behind and he was no match for them. Henry had chosen his companions well.

Henry was praising a magpie for its flight and asking if there were magpies in England. He looked into the sky, narrowing his eyes as two of the birds flashed overhead. 'I am told they are very brave, but cruel.'

'Why has he taken me with him?' Robin wondered. 'He thinks I am not to be trusted, so why has he chosen me?'

They rode through a village where a pack of mangy dogs

rushed out barking and snapping at the horses' ankles and making sufficient commotion to alert the whole countryside of the presence of strangers. A stream ran through the village but there was only a thin trickle of water now and children played among the smooth white boulders. As the party rode by the children pelted them with pebbles to the toothless amusement of two ancients sitting on a bench.

'Let me go back and punish them!' Robin said.

'Save your courage,' Henry answered.

It was hot. This was a damnable country in summer. Dust rose from the baked mud track and in the distance trees furred and wavered until Robin could not tell whether they were in fact trees or marching men. His throat was so parched he had difficulty in swallowing. He would have sold his soul for a drink of water had he still a soul to sell. He squinted up at the sky, deep blue and cloudless.

Henry was talking about the Romans now; did he think those were Roman legions there in the distance, shimmering and bobbing about? Robin croaked, 'Those are trees, Sire.'

'What are trees?' Henry frowned.

'I am sorry, Sire,' Robin began to babble. 'I fear for you and so my imagination plays tricks on me.'

'But what do you fear?'

'That we might be pursued. It is because . . . because of that other time when I rode with you across that desolate place. I feared for you then, Sire, and stayed close by you.' Surely Henry would remember and be touched as Robin himself was now so touched that tears smarted in his eyes.

Henry said tersely, 'But that was a long time ago and you have ridden with me often since then without being afraid of trees.'

'I am afraid that you may be harmed. Do you recall how I nursed you that time in Brittany? You had a high fever and we all feared for you.'

'I remember the fever. But that pretence will not serve now, Rob.' Henry spoke gently and Robin was pleased. He resolved not to kill Henry. He would spare his life and Henry would take him to France and he would be his very good servant.

'If I have ever failed you, Sire, I ask your forgiveness. It was but weakness; no one could desire your well-being more. . . .'

'What nonsense is this?' Henry's voice was as sharp as if he had bitten on a nerve. 'This is no time for melancholy.' He rode for several paces with his lips tightly compressed; his horse tossed its head and began to prance fretfully, the muscles in its flanks quivering. Henry ran a hand down the side of the taut neck murmuring, 'Easy, easy.' As if to soothe the animal he

began to talk about some ancient stones which had been placed
in a mysterious configuration by people who were in this land
long before the Romans came; some of the stones were very
large and no one knew how they had come there or to what use
they had been put. 'Some say they were part of a temple to
heathen gods.' His voice droned on; Robin had never known
him talk so much to so little purpose. Henry said he had seen
the stones once but could not remember where they were
situated; he looked around him as though searching for them
and the horse strained its neck uneasily. Then, from the direction
of the village through which they had passed, there came the
frantic barking of the dogs. Henry said, 'The trees!' but he
scarce had need of the words for they were all of one mind and
rode hard for the shelter of the trees.

A change had come over the party now. They followed first
one track and then another through the wood; yet although they
proceeded as if negotiating a maze, there was nothing aimless
about the manoeuvre. Robin felt he was taking part in an
intricate ritual each movement of which had a precise meaning
known to all save him. They turned off the path, dismounted,
and led their horses between the trees, treading down the
dappled light, boring their way into a deep green tunnel. They
moved quietly for this was a pine wood and the ground was soft.
There seemed to be no bird or animal life and Robin thought it
an unnatural place. Eventually they came to a small clearing
where one of the great trees had fallen. Henry handed the reins
of his horse to one of the men; then he took off his cloak and
tossed it on the ground in front of Robin. He said:

'You are much thinner now, Rob. I think your clothes would
fit me and you have often thought you would do very well in mine.'

Duncan and his companion stepped up to Robin and began
to hustle him out of his clothes. 'But why . . .' he blustered. 'I
don't understand. . . .'

'Never mind about understanding, just be quick!' Duncan
said roughly.

Henry, being more eager and more agile, was more quickly
changed and had time to move around as though easing himself
into Robin's skin. Had I not to be a king, I'd as like be a fool,
he thought; or perhaps I'd be a strolling player, or a rogue like
this fellow here. How will he enjoy playing my part? He looked
wryly at Robin, who was squirming and struggling as they tried
to drag the doublet over his head; when his head emerged there
was some trouble trying to get his left arm into the sleeve.
'What kind of a claw is this?' Duncan said as the crooked wrist
emerged. They were all too busy to notice Henry, which was

just as well. The sight of that broken wrist caught him like a blow in the stomach; he turned away and was sick. The sickness was followed by intense anger with himself. Were any soldier of my company to betray such weakness I could afford to show him no mercy, he thought.

'What will happen to me?' Robin whined.

Henry turned. His face was pale, the narrow eyes like glass. 'You will ride out and take the direct route to Anjou. Piers and Martin will accompany you. Ride hard.'

'But if I am taken?'

'No matter, provided you give them a good day's hunting.'

'But, Sire, they will kill me.'

But Henry had turned away and was leading his horse between the trees. The others followed him and when they came to the edge of the wood their ways divided. Henry and his two companions remained in the shelter of the trees and watched the other three ride into the open country. Duncan, watching Robin, laughed and said, 'King Hob o' the muirs!'

'We'll have time to laugh when we are in Anjou,' Henry said. For the present, he scarce gave them time to draw breath. If they thought that they must restrict their pace to his, they now had good cause to revise their assessment of his abilities as a horseman and his endurance as a man. 'The Devil was in him,' Duncan would say afterwards on the numerous occasions when he recounted the story of their flight. In fact, their exploits became so magical that his hearers would sometimes ask, 'Are you sure it was Henry Tudor and not Robin Goodfellow that rode with you, Duncan?'

Henry crossed into Anjou the next day, but Robin remained in Brittany. The men who captured him spared the two servants but Robin was hacked near to death and left in fields some twenty miles from the pine wood. He had given his pursuers a good day's hunting. Now it was dark and looking up at the night sky he whispered, 'I'm not . . .' but he could not think who it was that he was not, or who he was, and he was still puzzling about it when the stars blinked and went out.

Chapter 18

*

The clouds moved slowly across the sky. One was shaped like a crouching boar with a savage tufted tusk and it grew and grew until it dominated the sky; but the wind chased and worried it as relentlessly as hounds tearing at its extremities until it broke apart. Then the wind built up turrets and temples and gorgeous palaces, all for the pleasure of pulling them down. In the fields the wind combed the grass this way and that so that it was never the same from one second to another; and over the moors sun and cloud made an endless shadow play. And all the time the adversaries rolled across the sky, billowing up threateningly or feigning innocence as when a tiny scrap of white on the horizon scudded in and turned the whole sky black. The formations of the sky had no permanence, they loomed up, dark and ominous, moved on, dissolved. Only change was constant.

On earth, things were to be better ordered. King Richard was at work bringing stability to his realm. In the first instance, he looked to that most stormy part of his kingdom, the north. He had won support from the north, but this was a personal achievement rather than a mark of attachment to the crown or a desire for the establishment of law and order throughout the realm. Now, he planned to control this most turbulent but well-loved part of his kingdom. He, too, would create his ramparts and turrets, his splendid towering achievements. He set up a Council of the North with jurisdiction over Yorkshire, Cumberland and Westmorland, and he made his nephew and successor, the Earl of Lincoln, who had no lands beyond the Trent, President of the Council. This Council was to be no airy, insubstantial creation, but something firm and solid that would endure as long as England should endure which, as Richard saw it, was to the end of time. Henry Percy, Earl of Northumberland, feared that at least it might endure during his lifetime which, however it might affect England, would go ill for the future of the Percys.

Richard rode about his northern territory, across land where the wind blew the soil away and nothing would grow save heather and stunted thorn trees all bowed the one way so that the tormentor seemed almost visible. The air was clear and one could see for miles ahead. There had been trouble with the Scots for some time but during this summer Richard's men had struck hard and now the Scots were ready to sue for peace. Richard felt himself in command, no longer Edward's able lieutenant but King of England by right of his own strength and power. Even that small scrap on the horizon which could scarce justify the name of 'cloud' kept a respectful distance, for Henry Tudor was involved in a shadow play of his own.

Henry's followers had been allowed to join him in France and now he must concentrate on winning the favour of the French king, Charles the Eighth, with whom he could claim kinship. Henry found little cause for rejoicing in his descent from Henry the Fifth's Queen Katherine, daughter of the mad king of France. Nevertheless, it was useful now to be of the line of the Valois and Henry's frugal nature did not allow him to neglect anything that could be of use to him. But it was wearisome, this need to be endlessly charming, to be modest about one's accomplishments while making sure that no one doubted them, to maintain a balance between natural aspiration and over-weening ambition, to contrive to be a suppliant without becom-ing too obviously a beggar. And all the time to smile, smile, smile. 'When I become king I hope never to smile again,' he said sourly to his uncle. 'Indeed, when I look at the state of my kingdom, I doubt I shall ever have cause to smile.' He saw England as so disunited as barely to justify the word 'kingdom' and he had no quarrel with Richard's view that the need to unify was of paramount importance; nor did he have much fault to find with the measures which Richard had so far taken. The difference between them was in the gifts they brought to bear on what was a common task.

In the summer evenings Henry would sit in the courtyard where he enjoyed being entertained by his fools. The slanting rays of the sun cast patterns on the stones and sometimes ideas would spring to his mind and he would move them about, manipulating them in that chequered light while the breeze shifted the dust from the ivy leaves. He liked to test his ideas thoroughly; he was not a rash man. The summer breeze was soft; it whispered messages in a voice that was dry and sweet, and told him that soon he would be king. It spoke of no effort. Henry's courtiers spoke softly, too, and told him how the people yearned for him to come to them. Henry was not so easily seduced. The people 'yearned' for a strong king so that they could get on with the business of their lives in peace, and only when he had demonstrated that he was that king would he earn their support. He would not have had it otherwise.

There were times when the summer seemed too long. Henry's resolution was not of the kind that dies with the heat of the day; and disappointment and delay would not wear away his courage. Inactivity, however, he found hard to combat. In his moments of enforced idleness, strange things slipped into his mind, things which had no place in the mind of a man so eminently self-disciplined and practical. Voices came out of the past—a boy saying 'It's only a puppy devil' and the image of a face, dark, vivid, faun-like, a face that did not belong to the world of everyday; behind that face were other faces, not so clearly remembered, faces of men who rode a winding path which led them further and further from the everyday into a misty, mountainous land where they sat over camp fires at night, spinning stories of a golden age; men who travelled light and served no master. Why should he envy such as these? More than envy, why should he feel they had spirited away something that should have belonged to him? He could not remember what it was, but he had always had a keen sense of possession and he felt the theft deep within himself.

These are demons that torment me, he thought; did they not tell me that demons haunt those mountains? He brought his wandering thoughts to heel and set about preparing himself for entry into his kingdom of England where dreams of a golden age had no place. He wrote to his friends in England assuring them that no Christian heart could be more full of joy and gladness at the thought of returning to his country, and asking what support they could promise him. The replies were encouraging.

The man who comes bloodily to power may in time be forgiven almost any crime if he proves himself a good ruler. But these were early days and Richard lacked the qualities which can quickly turn enemies into friends. He was not an adjustable person; because he felt at home in the north and had had some success there in the past, he put the problems of the north before those of the rest of the country. Trouble simmered in the south. It was now many months since the Princes had been seen and the rumours regarding their murder were spreading. In July a notice was fastened to the door of St Paul's 'The Cat, the Rat, and Lovell our dog, Rule all England under an Hog'.

But Richard was in the north where things seemed to go well for him. By September a peace treaty was being negotiated with the Scots and his Council of the North had been established. It was not until the end of October, when he was on his way to London, that a blow was struck which forced him to admit that there was another enemy with whom he must now come to a reckoning. The Earl of Oxford, who had been held prisoner since 1474 in Hammes Castle, near Calais, had escaped and had joined Henry Tudor. Oxford was the most powerful of the Lancastrian lords. Now that he was surrounding himself with men such as this, the Tudor must be taken seriously. The scrap of cloud was fast transforming itself into a dragon; a puffed-up dragon, perhaps, but one whose pretensions the boar must now prick. In December, Richard issued a proclamation against Henry Tudor who, ambitious and insatiably covetous, sought to usurp the throne 'whereunto he hath no manner of interest, right, title or colour, as every man well knoweth, for he is descended of bastard blood, both of father's side, and of mother's side. . . .'

Henry was by no means displeased when he heard this account of himself: recognition is always encouraging.

Richard spent Christmas at West Minster. The wind blew from the east. At night, Anne heard it knocking on the window pane like an importunate traveller who will not be turned away. A change had come over her and it was apparent to all those around her, save Richard, that she was no longer ill but dying.

Richard was extravagant with gifts this Christmas. Anne received his presents with a sadness too deep for tears. The gorgeous silks and velvets hung on her shoulders heavy as the weight of his despairing love. He was generous to Princess Elizabeth and her sisters, and Anne saw how others marked this generosity. She made it her business to be gay in company and to be particularly gay when Elizabeth was present and as her spirit had always been stronger than her body she succeeded very well. The time was coming, however, when she would have nothing left to give Richard and now, when they were alone, she began to talk about her death.

'You must not say such things!' he shouted.

'You behave as though death was a fate reserved especially for me,' she mocked him lightly. 'It will come to you, too. So why may we not speak of it?'

'You torment me!' he protested like a frightened child. 'You have always tormented me.'

'I want only to ease things for you, not to torment you. When I die you will marry again.'

He protested violently, but she said, 'Of course you must marry, there can be no question of that! Nor will you have far to look.' She spoke of Princess Elizabeth, hoping that by advocating this marriage at a time when it was unpalatable to him she might thereby prevent it. She did not want him to be denied comfort after she died, but she could not bear to be acquainted with the comforter. She hated herself for this weakness but could not overcome it.

People pointed at Elizabeth and whispered things in her ear that frightened her. But to whom could she look for deliverance? To Henry Tudor who had contracted to marry her? No one here took his chances of claiming such a bride very seriously. Even so, Elizabeth found herself wondering what kind of a rescuer he would be. Her half-brother, the Marquis of Dorset, had written to her describing Henry as 'a cold, unfeeling man who would bring little joy to any woman.' It was not very encouraging. She had her life still to live and there must be

8

love and joy because her heart commanded it. She wrote to her half-brother, saying, 'I would have you tell me what is good in this man.'

She had no reply, but her mother received a letter from him in which he sent a brief message to Elizabeth.

'I am to tell you that Henry Tudor is just, though why that should interest you, I can't imagine.'

'Just!' Elizabeth said in dismay. 'What is "just" to me?' But as 'just' was all she had, she tried to make a place for it in her heart. If a man is just, will he not be merciful and if he is merciful, will he not be considerate, kind and tender? And from these attributes surely in time, if a woman is patient, love and affection may grow.

Elizabeth wrestled with the problems of life and Anne set herself seriously to her dying. Richard was told that he must not share her bed for her sickness was contagious. The black winter days crept by. Sometimes he stole into her chamber, but she had little to say to him. His needs no longer roused her and his presence fretted her; she felt him trying to draw her back to life but had barely the strength to be sad for him. She knew herself of no use now to anyone and longed for the end to come.

'I wish the wind would cease,' she said.

'There is no wind today,' he answered.

'It is in my head, then. I hear it in my head.'

At first, the wind brought the stench of the sewers, but gradually this changed, and the wind carried to her the smell of the moorland and its sound was the sound of another wind, a wind that sang on a high, sustained note beyond the range of human sound addressing itself to the great blue vaults that lie between the sun and the stars. She pleaded to whoever was with her 'open the window; open the window wide!' She pleaded so incessantly that Richard would sometimes pretend to open the window. She had terrible coughing fits after which she was utterly exhausted; but the exhaustion seemed to bring content-ment and she would lie quite still, her tiny claws resting on the counterpane, her head turned to one side, her eyes gazing so raptly at the window that it seemed to Richard that there was something out there which might still at this late stage of her sickness bring about a miraculous recovery. But as he watched her, he saw that she was changing in a way that drew her further and further from him. Days before she died she was lost to him. She lay remote and serene, freed at last from all his claims on her. The lines on her face had been smoothed out and she looked young as he had never known her, and at peace as she had never been with him. It was as though at last all her hopes had been realized. She was beautiful. But she was not his Anne. His Anne's face had been marked with care and suffering and he wanted this Anne to be restored to him.

On the day she died it was dark. The sun was blotted out and people all over the country wondered what this might betoken. For Richard, the darkness seemed never quite to clear. When his brother Edward died, something had been taken from Richard which had never been replaced. Then his dear son had died and he, too, had taken something of Richard with him. Now that Anne had died, all his riches had gone. He sought for comfort and came across the Book of Hours for which he had pestered her and been so little grateful when she gave it to him that he had scarcely looked at it from that day to this. 'I shall keep it with me forever,' he swore. But the book alone was not enough. His agony was terrible, but it was all he had and he must offer it to God as others raise hymns of praise and adoration. He had composed for him a prayer which he himself transcribed in the Book of Hours.

'Of the blessed Julian. As you wished to relieve those burdened with sore afflictions, to redeem the captives, to free the imprisoned, to bring together those who are scattered, restore the pilgrims to their native land, to restore the contrite in heart, to comfort the wretched, to console those who grieve and mourn; deign to release me from the affliction, temptation, grief, infirmity, poverty and peril in which I am held, and give me aid. And you, O Lord, who restored the race of man into concord with the Father, and who bought back with thine own precious blood that forfeited inheritance of paradise, and who made peace between men and angels, deign to establish and confirm concord between me and my enemies. Show to me and pour out on me the glory of thy grace. Deign to assuage, turn aside, extinguish and bring to nothing, the hatred that they bear towards me. I ask you, O most gentle Christ Jesus to save me from all perils of body and soul by thy love and deign always to deliver and succour me, and after the course of this life deign to bring me to you, the living and true god. Who livest and reignest, O God, Through Christ, the true Lord Amen.'

With the penning of this prayer, some peace came to him.

Another spring came. The great festival of Easter was celebrated and nowhere more fervently than at Foxlow Priory. Already there were legends about Ormond, tales of flowers blooming all the year round near the place where he had been burnt. 'Heresy blooming all the year round more likely,' the prioress said grimly when her attention was drawn to these stories.

Princess Elizabeth watched for the willows to come out. There was one tree in particular which fascinated her. It was an old, gnarled tree borne down by heavy branches from each of which young twigs sprayed out, each making its own gesture, menacing, humorous, provocative. Although the branches dipped down, each twig thrust its tip upwards, and inside the tree a wily green creature had pushed its way up the trunk, along the branches, and now peeped out at each upthrust tip, gay, impudent, and, above all, joyous.

'Why do you keep looking at that tree?' Elizabeth's sister Cecily asked.

'It's so joyful.'

'How can a tree be joyful?'

'I don't know how, it just is.' The tree was so old, it had not found its joy, it had grown into it over many, many years. '*Look* at it. Can't you see?'

'I can see it is coming into leaf.'

'I wish I was like the tree,' Elizabeth sighed. This was a worrying time. It was known that Henry Tudor had pledged to marry her and there was the danger that her Uncle Richard might put a stop to that by marrying her himself. She prayed that Henry would come while the willow was still in leaf.

The days dragged on. Sometimes she was hopeful and sometimes she was so despondent she was not sure that she wanted Henry to come at all. Then she remembered what Anne had said about loving—'the seed is within *you* and you must nourish it.' She tried to set aside a time each day when she sat near the willow and composed herself to nourish her love. Sometimes she failed miserably and feared what the future might hold with this unknown man; but the days of the tree outnumbered the days of her weakness.

Summer came and the days lengthened, for several days the rolling sun stood still in the heavens; then, gradually, the days shortened and it was August. The wind was from the east. It scythed through the long grass beyond the castle of Ludlow; it screeched across the Marches and rampaged in the Welsh mountains.

From the mountains the small dark men looked down and saw a track like a line of cotton onto which had been threaded a procession of tiny coloured figures which wound through a narrow cleft and then gradually eased into a valley. The figures were so small it seemed that the wind must bear them away; but in spite of their frailty, the tiny creatures held on with surprising tenacity, their mothlike banners fluttering bravely. At the next pass they drew together. The cloud was dark over the pass and they were swallowed up in shadow, but later on they appeared again, winding down into a broad valley, threading their way slowly towards England.

At the van of the cavalcade, Henry Tudor looked up at the great dragon banner of Cadwallader flying above his head. He fingered his gift stone and hoped that the compact made so long ago would be honoured as more recent compacts had not been. He gave a little sigh, and his uncle, imagining him to be tired, said, 'Not so far to go now.'

Behind them the mountains grew smaller and the unfamiliar land of England lay ahead of Henry. He wondered whether it would prove unfriendly as well as unfamiliar. He needed friends in England. He had come with but three thousand men and had expected the powerful chieftain Rhys ap Thomas to join him before now. Thomas had in his time supported both York and Lancaster and Henry had cause for anxiety that he might not honour the promises he had made. It was a relief when, in Newtown, he was joined by Thomas. Even with the chieftain's support, Henry's force still numbered less than five thousand and much would depend on the Stanleys. He did not like what he had heard of them, even though Lord Stanley was his step-father. A week later, when he met Sir William, Lord Stanley's brother, at Stafford, he had no cause to change his mind.

Lord Stanley was not present at this meeting. Although Henry met him briefly a few days later at Atherstone, it was this encounter with Sir William that stayed in his mind. Sir William explained that Lord Stanley's son was in King Richard's hands and he dared not declare himself at this stage. 'But he pledges his loyalty to your cause.' Sir William paused to allow these weighty words to take their effect.

Henry pushed a finger against the side of his nose and studied Sir William. His nose was now pointing in a different direction to the rest of his face. Sir William thought one might have taken this young man for a buffoon had it not been for the grey eyes which held their direction uncommonly steadily. He went on quickly to state that Lord Stanley was encamped to the east of Shrewsbury with a large body of men while he, with no less a force, was encamped to the north-east. 'In time convenient' they would move to support Henry. Henry, looking at Sir William's thin face, the lids hooding the evasive eyes, thought that this was all very well; but *when* would time be convenient for the Stanleys, and would it be in time for Henry Tudor?

Henry had intended to march on London, but Sir William counselled against this. Henry listened to his reasons and put aside his dislike of the man. 'Richard is at Nottingham and will move quickly, as he has before now. If you march on London, you may well have him on your back and—which God forfend —if things go badly for you, you will be cut off from Wales where support for you is strong.'

'As it is not in England?'

'These are early days,' Sir William shrugged.

'They are the only days I have,' Henry retorted.

'There is another advantage in forcing a battle now. I have said that Richard will move quickly; but it is doubtful whether the same can be said of Northumberland, who has no love for Richard. Strike quickly, and you may find him unprepared for action.'

King Richard's problems and mine seem to be remarkably similar, Henry thought as he looked at Sir William. This was not a man who played for the highest stakes. He and his brother had ambitions which were practical and so there was some possibility of satisfying the Stanleys: they could be bought and at not too high a price. In an age which had produced far more dangerous men, it was not wise to get rid of the Stanleys; any man who hoped to rule must number such men among his supporters.

Henry said, 'It is your suggestion then that I march towards Leicester, rather than turning south towards London?'

Sir William nodded.

'And you and your brother will join forces with me?'

'We will move our forces in advance of you. This way, we shall not declare our intentions to Richard too soon.'

Henry could see that this would also enable the Stanleys to position their men to suit their own convenience. They could then sit the battle out and see which way it went and there was nothing that Henry Tudor or Richard Plantagenet could do about it. Henry bowed his head to hide the cold fury which possessed him. He vowed that, if he survived this battle, in future he would fight his kind of battle and on ground of his choosing. Now, however, he needed to know the odds against him. He said to Sir William: 'I have been informed that King Richard can be expected to bring to the field some six thousand men; and that the Earl of Northumberland, should he be more eager for battle than you imagine, will bring three thousand.

So, at the worst, we shall face armies totalling nine thousand. Do you agree?'

Sir William, a little taken aback that Henry should have available such accurate information, said that he agreed.

'And you, how many men do you bring?'

'Three thousand.'

'And your brother?'

'Three thousand, five hundred—perhaps four thousand.'

'I see.' Henry, who could only bring some five thousand men to the field, as against Richard's nine thousand, saw very clearly that he had small reason to hope if the Stanleys deserted him. When Sir William had taken his leave, he said to Jasper, 'If these are to be our "supporters" in England, may God have mercy on us!'

'They are the only English supporters of Richard who are pledged to join with you,' Jasper said wearily. 'You have no choice but to trust them.'

'They change sides too often for anyone to trust them.' It seemed to Henry that he was soon to fight a battle which, if numbers were of any consequence, he could have little expectation of winning. He would not forget the indecision of the Stanleys.

The next day he prepared to march to meet Richard.

'The Tudor is at Shrewsbury and no blow struck!' Richard made some small amend for this by striking the table with the flat of his hand. 'Why has Northumberland not alerted the men of York? What are the Stanleys doing?'

He sounded angry. Yet deep in his heart he was not as angry as Henry had been with the Stanleys. Henry might vow that if he won this battle he would deal with men like the Stanleys. But to Richard this was neither the beginning nor the end of the Stanleys' treachery but a process which had gone on all his life and which he seemed powerless to prevent. If he could have so ordered himself that he did not care it would have been better for him; but he still longed for the respect and loyalty of his subjects and the battle between hope and despair had wounded him sorely.

The news from York brought little comfort. The plague was spreading there and many of the members of the city council were staying outside the walls. They would send what men they could but their numbers were bound to be depleted. Richard headed for Leicester where he would join forces with the one commander of whose loyalty he had no doubt, the Duke of Norfolk. To his rear, the army of Northumberland was at last on the move; and the Stanleys, each with their own army, were approaching Leicester from the west. Five armies mustered in support of Richard would converge on Leicester; a formidable force, provided all the men could be brought to the field.

The commander of the sixth army now approaching Leicester was himself something short of confident. Henry Tudor had come to save England from the ravages of the Yorkists, but to his untutored eyes it did not look ravaged. Now that they had left behind the wilder border area, the countryside, in comparison with that of France, had a miniature neatness and an appearance of self-sufficiency. The sun was reddening the distant hills and long shadows fingered the fields. As Henry regarded this land which was completely alien to him, something more than fear, with which he was well-acquainted, weighed like a stone in his belly. What seeds could he sow in this soil and what would the land yield him in return? A breeze stirred the bushes and thistles at the roadside like a shiver of regret for the passing day. Henry saw that this land would yield him nothing; that it would take and take and take until he was harrowed to the bone. Why had he come?

These fears are the fears of all men before battle, he told himself. Yet his intelligence told him otherwise. His intelligence told him that a harder road lay ahead of him than any he had yet ridden down; it told him that soon Henry Tudor was to fight Richard Plantagenet for the right to feel the weight of the crown grow ever heavier on his brow; to fight Richard for his cares and disappointments, to take from him the betrayals, the hatred, the envy; to fight him that he, Henry, might be the one to grow old and bitter.

At this point in his melancholy reflections, Henry noticed that the people who rode with him were also looking anxiously about them. At first, he thought that they, too, were uneasy in this land of England. 'Now I must say something to reassure them,' he thought tetchily. 'They are like children.' While he was trying to think of something reassuring to say, one of his esquires said to him:

'There is a village with an abbey nearby which we should have passed through by now.'

Dear God, they were lost! The panic which now seized Henry quite cured him of any other ills which had beset him. He was separated from the main part of his army and had no idea where he was; for all he knew he might even be approaching the army of King Richard. To lose a battle is one thing, to ride into the enemy's camp because you have lost your way, quite another. In the whole course of human history could anyone have been so foolish? The long shadows had merged now and Henry watched the burnished sun slide quietly beyond the furthest hill. There was no question now as to *why* he had come; all that mattered was that he was here when he should have been there. One cannot expect men to go into battle behind a commander who has acquired a reputation for losing his whereabouts. Henry said calmly, 'Soon we shall come to a village where I expect to receive certain news and where we may spend the night.'

The 'news' he must contrive as best he could. England must provide the village; it seemed to have an inexhaustible supply of them. Sure enough, a turn in the road revealed the by-now familiar complex of cottages and church. Henry sent a man ahead to secure accommodation and waited for sounds of strife and glee, or whatever sounds men make when they capture an enemy without a battle. None came. Eventually the man returned. He had found an inn where accommodation, albeit crude, could be offered. The accommodation was indeed crude, but Henry had slept in worse places.

Before he lay down for the night, he despatched a rider to reconnoitre and report to him. By night, with any luck, the camp fires would indicate the position of his army. So it proved. The rider, who had been strictly instructed to return to Henry as soon as he had discovered the whereabouts of the army (Henry preferred to make his own explanation of his absence) returned in less than an hour to say that he had seen camp fires not far distant, and had heard men talking in Welsh and French. Henry thanked God for his deliverance.

Early the next morning he rode without unseemly haste towards Tamworth. There was a hint of autumn in the air; mist furred the contours of the landscape so that it lost that particular quality which it had seemed to possess the evening before and which had made it so alien. Now, Henry might have been riding down any country lane at any time. Ahead, accompanied by a jingle of harness and rattle of metal, something not at first clearly defined moved towards them, a strange patchwork weakly stencilled in the air, which gradually took the shape of a tinker on horseback followed by three ragged children. Henry shivered and thought of Robin. The wound was still there, and this was as it should be; it had been gained in his engagement with life and he needed it as an old warrior needs his itching battle scars to remind him of danger. But, in the raw air of this notable morning, it smarted so painfully one would have thought it newly made.

On the morning of Sunday, August 21st, the royal armies

gathered for battle under the banners of England and St George and the marching columns made their way through the country lanes towards Kirkby Mallory watched by a people who were tired of such spectacles. There had been too much of Death, he had stalked the country in one guise or another ever since the Black Death of 1349. Now, there was plague in York; Death was abroad again and little he cared for the White Boar, for honour and gallantry and valour. And the only answer to him that their rulers could contrive was this endless blood-letting! Too much blood had been drained away. The colour had run out of their days; the stuff of their very lives was thin and their faith was dark with fear. Richard's courage was of the kind that goes hand in hand with Death. Courage needed a new face, not so heroic perhaps, but quieter and less despairing; a hard face, for there were hard times ahead still, but a face with a leaven of humour, and above all a face that meant to survive into the sixteenth century. The army marched and the people turned their backs and went on with their work.

From Kirkby Mallory the columns marched on into the warm August afternoon and, climbing a high ridge, came to Sutton Cheney, some two miles south of the little town of Market Bosworth. Here Richard halted so that the army could be fed and he could confer with Norfolk and Northumberland. He had sent scouts out, and two were waiting for him here with news that the Tudor army was advancing down Watling Street from Atherstone. Richard, who was eager to do battle, was determined that the ground should be of his choosing. Before he talked to his commanders, he rode some way out of the town. Sutton Cheney was at the eastern edge of the ridge and to the west the land climbed to Ambien Hill, which must have been close on four-hundred feet. From here, Richard had a fine view of the area in which he must fight.

Beneath him, to the south, was Redmore Plain which was bisected north-west/south-east by a stream known as the Tweed which was shallow and fordable at several points, and bridged at its meeting with the Atherstone to Kirkby Mallory road. The plain was bounded to the north and south by more rolling country with here and there small hills which offered good vantage ground. Already, however, Richard had been denied freedom of choice. On the far side of the plain, to the south-west, Lord Stanley had taken up his position near Stoke Golding; while, to the north, facing his brother across the plain, Sir William Stanley was encamped at the village of Shenton. If Henry Tudor was allowed to fight in the plain, the Stanleys could come down from either side to support him. It was important, therefore, that, this night, Richard's armies should be so disposed as to discourage the Tudor from advancing into the plain. In order to do this, he decided that he must position one army in the centre of the plain and another on Harper's Hill which was on the southern boundary of the plain, to the east of Stoke Golding. An army stationed there would not only overlook the plain, but would be able to keep a watch on Lord Stanley's army from which it would be separated by some two miles and the Tweed river.

So far, so good. In this way he might hope to halt the Tudor advance and force them to camp for the night somewhere short of the plain. The disposition of his commanders, however, was another matter. He was silent, staring in front of him. His companions were used to his silence at such moments and thought little of it; perhaps it seemed to them that he was uncommonly grim, but this was a serious moment and he was apt to take serious things seriously. It was now late afternoon. Ahead, the level land stretched beneath him, uninhabited, uncultivated, and uneventful, a dullish green expanse shot with needles of light where the sun's rays glanced on the many streams which veined the plain. Away to the west, sunlight slanted like an arrow shot from the advancing Tudor army. Richard had looked down on grander scenes than this, but now, either weariness, or something more desperate which gnawed at his mind, humbled him. Once, he had felt that he had the power and strength of an eagle, that he would stretch his wings and encompass his kingdom; but he had no such flights of fancy now. As he looked at the hummocks rising almost playfully from the plain, he felt that these little hills must be engraved on his heart. In the morning, if the Tudor army had indeed been deterred from moving into the plain, he intended, while it was still dark, to move his main force to this hill of Ambien on which he now stood. If he could concentrate his forces here, he would be well-placed should Northumberland and the Stanleys fail him. In that case, the ideal plan would be for his army to remain on this ridge while Norfolk held the plain, and Northumberland moved to Harper's Hill. But to post Northumberland on Harper's Hill, where he would be in line with Lord Stanley's force, was too great a risk; nor could he trust him to hold the position in the plain. Oh, treason, treason, always treason! It seemed, as he surveyed the land, that all his life he had been prevented, hampered and hobbled until now the fetters had bitten so deep they had become bone of his bone.

It was best to leave Northumberland's army to guard the eastern end of the ridge at Sutton Cheney: in this position any failure on its commander's part would be damaging but not crucial. He would station Norfolk in the centre of the plain and himself camp for the night on Harper's Hill. He looked to his right where, not a mile away, he could see Sir William Stanley's army camped on low ground outside the village of Shenton. He did not think that Sir William was any more likely to act precipitately in support of the Red Dragon than of the White Boar; nevertheless, it would be disastrous were Sir William to send men to occupy Ambien Hill overnight.

When he returned to Sutton Cheney he discussed his plans with Norfolk and Northumberland. As the armies moved off, a small party of his own men were despatched to Ambien Hill with instructions that they were to light no fires at night. He did not wish to give the enemy advance warning of his intention to occupy the hill. His forces were now disposed and he must wait the arrival of the Tudor.

As twilight deepened into dusk the men on Ambien Hill saw the fires lit in the camps until they glowed like stones set in a giant horseshoe. Then, in the distance a column of lights moved from the south-west; slowly, the little glow-worm column advanced in the direction of the plain, then wavered, turned aside and finally halted facing the gap in the horseshoe. The men on Ambien Hill watched while the Tudor army set camp.

'And bloody fine they must feel if they can see all we can see!' the watchers thought. 'In the morning, we'll move in and crack them like a nut!'

Richard could see the lights flaring as the Tudor army made camp. He could also see Lord Stanley's camp much nearer and settled for the night. He sent a messenger to instruct his lordship to be prepared to join him before dawn if he valued the life of his son.

It grew darker and the stars came out. The soldiers grouped around the fires and sang their songs. Gradually, the fires died down and, humped around Ambien Hill, the armies slept. Richard prayed. His armies outnumbered his opponent's host by almost two to one, yet tonight he was but one man and felt the weight of the whole weary world against him.

'A king must rule,' he said. 'Young Edward could not have ruled; therefore I have taken nothing from him.' Yet later, his face livid in moonlight, he prayed, 'Lord God, if I have sinned, thou wilt punish me. If not, this day, by Thy hand, shall be mine.'

Three rolling miles and a river away, Henry Tudor pledged himself to the service of God and the people of England. He did not ask that the people should love him, or even that they should like him; he asked only that he might have their support because without it he would not be able to rule them. In return, he would give not his heart but his head, since his head was by far the better part of him. He had little passion to infuse into the dry stuff of administration, but he had great intelligence, steadfastness, and an unremitting patience which would survive when the energy of youth was spent and carry him through the years when the heart has ceased to sing. He had what England needed and must hope that God and England realized this.

Sometime, in the dead hour of the night, a message was scrawled on the door of Norfolk's tent:

Jack of Norfolk, be not too bold,
For Dickon, thy master, is bought and sold.

In their tents, Henry and Richard slept at last. Henry slept lightly and woke at the slightest sound. Richard slept heavily, dreaming that he was walking in full armour within a fortress he could not identify. It was night and there was no one about save for one man who walked beside him. The man, too, was in full armour, but when Richard looked at him the vizor was up and Richard saw that his face was terrible, yet beautiful. Although this made a strong impression upon him, he could not have described any feature of the face. They came to the wall of a watch tower and as they approached the tower Richard knew that they were trying to get out, not only of the fortress, but of the country in which it was situated. His companion suddenly took him by the shoulder and pushed him against the wall, only now it wasn't a wall, it was a portcullis and beyond it there were fields on the far side of the frontier. As they crouched there, footsteps rang on cobblestones. Richard, pressed against the iron spikes, heard the footsteps coming nearer and nearer and he felt helpless as though he was weak and naked as the day he was born. 'It is the night watchman,' he said. Then his companion drew him down to the ground and as they lay looking through the spikes at the fields beyond the frontier, Richard knew that the most terrifying moment of his life had come; he put his head down and seemed to regard the terror as though he was looking at it down a well, then he dived forward into it. His companion placed an arm around his shoulders. It grew darker and darker, but the arm around his shoulders held steady, and gradually Richard came to the core of the darkness and there was no fear there. Then he saw that they were on the far side of the portcullis. He said, 'We are free!' and the unknown friend laid a dark cloak over him.

A hand was shaking his shoulder and he woke with a start, disturbed that he should dream of escape at this of all times. It was not yet light, but the plan was that before dawn broke he and Norfolk would march to occupy Ambien Hill. He was still disturbed by the dream when he came out of his tent. A breeze was getting up which would soon clear mist from the valley; it stirred the flap of his tent and brought to his nostrils the rank smell of dead fires and the ordure of men and horses.

'Is there any movement from the Tudor camp?' he asked one of his esquires.

'No, Sire. Only a few lights.' As Richard turned away, the man muttered, 'We have no chaplains, Sire.'

'If God espouses our cause, it cannot but prosper; if not, to pray for victory were but idle blasphemy.' He paused, seeing dismay on some of the faces around him. In a surge of angry defiance, he shouted, 'Be of good cheer, as am I. Today will see an end to our long quarrel with the House of Lancaster. I promise you I WILL NOT QUIT THIS FIELD until my cause be proved!'

News came that Norfolk, who was nothing if not bold, was ready to march.

The day yawned in the east; light came stealthily over the plain, skirted the side of Harper's Hill and climbed up Ambien Hill; gradually it coloured the Tweed River so that it ran like a twisted blue ribbon from the west of Harper's Hill northwards across the valley to Shenton where Sir William Stanley's army still slumbered.

In Henry Tudor's camp the army was astir; but Richard had taken them by surprise and by the time they were formed to march Richard's army was taking up its position on Ambien Hill. Now there were three armies on the move, those of Richard, Norfolk, and Henry Tudor. Northumberland delayed, dishonoured in the eyes of his own men, and neither of the Stanleys had moved. The Tudor host moved eastward towards Ambien Hill; its trumpets sounded and the Earl of Oxford rode forward in the van, his banner of a star with streams unfurled.

The sound of the trumpets excited the men and sent larks protesting into the sky. Henry's blood ran cold. His horse pranced about and he calmed it, and then practised some defiance for his own comfort. 'Never fought a battle, is that what you are thinking of me now, Richard Plantagenet? Before I could walk I was hunted; my life has been spent in peril and in flight; I have known little of comfort or ease; there has been no standard to which I could rally—when I was hard-pressed, I was alone; I have been humiliated, scorned, betrayed, and never lost heart. Were these not battles? They were battles that I won, else I would not be here to do battle with you this day. Must I shout like a madman, wield an axe and lumber around a field weighed almost to the ground like some poor beast in order to prove myself a man?' In the distance he could see Oxford's standard raised where men were fording the river. On the far side of the river, on the slopes of Ambien Hill, Norfolk's men waited under his banner of the silver lion. Henry thought, 'If I must—why, then I shall.' He rode forward, putting his trust in God: it was doubtful if he could put it in the Stanleys. Sir William had still not moved. Lord Stanley who, in answer to Richard's command had replied, 'I have other sons,' was now moving his army across the plain; but the progress was so slow it was hard to decide whether Stanley was advancing in order to come to Henry's aid, or the better to observe his end.

Oxford's men had crossed the river and were attacking Ambien Hill. Norfolk's men surged down to meet them. Beneath the banners of the silver lion and the star with streams the spears struck, the axes rose and fell. Norfolk's force was hard-pressed at the centre, Richard sent in some of the reserve; now Oxford's men fell back, rallying to their standards. Clouds of dust dimmed the brightness of the day; the vigour of life ran out and stained the earth red.

On a hummock some little distance from the fighting, Henry Tudor watched, while Richard Plantagenet looked down from Ambien Hill. They were both young men, and who could guess at this point in the battle that Henry was at his beginning and Richard at his end? Certainly not Henry. Before the sun had set the crown of England would be his, but between that time and this he must live through the worst moments of his life. He looked through the dust of battle to that area from whence no help came; Sir William Stanley's cavalry was not yet formed to charge. Lord Stanley's men were making heavy weather of fording the river. Henry felt he had outdistanced hope. And yet, in spite of his dismay, there was in his eyes as he looked about him something of the grim resolution of the man who, when the carnage has ceased, must pick up the pieces of life again.

Even when he heard the great cry that went up when Norfolk fell, Henry did not realize what had happened. But Richard knew. He looked down the hill at the broken standard of the silver lion and knew that his moment had come. He called the members of his household to him and mounted his horse. They were grouped high on the hill, above the dust of battle. The

day was brilliant, the sun had called all its colours to its
standard. The deep blue sky had bands of thin cloud across it,
formally patterned above the emerald of the distant hills; there
was a sense of something planned, written in the heavens. Oh,
hope was difficult to resist! He felt those old enemies, hope and
despair, war within him as he urged his charger forward and
then, as the pace quickened, the ranks of his army parted before
him and below the plain opened out for him thick with men, a
harvest to be reaped but one single ear of corn to be gleaned.
He cried, 'The Tudor!' and raised his arm, holding the great
battle-axe high. Now it was all or nothing, and all and nothing
were one. The baited animal had sprung the trap of lineage and
duty; the last sprig of broom had wrenched free of rooted earth.
Hope and despair fused in joy.

The wind surged past him; the sun glinted and danced on
the steel of Sir William Stanley's cavalry as it charged down
the hill. The standard of the White Boar dipped and swayed
and fell. The wind raced on in pursuit of other sport. The
battalions of the sky formed and reformed. Everything was
movement and change.

Only now that the frame is set about the picture, the movement ceases, the last breath of life rattles out of the figures.
They are left to history which tries to impose a pattern on the
brilliant fragments, to assemble a cast of good and bad kings,
of men who were ambitious and others who were avaricious, of
humble folk, mute, downtrodden; all static figures in a static
landscape, incapable of the turbulent emotions, the whirlwind
hopes and terrors, the glorious inconsistency of the living.

But the streams flow on and mingle with the river, mirroring
meadow-sweet and heather-purpled hills and motley men and
women passing over bridges, a willow decked with spring and
a truant child at play under the hunter's moon; the wind
breaks the images which are tossed about like heaps of brightly-
coloured glass and the river carries this living mosaic down to
the sea.